The Accidental Hero

A group of men had come out of the copse and were running up towards the fire. Vizqash was saying something to them. Barnevelt could hear his voice but could not make out the rush of Krishnan words.

"They don't look friendly to me," said Barnevelt. "We may have to fight or run."

"Nonsense, cobber. You're being romantic . . ."

All the men, including Vizqash, started running towards the two Earthmen, swords in hands, all but one who carried a bow instead.

"Blind me," said Tangaloa, "it does look like trouble!" He picked up a couple of softball-sized stones.

Barnevelt put his back to the wall and drew his sword. Although the blade came out with a satisfying *wheep*, it occurred to Dirk that reading a historical adventure story about a dauntless hero fighting with archaic weapons against desperate odds is by all means a more satisfactory occupation than trying to enact the role in person.

L. SPRAGUE DE CAMP

THE HAND OF ZEI

*Interior Illustrations
by Edd Cartier*

THE HAND OF ZEI

A Baen Books Original

Baen Publishing Enterprises
260 Fifth Avenue
New York, N.Y. 10001

ISBN: 0-671-69865-6

Cover art by Edd Cartier and Tom Kidd

First Baen printing, March 1990

Distributed by
SIMON & SCHUSTER
1230 Avenue of the Americas
New York, N.Y. 10020

Printed in the United States of America

To Phil Sawyer
one of the devoted readers who enable me to live without working.

NOTE ON PRONUNCIATIONS

The reader may render the exotic names in this story as he likes. The author, however, had in mind the following pronunciations of names in Gozashtandou and other Varasto languages: *a* and *á* as in "add" and "wad" respectively; other vowels about as in Spanish. Among consonants, *k* and *q* as in "keep" and "quote" regardless of adjacent sounds; *gh* = French uvular *r*; *kh* = *ch* in German *ach*, Scottish *loch*; ' = a glottal stop or cough; others as in English. Stress usually falls on the last syllable if the word ends in a diphthong or a consonant; otherwise (with exceptions) on the next to the last. Sotaspé is "saw-**TASS**-peh"; Sadabao is "sad-ab-**OW**"; Qirib is "keer-**EEB**" (with a guttural *k*); Douri is "**DOE**-ree"; Dejanai is "ded-ja-**NIGH**"; Gozashtandou is "gaw-zash-tan-**DOE**"; Gizil is "giz-**EEL**." Gavao rhymes (approximately) with "avow"; Káj with "dodge"; Zair with "fire"; Zei with "hay." Sheafasè is "shay-ah-fah-**SEH**." Castanhoso, a Portuguese name, is about "kush-**TAH**-nyew-soo."

Dirk Barnevelt hunched his mooselike form over his typewriter and wrote:

Twenty-five degrees north of the equator on the planet Krishna lies the Banjao Sea, the largest body of water on this planet. And in this Sea is found the Sunqar, home of legend and mystery.

Here under the scorching rays of the hot high sun, the beaked galleys of Dur and the tubby roundships of Jazmurian slowly rot in the unbreakable grip of a vast floating continent of the terpahla sea vine. Even the violent storms of the Krishnan sub-tropics no more than ruffle the surface of this immense floating swamp—which, however, sometimes heaves and bubbles with the terrible sea life of the planet, such as the gvám or harpooner.

Barnevelt sat back to wonder: For a couple of years he'd been writing about the places that Igor Shtain explored; would he ever see any of them? If his mother died . . . But that was unlikely. With modern geriatrics she'd be good for another century. He still had a great-great-grandfather alive in the Netherlands. Besides, he thought guiltily, that was no way to think about one's mother. He resumed:

Nothing, once caught in this web of weed, can escape unless it can fly like the aqebats that wing over from the mainland to prey on the smaller sea life of the Sunqar. Here time means nothing; nothing exists save silence and haze and heat and the stench of the strangling vine.

At least, thought Barnevelt, this hack writing was better than trying—as he had once tried—to ram the glories of English literature down the unwilling throats of rural adolescents with only two interests: sex, and escape from the toils of the public school system.

To the heart of this forbidding place Igor Shtain, most celebrated of living explorers, plans to penetrate on his forthcoming Krishnan expedition, to clear up once and for all the sinister rumors that for years have issued from this undiscovered country.

Barnevelt gazed into space, like a moose that has heard the mating cry of its kind, while waiting for the next sentence to form. A hell of a thing if Shtain never showed up to carry out his expedition! He, Dirk Barnevelt, couldn't release this publicity puff until the missing explorer was found.

Well, you may say, why cannot Shtain simply ask the skipper of a spaceship to set him down near the Sea, and fly over it in his helicopter, cameras whirring and guns ready? Because Krishna is a Class H planet, and the Interplanetary Council regulations forbid visitors from other planets to reveal mechanical devices and inventions to its egg-laying but human-looking natives, who are deemed on one hand too backward and warlike to be trusted with such things, and on the other intelligent enough to take advantage of them.

So there will be no helicopter, no guns. Dr. Shtain will have to do it the hard way. But how? For the Sunqar can neither be walked over nor sailed through. . . .

Barnevelt jumped like a tripped mousetrap as Mrs. Fischman said over his shoulder: "Time for the meeting, Dirk."

"What meeting?"

Mrs. Fischman, the secretary of Igor Shtain, Ltd., rolled her eyes up as she always did when Barnevelt showed his balmier side. "The directors. They want you."

2

§ § §

He followed her into the board room, bracing himself for unpleasant surprises like a man summoned to hear the verdict of a court-martial. The three directors of Igor Shtain, Ltd. were present: Stewart Laing, who was also vice-president and business manager; the banker Olaf Thorpe; and Panagopoulos, also treasurer. Mrs. Fischman, the secretary, completed the list of executives since Shtain had disappeared.

Even though the firm's president was missing, his likeness looked out at them from the colored bathygraph on the wall: a square-jawed, brick-red face seamed with many small wrinkles; coldly glittering china-blue eyes; a close-cut brush of coppery hair speckled with gray.

On the unofficial side there were, besides Barnevelt, the little Dionysio Perez the photographer, the large brown George Tangaloa the xenologist, and Grant Marlowe the actor, looking much like the picture on the wall even without the makeup he wore when impersonating Shtain on the lecture platform.

"What ho, ghost!" said Tangaloa, grinning.

Barnevelt smiled feebly and slouched into the remaining chair. Though he, like the others, was a stockholder in the company, his holdings were so small that he, a minnow among muskellunges, did not speak with any authority. However, this was not a formal directors' or stockholders' meeting, but an informal assembly of worried specialists who coöperated to put before the public that synthetic entity known as "Igor Shtain," of which the real Shtain was only a part—albeit the most important part.

"Well, Stu?" said Marlowe, lighting his pipe.

Laing said: "No news of the Old Man."

Mrs. Fischman rasped: "Those damn detectives! Hundreds of bucks a day for weeks, and not one lousy thing do they find. I bet they never did anything but trail wayward husbands before we hired them."

"Oh, no," said Laing. "Ugolini has fine references."

"Anyway," she continued, "if we don't get going, that contract with Cosmic Features won't be worth a last year's snowball."

Laing said: "Ugolini does have a theory that the Old Man has been taken to Krishna."

"How does he figure?" said Marlowe, puffing.

"Igor was hoping to clear up those rumors about a connection between the Sunqar and the *janrú* racket. The Division of Investigation hasn't been able to get a man in there—or rather those they sent never came out. So the W.D.I. hoped that the Old Man, as a private citizen, could learn something. Well, thanks to Dirk, Igor gets plenty of publicity about his safari. Now, let's suppose the main connections of the janrú ring are on Earth because of the effect of the stuff on human beings."

(Perez looked as if he were going to cry.)

Laing continued: "Then why shouldn't the ring, hearing of this expedition, decide to put the Old Man on ice?"

Barnevelt cleared his throat, his long equine face taking on the embarrassed look it always assumed before his superiors. "How d'you know they haven't murdered him? I've often wanted to myself."

"We don't, but it's not easy to dispose of a body completely, and there's no trace of his body on Earth."

Tangaloa's organ-bass voice broke in: "Blokes have been smuggled past the Viagens Interplanetarias security measures before."

"I know," said Laing. "However, we've got private, city, state, national, and international police looking for Igor, and that's all we can do in that direction. Our immediate concern is that contract. All I can see is for some of us to go to Krishna and carry out Igor's plans. Get the 50,000 meters of film—a quarter of it in the Sunqar—turn it over to Cosmic, and by then we shall know if the firm's going to continue. If Shtain's on Krishna, rescue him if possible."

Laing's sharp eyes swept the room. All nodded.

"So," he continued, "the next question is: Who?"

Most of those present looked away, assuming the detatched air of people who didn't work there at all, but had just dropped in for a visit.

George Tangaloa patted his paunch. "Dio and I can do it."

Perez jumped up. "I no go! I no go until thees trouble with my wife is feexed. That damn drug, thees damn woman use on me, not my fault . . ."

"Yes, yes," interrupted Laing. "We know about your trouble, Dio, but we can't send one man alone."

Tangaloa yawned. "I presume I could manage by myself. Dio has checked me out on the Hayashi camera."

Mrs. Fischman said: "If we send George alone we won't get enough film to wrap around your finger. He'll settle down the first place they got good steaks and beer and . . ."

"Why Ruth!" said Tangaloa with ostentatious innocence. "Are you insinuating I'm indolent?"

"Damn right you're indolent," said Marlowe the actor. "Probably the laziest hunk of meat that ever came out of Samoa. You need somebody like Dirk to keep an eye on you. . . ."

"Hey!" cried Barnevelt, shyness dropping from him like a discarded cloak. "Why me? Why not you? Matter of fact you not only look like Igor, you can even imitate that foul Russian accent of his. It is you who should gaw, my frand . . ."

Marlowe waved a hand. "I'm too old for roughing it, just a mass of flab, and I never had any training at that sort . . ."

"Neither have I! And you said yourself the other day I was an impractical intellectual, so who am I to clear the dark places and let in the law?"

"You can work the Hayashi, and you yacht, don't you?"

"Oh, foof! Only on a friend's boat. You don't think I own a yacht on *my* pay, do you? Of course if you wanted to raise it, . . ."

Marlowe shrugged. "It's the experience that counts, not how you got it. And being brought up on a farm you know about the simple life."

"But we had electricity and running . . ."

"Furthermore, all of us have dependents except George and you."

"I've got my mother," said Barnevelt, his naturally ruddy face turning a lobsterish red. References to his rural background always embarrassed him; for, while he preferred city life, he had never gotten over the feeling that to these born city slickers he was a figure of fun.

"Bunk!" said the acid voice of Mrs. Fischman. "We know all about your old lady, Dirk. Best thing for you would be to get away from her apron strings."

"Look here, I don't see what business . . ."

"We'll pay her your salary while you're gone, if you like, so she won't starve. And if you put it over there'll be enough dividend to get you out of those debts she got you into."

"Enough," added Marlowe, "so you'll be able to afford a fancy duplex apartment with an Oriental man-servant."

Tangaloa put in: "Don't you think he'd get more fun out of a French maid?"

Barnevelt, now scarlet, shut up. It was always a mistake to bring up his mother. On one hand he felt he ought to defend her, while on the other he feared they were right. If only his father, the Dutchman, hadn't died while he was still a boy. . . .

"Besides," Marlowe went on, "I know my limitations, and I shouldn't be any better at Igor's job than he was at mine in New Haven."

"What's this?" said Thorpe. "Don't think I know that story."

Laing explained: "You know Igor's the world's worst public speaker, so Grant takes his place on the platform, using his films, just as Dirk ghost-writes his books and articles. For emergencies we procured a little mechanical speaker that looks like a flower on the lapel and made recordings of some lectures, written by Dirk and spoken by Grant. Then we trained Igor to stand there moving his mouth in synchronism with the speech coming out of the speaker."

"And then?"

"Then two years ago Grant got sick, and Igor undertook the job with this gadget. But when he stood up and started the speaker, the thing had gotten out of adjustment and played the same line over and over: '. . . happy to be here . . . happy to be here . . . happy to be here . . .' Like that. It ended with Igor dancing on the gadget and howling Russian curses."

While Thorpe laughed, Laing turned to Barnevelt. "It's a lot to ask, Dirk, but there's no way out. Besides, if you're Igor's ghost, don't you want your body back?"

Tangaloa, grinning like a large Polynesian Billiken, sang: "Bring back, bring back, oh bring back my body to me, to me!"

All laughed save Barnevelt.

"No," he said with the exaggerated firmness of a man who feels his inner defenses beginning to crumble, "I can make a perfectly good living on Earth without Igor Shtain Limited—better than I'm making now . . ."

"Wait," said Laing. "There's more to it. I had a talk with Tsukung of the Division of Investigation, and they're really worried about the janrú racket. You know what it did to Dio, and you read about the Polhemus murder. The extract is so powerful you can hide a hundred doses in a tooth-cavity. It's diluted thousands of times over, and finally appears in perfumes with names like *nuit d'amour* and *moment d'extase*. But with the janrú added, they really do what the names imply. A woman can squirt herself with the stuff, and as soon as a man gets a whiff he goes clean daft and she can make him jump through hoops as if he were under Osirian pseudohypnosis.

"But that's not all. It only works when a female uses it on a male, and the way the stuff's getting spread around, Tsukung's afraid the women will completely dominate the men of the world in a couple of decades."

"That wouldn't be so bad," said Mrs. Fischman. "I could use some on that nogoodnik husband of mine."

"So," continued Laing, "you can save the male half of the human race from a fate worse than death—or at least a fate like the one your mother's been inflicting on you. Isn't that worth while?"

"Come to think of it," said Marlowe, "are you sure Dirk's mother hasn't been using it on him?"

Barnevelt shook his head vigorously. "It's just that she got the psychological jump on me long ago. But what do I get out of this? I'm a peasant slave already."

"You'd get away from her," said Laing.

Tangaloa said: "You don't want to see the women enslave the men, the way you Westerners used to do to your women, do you?"

"It'll make a man of you," said Marlowe. "Anybody your age who's never been married needs something drastic."

"It'll give you real experience to write about," said Mrs. Fischman.

"Better get in your adventures now, while you're young and unattached," said Thorpe. "If I had your chance . . ."

"We'll raise your salary," said Panagopolos. "And with your expense account on Krishna, you can . . ."

"Think of all the screwy animals you'll see," said Tangaloa. "You're crazy about queer beasts."

"And," said Laing, "it's not as though we were asking you to go to Odin and live among those over-sized insects with an oxygen mask on your face. The natives look almost human."

"In fact, the females . . ." said Tangaloa, making curving motions in the air with his hands.

"Oh, hell, I'll go," said Barnevelt at last, knowing that they'd talk him around in the end. Anyway, hadn't he promised himself an adventure like this years ago when he was a boy on the farm in Chautauqua County? Served him right.

"**G**eorge," said Barnevelt, "What do I do now? Increase my insurance?"

"Oh, it's all arranged," said Tangaloa. "I have reservations on the *Eratosthenes* leaving Mohave day after tomorrow."

Barnevelt stared. "You mean—you mean you actually had this all cooked up in advance?"

"Certainly. We knew you'd come round."

Although Barnevelt turned red and started to sputter, Tangaloa added calmly: "When can you be packed?"

"That depends. What do I bring, ear muffs?"

"Just ordinary clothes for a couple of months. I've got the cameras and other special gear, and the rest we buy at Novorecife. No use paying freight on more luggage than we can help."

"Where's the *Eratosthenes* bound for? Pluto?"

"No, Neptune's now the staging-planet for the Cetic planets. The *Amazonas* takes us over the long jump to Krishna."

"What do I do about my mother?"

"Why, nothing!"

"But if she finds out she'll forbid the trip, and I can't defy her. That is, I can, but it never works."

Tangaloa grinned. "Tell her you're going on a cruise with that sailing friend of yours."

"Good. I'll say we're going to visit my great-grandmother Anderson in Baltimore. Matter of fact I'd better call Prescott. There's nothing like getting your lies straightened out in advance." He dialled his wrist' phone. "Harry? Dirk. Could you do me a favor? . . ."

When Barnevelt let himself into his apartment, he was relieved to find his mother out. No doubt she was downtown enjoying her usual hobby of overdrawing her charge accounts. With guilty haste he packed a suitcase, bid goodbye to the cat, the goldfish, and the turtle, and in half an hour was tiptoeing out, feeling much like a tyro at burglary.

But, as the front door closed behind him, a bugle blew through the caverns of his mind. His stoop straightened; after all, man is man and master of his fate. If all went well, he wouldn't see his mother again before leaving. He would, for the first time in his thirty-one years, be really on his own.

But was it right? A spasm of doubt assailed him . . .

And so he made his way by subway and bus to Tangaloa's flat, the two sides of his nature contending. As he entered, the Oedipean side was uppermost.

"What are you looking so downcast about, cobber?" said Tangaloa. "Anybody'd think you were a Cosmotheist whose guru had just died. Do you want to spend your whole life on Earth?"

"No," said Barnevelt, "but my conscience won't let me walk out this way. Our one white lie sits like a little ghost here on the threshold of our enterprise. Maybe I'd best call her . . ." and he pulled the stylus out of its clip to dial.

"No you don't!" said Tangaloa with unwonted sharpness, and shot out a large brown hand to grip Barnevelt's wrist.

After a few seconds Barnevelt's eyes fell. "You're right. In fact

I'd better disconnect my 'phone." He fitted the screwdriver end of the stylus into the actuating slot, and turned it with a faint click.

"That's better," said Tangaloa, turning back to his packing. "Have you ever been psyched?"

"Ayuh. Turned out I was a schizoid Oedipean. But my mother stopped it. She was afraid it might work."

"You should have grown up in a Polynesian family. We're brought up by so many different people at once that we don't develop these terrific fixations on individuals."

Tangaloa folded shirts to fit his bag, whistling "Laau Tetele," and began fitting special gear into appropriate compartments. First medicines and drugs, including the all-important longevity capsules without which no man could expect to attain his normal ripe age of 200 plus.

Then six Hayashi one-millimeter cameras, each mounted in a large ornate finger-ring that effectively camouflaged it. A pair of jeweller's monocles and tiny screwdrivers for opening the cameras and changing the film.

Then a couple of König and Das notebooks with titaniridite sheets, a magnifier for viewing the pages, and a folding panto-graph for reducing the hand motions of the writer to almost microscopic size. By writing small and using the Ewing digraphic alphabet, a skilled note-taker like Tangaloa could crowd over 2,000 words on to one side of a six-by-ten centimeter sheet.

Barnevelt asked: "Will the Viagens people at Krishna actually let us take the Hayashis out of the reservation?"

"Yes. By a strict interpretation of Regulation 368, they're not supposed to, but they wink at the Hayashi because the Krishnans don't notice it. Besides it contains a spring destructor, so if one of them tried to take it apart it would fly into little bits. Put this microfilm spool in your bag."

"What's that?"

"Elementary Gozashtandou. You can work at it enroute, and here's a stack of records." He handed Barnevelt a disk about two centimeters thick by six in diameter. "They have players on the ships. Up stick, laddie!"

At New York Airport, four women came to see Tangaloa off: his current mistress, two ex-wives, and a miscellaneous girlfriend. Tangaloa greeted them with his usual fuzzy amiability, kissed them all soundly, and strolled out to the bus.

Barnevelt, after saying good-bye to the lovely quartet, followed Tangaloa, reflecting morosely that to him that hath shall be given. In looking out of the bus window to give one last farewell wave to the girls, he spotted a small gray-haired figure pushing its way to the front of the crowd.

"Zeus!" he said, quickly turning his face away.

"What ails you, pal?" said Tangaloa. "You're white!"

"My mother!"

"Where? Oh, *that* little female! She doesn't look very formidable."

"You don't know her. Why doesn't that fool driver start?"

"Don't get off your bike. The gate's closed, so she can't get in."

Barnevelt cowered in his seat until the bus lurched into motion. In a minute they were at the ship. The companionway, like a tall stairway on wheels, stood in position. Barnevelt went up quickly, Tangaloa wheezing behind as his weight told and grumbling about elevators.

"You want syrup on your shortcake," said Dirk.

Now that he could no longer see individuals among the crowd at the gate, because of the distance and the gathering darkness, he was beginning to feel himself again.

Inside the fuselage they climbed down to their seats, swivelled to allow them to sit upright even though the ship for the Mohave Spaceport was standing on its tail.

Barnevelt remarked: "You sure take it coolly, leaving all those women."

Tangaloa shrugged. "There will always be another along in a minute."

"Next time you're discarding a set of such sightly squids, you might offer me one."

"If they are willing, I shall be glad to. I suppose you prefer the Pink—or as you Westerners prefer to call it the White—Race?"

An airline employee was climbing down, rung by rung, to

punch tickets. He called out: "Is there a passenger named Dick Barnwell on the 'plane?"

"I suppose you mean me," said Barnevelt. "Dirk Barnevelt."

"Yeah. Your mother just called us on the tower radio, saying for you to get off. You'll have to let us know right away so we can put the companionway back."

Barnevelt took a long breath. His heart pounded, and he felt Tangaloa's amused eyes upon him.

"Tell her," he croaked, "I'm staying on."

"Good-o!" cried Tangaloa. The man climbed back up.

Then the hurricane rumble of the jet drowned all other sounds, and the field dropped away. The New York area, spangled with millions of lights, came into view below; then all of Long Island. To the West the sun, which had set half an hour before, rose into sight again. . . .

U p ahead, around the curve of the corridor, the door of the airlock clanged open. Loudspeakers throughout the *Amazonas* began their chant: *"Todos passageiros fora—*all passengers out—*todos passageiros . . ."*

Dirk Barnevelt, standing beside George Tangaloa in the line of passengers waiting to disembark, automatically moved forward to close up the distance between himself and the man in front of him. Through the invisible open door in the nose of the ship came a breath of strange air: moist, mild, and full of vegetal smells. So different from the air of a spaceship in transit, with its faint odors of ozone, machine oil, and unwashed human beings. Lighters flared as the passengers eagerly lit up their first smokes since leaving Neptune.

The line began to move forward. As they neared the lock, Barnevelt heard the rush of wind and the patter of rain over the shuffle of feet. Finally the outside world came in sight, a rectangle of pearl-gray against the darker tone of the bulkheads.

Barnevelt muttered: "I feel like a mummy escaping from its

tomb. Didn't know space travel was such a bore."

As they neared the lock, he saw that the gray exterior was the underside of a rain cloud driving past. The wind flapped the canopy over the ramp, and rain drove through the open sides.

As he in turn stepped through the lock, Barnevelt heard below him the thump of trunks and suitcases as grunting crewmen heaved them out the service lock into the chute beneath the ramp, and the swish of the baggage taking off down the chute. A glance over the rail startled him with the distance to the ground.

The wind thrummed through the spidery ramp structure and whipped Barnevelt's raincoat about his knees. At the foot of the ramp he found he still had several minutes' walk to the customs building. The walkway with its canopy continued on little stilts across the field, an expanse of bare brown earth dotted with puddles. In the distance, a scraper and a roller were flattening out the crater left by the last takeoff. Behind him the *Amazonas* stood like a colossal rifle cartridge on its base. As they walked towards the customs building, the rain stopped and Roqir showed his big yellow buckler between towering masses of cloud.

A uniformed Viagens man was holding open the door of the customs building and saying in the Brazilo-Portuguese of the spaceways: "Passengers remaining on Krishna, first door to the right. Those proceeding on to Ganesha or Vishnu . . ."

Nine of the fourteen passengers crowded through the first door to the right and lined up before the desk of a big scowling man identified by a sign as Afanansi Gorchakov, Chief Customs Inspector.

When their turn came, Barnevelt and Tangaloa presented their passports to be checked and stamped and entered while they signed and thumb-printed the register. Meanwhile Gorchakov's two assistants went through baggage.

When one of them came across the Hayashi ring-cameras he called to Gorchakov, who examined them and asked: "Are these equipped with destructors?"

"Yes," said Tangaloa.

"You will not let them fall into Krishnan hands?"

"Certainly not."

"Then we'll let them through. Though it is technically illegal, we make an exception because Krishna is changing, and if pictures of the old Krishna are not made now they never will be."

"Why's it changing?" said Barnevelt. "I thought you fellows were careful to protect the Krishnans against outside influences."

"Yes, but they have learned much from us nevertheless. For instance, back in 2130 Prince Ferrian of Sotaspe established a patent system in his kingdom, and it has already begun to show an effect."

"Who's he?"

"The rascal who tried to smuggle a whole technical library into Krishna in his ancestor's mummy. When we blocked that, he put this patent idea into practice, having picked it up on his visit to Earth."

Tangaloa asked: "Who is counselor to visitors?"

"Castanhoso. Wait, and I will present you."

When all the incoming visitors had been medically examined, Gorchakov led Shtain's men down the hall into another office harboring Herculeu Castanhoso, Assistant Security Officer of Novorecife.

When Gorchakov had left, Tangaloa explained the purposes of the expedition, adding: "Can we trust the young lady? We don't want our plans noised among the aborigines." He nodded towards Castanhoso's pretty secretary.

"Surely," said Castanhoso, a small dark man.

"Good-o. Has anybody like Dr. Shtain come through in recent months?"

Castanhoso examined the bathygraph of Igor Shtain. The three-dimensional image stared back coldly.

"I don't think—wait, there was one on the last ship from Earth, one of three who said they'd been hired by the King of Balhib to survey his kingdom."

"How could they do that without violating your rules?"

"They would be limited to Krishnan methods of surveying. But even so, they said, they are still much more accurate than

15

any Krishnan. Now that I think of it, their story did sound thin, for it's notorious that ever since Sir Shurgez cut off his beard, King Kir has had a mania against strangers. I'll ask him. Senhorita Foley!"

"*Sim?*" The girl turned, revealing large blue eyes. She looked at Castanhoso with a breathless expression, as if expecting him to reveal an infallible method of winning at swindle-bridge.

"A letter, *por favor*. From Herculeu Castanhoso, etcetera, to his sublime altitude, Kir bad-Baladé, Dour of Balhib and Kubyab, hereditary Dasht of Jeshang, titular Pandr of Chilihagh, etcetera, etcetera. May it please Your Serene Awsomeness, but the Viagens Interplanetarias would appreciate information respecting the following matter, namely, that is, and *videlicet: . . .*"

When he had finished he added: "Translate it into Gozashtandou and write it in longhand on native paper."

"She must be a right smart girl," said Barnevelt.

"She is." (The girl glowed visibly at this brief praise.) "Senhorita, these are our visitors the Senhores Jorge Tangaloa and Dirk Barnevelt; Mees Eileen Foley."

Barnevelt asked: "What about the king's beard? These people must have rugged ideas of humor."

"You do not know the tenth of it. This Shurgez was sent on a quest for the beard because he had murdered somebody in Mikardand. Kir was mad with rage, because Krishnans have practically no beards and it had taken him all his life to grow this one."

"I can see how he'd feel," said Barnevelt, remembering how his classmates at Teachers' College had forcibly demustached him. "When was this?"

"In 2137, just before Ferrian's stunt with the mummy and the Gois scandal." Castanhoso told what he knew of the singular story of Anthony Fallon and Victor Hasselborg, adding other details of recent Krishnan history.

"Sounds as complicated as an income-tax form," said Barnevelt. "I don't remember any of this in my briefing."

"You forget, Senhor Dirk, the news had not reached Earth when you left, and that you have been traveling twelve Earth years, objective time."

"I know. I have to keep reminding myself of the Fitzgerald effect. Actually I don't feel that much older."

"No, because physically you aren't—only three or four weeks older. You passed Hasselborg on his way back to Earth."

Tangaloa said: "Ahem. Let us get to the point, gentlemen: How do we get to the Sunqar?"

Castanhoso walked over to the wall, where he pulled down a roll-map. "Observe, Senhores. Here are we. Here is the Pichidé River, separating the Gozashtandou Empire on the North from the Republic of Mikardand on the South. Here to the East lies the Sadabao Sea. Here is Palindos Strait opening into the Banjao Sea to the South, and here is the Sunqar.

"As you see, the port closest to the Sunqar is Malayer on the Banjao Sea, but there is war in those parts and I seem to remember hearing that Malayer is under siege by the nomads of Qaath. Therefore you must go down the Pichidé to Majbur, then take the railroad down the coast to Jazmurian, and thence travel by road to Ghulindé, the capital of Qirib. From there I suppose you will go by water—unless you prefer to sail to Sotaspé," (he pointed to a spot on the map far out in the Sadabao Sea) "to borrow one of Ferrian's rocket gliders.

"If you ask me how to proceed from Ghulindé, frankly I don't know how you can get into that continent of *sargaço* without at least getting your throats cut. However, you will find Qirib comparatively unspoiled by Earthly influence, and I hope you decide it is picturesque enough for purposes of cinematography."

Tangaloa shook his head. "The contract says the Sunqar. But how do we get to this Ghulindé?"

"What we mean," said Barnevelt, "is: How do we travel? Openly as Earthmen?"

"I would not, even though some have gotten away with it. Our barber can give you disguises: artificial antennae, points to your ears, and green dye for your hair."

"Ugh," said Barnevelt.

"Or, if you dislike dyeing your hair, which entails taking along extra dye for when your hair grows out, you could go as men from Nyamadzë, where they shave their scalps completely."

"Where's Nyah-whatever-it-is?" asked Barnevelt. "Sounds as if it might be Igor Shtain's home town."

"Nyah-mah-dzuh. It's in the South Polar Region, thousands of hoda from here, as you can see on this globe. You shall be Nyamen. They seldom get to this part of the planet, and if you pretended to be such, it might avert suspicion if you speak with an accent or seem ignorant of local matters."

Tangaloa asked: "Have you facilities for intensive linguistic training?"

"Yes, we have a flash-card machine and a set of recordings, and Senhorita Foley can give you colloquial speech practice. You should spend a few days anyway brushing up on Krishnan social behavior."

When they had agreed to his suggestion of going as Nyamen, Castanhoso said: "I shall give you Nyami names. Senhor Jorge, you are—uh—what are a couple of good Nyami names, Senhorita?"

The girl wrinkled her forehead. "I remember there were a couple of famous Nyami adventurers—Tagdë of Vyutr and Snyol of Pleshch."

"Bom. Senhor Jorge, you are Tagdë of Vyutr. Senhor Dirk, you are Snyol of Pleshch. PLESH–TCH, two syllables. Now, do you ride and fence? Few Earthmen do."

"I do both," said Barnevelt. "Matter of fact I even tell stories in Scottish dialect."

Tangaloa groaned. "I had to learn to ride on that expedition to Thor, though I'm no horseperson. But as for playing with swords, no! Everywhere except on these flopping Class-H planets you can go where you must in an aircraft and shoot what you must with a gun, like a sensible bloke."

"But this is not a sensible planet," replied Castanhoso. "For instance, you may not take that bathygraph of Senhor Shtain with you. It's against regulations, and any Krishnan who saw that three-dimensional image would know that here was the magic of the Earthmen. But you may have an ordinary photographic flat print made and take that.

"Let me see," the Viagens official continued. "I shall give you a letter to Gorbovast in Majbur, and he can give you one to the Queen of Qirib, who may be willing to help you thenceforward. If she is not to know you are Earthmen, what excuse should you give for yourselves?"

Barnevelt asked: "Don't people go to the Banjao Sea on legitimate business?"

"But yes! They hunt the gvám for its stones."

Tangaloa said: "You mean that thing something like a swordfish and something like a giant squid?"

"That is it. You shall be gvám hunters. The stones from their stomachs are priceless because of the Krishnan belief that no woman can resist a man who carries one."

"Just the thing for you, Dirk," said Tangaloa.

"Oh, foof!" said Barnevelt. "Having no faith in the thing, I'm afraid it would be priceless to me but in the other sense. What time is it, Senhor Herculeu? We've been cooped up in that egg crate so long we've lost touch with objective time."

"Late afternoon—just about our quitting-time."

"Well, what d'you do for that seventeen o'clock feeling?"

Castanhoso grinned. "The Nova Iorque Bar is in the next compound. If you gentlemen . . ."

The greenish sky had almost cleared; the setting sun threw reds and purples on the undersides of the remaining clouds. The plain concrete buildings were arranged in rectangles whose outsides were blank wall, all the doors and windows opening on to the central courts.

In the bar Castanhoso said: "Try a mug of kvad, since that is the chief distilled liquor of Krishna."

"I hope," replied Barnevelt, "it's not made by native women chewing and spitting, the way they do where George comes from."

Castanhoso made a face. As they ordered, a high, harsh voice

19

called out: *"Zeft, zeft! Ghuvoí zu! Zeft!"*

Barnevelt peered around the partition between their booth and the next and saw a large red-yellow-and-blue macaw on a perch.

"That is Philo," said Castanhoso. "Mirza Fateh brought him in on the last ship, the one that also landed the man who might be your Dr. Shtain."

"Why did he leave the bird here?" asked Barnevelt.

"The regulations made us keep that bird for a quarantine period, and Mirza was in a hurry to get to a convention of his sect in Mishé. So he gave the parrot to Abreu, my chief, who gave him to me after he had bitten Senhora Abreu. You gentlemen don't need a parrot, do you?"

As the explorers shook their heads, the macaw shrieked: *"Zeft! Baghan!"*

"Somebody taught him all the obscenities of Gozashtandou," said Castanhoso. "When we have proper Krishnan guests we hide him."

Barnevelt asked: "Who's this Mirza Fateh? Sounds like an Iranian name."

"It is. He is a Cosmotheist missionary, a little fat fellow who wanders back and forth among the Cetic planets promoting his cult."

"I've been in Iran," said Tangaloa. "Hang of a country."

Castanhoso continued: "We hadn't seen Senhor Mirza for many years, since he went back to Earth to get the Word from the head of his cult."

Tangaloa said: "You mean that Madame von Zschaetzsch? Who claims to be a reincarnation of Franklin Roosevelt and to get her inspiration by telepathy from an immortal Imam who lives in a cave in the Antarctic ice-cap?"

"The same. Anyway, Mirza has been working this region for over a century. A curious character: sincere, I think, in his supernatural beliefs, and kind-hearted, but not to be trusted for a minute. He was caught cheating at gambling on Vishnu."

Barnevelt said: "A rogue in grain, veneered in sanctimonious theory."

"So-yes? He has his troubles too, poor fellow. A couple of decades ago, just before he returned to Earth, he lost his wife and daughter here on Krishna."

"I thought Cosmotheists were celibates?"

"They are, and I have heard Mirza explain with tears running down his fat face that his misfortune was the result of violating that tabu."

"How'd it happen?"

"They were going by train from Majbur to Jazmurian (where you will be going) when a band of robbers ambushed the train. Mirza's wife was killed by an arrow. Mirza, who is not notable for courage, escaped by shamming dead, and when he opened his eyes the little girl was gone. No doubt the robbers took her to sell into slavery."

Tangaloa said: "Fascinating, but tell us more about Qirib."

"To be sure. Qirib is called a kingdom, but I suppose it should be 'queendom.' It's a matriarchal state, founded long ago by Queen Dejanai. Not only do the females run the country; they have a strange custom: The queen chooses a man for her consort, and after he has served for a year they kill him with much ceremony and choose another."

Tangaloa exclaimed: "Like some early agricultural cultures on Earth! Ancient Malabar, for instance . . ."

"I shouldn't think," said Barnevelt, "there'd be much competition for the siege perilous. There must be an easier way to make a living, even on Krishna."

Castanhoso shrugged. "The poor men have nothing to say. They are chosen by lot, though I hear the lots are sometimes rigged. There is a movement to replace the actual execution by a symbolic one—they would just nick the outgoing king a little—but the conservatives of course object that such a change would enrage the fertility goddess, in whose honor this gruesome ceremony is observed."

Barnevelt asked: "Is there any chance they'd choose one of us for the honor? It's one I could stand missing."

"No, no, only citizens of Qirib are eligible. However, you must take some sort of present for Queen Alvandi."

"Hm," said Barnevelt. "Well, George, I suppose the expense account will have to take another sock . . ."

"Wait a spell!" said Tangaloa, looking with liquid eyes towards the macaw. "How would that cockatoo do? I don't suppose the queen has any Earthly birds, has she?"

"Just the thing!" said Castanhoso. "It will cost you nothing, for I am glad to get rid of the creature."

"Hey!" said Barnevelt. "Much as I love animals, I'm allergic to feathers!"

"That's all right," said Tangaloa. "I shall carry the cage, and you the rest of our gear."

Castanhoso added: "You must warn the queen that Philo is not to be trusted."

Barnevelt said: "Actually he's probably grumpy because he hasn't seen a lady macaw in a long time."

"That may be, but as the nearest one is twelve light-years away, he will have to put up with it."

"How about his vocabulary? The queen might not like that *avant-garde* language he uses."

"That is nothing. She is said to have a pretty rough tongue herself."

"Come on," said Barnevelt sharply next morning. "You can't lie around digesting your breakfast all day like one of my old man's hogs."

And he bullied and dragged the unwilling Tangaloa into the Novorecife gymnasium. Although Tangaloa was nominally his superior, Dirk found he had to take more and more of the responsibility for the expedition if they were to get anywhere.

In the gym they found a stocky, balding, blue-eyed man chinning himself on a bar, who said his name was Heggstad.

"Vot do you vont? Massage?" asked this one, standing on his head.

"No, some fencing," said Barnevelt.

"Going out, eh? I got yust the thing for you," said Heggstad, doing deep-knee bends. The gymnast took time out to get out a pair of masks, jackets, gloves and épées.

"A little heavier than the Earthly épée," he explained, spreading his arms and doing a one-leg squat. "That's so it corresponds to the Krishnan rapier, which must be heavy to get through armor. You know the firsht principles?" he added, doing push-ups.

"Ayuh," said Barnevelt, pulling on the jacket. "Get 'em on, George, unless you want me to carve my initials in your hide with my *point d'arrêt*."

Tangaloa grumbled: "I have already informed you I'm a hopeless dub at all sports, except perhaps cricket."

"Oh, foof. You swim like a fish."

"That's not a sport, but a utilitarian method of crossing water when one has neither bridge nor boat. How do I grasp this archaic object?"

Barnevelt showed him, while Heggstad did a hand-stand on a pair of parallel bars.

"I'm exhausted just observing Mr. Heggstad," said Tangaloa, holding his blade listlessly.

"Vun of these dissipated high-liversh, that's the matter vit you," snapped Heggstad, standing on one hand. "Smoking, drinking, late hoursh, all that sort of thing. If you vould put yourself in my hands I could make a new man of you. Then you'd learn to really enyoy life."

"I enyoy it so much now I don't believe I could endure any more," said Tangaloa. "Ouch!"

"He vill never make a fencer," said Heggstad, leaping into the air, turning a somersault, and coming down on his feet again. "He has no killer instinct, that's the trouble. He takes it as a yoke."

"Of course I have no killer instinct, you Norwegian berserker!" said Tangaloa in an aggrieved tone. "I'm a scientist, not a bloody gladiator. The only time I ever smeared anybody was that time on Thor when they thought we'd stolen the sacred pie and we had to shoot our way out."

And in truth Tangaloa did not prove a promising pupil. He seemed slow, awkward, and not much interested.

"Come on, you big mass of lard," said Barnevelt. "Get that

arm out! What would d'Artagnan think?"

"I don't give a damn what any unwashed seventeenth-century European thinks, and I am not obese," said Tangaloa with dignity. "Merely well-fleshed."

After half a Krishnan hour Barnevelt gave up and asked Heggstad: "Like a few touches?"

They went at it. Tangaloa, sweating hard, sat down on the canvas with his back to the wall and watched. "A more appropriate rôle for one of my contemplative temperament. I shall observe while the medieval romanticists perform the work."

"He is yust lazy and trying to hide it vit big vords," said Heggstad. "Now you are pretty good, even though you look kind of awkvard. *Touché!*"

"Practice makes perfect," said Barnevelt, getting home again with a *double degage.* "The game George has had the most practice at won't help us on Krishna."

Heggstad said: "Those Krishnans are not so good. They use a complicated drill, very formal, vit diagrams on the floor. *Touché!*"

Barnevelt finished his fencing and gave Heggstad back his gear.

Tangaloa yawned. "I presume our next objective will be to rout out Castanhoso for advice on equipment."

Castanhoso said: "Do not apologize! This is part of my job."

"Can I come?" asked Eileen Foley, casting sheep's eyes at Castanhoso.

"So-yes," said Castanhoso, and led them out of his office, across the compound, and into the Outfitting Store, where they were met by the first Krishnan whom Barnevelt had seen close up.

The young fellow looked superficially human, though his bright-green hair, large pointed ears, and smelling antennae sprouting from between his eyebrows made him look as if he had stepped out of an Earthly children's book about the Little People. As Barnevelt scrutinized the Krishnan, he began to notice other little differences as well: details of color and shape of teeth, fingernails, eyes, and so on. The Krishnan was small compared to Barnevelt but wiry and well-muscled, with a scar on his face that crossed his flattish nose diagonally.

"This is Vizqash bad-Murani, one of our tame Krishnans," said Castanhoso. "He will sell you any outfits you need. Vizqash, these gentlemen are going out as Nyamen."

"I have just the thing, gentlemen," said the Krishnan in a curious rasping accent. With immense dignity he led the way to a rack of bright fur-lined suits that might have been made for a squad of Earthly department-store Santa Clauses.

"Oh, no!" said Castanhoso. "I didn't mean they were going to Nyamadzé. They are going to Qirib, which is much too hot for those!"

"To my old country?" said the Krishnan. "They don't wear *clothes* there!"

"You mean they go naked?" said Barnevelt in alarm, for he had been brought up as a non-nudist and did not regard his own long knobby form as a thing of beauty.

"No, except for swimming," said Castanhoso. "He means the Qiribuma do not tailor clothes to fit them as we and the Gozashtanduma do. They wrap a couple of squares of goods around themselves, pin them in place, and consider themselves dressed. Of course if you go farther south, you find Krishnans who regard any clothes as indecent."

Eileen Foley said: "Boy, I'd like to see you disguised as one of those!"

"You'd be disappointed," said Barnevelt, blushing.

"How d'you know what I'd expect?"

"I'd only look more like a horse than ever." A fresh little snip, thought Barnevelt.

Castanhoso warned: "Stay away from such people, because you couldn't fool them as to your species. I think the best thing would be summer-weight Gozashtando suits."

"Size forty-four long," added Barnevelt.

Vizqash accordingly brought out outfits comprising tight jackets, legwear somewhere between divided kilts and longish shorts, trunk hose to go under these, calf-high soft-leather boots, and stocking caps whose tails were designed to be wound turbanwise around the head.

"When you get to warmer country you can go without the hose," said Vizqash. Staring at Tangaloa he added: "I fear we have nothing large enough for you. I shall have to have our tailor . . ."

"Here's a big one," said Barnevelt, rummaging.

"*Ohé*, I had forgotten! A hundred-kilo Earthman ordered it and then died before we could deliver."

Tangaloa put the suit on, and Barnevelt said: "George, you're a sight to shake the midriff of despair with laughter."

"At least my knees aren't knobby," retorted the xenologist.

"Now for arms and armor," said Castanhoso.

"This way," said Vizqash. "If you could tell me just what you plan to do . . ."

"Observing people and customs," said Barnevelt. "A general xenological survey."

"You want to know things like Krishnan history and archeology?"

"Yes, and also ecology, sociodynamics, and religion."

"Well, why not start by visiting the ruins west of Qou? That is only a short way from here—big ruins with inscriptions nobody can read. Nobody knows who built them."

"Let's all go there tomorrow for a picnic," suggested Eileen Foley. "It's Sunday, and we can borrow the big V.I. rowboat."

Barnevelt and Tangaloa looked questioningly at one another.

"A good idea," said Castanhoso. "I cannot go, but it will give you two practice at being Krishnans. I suggest that Vizqash go along as your guide."

Barnevelt suspected that Castanhoso was politely urging them to get out of his hair, but saw no objections. When the details of the picnic had been settled, he let Vizqash sell him an undershirt of fine link mail, a rapier, and a dagger. Tangaloa balked at the sword.

"No!" he said. "I'm a civilized man and won't load myself down with primitive ironmongery. Besides, where we're going, if I can't talk us out of trouble it's unlikely we shall be able to fight our way out either."

"Anything else?" asked Vizqash. "I have some fine curios —charms in the form of the Balhibo god Bákh. You can wear them anywhere but Upper Gherra, where it's a capital offense. And Krishnan books: dictionaries, travel books . . ."

"What's this?" inquired Barnevelt, untying the string that held together the two wooden covers between which a book, a single long strip of native paper, was folded zigzag. "Looks like a Mayan codex."

"A navigational guide published in Majbur," said Vizqash. "It has tables showing the motions of all three moons, the tides, the constellations, an almanac of lucky and unlucky days."

"I'll take it."

They paid, made a date with Miss Foley for a language lesson, and departed for the barber shop to receive their disguises.

In charge of the Viagens boathouse was a tailed man from the Koloft Swamps, hairy and monstrously ugly. Eileen Foley handed him a chit from Commandate Kennedy and inquired: "Any robbers on the Pichidé lately, Yerevats?"

"No," said Yerevats. "Not since great battle. I there. Hit robber on head, like this . . ."

"He tells that story to everybody who'll listen," said Eileen Foley. "Let's take this boat."

She indicated a rowboat with semicircular hoops stuck in sockets in the thwarts, forming arches over the hull.

"Why not that one?" asked Tangaloa, pointing to a motorboat.

"Good heavens, suppose it fell into the hands of the Krishnans! That's for emergencies only."

Barnevelt stepped into the boat and held out a hand to Miss Foley. Vizqash climbed in holding his scabbard. The boat settled markedly as Tangaloa added his weight to the load. Yerevats handed down the lunch basket, untied the painter, and pushed them out of their slip with a boathook.

As they emerged into the open, Tangaloa said: "While I'm no ringer on the local meteorology, I should hazard a conjecture

27

that rain in the near fut—"

A crash of thunder drowned the rest of the sentence, and a patter of large drops made further comment unnecessary. Vizqash got a tarpaulin out of a compartment in the bow, and they wrestled it into place over the arches.

"The wettest summer since I was hatched," said the Krishnan.

Tangaloa said: "Whoever takes the tiller will get wet, I fear."

"Let Vizqash," said Barnevelt. "He knows the way."

Grumbling, the Krishnan wrapped himself in his cloak and took the tiller while the Earthmen unshipped the oars. Tangaloa took off the camera ring he was wearing and put it in his pocket. He said: "This reminds me of a picnic I attended in Australia."

"Is that a place on your planet?" asked Vizqash.

"Right-o. I spent some years there—went to school there in fact."

"Did it rain on this picnic too?"

"No, but they have ants in Australia: *that* long, with a sting at both ends . . ."

"What is an ant?"

By the time the Earthmen had explained ants, the rain had stopped and Roqir was again shining in a greenish sky crowded with deeply-banked clouds. They threw back the tarpaulin. The current had already carried them down the Pichidé out of sight of the Novorecife boathouse. Presently they came to the end of the concrete wall that ran along the north bank of the river and protected Novorecife from surprise.

Tangaloa said: "Tell us about Qirib, Senhor Vizqash, since you come from there."

"Stay out of it," rasped Vizqash. "A—how do you say?—lousy country. The women's rule has ruined it. I escaped many years ago and don't intend to go back."

The terrain along the south bank became lower until all that could be seen between water and sky was a dark-green strip of reeds, with odd-looking Krishnan trees here and there.

"That's the Koloft Swamp, where Yerevats's wild relatives live," said Eileen Foley.

Tangaloa looked at his hands, as if fearing blisters, and said:

"It will not be so easy rowing back upstream as down."

"We shall come back along the edge of the river, where the current is weak," said the Krishnan.

A V-shaped ripple, caused by some creature swimming under water, cut swiftly across their bow and disappeared in the distance.

Barnevelt asked: "Are we going all the way to Qou?"

"No," said Vizqash, "there is a landing on the south side before we reach Qou."

A pair of aqebats rose squawking from the reeds, circled on leathery wings to gain altitude, and flew away southward. Vizqash now and then let go the tiller ropes to slap at small flying things.

"One nice thing," said Miss Foley, "the bugs don't bother us. Our smell must be different from poor Vizqash's."

"Maybe I should go to your planet, where they would not bother me either," said the sufferer. "I see our landing."

The reeds along the south side of the river had given place to low brown bluffs, two or three times the height of a man.

"How d'you tell time?" said Barnevelt. "Castanhoso wouldn't let us bring our watches."

Visqash unclasped a bracelet from his arm, clicked it shut again, and dangled it from a fine chain. "It is the ninth hour of the day lacking a quarter, as you would say three-quarters of an hour past noon, though since your days and hours are different from ours I do not know what the exact equivalent would be. The sun shines through this little hole on these marks on the inside, as it did through the arrow slot in the haunted tower in the romance of Abbeq and Dangi. Perhaps I could sell you one of these back at Novorecife?"

"Perhaps." Barnevelt shipped his oars and hunkered forward.

A simple pier, made of a stockade of short logs with a gravel fill, extended out into the river at this point. Two other boats, of obvious Krishnan design, were tied to it with large padlocks. From a pier, a narrow dirt road ran back inland through a notch in the bluff. As the Viagens craft nosed in to shore, a couple of small scaly things slipped into the water with slight splashes.

When they had climbed out and secured the boat, Vizqash led

them up the road, which curved left towards Qou. Something roared in the distance, and the small animal noises, the rustlings and chirpings from the vegetation lining the road, stopped.

"It is all right," said Vizqash. "They seldom come this close to the village."

Barnevelt said: "Don't you wish you'd bought a sword now, George? Without mine I'd feel like a lawyer without his briefcase."

"With you and Vizqash to protect me I'm sweet enough. Here, you carry the basket."

Barnevelt took the basket, wishing he had the gall always to hand the heaviest burden to somebody else. The heat and the roughness of the path soon left them little breath for chatter.

Finally Vizqash said: "Here we are," and pushed through the shrubbery on the left side of the road.

They followed him. Since the country was of open savannah type, they found the going not too difficult. After some minutes they came to an area like a terminal moraine, strewn with stones and boulders. As Barnevelt looked, he perceived that the stones were of unnaturally regular sizes and shapes and arranged in rows and patterns.

"Up here," said Vizqash.

They climbed a conical heap, the remains of a circular tower long fallen into a mass of rubble but affording a view of the whole area. The ruins extended to the river. A fortress or fortified camp, Barnevelt surmised . . .

"Here," said Vizqash, pointing to the remains of a statue thrice life size. The pedestal and one leg still stood, while among the rocks and boulders scattered about the base Barnevelt could make out a head, part of an arm, and other pieces of the statue. He remembered:

"I met a traveler from an antique land
Who said: Two vast and trunkless legs of stone
Stand in the desert . . . Near them, on the sand,
Half sunk, a shattered visage lies, whose frown,
And wrinkled lip, and sneer of cold command,

Tell that its sculptor well those passions read
Which yet survive, stamped on these lifeless things . . ."

"What are you muttering?" said Eileen Foley.

"Sorry," said Barnevelt. "I was just remembering . . ." and he recited the sonnet.

Tangaloa said: "That's by those English blokes Kelly and Sheets, is it not? The ones who wrote *The Mikado?*"

Before Barnevelt had a chance to straighten out his colleague, Vizqash broke in: "You should know the great poem of our poet Qallé, about a ruin like this. It is called *Sad Thoughts* . . ."

"How about some tucker?" said Tangaloa. "That row has given me an appetite."

"It is called," said Vizqash firmly, "*Sad Thoughts Engendered by Eating a Picnic Supper in the Moss-Covered Ruins of Marinjid, Burned by the Balhibuma in the Year of the Avval, Forty-Ninth Cycle After Qarar.*"

Tangaloa said: "With all that title, I'm sure we shan't need . . ."

But the Krishnan burst into rolling, guttural Gozashtandou verse, with sweeping Delsartean gestures. Barnevelt found that he could catch perhaps one word in five.

Tangaloa said to Eileen Foley: "That's what we get for going out with a pair of bloody poetry enthusiasts. If you'd care to take a walk with me while they get it out of their systems, I'm sure I can find some more entertaining . . ."

At that moment Vizqash ran down, saying: "I could go on for an hour, but that gives you the idea."

He then elected himself chef and rummaged for dry wood. Although his pile of twigs did not look promising, he picked some weedy plants with pods. He broke these open and shook a fine yellow dust on to his heap of sticks.

"The *yasuvar*. We use this powder for fireworks," he explained.

He got out a small cylinder with a piston that fitted closely into it and bore a large knob at its upper end. From a small box he shook a pinch of tinder into the cylinder, inserted the piston into the open end of the cylinder, and smote the knob with his palm, driving the piston down into the cylinder.

"I like these better than those mechanical flint-and-steel lighters such as the one you bought," he said. "There is less to get out of order."

He took the piston out of the cylinder and shook smoldering tinder onto the fire. The fragments lighted the yellow powder, which blazed up with crackling sounds and ignited the rest.

Meanwhile Eileen Foley laid out the contents of the basket. From among these, Vizqash took a package wrapped in waxed paper. When the paper was unwrapped, there came into view four jointed creatures something like small crabs and something like large spiders.

"This," said Vizqash, "is a great delicacy."

Barnevelt, gulping, felt Tangaloa's amused eyes upon him. The Samoan ate everything; but he, Barnevelt, had never developed the catholicity of taste that marks the true traveler. However, he controlled his features; they might have to eat odder things yet. If he had thought of this aspect of interplanetary exploration sooner, though, he might have put up a stouter resistance to the project.

"Fine," he said with a weak smile. "How long will they take?"

"Five or ten minutes," said Vizqash. He had fitted together a wire grill so that his four bugs were inclosed between the two grids. They sizzled and sent up a sharp smell as he toasted them.

From the direction of the road, a dozen flying creatures rocketed up out of the shrubbery with hoarse cries. Barnevelt idly watched them fly away, wondering if some prowling carnivore had disturbed them. The small animal noises seemed to have died down again.

"Vizqash," he said, "are you sure there are no more bandits around here?"

"Not for years," said the Krishnan, jiggling his grill over the fire and poking additional twigs into the flames. "Why do you ask?" he added sharply.

Tangaloa, aiming his Hayashi at bits of ruin, said: "Let's walk down towards the river, Dirk. There is some solid-looking masonary at the end of the block."

"These will be ready soon," said Vizqash in tones of protest.

"We're not going far," said Tangaloa. "Call us when they're nearly done."

"But . . ." said Vizqash, in the manner of one who struggles to put his wishes into words.

Tangaloa started for the river, and Barnevelt followed. They picked their way among the rocks to the north end of the ruin, on the top of a low bluff sloping down to the water. Near the line of the boundary wall stood a big slab, half sunk in the earth and leaning drunkenly, its face covered with half-obliterated carvings.

Tangaloa shot a few centimeters of film, saying: "In a couple of hours the sun will bring out these carvings . . ."

Barnevelt looked back towards the fire, and paused. Vizqash was standing up and waving an arm.

"I think he wants us . . ." Barnevelt said, and then realized that the Krishnan was waving his far arm as if beckoning to somebody on the other side, towards the road.

"Hey!" said Barnevelt. "Look, George!"

"Look at what?"

"What's that moving in that copse?"

"What? Oh, I suppose some local friends of his . . ."

A group of men had come out of the copse and were running up towards the fire. Vizqash was saying something to them. Barnevelt could hear his voice but could not make out the rush of Krishnan words.

"They don't look friendly to me," said Barnevelt. "We may have to fight or run."

"Nonsense, cobber. You're being romantic . . ."

All the men, including Vizqash, started running towards the two Earthmen, swords in hands, all but one who carried a bow instead.

"Blind me," said Tangaloa, "it does look like trouble!" He picked up a couple of softball-sized stones.

Barnevelt put his back to the wall and drew his sword. Although the blade came out with a satisfying *wheep*, it occurred to Dirk that reading a historical adventure story about a dauntless hero fighting with archaic weapons against desperate odds is by

all means a more satisfactory occupation than trying to enact the rôle in person.

It also struck him that something was drastically wrong with the picture. Eileen Foley had been standing across the fire from Vizqash when he beckoned his friends out of the bushes. She had continued to stand there, without sign of alarm or excitement, as they ran past her, paying her no more heed then one person pays another in a subway crush. Now she was trailing them towards the river at a walk.

"Drop your sword!" cried Vizqash. "Put down those stones and you shall not be hurt!"

"What kind of picnic d'you call this?" asked Barnevelt.

"I said, give up your weapons! Otherwise we will kill you."

The men—nine counting Vizqash—halted out of reach of Barnevelt's blade. After all, he and his companion were both well over average Krishnan stature.

"And if we do?" said Tangaloa softly.

"You will see. You must go with these men, but no harm shall come to you."

"Please give up," said Eileen Foley from behind the Krishnans. "It's the best way."

"We have given you your chance," said Vizqash. "If anybody is hurt it will be your fault."

Barnevelt said: "What's your connection with this, Eileen?"

"I—I . . ."

"*Manyoi chi!*" cried Vizqash in his harsh voice, switching from Portuguese to his native Gozashtandou.

However, instead of all rushing in at once—which would have ended the encounter right then—the men inched forward, looking at one another as if each were waiting for the other to take the first shock.

Tangaloa let fly one of his stones with a mighty heave.

"*Mohoi raf!*" shrieked Vizqash.

Crunch! The stone struck the archer in the face just as he was reaching back over his shoulder for an arrow. He fell backwards, his face a mask of blood.

Barnevelt, scared but determined, remembered the old platitude about the best defense. He accordingly launched a furious *attaque-en-marchant* at the nearest Krishnan. Eileen Foley screamed.

Tangaloa threw his second stone at Vizqash, who ducked and stooped to pick up another.

Barnevelt caught his opponent's blade in a whirling *prise* and drove him backwards. The Krishnan stumbled on a stone and fell sprawling. As he started to sit up, Barnevelt ran him through the body.

At that instant Barnevelt felt a sharp pain in his left side, towards the rear, and heard the sound of tearing cloth. He spun. He had driven right through the line of foes, one of whom had thrust at him from behind. He parried a second thrust and knocked up a blade coming at him from still another direction. He knew that even a much abler fencer than he would stand no chance against two at once.

Tangaloa had thrown another stone and vaulted to the top of the wall. Three Krishnans were running towards him and in a couple of seconds would skewer him.

"Run!" bellowed Tangaloa, dropping off the wall to the slope below.

Two Krishnans were threatening Barnevelt, and others were crowding forward. Since Eileen seemed to be on the other side in this game, he could leave her with a clear conscience.

One Krishnan stood directly between him and the wall; the other was boring in from his right. Barnevelt threw himself forward into a *corps-a-corps*, and during the instant that his antagonist's body shielded him he punched the man with his left fist, hard and low. As the Krishnan started to double up, Barnevelt shoved him out of the way and leaped to the top of the wall, just as a sweeping slash from another sword carried away his cap.

Tangaloa was already halfway down the slope and, to Barnevelt's right, several Krishnans were climbing over the wall in pursuit. Barnevelt jumped off the wall and bounded down the slope in giant strides, his heels sinking into the loose earth at each step. Ahead of him Tangaloa kept right on through the reeds that bordered the river, his boots swishing through the plants, and into the river itself.

Barnevelt knew he was too encumbered to swim well, but the Krishnans would hardly hold off while he sat down to wrestle with his boots. He threw his sword at the nearest, cast aside baldric and scabbard, and plunged in after his colleague, who was already wallowing swiftly out towards midstream like an overdressed porpoise.

Whsht-plunk! Something struck the water beside Barnevelt. A glance back showed that one of the Krishnans had picked up the bow of the man whom Tangaloa had downed with the first stone, and was shooting from the top of the wall. Eileen Foley was looking on while Vizqash ran about waving his sword and shouting orders.

Whsht-plunk! A couple of Krishnans at the edge of the water

37

were throwing off coats, shoes, and other impedimenta.

"Duck!" Barnevelt called to Tangaloa, who immediately disappeared.

Barnevelt did likewise. Through the water the sandy bottom, little over wading depth, could be seen below. Water plants waved gently in the current.

When Barnevelt began to yearn for air he drove himself back up to the surface, shaking his head to throw non-existent hair out of his eyes. He glanced back. Half a dozen Krishnans, it seemed, were stripping to swim or were already splashing into the water after him. Ahead, Tangaloa's big brown head broke the surface, puffing like a grampus.

Whsht-plunk! Barnevelt took a deep breath and ducked under again. The bottom was now almost invisible, meters below. Another arrow darted down into the water near him from the quick-silvery surface above, trailing a comet-tail of bubbles. It lost speed within a meter and drifted back up to the surface where it hung, point downward, like a little buoy.

This time he came up out of effective range. However, five or six Krishnans were now swimming out from shore, plodding along with sedate breast strokes. The current had already carried Barnevelt and Tangaloa quite a way downstream. Barnevelt had no great fear of Krishnans in the water; he was a good swimmer and Tangaloa a superb one. But . . .

"George!" he called. "If we let those buggers follow us to the north side, they'll get us sure."

Tangaloa spat water. "We could wait in the shallows and stoush them as they crawl out."

"Then they'll spread up and down stream, so while we're conking one the others would get to shore. How about taking care of them right here?"

"Can you swim back to the first one under water?"

"I think so."

"All right—you take number one."

Tangaloa went under in a porpoise-roll, his feet showing momentarily. Barnevelt followed suit and swam towards the nearest pursuer. Ahead of him Tangaloa barreled along, gaining fast and heading for the second.

From below the pursuers looked like headless men. Barnevelt planned how to meet his antagonist. The man had stripped down to his underwear, a kind of diaper that flapped about his loins as he swam. The hilt of the Krishnan's dagger protruded from the waistband of this garment.

Barnevelt kicked himself into position below and in front of this Krishnan and then, as his natural buoyancy wafted him upwards, drew his own dagger. He had timed his approach carefully, and as the man came overhead he brought his legs together in a scissor kick and drove his dagger into the other's belly.

At once the water became dark with blood and opaque with bubbles as the man thrashed wildly. At that instant Tangaloa seized the ankles of the second swimmer and dragged him under.

Barnevelt thrust his head out for a long breath beside the man he had stabbed. The other swimmers were all looking towards the scene with alarmed expressions. By now they had all drifted down-stream out of sight of the ruin.

The stabbed man, lying limply face-down on the surface, was beginning to slide under. Tangaloa's head bobbed up near where he had pulled the second man under, but of his victim there was no sign.

"Take the next two?" said Tangaloa.

The other Krishnans, however, all turned and splashed back for the shore whence they had come. Barnevelt and Tangaloa struck out for the north side of the river. A long swim, but they could now take their time about it. They shed their outer clothing.

"Good thing they didn't have the rowboat handy," said Barnevelt. "A rowboat's as good as a cruiser if the other guy's swimming."

"What's back of this?" said Tangaloa. "The sheila seemed to be in with the push."

They swam silently until the bottom again came into sight below them, and presently they waded out and sat down on a log to rest. Their pursuers had disappeared.

Barnevelt said: "Hey, you're cut too!"

Tangaloa looked at the wound on his left arm. "A scratch; let's see yours."

Barnevelt's own wound had begun to throb painfully, and blood was still flowing since it had not had a chance to dry. Examination, however, showed that the point of the Krishnan sword had slid along a rib instead of going between the ribs into the vitals.

Tearing his shirt into strips for a bandage, Barnevelt said: "Next time maybe you'll bring a sword. You can't buckle a swash with your bare hands."

"Maybe. But if we had worn those mail shirts, we should have drowned. I wonder what those blokes will do now? They can't go back to Novorecife, knowing we shall be along to accuse them."

Barnevelt shrugged. "Unless they've cooked up some fancy disk, to the effect that we're janrú smugglers, or . . . Matter of fact, d'you suppose this is what happened to Igor?"

"It might be."

"Let's think about it. Meanwhile there sinks that nebulous star we call the sun, and we'd better shove before the dragon wing of night o'erspreads the earth."

"That damned energy of yours, battler," groaned Tangaloa, heaving his bulk to his feet. "Always rush, rush, rush. We Polynesians are the only people who know how to live."

The guard said: "Wait till I call the River Gate to confirm your story."

The River Gate did indeed confirm the fact that Messrs. Barnevelt and Tangaloa, alias Snyol of Pleshch and Tagdë of Vyutr, had gone out through the gate the morning past, on their way to a picnic with Miss Foley of the Security Office and Mr. Vizqash of the Outfitting Store. What did these gentlemen look like? . . .

"Pass on in," said the guard at last. "Anybody can see you're Earthmen."

"Is it as obvious as that?" said Tangaloa to Barnevelt. "Come to think of it, one of your feelers is coming loose. Better give the barber hell."

Barnevelt replied: "I'm more interested in giving Vizqash and the fair Eileen the wholesome boon of gyve and gag."

"Oh, them? I've forgiven them already. It is rather amusing to look back upon."

"As amusing as a funeral on Christmas Eve! I'm going to Castanhoso's office."

Barnevelt marched through the settlement, ignoring stares at his half-naked state, until he came to the compound next to the spaceport where the Security Force had its offices.

He strode in the front entrance and down the hall to Castanhoso's office. The door was ajar, and he was about to stalk in when the sound of voices from within stopped him. He held up a hand to halt Tangaloa, lumbering behind.

". . . we warned them," said the voice of Vizqash, "but no, they said they had not swum since leaving Earth. So they threw off their clothes and jumped in, and the next we knew one of them screamed and disappeared, and then the other did likewise."

"It was awful," said Eileen Foley's voice, quivering with pathos and sincerity.

Castanhoso could be heard clucking. "This will cause no end of trouble. These Earthmen were important people, and I liked them personally. And the forms we shall have to fill out! It is odd, though, that both should be taken—one at a time is all an avval usually seizes."

"Unless there is a pair in the Pichidé," said the Krishnan.

"True, but that does not bring back those splendid—"

Barnevelt stepped into the room, saying: "I'm glad our loss isn't permanent, Senhor Herculeu. The picnic was called because of a rain—of arrows. Actually—"

Eileen Foley jumped up with a shriek like that of a Vishnuvian siren-squirrel. Vizqash leaped to his feet also with a resounding oath and ripped out his sword.

"It shall be permanent this time!" he yelled, rushing upon the two Earthmen in the doorway.

Barnevelt had a flash of panic. His dagger would be of little use against the sword; the nearest chair was out of reach; if he stepped back he would merely bump into George. He could neither run nor fight, and after preserving his life with such effort he was now liable to lose it through a trivial lack of precautions . . .

The point of the rapier was a bare meter away, and Barnevelt was drawing his knife as a last resort, when a pistol shot crashed deafeningly. The Krishnan's sword spun out of his hand and clattered across the room. Vizqash was left standing weaponless, wringing his hand and looking foolish.

Castanhoso rose with the pistol he had snatched from his desk drawer in his hand.

"Do not move, *amigo*," he said.

The hall outside was suddenly full of people, male and female, human and Krishnan, uniformed and in civilian clothing, all jabbering. Vizqash assumed the air of an insulted grandee.

"My good Castanhoso," he said, "instruct your men to treat me with due respect. After all, I am who I am."

"Precisely," snapped Castanhoso. "Lock him up."

The long Krishnan day had ended when Barnevelt and Tangaloa were finally dismissed. Castanhoso said: "Get dressed, senhores, and have dinner. I must grill the prisoners. Shall we meet in the Nova Iorque afterwards?"

"Fine," said Tangaloa, "I could utilize a bit of tucker. We never did consume that lunch."

Two and a half hours later the explorers, back in Earthly garb and improved by a much-needed meal, were sitting in the bar. Barnevelt had suffered a delayed fright reaction from his experience, and had been on the verge of throwing up the expedition and his job. But Tangaloa had garruled cheerfully throughout dinner without giving him an opening, and now the feeling had gone. They saw Castanhoso enter, look around, and come to their booth.

"She has broken down," the Brazilian chortled.

"I hope you weren't brutal with the poor little squid," said Tangaloa.

"No, no, merely some sharp questioning under the metapolygraph. She does not really know who this Vizqash is—if that is his real name, which I doubt—but she thinks he is one of the janrú ring. Everybody suspects everybody of smuggling janrú nowadays."

Barnevelt grunted assent while lighting a Krishnan cigar. Though he had always smoked cigarettes and pipes, he would have to learn to like cigars here.

"Why was Miss Foley involved?" asked Tangaloa. "Such a bonzer little sheila . . ."

"That is a strange story," said Castanhoso, looking at his fingernails with an expression of embarrassment. "It seems that she was—ah—in love with—uh—*me,* of all people, though she had plenty of admirers and knew perfectly well I was married."

"And you loathed the bright dishonor of her love?" said Barnevelt with a grin.

"It is not funny, my dear sir. This Vizqash had promised her a bottle of perfume doped with janrú to use on me. All she had to do was come along on this picnic, and after you two had been disposed of, go back to Novorecife and confirm his story about the avval."

"What's that?" asked Barnevelt.

"A great snaky thing that lives in water. You can call it a giant armored eel or a legless crocodile. There has been one in the Pichidé for some time. Only last week it carried off a woman of Qou."

"Guk! You mean we went swimming with *that?"*

"Yes. I should have warned you. After Vizqash had sent his men in pursuit of you—I suppose he did not tell them about the avval—you swam so far out you could no longer be clearly seen from shore. Then they came back, saying that two of their number and both of you had perished. I imagine they lied because they feared that if they told Vizqash the truth he would be angry and withhold their pay. But if they had told him the truth, he and Miss Foley would not have rowed back to Novorecife with that story about the avval."

"What will they do with the poor little thing?" said Tangaloa.

Barnevelt said: "George, I find your sentimental solicitude for this young Lady Macbeth tiresome."

"You are merely maladjusted, Dirk. What will they do?"

Castanhoso shrugged. "That is up to Judge Keshavachandra. Meanwhile you had better replace your lost equipment and find another language teacher."

They settled the details of their passage to Qirib: by boat down the river to Majbur, by rail to Jazmurian, and by stagecoach thence to fabulous Ghulindé.

"With that damned macaw making me sniffle," said Barnevelt. "And then we face the foam of perilous seas in faery lands forlorn."

"Well," said Castanhoso, "do not go swimming in them until you know what sort of swimming companions you have. Here is to your success."

"By the way," said Barnevelt, "what does Vizqash himself say?"

"I do not know yet. This will be much more difficult, because the metapolygraph will not work on Krishnans." The Brazilian looked at his watch. "I must get back to question this rascal . . . Yes?"

Another man in the Security Force uniform had come in and now whispered in Castanhoso's ear.

"Tamates!" cried Castanhoso, leaping up and clapping a hand to his head. "The unspeakable one has escaped from his cell! I am ruined!"

And he rushed out of the Nova Iorque Bar.

Again the dark-green rampart of reeds that marked the Koloft Swamp slid past Dirk Barnevelt and George Tangaloa. This time, however, they lounged on the bow of a river barge, the *Chaldir*, which wafted down the Pichidé on the convection of the current and the pull of a single triangular sail slung at the bow from one stubby mast. The prevailing westerly carried the smoke of their cigars down the river. Less welcomely it also brought them the smells of the cargo of green hides and of the team of six-legged shaihans on the fantail, who at the conclusion of the journey

44

would pull the boat back upstream by the tow-path. They chain-smoked to offset the stench.

Now came into view the landing where they had tied up on the ill-omened picnic the week before, and then the ruin, still keeping to itself whatever secret it harbored. Then Qou, small and squalid, opened into view on the south bank and as quietly glided out of sight again.

"*Zeft! Ghuvoí zu!*" shrieked Philo the macaw from his cage.

Barnevelt, practicing lunges, said: "I'm still surprised how human these Krishnans seem to be."

Tangaloa had weakened to the point of buying a mace, half a meter long, with a stout wooden shaft and a spiked iron head. The shaft he had now stuck through his belt. He sat crosslegged like a large bronze Buddha with his back against their duffel bag, looking, with his brown skin and Mongoloid cast of features, Dirk thought, a lot more authentically Krishnan than he himself.

Tangaloa cleared his throat, indicating that a lecture was taking form, and began: "That has been figured out, Dirk. A civilized species must have certain physical characteristics: eyes to see and

at least one arm or tentacle to manipulate with, for instance. And it can't be too large or too small. Well, it works out similarly with mental characteristics. Intelligence alone is not sufficient. If the species is too uniform in its mental qualities it won't achieve the division of labor needed for a high culture—while, if it's too variable the smart ones will tyrannize too easily over the rest, which again results in a static society. If they're too erratic or maladjusted they will be unable to coöperate, whereas if they are too well-adjusted they won't produce schizoid types like you to create new ideas."

"Thanks for the implied compliment," said Barnevelt. "Any time I feel the stirrings of genius I'll let you know."

"Even so," continued Tangaloa, "there is much variation among extraterrestrials, like those things on Sirius Nine with their ant-like economy. It just happens that of all intelligent species the Krishnans are the most humanoid . . ."

"Har 'immá! Har 'immá!" screamed Philo.

"If that actually means what I think," said Barnevelt, "Queen Alvandi will have to be pretty broad-minded to put up with it."

"She may not even understand him. The Qiribo dialect differs a lot from standard Gozashtandou, you know. It preserves the middle voice in verbs . . ."

Barnevelt ended his practice and went forward to look at the shaihans, with whom he had made firm friends, and to scratch their shaggy foreheads.

At night they anchored in the shallows, there being no settlement near. Roqir sank beneath the low horizon in the polychrome glory of a Krishnan sunset; the master's wife prepared the evening meal; the night noises of the small things that lived in the reeds came over the water, and the boatmen set up their little altars and prayed to their various gods before turning in.

So passed the days while they followed the Pichidé as it wound across the Gozashtandou Plain on its leisurely way to the Sadabao Sea. They considered how they should approach Gorbovast in Majbur, and Queen Alvandi in Ghulindé, and what means they should employ to overcome the perils of the Sunqar. Dirk Barnevelt acquired a sunburned nose, the knack of wearing a sword without getting fouled up in it, a fair facility with his new languages, and a certain hard self-confidence he had never known on Earth.

He wryly debated with himself whether this feeling came from a chance to indulge a long-suppressed romanticism; a chauvinistic feeling of superiority to the Krishnans; or simply getting away from his mother. He was relieved to discover that his killing of two Krishnans brought on no violent emotional reaction, then or later. On the other hand he suffered occasional nightmares wherein he fled, yelling for his mother, from a swarm of huge hornets.

He knew, however, that it did no good to unburden himself to Tangaloa, who would merely make a joke of his broodings.

While George had a remarkable mind (he showed an amazing flair for languages and had soaked up a vast deal of xenological lore) he would not bother with anything he found hard, like working when he did not feel like it, perhaps because some things were so easy for him, or perhaps because of his indulgent Polynesian upbringing. Though kind and good-natured in a vague impersonal way, he had no emotional depth or drive; brilliantly superficial, a facile talker but a feeble doer, and no man to lead enterprises of great pith and moment. Barnevelt was sure that, though George was older than he and his nominal superior, the whole responsibility would sooner or later come to rest upon his own bony shoulders.

At last the river broadened out until from one side the houses on the other were as matchboxes, and the folk as ants. The *Chaldir* followed the bank past the villas of the rich of Majbur, whose young played piggy-back polo on the lawns or pushed each other off the docks with shrieking and loud laughter. Here much water traffic was to be seen: anchored rowboats with men fishing from them; another river barge like their own, wallowing across the river under sail to set her team ashore on the tow-path on the northern side.

Since the tubby *Chaldir* had but small powers of maneuver, the master asserted his right-of-way by banging a gong of dented copper whenever they neared another vessel. They almost collided with a timber raft which, being even less agile, drifted tranquilly in their path until the raftmen and the *Chaldir*'s crew were forced to hold off from each other with poles, shouting abuse until the Earthmen half expected the two crews to fall upon each other with knives, and the shaihans in the stern bellowed uneasily. However, once the barge had been poled around the raft so that the way again lay clear, all passed off amiably enough.

The villas gave way to suburbs and the suburbs to the central city: with neither the onion-domed opulence of Hershid nor the frowning gray fortress-look of Mishé, but a character of its own. It was a city of many graceful arches with intricate and fantastic carvings, buildings of five and six stories, and a seething timeless traffic tangle.

Along the shore appeared wharves and piers at which were tied up many barges like their own. Beyond them, Barnevelt saw the spiky tangle of masts and spars of the port's deep-water shipping. The *Chaldir*'s master, spotting a vacant place, brought his craft angling in to shore, a couple of her people grunting at long sweeps to counteract the current. A fishing craft with sails sprouting at all angles, like a backyard on Monday, had marked the same parking space and tried to nose out the barge, but not quickly enough. Philo the parrot added screeches to the imprecations of the crews of the two vessels.

The sun was high in the heavens when the barge tied up at last. Barnevelt and Tangaloa bid good-bye to the master and his people and climbed on to the wharf to search out the office of Gorbovast, Barnevelt with the usual feeling of butterflies in the belly that afflicted him whenever he was called upon to walk in on a stranger and introduce himself.

He need not have worried. Gorbovast received them, Barnevelt thought, "with garrulous ease and oily courtesies" on the strength of their letter from Castanhoso. This sleek Krishnan gentleman had long defied the dictum about the difficulty of serving two masters; for, while acting as the commissioner for King Eqrar of Gozashtand in Majbur, he had also for years augmented his income by sending information to the Viagens Interplanetarias Security Force at Novorecife.

"*The* Snyol of Pleshch? And gvám-hunting in the Sunqar, eh?" he said, pronouncing Barnevelt's Nyami name "Esnyol"—as for that matter did all Gozashtandou-speaking Krishnans. "Well, his the riches whose is the risk, as it says in Nehavend's proverbs. You know the Banjao Sea has become a nest of most irregulous bloody pirates, and there's no putting 'em down because Dur in its arrogance subsidizes 'em with tribute so they'll hurt the trade of smaller powers like Majbur and Zamba. Moreover rumor links these same knaves to the janrú trade, which makes every independent man shudder o' nights."

Barnevelt told him a little about the unmasking of Vizqash at Novorecife.

"So," said Gorbovast, "the cullions have been operating in these parts, eh? Well, well, and well. 'Twill do no harm to slip a word to the Chief Syndic, for the folk of Majbur mortally fear the stuff should spread among 'em and give their women the upper hand. While we be not so susceptible as the silly Earthmen, whom the merest whiff reduces to servile jelly, still much havoc could be wrought upon us by this subtle means. As to a letter to the Douri of Qirib, you shall have it straight. 'Twere well to hasten if you would deliver it."

"Why, is the old man-eater dying?"

"Nay—because, so 'tis said in the mughouses, she intends, once her present consort be unheaded in accordance with their barbarous and bloody custom, the throne in favor of her daughter Zei to resign."

Barnevelt raised his eyebrows, and his glued-on antennae rose with them. Qirib under a young and newly-enthroned queen sounded more attractive than under a tough old Tatar like Alvandi. "I hadn't heard that angle. Perhaps, Master Gorbovast, you'd give us two letters of introduction, one to each dame."

"The very thing. And watch well your step among these masterful dames, for 'tis gossip that they keep their men subdued by this same drug. . . ." And he told them what they needed to know about tickets and train times, adding: "As the glass shows that the celestial wheel has not yet turned to the meridian, you'll have time to view our jewel of a city ere sallies forth the south-bound daily express."

And view it they did, wandering down to the waterfront to photograph the ships—mere dories compared with Earthly ships, but impressive enough in their own setting. There were high-sided square-riggers from Dur in the Va'andao Sea, lanteeners from Sotaspé and other Sadabao ports, and even a catamaran with a crescent sail from Malayer in the far South. And long low war galleys, outstanding among them the pride of Majbur's navy, the quinquireme *Junsar*, with her bank of five-man oars belayed to her sides, her high gilded stern, and her toothed ram pro-jecting at the waterline forward.

They braced themselves to withstand the odors of the seafood market and sampled one of the lunches the counters of this section offered.

Barnevelt soon regretted his curiosity, for the object placed before him in a bowl of soup, a sea creature something like a large slug with tentacles, had the curious property of remaining alive and wriggling for some time after being cooked. He got down a couple of writhing bites before his gorge rose and in-terrupted the experiment.

"You effete Westerners," chuckled Tangaloa, finishing his sea slug and wiping his mouth.

"Damn you," growled Barnevelt, and doggedly resumed his assault until his organism, too, was gone.

Then they took in the municipal zoo. Barnevelt, remembering his swim in the Pichidé, winced at the sight of a half-grown avval in a tank. But then he would have loitered all afternoon watching the things in the cages until even Tangaloa, who almost never hurried, had to remind him of train time and drag him away.

In the park they came upon an open-air performance by a ballet troupe of dancers from the temple of Dashmok, the Free City's own special god of commerce. A priest was passing the hat—or rather a gourd-like container—as part of the temple's drive for some fund. Watching the leaping girls, Barnevelt felt a blush of embarrassment sweep over his face. Chautauqua

County was never like this.

Tangaloa dryly remarked: "You see, Dirk, different cultures differ as to what should be covered. Few cultures other than your own Western one have that violent nudity-tabu that came into it from the old Syriac civilization via Judaism and its offshoot, Christianity . . ."

A shower ended the dance and scattered the audience. The Earthmen made their way to the terminal, to find that the train was not made up yet and would not leave for at least a Krishnan hour after its scheduled time. Since the station agent could give them no more definite statement than that, there was nothing to do but sit and smoke while waiting.

Presently a man in a pale-blue costume, wearing a light and strictly ornamental silver helmet with a pair of silver aqebat-wings sprouting from its sides, strolled in with a big bag over his shoulder and took a place on the bench next to the Earthmen.

While Barnevelt had never had much talent for picking up conversations with strangers, the uninhibited Tangaloa was soon in animated discussion with the helmeted man.

"This," said the Krishnan, pointing to his helmet, "means I toil for the Mejrou Qurardena, bearing fardels hence to thither." (The name meant roughly Reliable Express Company.) "Our Company's motto is 'Neither storm, nor night, nor beast of prey, nor men of evil intent stay our carriers in the swift performance of their duties.' "

"A fine motto," said Barnevelt. "Matter of fact it sounds familiar."

"No doubt word of our company has reached far Nyamadzë," said the courier. "And some day shall we extend our services even unto that chilly clime. O masters, I could tell you tales of the deeds of our people that would make your antennae stand upright with terror. At the time my friend Gehr carried a parcel into the heart of the dread Sunqar and delivered it to the chief pirate himself, the fearsome Sheafasè."

Both Barnevelt and Tangaloa leaned forward, the former saying: "What sort of person is this She— this pirate king?"

"As to that, my friend Gehr knows no more than you, for

Sheafasè shows himself to none but his own subjects. But since Gehr could not leave ere the consignee signed his receipt, 'twas finally arranged that the arch-robber should thrust his hand through a gap in a curtain to wield the pen. And Gehr thus caught a glimpse—ah, masters, what a dreadful thing was that! No human hand, but a shuddersome structure of claws and scales, like the foot of the fearful pudamef that haunts the glaciers of your own land. So Sheafase must be a creature, not of our own honest world, but of some depraved unwholesome other planet in the deeps of space—like that called Earth, for instance, the home of all the baneful and goetic sorceries . . ."

"*Pun dessoí!*" called the gatekeeper.

The expressman got up and shouldered his parcel sack, and the Earthmen picked up their duffel bag and birdcage. So Earth was a depraved and unwholesome planet, eh? thought Barnevelt, amused and patriotically irked at the same time. Unfortunately he was in no position to start waving the checkered World Federation flag.

The train consisted of five little four-wheeled carriages: two flatcars heaped with goods, and three passenger cars that looked like converted stagecoaches, running on a track of about one-meter gage. The locomotive was a bishtar, hitched to the leading car by a rope harness. The beast stood, swinging its two trunks, switching its tail, and swivelling its trumpet-like ears.

The rearmost car was occupied by a noisy family comprising a small male, a large female, three young, and one of the portable incubators in which Krishnans carried their unhatched eggs. To avoid the woman's chatter, Barnevelt and Tangaloa and their new acquaintance took the foremost car.

When all the waiting passengers were stowed, the mahout on the bishtar's neck blew a little trumpet and whacked his beast with his goad. The links between the cars clanked as the slack was taken up, and the car occupied by the Earthmen started with a jerk. They clicked over switch points and rolled past a bishtar moving cars on an adjoining track, so close that Barnevelt, had he been so rash, could have reached out and touched one of its six columnar legs.

They rolled out of the yard, along a right-of-way between building lots, and finally out on to one of Majbur's main streets, down whose middle ran two tracks. Presently they passed a local headed in the opposite direction and standing at an intersection to discharge passengers.

Other Krishnans swarmed the street, some on scooters, some on short six-legged ayas or tall four-legged shomals, and some in carriages. A team of six ayá pulled a great double-decked contraption, evidently a public omnibus. At a main intersection an official-looking Krishnan in a helmet directed traffic with a sword, which he waved with such verve that Barnevelt half expected to see him slice an ear from some passing pedestrian.

Barnevelt quoted: "New things and old co-twisted, as if time were nothing."

Gradually the traffic thinned and the houses got smaller. The railroad left the middle of the street for its own right-of-way again, and a branch line curved off to the right, up-river. The city turned to suburbs, and then houses alternating with cultivated plots. The two tracks became one, and they were in open country. Once they stopped to let the frontier guards of the Republic of Mikardand, men in Moorish-looking armor, look them over and wave them through.

The ride was uneventful, save when they stopped at a nameless hamlet to water the bishtar and let the passengers eat a snack and otherwise care for their comfort, and the oldest child of the noisy family aft stealthily uncoupled the rearmost car, so that when the train started up it was left standing with the fat woman screeching louder than Philo. The train halted, and the male passengers pushed the abandoned car along the track until its connection with the train was reëstablished, the conductor all the while calling upon Qondyor, Dashmok, Bákh, and other deities to destroy the young culprit in some lingering and humorous manner.

The expressman explained why he merely showed a pass instead of presenting a ticket: The Mejrou Qurardena had an arrangement with all the main transportation media like the railroad to carry its couriers on credit and then bill the express company for mileage.

They stopped the first night at Yantr, where a train going the other way was standing on a siding to let them by; and the next night at another village. At the end of the third day they reached Qa'la, where they again came in sight of the waves of the Sadabao Sea. The climate was noticeably warmer, and they began to see people dressed in Qiribo fashion, in wrap-around kilts and blanketlike mantles.

Next morning they were taking their places in the train when a deep voice said: "Be this seat occupied?"

A tall young Krishnan with a face like a fish, dressed much like themselves but more expensively, climbed aboard. Without waiting for an answer he kicked the Earthmen's duffel-bag off the empty seat it occupied and tossed his own bag on the rack above that seat. Then he unfastened his scabbard and leaned it in the corner, and sat down on the crosswise seat facing the Earthmen.

Another would-be passenger, looking through the cars for a choice seat, put his head into the one where Barnevelt sat.

"All filled!" barked the new arrival, though there was obviously room for one more. The passenger went away.

Barnevelt felt himself grow cold inside. He was about to say: "Pick that up!" and enforce his command, if need be, by tearing the young man limb from limb, when Tangaloa's musical voice spoke up: "Do my senses deceive me, or are we honored with the companionship of one of rank?"

Barnevelt stole a quick look at his companion, whose round brown face showed nothing but amiable interest. Where xenological investigations were concerned, George could take as detached and impersonal an attitude towards Krishnans as if they were microörganisms under his microscope. Their amiabilities and insolences were alike mere interesting data, not touching his human emotions in the least. In that respect, thought Barnevelt, George was one up on him, for he tended to react emotionally to the stimuli they presented.

"A mere *garm*," replied the youth briefly, but in a slightly less belligerent tone. "Sir Gavao er-Gargan. Who be you?"

"Tagdë of Vyutr," said Tangaloa, "and this is my trusty companion in many a tight predicament, answers to Snyol of Pleshch."

"*The* Snyol of Pleshch?" said Sir Gavao. "While I've no use for foreigners, the Nyamen are well spoken of, save that they bathe less often than is meet for folk of culture."

"It's a cold country, sir," said Tangaloa.

"That could be the way of it. As 'tis, I must spend a ten-night amongst these effeminate Qiribuma, who let their women rule 'em. Be you bound thither also?"

The expressman said "Aye."

Barnevelt wondered at the phrase "*The* Snyol of Pleshch"; he thought he'd heard it from Gorbovast, too. When Castanhoso had bestowed the *nom-de-guerre* upon him, he had assumed that it was that of some ancient gloop. If the authentic Snyol were still about, the consequences might, to put it mildly, be embarrassing.

"Have a cigar?" he said. "Where do you come from?"

"Balhib," said Sir Gavao. He drew on the cigar, looked at it with distaste, and threw it away. He then got out a jewelled case, took out and lit one of his own and put the case away. Barnevelt gritted his teeth, trying to take George's detached view.

Tangaloa purred: "Balhib, eh? Do you know anything about a survey of the kingdom ordered by the king?"

"Not I."

"We heard a most fascinating tale about that land," continued the xenologist. "Something to do with the king's beard."

"Oh, that!" Gavao's face cracked in its first smile. " 'Twas indeed a saucy piece of ropery, that this Sir What's-his-name from Mikardand did commit. Were't not that the Republic outweighs us five to one, there would have been robustious war betwixt us. Serves old Kir right for being so free with dirty foreigners."

"How did Sir Shurgez get close enough to the king?" asked Barnevelt.

"By a crafy cautel. He came disguised as an expressman like our friend here, saying he bore a package marked for special personal delivery, to be yielded only on signature of a receipt by His Altitude himself."

" 'Tis nothing special," said the expressman, "but our routine procedure, to avoid suits for non-delivery of parcels."

"Be that as it may," Gavao went on, "as the king was posing his seal ring upon the document—for he, a warrior true, can neither read nor write—did the feigned courier whip from the packet a pair of shears wherewith he did effect his zany lune. He sneaped the whisker and, ere any could stay or smite, did this bold bully-rook flee forth from the court with wightly step and gallop off upon his aya."

"A most perverse and unjust antic!"exclaimed the expressman.

"My company has lodged an action at law against this same Shurgez for his impersonation. Ever has this garb been known as a badge of probity and discretion, so that messengers of the Mejrou Quarardena can safely penetrate whither none other can go. But now if these braggartly japers be granted leave ourselves to personate, what becomes of our immunity?"

" 'Twill go whither went the scarecrow's ghost in Daghash's ballet," said Gavao. "Namely and to wit, into the nothingness of nought. But you, my masters, since you're in the mood for personalities, tell me whence and whither travel *you* and why?"

"We're planning a gvám-hunting expedition," said Barnevelt.

"Then I suppose you'll set forth from Malayer?"

"No, we were thinking of organizing in Ghulindé. We heard Malayer was under siege."

"It has fallen," said Sir Gavao.

"Really?"

"Yes. 'Tis said the renegade Kugird took it by some foul mitching means, using a baleful new invention 'gainst the walls."

"What sort of invention?"

"I know not. To me they're all one, devices of Dupulán to ruin the fine old art of war. All inventors should be slain on sight, say I. Methinks 'twere a meritorious deed to start a secret society for the prevention of inventions in warfare. Do we not such precaution take, 'twill not be long ere war's as unvalorous and mechanical as among the cursed Earthmen. Why, 'tis said that there the noble martial art became so noxiously machinal that the Terrans abolished it—setting up a planetary government this prohibition to enforce. Canst fancy anything more dismal?"

The expressman said: "We should destroy those Earthmen slinking amonst us in disguise, ere we're hopelessly corrupted by their evil magic."

"An interesting idea," said Barnevelt. "However, I think we'll still set out from Ghulindé, for Malayer would be pretty disorganized yet after having been besieged and sacked."

Gavao laughed. "Good hunting to you, but ask me not to patronize your product, for never yet have I found the gvám stone necessary to the enjoyment of life's elementary pleasures. Why, ere I quitted Qa'la . . ."

And Gavao was off on the one subject on which he was truly eloquent. For hours he regaled his companions with tales of exploits which, if true, made him the planet's leading boudoir athlete. He was a mine of information on the more intimate customs and characteristics of the females of the various races and nations of Krishna. Barnevelt realized that he was in the presence of a great specialist. However, he became bored after a while, and there was nothing he could do short of assault to staunch the flow of amorous anecdote.

All went smoothly enough as they stopped the night at another village and rolled on next day along the coast towards Jazmurian.

As they neared their destination they came to another border, from Mikardand into Qirib. As the train halted, Barnevelt became aware that the guards on the Qiribo side were women in musical-comedy outfits of pleated kilts and brass helmets and brassieres. Some of them sported shields and spears as well.

"Stand by your cars," said a beamy specimen (evidently the commanding officer) in Qiribo dialect. "Ah, you there!" She pounced on Barnevelt and his companions. "Hither, Na'i! Seal these fellows' swords into their sheaths, for we let no males go armed in this our land. As for you with the mace . . ." She picked her teeth with a twig as she pondered. "Since it has no sheath, we'd best fasten it to your belt. Then if you'd use that ugly thing it must needs be at the cost of your breeches, which would enhance neither your prowess nor your dignity."

"That, madam, depends on what you mean by prowess," said Tangaloa. The Amazon went off scratching her head, while the other men suppressed their mirth.

The girl called Na'i came over with a kit and belayed the swords of Barnevelt and Gavao into their sheaths with several turns of stout iron wire wound around the guard and through one of the scabbard rings. The ends of the wire were then clamped together in a little gadget that left them buried in a lead seal like that used on Earthly freight cars.

The customs guard added severely: "Should these seals be

broken, you must answer to our magistrates forthwith. And your excuse had better be good, or else . . ." She drew a finger across her throat. "Now get in line to pay your tariffs."

Then they were off for Jazmurian again. They were no sooner out of sight of the frontier station than Sir Gavao brought out an apparatus of his own. First he pulled on the wire until he had some slack in one length of it. Then he snipped it with a small pair of pliers and twisted the ends together. Then out of a tiny container he dug a fragment of dark waxy substance which he rubbed over the splice until only the most careful examination would show that the wire had been tampered with.

"Now," he said with a sly piscene grin, "does trouble impend, I have but to give my hilt a good tug, and the wire parts and out comes my lady fair. 'Tis the wont of gentry forced to travel through this noisome province of . . ." He used a badly anatomical term to describe the matriarchate.

"How about doing the same to ours?" said Barnevelt, for Gavao was putting away his kit.

"Oh, very well." And soon the Earthmen, too, had their weapons freed in this manner.

"Thanks," said Tangaloa. "What sort of place is Jazmurian?"

"A reeky hovel where honest men durst not wend abroad o' nights save in pairs or more. While 'tis under the rule of Qirib like the other land hereabouts, 'tis an international garbage heap, swarming with the vermin of the five seas, and Queen Alvandi's she-officers can no more cope with it than you can catch an avval with a fishhook."

Before reaching Jazmurian, late in the day, the railroad detoured inland until it came to the Zigros River, then turned east again and followed the river as it wound towards the town. The sun, setting behind the creaking cars, was reflected redly in the rough native glass of many windows. The second largest port of the Sadabao Sea did not prove quite so bad as Gavao's words, though indeed it showed a less prepossessing face than Majbur, being a sprawled-out city of slums, grog shops, and dilapidated-looking characters of varied hue and garb.

"Where are you staying?" Barnevelt asked Gavao.

"Angur's Inn, across the street from the station. 'Tis the only hostelry where the stench assailing the antennae is not such as to turn a gentleman's second stomach."

Barnevelt exchanged a glance with Tangaloa. Gorbovast in Majbur had recommended this same place to them, for here they would have to stop overnight before taking the stage for Ghulindé in the morning.

The train ground to a stop with squealing brakes. As the Earthmen gathered their baggage and got out of their little car, somebody on the splintery boardwalk beside the train said: "Pictures, my lords? Magic pictures?"

It was a shabby oldster with a straggle of hairs on his chin and a large box on a tripod.

"By the green eyes of Hoi," said Barnevelt, practicing a Krishnan oath, "look at that!"

"What the devil is it?" asked Tangaloa.

"A camera." Barnevelt had recognized an apparatus like those used centuries before on Earth in the pioneering days of photography. He could not help stealing a glance at the little Hayashi secure in its setting on his finger. "Wonder how he can get a picture in this light?"

He gazed up-river where the line of the plain already drew a cord across Roqir's red disk, and continued: "This must be a product of Prince Ferrian's scientific revolution. No thanks," he told the photographer and started to move off, when a shrill explosion of speech made him pause.

A beefy policewoman in scarlet and brass was bawling out the photographer for violating some ordnance by soliciting business on the railway platform. She ended:

". . . now go, you rivelled wretch, and thank the Mother Goddess you do not pass the night in our dankest dungeon!"

Barnevelt started to go too, but was halted by another outcry: "Stand fast, you! I do perceive you are a stranger and therefore ignorant—but no excuse does ignorance of the law provide. Know that we of Qirib do take it amiss to hear the false goddess Hoi sworn by. 'Tis classed as conduct disorderly, wherefor penalities most codign are stablished. Let's see those weapons!"

She examined the seals on Barnevelt's sword and Tangaloa's mace. Barnevelt's heart rose into his mouth; he was sure she would notice the place where Gavao had cut and spliced the wire. But, whether from perfunctory haste or from the weak waning sunset light, she failed to do so and sent them on their way with a final: "Go about your legitimate concerns, aliens, but watch your step!"

Angur's Inn stood in plain sight of the station, with the skull of some long-fanged carnivore over the doorway to identify its line of business. It was a three-story building built out over the sidewalk, a row of arches holding up the overhanging second story. All the ground floor of the building, save an entrance and a small office space at one side, was taken up by an eatery.

The travelers pushed through a crowd watching a sidewalk magician produce a baby unha from his hat and entered the door at the side. A tap on the little gong that hung in the upper part of the cashier's window brought a flat Krishnan face into the opening; a face to which a pair of unusually long antennae gave rather the look of a beetle.

"Angur bad-Ehhen, at your service," said the face.

"Baghan!" yelled Philo from his cage.

"Well—really, my masters . . ."

"It was not we," said Barnevelt hastily and, embarrassed, plunged into a typically fustian Krishnan speech: "It is this wretched beast from distant lands, whose brutish humor 'tis to cry out words in human tongues the meanings whereof he is as ignorant as you or I of the inmost secrets of the very gods. Therefore take no offense. May your lucky star ever be in the ascendant. Know that I am Snyol of Pleshch, a traveler, and this my companion Tagdë of Vyutr."

He paused, slightly out of breath but proud of his performance.

While they were settling the matter of the room, Angur kept

craning his neck through the opening to look at the macaw. "Truly, sirs, never have I seen a creature clad in fur of such strange abnormous form. Whence comes it?"

"From the loftiest mountains of Nyamadzë," replied Barnevelt, realizing that feathers were unknown on this planet, and hoping his adopted fatherland *had* mountains for Philo to come from. The lack of feathers was all to the good: there would be no feather pillows to give him hay fever.

"Garrrrk!" said Philo, half opening his wings.

"It flies!" cried Angur. "And yet it be no aqebat nor bijar nor other flying beast of form familiar. 'Twould make a rare attraction for my hospice, could you to part with it persuaded be."

He thrust out a tentative finger, then snatched it back as Philo lunged at it with gaping beak.

"No," said Barnevelt. "Regret it though we shall in aught to contravene you, yet when we—uh—bought the creature, did a great astrologer assure us that our fates were linked to his, and woe betide the day we parted from him."

" 'Tis pity," said Angur, "but 'tis plain as the peaks of Darya that you do have good reason for your answer, as the witch of the forest said to Qarar in the story. Here's your key. Share your chamber with another of my guests, by name Sishen, you must or sleep elsewhere. But let it vex you not, for he is of another world and uses not the bed. Ere you break your fast, would you crave company to comfort you?"

"No thanks," said Barnevelt.

"But we have licensed . . ."

"No thank you!" said Barnevelt and headed up the stairs.

Tangaloa remarked apologetically: "You see, Master Angur, I suspect my friend of leading a single life." Then he followed Barnevelt, saying: "Wowser! You needn't have been so precipitate. Still, you handled that jolly well. I wonder who is this joker he's putting in with us?"

"He said not of this world, which sounds like a ghost."

"Then you and he could hold a convention. Are you sure it *is* a he? The personal pronouns don't always distinguish gender."

"No, but we shall see. How do these oil-lamps work?"

When they had adjusted the lamp, they looked for clues to the nature of their fellow-roomer. In one corner lay a small bag with oddments of personal possessions sticking out. On one windowsill reposed three small jars, stoppered, and another open with handles protruding. Barnevelt found that the handles were those of small paint brushes.

He exchanged glances with Tangaloa and shrugged. They stowed their gear, washed up, and checked their disguises. While looking at himself in the mirror, Barnevelt saw over his shoulder something white against the door. It was a posted notice. By working on the Gozashtandou curleycues at the same time, he and Tangaloa managed to translate it:

NOTICE

Rites of Love shall be observed only in accordance with the Regulations of the Governing Council of the Cult of the Goddess Varzai, namely and to wit: They shall be preceded by the Short Prayer to the Mother Goddess and followed by the Lesser Ritual Mundification. A Love-Offering of one kard (Qiribo) for the Mother Goddess shall be left with the Innkeeper. By Order of Sehri bab-Giráji, High Priestess.

"Well!" said Tangaloa. "That is the first time I ever saw anybody put a tax on *that*."

Barnevelt grinned. "Just as well we turned down Angur."

"A bigoted lot of henotheists, these Qiribuma. I wonder how the tax collectors can check up?"

"Probably a custom more honored in the breach than the observance," said Barnevelt.

From the tavern came the sounds of weird music. An orchestra of four Krishnans—two men with tottle-pipes, another with a drum, and a girl with a harp-like instrument—were giving it out while in the dimly-lit middle of the room a young female Krishnan was performing a dance in the course of which she was winding herself up in an endless length of gauze, like a caterpillar spinning its cocoon.

"She seems to be doing a strip act in reverse," said Tangaloa. "We should have got here sooner."

Barnevelt replied: "Matter of fact, I half expected to see a male Qiribu stripping to an audience of these Amazonian females."

The room, smelling of Krishnans and of nameless drugs and liquors, had benches extending around most of the wall. Some diners were already at work with their little eating-spears. A mixed lot, thought Barnevelt, but predominantly bourgeois, with a masked couple in the corner in aristocratic silky stuff.

In accordance with custom, the Earthmen gave their orders over the counter to the cook, who sweated at his task in sight of all. Then they sidled around the edge of the room and slid into a vacant place. The waiter brought them their kvad, and they sat and sipped while the girl with the gauze continued her gyrations.

The girl finished. As the audience cracked their thumb joints by way of applause, several more customers came in, and on their heels one who hardly fitted: a dinosaurian creature, a head taller than a man, walking on birdlike legs with a tail as long as the rest of it stuck out behind to balance. Instead of clothes, the newcomer bore upon its body an intricate design of interwoven stripes painted on its scales.

"An Osirian!" said Barnevelt. "And a male from his wattle. Jeepers, I didn't expect to see one of those here!"

Tangaloa shrugged. "There are quite a few on Earth. Not a bad lot, though tending towards hypomania: impulsive and excitable."

"I've seen them, but I don't know any. I once took a girl who was deathly scared of snakes to see Ingrid Demitriou in *Lust Incorporated*, and when the lights went on an Osirian was sitting next to her and she fainted."

"They are mostly harmless," said Tangaloa, "but if you ever get in an argument with one, don't let him look you in the eye, or he will have you under pseudohypnosis before you can say 'thalamus.' Unless you are wearing a silver skullcap next to your scalp."

"Say, George, d'you suppose that's our roommate?" Barnevelt caught the waiter's eye and beckoned.

The servitor approached and murmured: "Seeing that you're Nyamen, my lords, perchance you'd like a brazier of nyomnigë; we have a secluded alcove for the purpose . . ."

"No thanks," said Barnevelt, not sure what nameless vice the waiter was trying to tempt him into. "Who's the fellow with the tail?"

"That's Sishen, who dwells here," said the waiter. "A generous tipper, for all his horrid form."

"Well, let's hope the species is honest. When will our chow be ready?"

The Osirian made it plain that the gulf that divided intelligent beings with tails from those without was one not easily crossed. After filing his order in a shrill whistling accent that the cook could hardly understand, he squatted in a corner facing the wall, his tail lying along the floor out into the room, and he looked up nervously every time somebody walked near. The waiter brought him his drink in a special vessel like a large oil can.

Barnevelt, glancing in the other direction, said: "Oh-oh, if there are ghosts around, this would seem to be it. At least he's haunting us."

It was the whiskered ancient with the box camera. He had been speaking to the man in the mask and now came over to the Earthmen, quavering: "Pictures, my lords? Magic pictures?"

"Let's give the old sundowner a break," said Tangaloa. "The swindle-sheet will stand it." He turned to the photographer. "How soon can you deliver prints?"

"Tomorrow morn, good my lord. I'll toil and swink all night . . ."

Barnevelt felt like objecting, for several reasons. But he held his peace, not wishing always to be cast in the role of penurious fussbudget by his colleague's easygoing ways. Besides, it was a chance to see what Earthly pioneers in photography like Daguerre and Steichen had had to go through.

The photographer spent some minutes focussing, moving first

one leg of the tripod and then another. Then he got out a little tray with a handle protruding from the center of its lower surface and a ball of string. He cut off a length of the string and caught one end of the piece under a little cleat on the upper surface of the tray.

Then he brought out a phial from which he sprinkled on the tray a yellow powder like that which Vizqash had extracted from the pods at the start of the abortive picnic. He stoppered and put away the phial, still holding the tray by its handle so that its powdered surface remained level. Then he brought out a flint-and-steel lighter, which he snapped against the dangling end of the string until the latter caught and sizzled. It was a fuze.

"Hold ye still, noble sirs," he said, reaching around to the front of the camera and flipping a switch.

The old man stepped back, holding the tray over his head. The fuze burned with little spitting sounds, the flame running up the string and over the edge of the tray out of sight.

Foomp!

A bright flash lit up the room, and a mushroom of thick yellow smoke boiled up from the tray. As the photographer reached around the camera and again flipped the shutter-switch, a clatter drew eyes down the room to where Sishen the Osirian had leaped to his feet in startlement and upset his drinking-vessel.

The Osirian took two long steps towards the photographer who, peering up, seemed to see the creature for the first time.

"*Iyá!*" howled the old man. Snatching up tray and camera, he rushed from the tavern.

"Now wherefore did he thus?" asked Sishen. "I did but mean to ask him if he would take one of me as well, and off he goes as though Dupulán were hard upon his trail. These Krishnans are difficult folk to fathom. Well, sirs, be you my new roommates? For by your shaven polls I do perceive you are Nyamen, and Angur has but now advised me that I'd share my quarters with such this night."

"It seems so," said Barnevelt.

"Yes? Then let us hope you come not in twixt midnight and morn, in riotous mood to rouse me from my rest. We'll meet

66

again, fair sirs."

As the Osirian returned to his place, Barnevelt said: "It occurs to me old Wiskers might be another janrú man."

"You're too suspicious," said Tangaloa. "It's as Castanhoso told us: Everything out of the ordinary gets blamed . . . Look, here comes our fish-faced friend with the bad manners."

The tall Sir Gavao er-Gargan was pushing his way in. He spotted the Earthmen and approached with a cry of: "What-ho, O Nya-men! As a reward for the due deference you've shown my rank, I permit you to eat with me." And he flung himself down. "Waiter!" he boomed. "A cup of buhren, and sprackly! Where's our Mejrou man? The parcel-carrier?"

"Haven't seen him," said Barnevelt, and to the waiter: "The same for us."

"Ah well, small loss. An ignorant wight, crediting the myths of magic powers of the accursed Earthmen. I, now, am emancipate from superstitious follies, in which I do include all talk of gods, ghosts, witches, and powers thaumaturgic. All's governed by unbending laws of nature, even the damned Terrestrials."

He stuck a finger in his drink, flicked a drop to the floor, muttered a minor incantation, and drank.

Barnevelt said in English: "Watch this guy. He's up to no good."

"What say you?" barked Gavao.

Barnevelt answered: "I spoke my native language, warning Tagdë against such incautious over-indulgence as cost us dear in Hershid."

" 'Tis the first I ever heard of hardened mercenaries counting costs with such unwarlike clerkly caution, but 'tis your affair. At whom do you stare so fixedly, fat one?"

Tangaloa looked around with a grin. "The little dancer over there. Either my old eyes deceive me, or she's giving me the high-sign."

Barnevelt looked in the direction indicated. Sure enough, there sat the dancer, still wrapped in her meters of gauze.

"This bears looking into," said Tangaloa. "You order dessert for me, D— Snyol."

"Hey . . ." said Barnevelt weakly. While he did not like to see Tangaloa headed for some escapade, he knew George would be hard to stop. Therefore he sat still and unhappily watched Tangaloa's broad back recede into the shadows in pursuit of the dancer, in temper amorous as the first of May.

"*Ao*, here comes the singer!" said Gavao, pointing.

" 'Tis Pari bab-Horáj, well-known along the Sadabao Coast for her imitations. I mind me of the time I was in an Inn in Hershid with a singer, a dancer, and a female acrobat, and in order to decide . . ." and Gavao was off on another of his Paphian anecdotes.

A young female Krishnan with the bluish hair of the western races had dragged in a stool of intricate workmanship and now seated herself upon it. Her costume consisted of a square of thin purple stuff, a little over a meter on a side, wrapped under one armpit and fastened with a jewelled clasp over the opposite shoulder. She carried an instrument something like an Earthly child's toy xylophone and a little hammer to strike it with.

She seated herself on the stool with the instrument in her lap and cracked a couple of jokes which caused many to make the gobbling sounds that passed here for laughter, though between the dialect and the speed of her speech Barnevelt could not understand them. (He lived in dread of running into a real Nyamë who would insist on conversing with him in the difficult Nyami language.)

Barnevelt caught a flash of motion out of the corner of his eye. As he looked around, his companion's arm resumed its former position. But Barnevelt could have sworn Gavao had made a quick pass over his, Barnevelt's, mug. A knockout drop?

Barnevelt had a supply of capsules and pills of various kinds in a pouch next to his skin, but he could not get through the tight Krishnan jacket without attracting attention.

The girl now beat upon her instrument, which gave forth clear bell-like tones, and sang in a voice dripping with melancholy and nostalgia:

> *"Les tálda kventen bif orgát*
> *Anevorb rottum aind . . ."*

Though to Barnevelt the tune sounded vaguely familiar, he could make no sense of the words. *Kventen* would be the present passive infinitive of *kventer*, "to drink" . . .

Then he snorted as it hit him. By Zeus, he thought, I come eleven light-years to hear a dame sing "Auld Lang Syne" in a dive! Wasn't there any place in the universe where you could get away from Earthly influence? The next planet he visited would be one where the folk had tentacles and lived in a sea of sulphuric acid.

There still remained, however, the problem of his possibly doped drink. If he simply sat without drinking he'd arouse suspicion . . .

Then it occurred to him that two could play at that game. He caught Gavao's arm and pointed: "Who's the fellow with the mask? The Lone Space-Ranger?"

As Gavao looked, Barnevelt switched mugs with him.

"Those?" said Gavao. "I know not. 'Tis the custom of the local gentry to mask themselves when mingling with the general. As I was saying, when we awoke . . ."

Barnevelt took a gulp of Gavao's liquor, which tasted something like a whiskey sour made with tomato juice. Gavao drank likewise. The singer started off again.

> *"Inda blu rij maonten zovor jinyá*
> *Ondat relo va lounsom pain . . ."*

Whoever wrote that old clinker about the Lonesome Pine would never know it, thought Barnevelt, watching Gavao for signs of the effect of his drink. The singer worked her way through "Die Lorelei," "La Cucaracha," and "Drink to Me Only," and was starting on:

    "Jingabelz, jingabelz, jingel ollavé . . ."

when the Krishnan wiped his mouth and his sleeve and muttered:

"That potation must have turned my second stomach. I feel unwell. When I recover I'll seek out the unha responsible and skewer him in despite for such unmannerly dealing with a collared knight . . ."

By the time Tangaloa appeared with the expression of a canariophagous cat, Gavao's insensible head was pillowed on his hands on the table. Tangaloa said:

"What's wrong with the skite, stonkered already? I'm thirsty . . ."

Barnevelt shot out a hand and covered Tangaloa's mug, saying quietly: "Don't—it's doped. We had a visit from one Michael Finn, and I switched 'em. Let's go."

"Are you mad? We are in the midst of the most fascinating investigation of an alien culture, and you want to go! Here comes the band again. Let's see what they have to offer."

"Excuse me while I shudder."

"Don't you dance? If I had my third wife here I would show you . . ."

The four Krishnans with the instruments filed in and began emitting an eerie, exotic tune which, after a while, Dirk Barnevelt recognized as that scourge of the radio waves, "I Don't Need No Blanket (When I Got My Baby)" which had been popular on Earth three years before he left it.

He turned a grimace to Tangaloa. "Every time I begin to imagine I'm in the Mermaid Tavern in Shakespeare's time, they spring something like that!"

"A hopelessly parochial point of view," said Tangaloa. "You should take things as they come, as I do."

"You certainly do!" said Barnevelt in a marked manner.

The masked couple got up and danced a slow Krishnan dance that consisted mainly of bowing to each other. Barnevelt got his first good look at them: the man lithe and well-muscled despite his small size and androgynous garment, a tunic of pale pink gauze that left one shoulder bare. The woman was similarly clad, with one difference: She wore a shortish broadsword slung at her side.

Barnevelt said: "You can't say the women wear the pants in Qirib, but they do wear the swords. There's something familiar about that bleep. Wish I could place him."

Other couples got up to dance too. Then the Osirian stood up, belched, and teetered on his birdlike feet over to the harpist.

"Come," he burbled, "since you play an Earthly tune, let me show you Earthly dancing . . ."

Presently the reptile and the entertainer appeared upon the floor, the latter bearing the expression of one who is only doing this to avert worse trouble. The Osirian started to spin round and round in the steps of the popular Earthly zhepak, and his tail whacked the masked man in the fundament just as the latter was bowing again to his lady.

"*Hishkako baghan!*" roared the masked man, recovering his balance.

"I apologize . . ." began the Osirian, but the masked man snatched his partner's sword from its sheath, grating:

"I'll apologize you, you scaly horror! 'Twill pleasure me to see your hideous head, shorn from its vile trunk, leaping like a football adown the planching of the floor!"

He stepped forward, swinging the heavy blade around for a slash.

Barnevelt picked up his empty mug. It was a solid piece of ceramics, the outside banded with reliefs of men chasing women or vice versa. Dirk drew back his arm and let fly.

The mug shattered against the back of the masked man's head, and the latter's leading leg buckled under him, so that he fell forward to hands and knees. The Osirian darted out the door.

The room was full of babel. Angur hauled the masked man to his feet and tried to pacify him, while Barnevelt, having resumed his seat, looked innocent but kept his sword hilt within reach. The masked man glared around the room, saying:

"Fainting fit, my eggless aunt! Some villain did most discourteously yerk me upon the pate from behind, and when I catch the varlet I'll clapper-claw him fittingly . . . Saw you the miscreant, madam?" he asked his companion.

"Nay, for my eyes were upon you, my lord."

The eyes behind the mask came to rest on Barnevelt. "What . . ." the masked man began, and looked around for the sword he had just been using.

Angur and the waiter, one on each side of him, uncovered short bludgeons. The former said: "Nay, brawl not on my premises, my lord, or I'll have the watch in despite your status. Do you be good, now."

"*Chá!* Let's forth, madam, to seek entertainment meeter for our rank. After all, I am who I am!"

"That was our friend Vizqash bad-Murani!" said Barnevelt. "Remember the last time he used that expression?"

Since Tangaloa at last agreed to depart, they paid and went to their room, leaving the somnolent Gavao still sprawled upon the table. As they opened their door, Sishen the Osirian was bending over the macaw's cage, and as they stepped into the room he twitched aside the cloth that covered it. Philo opened his eyes, flapped his wings, and uttered an earsplitting "*Yirrrrk!*"

The Osirian jumped back, turned, and leaped upon Tangaloa, seizing him around the waist with his long hindlegs and around the neck with his arms. From his reptilian throat came a whistling approximation of Gozashtandou for "Save me!"

"Get down, damn it!" cried Tangaloa, struggling under his burden, in a voice muffled by the creature's terrified embrace.

Sishen got, drooling the Osirian equivalent of tears.

"Sorry am I," he hissed, "but the events of this eve—the flash of light, the brabble with the masked gentleman, and now the uncanny outcry of this kindless monster—have unstrung me quite. Were not you those who succored me when that fellow sought to slay me for a trivial gaffe?"

"Yes," said Barnevelt. "Why didn't you fix him with your glittering eye?"

Sishen spread his claws heplessly. "For the following reasons: Item, ere we Sha'akhfi be allowed on Earth or the Earthly space line, we must pledge ourselves the use of this small talent to

forswear. And since our own space line runs not hitherward
nigher than Epsilon Eridani, to visit the Cetic planets must we
of the Procyonic group to this pledge subject ourselves. Item:
I'm far from the most effective of my species in the employ of
this mental suasion, though given time I can cast the mental net
or lift it as well as others. And item: Krishnans are less liable to
our guidance than men of Earth, wherefore I'd not have had
time this bellowing bully to subdue before my own life were sped.
Hence came your intervention in time's nick. Now, if you would
aught in recompense of Sishen, speak, and to the length of my
poor ability shall it be given."

"Thanks—I'll bear that in mind. But what brings you to Jazmurian? Not a lady Osirian, surely."

"I? I am a simple tourist visiting places far and strange for the
satisfaction of my longing after new experience. Here am I stuck,
for three days ago was my guide, poor lad, fished from the
harbor with a knife wound in his back, and the travel agency yet

essays to find me another. So meager is my command of these tongues that I dare not journey unaccompanied. This loss made good, I will onward press to Majbur, where it's said there stands a temple of rare workmanship." The Osirian yawned, a gruesome sight. "Forgive me, gentles, but I am fordone. Let us forthwith to our rest."

And Sishen unrolled the rug he used in lieu of a bed and flattened himself down upon it, like a lizard basking in the sun.

Next morning Barnevelt found it necessary to rouse Tangaloa, the world's soundest sleeper, by bellowing in his ear:

> *"Wake! For the Sun, who scatter'd into flight*
> *The Stars before him from the Field of Night . . . ."*

They left while Sishen was still touching up his body paint, a task that apparently consumed much of his waking time. When they came downstairs, they found Angur arguing with three rough-looking youths with cudgels.

"My masters!" cried Angur. "Explain to these jolt-heads that the pictures the old photographer left this morn are yours, not mine, and deal with the matter howso you will."

"What's this?" said Barnevelt.

The biggest of the three said: "Know, O men of Nyamadzë, that we're a committee from the Artists' Guild, which has resolved to root out this fiendish new invention that otherwise will rape us of our livelihood. For how can we compete with one who, possessing neither skill nor talent, does but point a silly box and **click!** his picture's done? Never did the gods intend that men should limn likenesses by such base mechanical means."

"Good Lord," muttered Barnevelt, "they actually worry about technological unemployment here!"

The Krishnan went on: "If you do but yield the pictures the old coystril made, all shall be well. Should you wish portraits of yourselves, our Guild will rejoice to draft or daub 'em for a nominal fee. But these delusive shadows—*chá!* Will you give them up like wights of sense? Or must we to robustious measures come?"

Barnevelt and Tangaloa exchanged a long look. The latter said in English: "It does not really matter to us . . ."

"Oh, no!" said Barnevelt. "We can't let 'em think they can push us around. Ready?"

Tangaloa sighed. "You have been eating meat again. And you were such a peaceful chap on Earth, too! *Coo-ee!*"

Barnevelt hauled on his hilt. The wire parted and the sword swept out. With a mighty blow he brought the blade down flat-wise on the head of the spokesman for the Artists' Guild. The Krishnan fell back on the cobbles, dropping his club. Tangaloa at the same time tugged out his mace and advanced upon the other two, who ran like rabbits. The fallen man scrambled up and fled after them. The Earthmen chased them a few steps, then returned to the inn.

"One damn thing after another," said Barnevelt, after looking around to make sure no Qiribo policewoman had observed the fracas. "Let's see those pictures—jeepers cripus, if I'd known they were as bad as that I'd have given them to those guys. I look like a mildewed mummy!"

"Is that bloated gargoyle I?" said Tangaloa plaintively.

Reluctantly they gave Angur the money for the photographer, wired up their weapons again, gathered their gear, and set out across the main boulevard of Jazmurian for the railroad station.

On the boulevard, beside the depot, a big stagecoach drawn by six horned ayas stood waiting. The expressman who had ridden with them from Majbur was already there, talking with the driver, but of Sir Gavao there was no sign.

Barnevelt asked the driver: "Is this the diligence for Ghu-lindé?"

Receiving the affirmative head motion, he and Tangaloa gave the man the remaining stubs of their combination rail-and-coach tickets. They stowed their bag on top (the baggage-rack at the rear being full) and climbed in with their birdcage.

The interior of the coach seated about a dozen and, by the time the vehicle left, it was somewhat over half full. Most of the passengers wore the wrap-around garb of Qirib, which reminded Barnevelt of the patrons of a Turkish bath instead of the tailored garments of the more northerly regions.

The driver blew his trumpet and cracked his whip. Off they went, the wheels rattling over cobblestones and splashing through puddles. Since the load was comparatively light, the springs were stiff and gave the passengers a sharp bouncing.

Barnevelt said: "I think both Vizqash and Gavao are agents of the Sunqar crowd, with orders to get us."

"How so?" said Tangaloa.

"It all fits. The plan last night was for Gavao to dope us, and then he and Vizqash, claiming to be dear old friends of ours, would lug us out into the alley and cut our throats. When I doped Gavao instead, Vizqash didn't know what to do about it. You saw how he stood there glaring at us?"

"That sounds reasonable, Sherlock. And speaking of Sishen . . ." Tangaloa switched languages and asked the expressman: "Did you tell us that the mysterious Sheafasè, who rules the Sunqar, has a scaly hand with claws?"

"Even so, good my lords."

"My God!" said Barnevelt. "You actually think Sishen is Sheafasè, and we slept in the same room with him? That's worse than swimming with the avval!"

"Not necessarily. That quarrel looked genuine. But suppose you'd known the two were the same, what would you have done about it?"

"Hell, I don't know—you can't erase a passing stranger on mere suspicion. It seems unlikely the real head of the Sunqar gang would prowl around incog like that Caliph in the *Arabian Nights*."

"We shall no doubt learn in time."

"Ayuh, though I like this job less and less. To catch a dragon in a cherry net, to trip a tigress with a gossemer, were wisdom to it."

Barnevelt offered a cigar to the expressman, who took it but said: "To smoke herein is forbidden, my masters. Therefore will I wait for a halt to clamber to the top."

Barnevelt found the smell of a lot of Krishnans in an inclosed space oppressive, something like that of a glue factory. He wished the Interplanetary Council in one of its spasms of liberal-mindedness would let knowledge of the art of soap-making into the planet. After all, they had let in printing, which was much more revolutionary.

He was glad when they stopped at a hamlet to drop a passenger and a couple of packages. He got out, lit up, and climbed to the top along with Tangaloa and the expressman. The coach started up again, following the railroad around the shores of Bajjai Bay, crossing creeks and embayments. At Mishdakh, at the base of the Qiribo peninsula, the road swung to the left, or east, along the northern shore of the peninsula, while the track disappeared to the right towards Shaf.

The road now began climbing to the high ground on the south side of the bay, where rocky headlands crested with small wind-warped trees overlooked leagues of choppy green water. Once the grade was so steep the male passengers had to get out and push. They wound along a hilly coast road, up and down and around stony points and prominences. The trees were bigger and more numerous than any the Earthmen had yet seen on Krishna, with trunks of glossy green and brown and purplish hues. Sometimes branches projecting over the road barely cleared their heads. The coach rocked and the wind whistled.

They had been rattling along this way for some time when a sudden onset of sounds drew their attention. Out of a clump of trees galloped a dozen armed men on ayas.

Before the passengers could react to their presence, the leading pair of the group had come up alongside the coach. On the starboard side rode the Earthmen's late train companion Gavao er-Gargan, shouting: "Halt! Halt ye on pain of death!"

On the other side came one whom Barnevelt did not recognize, a leathery-looking fellow with one antenna missing, who caught the hand holds on the sides of the coach, hoisted himself adroitly off his mount, and started to climb to the top with a knife between his teeth in the best Captain Blackbeard style.

Barnevelt, who had been daydreaming, was slow to take in the import of this visitation. He had only begun to pull himself together and reach for his sword when the iron head of Tangaloa's mace came down with a crunch on the boarder's skull. A second later came a twang as the driver discharged a crossbow-pistol at Gavao. The bolt missed the rider but struck the mount, which bleeped with pain, bucked, circled, and dashed off the road towards the rocks of the shore below.

The driver stuck his weapon back in its bracket and cracked his whip furiously, yelling: *"Hao! Hao-qai!"*

The six animals leaned forward in their harness and pulled. Away the coach rattled, faster and faster. Behind it, the pursuers were thrown into momentary confusion by the bolting of their leader's mount. Some halted at the body of the man whose skull Tangaloa had stove, and one pulled up so quickly he fell off his aya. Then a bend hid them.

"Hold on," said the driver as they took a turn on two wheels. From the interior of the coach below came a babble from the other passengers.

Barnevelt, gripping the armrest at the end of his seat, looked back. As the road straightened momentarily, the pursuit appeared, though they were now too far behind to recognize individuals. Stones from thirty-six hooves of the team rattled against the body of the coach. Another bend, and they were again out of sight of their attackers.

Barnevelt asked the driver: "How far to the next town?"

"About twenty hoda to Kyat," was the reply. "Here, load my arbalest!"

Barnevelt, wrestling with the crossbow-pistol, said to Tangaloa: "At this rate they'll catch us long before we get to the next town!"

"That's fair cow. What shall we do?"

Barnevelt looked at the tall trees. "Take to the timber, I guess. Grab the next branch that comes near and hope they go by without seeing us." He turned to the driver, saying: "They want us, and if you'll slow up when told we'll relieve you of our perilous presence. But don't tell 'em where we left, understand?"

The driver grunted assent. The pursuers, nearer yet, came into sight for a few seconds. More arrows whistled; one struck home with a meaty sound. The expressman cried: "I am slain!" and fell off the coach into the road. Then the riders again were hidden.

"This one's too high," said Tangaloa, eyeing a branch.

The coach rocked and bounced along behind its straining team. The whip cracks and shouts of the driver never stopped.

Barnevelt said: "This one's too thin."

Suddenly he had an idea. He seized their duffel bag and hurled it as far as he could from the coach, so that it fell into a clump of shrubs that swallowed it up.

"How about the cockatoo?" said Tangaloa.

"He's below, and anyway he'd give us away by yelling. Here, this one'll do. Slow down, driver!"

The driver pulled on his brake handle; the coach slowed. Barnevelt climbed to the seat on which he had been sitting and stood precariously balanced, swaying with the motion of the vehicle. The branch came nearer and nearer.

"Now!" said Barnevelt, launching himself into space. The branch struck his arms with stinging force. Then with a grunt and a heave he was up on top of it, then standing on it and holding another to balance himself. Tangaloa was slower in struggling up. The branch sank with the weight, so that whereas it had been about level before they seized it, they now had a sharp grade up to the tree trunk.

"Hurry, dammit!" said Barnevelt, for his companion was having an awkward time keeping his footing on the slick bark. Any second the pursuit would come around the last bend, and it wouldn't do to have them teetering in plain sight.

They scrambled up to the trunk and slipped around it just as the kettledrumming of hooves and clank of scabbards told that Gavao's gang was coming up. They went past almost close enough to spit on, Gavao again in the lead. Barnevelt and Tangaloa held their breaths until the Krishnans were out of sight.

Tangaloa wiped his forehead with his sleeves, his face a noticeably lighter shade of brown. "Didn't know I could perform a feat like that at my age and weight. Now what? When that push catches the coach they will find out we are not aboard, and they'll be back on our hammer in no time."

"We'll have to head inland and try to lose 'em on foot."

"Let's get our dilly bag first—good God, here they come already!" For the sound of hooves had begun to rise again.

"No," said Barnevelt, peering, "it's the coach! What the devil's it coming back for?"

Tangaloa said: "It's another coach entirely. Let's catch it back to Jazmurian, what say?"

"Okay." Barnevelt swarmed down the tree and ran out into the road just as the coach came by.

The brake screeched as the vehicle slowed. The Earthmen ran alongside, caught the hand holds, and hoisted themselves up.

"Slow down just a minute!" called Barnevelt. He dropped off, ran to the side of the road to seize the duffel bag, and rejoined the coach. He tossed the bag onto the stern rack and grabbed the hand holds again.

"All aboard," he said, hauling himself to the top and panting for breath. "What's the fare to Jazmurian?"

As he accepted their money, the driver said: "By the left ear of Tyazan, ye gasted me nigh out of my breeches, leaping out like that. Had ye aught to do with the commotion back yonder?"

"What commotion?" asked Tangaloa innocently.

"I was waiting at the turnout for the eastbound coach to pass, when it came by ahead of time, racing as though Dupulán were after it. Then just as I was about to move out onto the queen's highway, along came a troop of armed men, riding like fury after the other coach. Misliking their looks, I've been driving with utmost dispatch ever since. What know ye of these?"

They assured him with nervous glances to the rear that they knew nothing at all.

Tangaloa said: "Dirk, how *are* we to get to Ghulindé with these doers haunting the line?"

Barnevelt asked the driver: "Is there any shipping between Jazmurian and Ghulindé?"

"Certes. There's much haulage of falat wine to all the ports of the Sadabao Sea, for example."

And so it came about that evening found them putting out into Bajjai Bay aboard a tubby wallowing coastal lateener, the *Giyám*, so laden with wine jars that her freeboard could only be measured in centimeters. The master laughed at their obvious apprehension when a lusty wave sent a sheet of water racing across the deck.

"Nay," he said, " 'twill not be the season of the hurricane for several ten-nights yet."

For want of anything better to do, Barnevelt dug out of the bag the navigational handbook he had bought in Novorecife and tried to work out a line-of-position from the meager data provided by the ship's compass (which spun this way and that in maddening disregard of direction), the time as given by his pocket sundial, and Roqir's altitude as worked out by an improvised astrolabe. With so many sources of inaccuracy, however, his calculations showed the ship hundreds of hoda up the Zigros River, between Jeshang and Kubyab.

"Reading's useless baggage for the true sailorman," said the master, watching Barnevelt's struggles with amusement. "Here I have never learned the clerkly art, and look at me! Nay, 'tis better to spend one's time watching wave and cloud and flying thing, and becoming wise in their ways—or yet in learning the habitudes of the local gods, so that ye please each in his own bailiwick. Thus in Qirib I'm a faithful follower of their Mother Goddess, but in Majbur I'm a votary of jolly old Dashmok, and in Gozashtandu ports a devotee of their cultus astrological. Did our seas reach to your cold Nyamdzë, I'd doubtless learn to adore squares and trigons as do the sour Kangandites."

It was high time, Barnevelt thought, that he and George decided how they were going to gain access to the Sunqar. After some casting about for ideas, they resolved to combine those that had already been suggested to them by their friends and acquaintances on Krishna. In other words, they would seek entry with one or both of them disguised as expressmen of the Mejrou Qurardena with a package to deliver.

The wind held fair and true, and the morning of the third day found the *Giyám* heading into the harbor of Ghulindé. As the sun rose out of the sparkling sea, Barnevelt stared in silent wonder.

Before them lay the port, not properly Ghulindé at all but the separate city of Damovang. Southwest of Damovang rose tall Mount Sabushi. In times long past, before the matriarchate had elevated the cult of the fertility goddess and suppressed its competitors, men had carved the mountain into an enormous squat likeness of the war-god Qondyor (called Qunjár by the Qiribuma) as though sitting on a throne half-sunk in the earth, to the height of the god's calves. Time had blurred the sculptors' work, especially around the head, but the city of Ghulindé proper with its graceful forest of spiky spires lay in the great flat lap of the god.

Finally, far behind Mount Sabushi, against the sky rose the towering peaks of the Zogha, the range from which came the mineral wealth that gave the matriarchal kingdom a power out of proportion to its modest size.

Another hour and they were climbing the steep hill that led up the apron of Qondyor to the city of Queen Alvandi, through a crowd of Qiribuma, whose dress convention seemed to be that if one had a piece of fabric with one, one was clad—even though one merely draped it over one arm. Barnevelt observed that, whereas the women dressed with austere simplicity, the men went in for gaudy ornaments and cosmetics.

"Now," said Barnevelt, "all we need is a present for the queen to replace that damned macaw."

"Do you think the stage-coach line would have kept it? I don't suppose they have a lost-and-found department."

They sought out the coach company and inquired. No, they were told, nobody knew anything about a cage containing an unearthly monster. Yes, that stage held up between Mishdakh and Kyat had come in again, but the driver was off on a run at the moment. If they had left such a cage on the diligence, the driver had probably sold it in Ghulindé. Why didn't the gentlemen make the rounds of the pet shops?

There were three of these in town, all in the same block. Before they had even entered one, the Earthmen knew where their quarry was by the shrieks and obscenities that issued from the shop harboring Philo.

Inside there was a tremendous noise. In a cage near that of Philo, a bijar rustled its leathery wings and made a sound like a smith beating on an anvil, while in another a two-headed rayef brooded over a clutch of eggs and quacked. A big watch-eshun scrabbled at its wire netting with the front pair of its six paws and howled softly. The smell was overpowering.

"*That* thing?" said the shopkeeper when Barnevelt told him he was interested in the macaw. "Take it for half a kard and welcome. I was about to drown the beast. It has bitten one of my best customers, who was minded to buy it ere he learned of its frampold disposition, and it screams insults at all and sundry."

They bought back their bird, but then Barnevelt wanted to linger and look over the other animals. He said: "George, couldn't I buy one of these little scaly things? I don't feel right without a pet."

"No! The kind of pet you need walks on two legs. Come on." And the xenologist dragged Barnevelt out. "It must be that farm background that makes you so fond of beasts."

Barnevelt shook his head. "It's just that I find them easier to understand than people."

At last, when Roqir was westering in the sky and the folk of Ghulindé stopped their work for their afternoon cup of shurab and snack of fungus cakes, Dirk Barnevelt and George Tangaloa, weary but alert, entered the palace. Barnevelt repressed his terror at the prospect of meeting a lot of strangers. After passing between pairs of woman guards in gilden kilts and brazen helms and greaves and brassieres, they were run through a long series of screening devices before being ushered into the presence of Alvandi, Douri of Qirib.

They found themselves in the presence, not of one woman, but two: one of advanced years, square-jawed, heavy-set; the other young and—not exactly beautiful, but handsome in a bold-featured way. Both wore the simple unoppressive sort of garb that ancient Greek sculptors attributed to Amazons, which contrasted oddly with the flashing tiaras they bore upon their heads.

The Earthmen, having forehandedly boned up on Qiribo protocol, knelt while a functionary presented them.

"*The* Snyol of Pleshch?" said the elder woman, evidently the queen. "An unexpected pleasure, this, for my agents had reported you slain. Rise."

As they rose, Tangaloa launched into his rehearsed speech of presentation, displaying the macaw. When he had finished, the functionary took the cage from him and retired.

"We thank you for your generous and unusual gift. We'll bear in mind what you have told us of this creature's habits—a *bord,* you said it was called upon its native planet? And now, sirs, to your business. You shall deal, not with me, but with my daughter, the Princess Zei, whom you see sitting here upon my left. For within a ten-night comes our yearly festival called *kashyó,* after which I'll abdicate in favor of my dutiful chick. 'Tis meet, therefore, that she should gain experience in bearing burdens such as sit upon our shoulders, before responsibility in very truth descends upon her. Speak."

Barnevelt and Tangaloa had agreed in advance that, while the latter made the first speech, the former should make the next. As he looked at the women, however, Dirk Barnevelt found himself suddenly tongue-tied. The seconds ticked away, and no words came.

The reason for this was not that Zei was a rather tall, well-built girl, rather dark of skin, with large dark eyes, a luscious mouth, and a nose of unusual aquilinity for a Krishnan. She might in fact have stepped off a Greek vase painting except for the antennae, the dark-green hair, and the leprechaunian ears.

Now, Barnevelt had seen striking girls before. He had dated them too, even though his mother had always managed to break things up before they got serious. The real reason he found himself unable to speak was that Queen Alvandi, in tone and looks, reminded him forcibly of that same mother, only on a larger, louder, and even more terrifying scale.

As he stood with his mouth foolishly half-open, feeling the blush creep up his ruddy skin, he at last heard the soft voice of Tangaloa break into the embarrassing silence. Good old Geroge! For having rescued him in that horrid moment, Barnevelt would have forgiven his colleague almost anything.

"Your Altitude," said Tangaloa, "we are but wandering adventurers who beg two favors: first, to be allowed to present our respects to you, as you have generously permitted us to do. The second is to raise in Ghulindé a company to sail into the Banjao Sea in search of gvám stones."

The girl cast an appealing glance at her mother, whose face remained stony. Finally Zei answered.

"Gorbovast tells us of your gvám-hunting proposal in this his letter." (She touched the paper on her desk.) "Not sure am I, however, that the gvám-stone quest is sanctioned by the Mother Goddess, since if the common belief respecting it be true, it affords the male an advantage contrary to the principles of our state. . . ."

While she hesitated, Queen Alvandi prompted her in a stage whisper: "Tell 'em 'tis lawful sobeit they pay our taxes and sell their baubles far from here!"

"Well—uh—however," said Zei, "we can extend permission on two conditions: that you sell not the stones within the bourne of Qirib, and that you pay, from your profits on this transaction, subject to the scrutiny of our auditors, one-tenth to the treasury of the realm of Qirib, and an additional tenth to the coffers of the Divine Mother."

"Agreed," said Barnevelt, recovering his voice at last. It was easy enough to promise a cut on the gvám-stone profit when he and George knew there wouldn't be any such profit.

"Make 'em put up a bond!" hissed Alvandi. "Otherwise how shall we collect our money, once they've got their stones and are beyond our reach?"

"A—a slight bond, sirs, will be required," said Zei. "Of—of, let's say, a thousand karda. Can you meet it? On your return, all above the amount of our tax shall be returned to you."

"We can meet it," said Barnevelt after some fast mental calculations.

"I'd have mulcted 'em for five thousand," grumbled Alvandi. "Oh, well, Snyol of Pleshch always bore the reputation of . . ."

At that instant a round-faced young Krishnan strode in unceremoniously, saying loudly in a high voice: "A bearer of ill tidings I, fair Zei, for the Prefect and his lady are laid low by some tisick and cannot come tonight . . . . I crave pardon. Do I interrupt an audience of weight and worth?"

"Worth enough," growled Alvandi, "to make one of your graceless intrusions more vexing than is its usual wont. Here we have a pair of perfect gentle cutthroats from the regions of the nether pole, where folk have names none other can pronounce and where a bath is deemed a shocking heathen custom. Yon gangler on the left hight Snyol of Pleshch, while this unwieldy mass of flesh upon the right gives as his barbarous appellation Tagdë of Vyutr. This lown who into the flow of your eloquence has broken, my widely-traveled friends, is Zakkomir bad-Gurshmani, a ward of the throne and my daughter's familiar."

"General Snyol!" cried Zakkomir, his round made-up face taking on a reverent expression. "Sir, may I grasp your thumb in abject homage? Long have I followed your deeds in admiration. As when with but a single wing of troops having upon their feet those boards you use for sliding on snow—skids, I think they're called—you did overthrow and rout the wretched rabble of Olñega . . . But I looked to see you one of greater age?"

"We come of a long-lived family," said Barnevelt gruffly, wishing he knew more about the man he was impersonating. Although he was not too favorably impressed by this painted youth, the latter's admiration seemed unbounded.

Zakkomir addressed Zei: "Princess, 'twere unworthy of us to deal with one of such eminence as though he were a common hilding, merely because the false cult of the Kangandites has driven him forth from the realm he served so well—to become a wanderer upon the planet. Since the Prefect and his dame be indisposed, let's have these masters in their stead tonight. What say you?"

"An idea worth pondering," said Zei. " 'Twould give us a full table of *chanizekash*."

"Ever a creature of whim," said Alvandi. "Such an invitation before even have their bona fides been confirmed! Oh, have 'em in, since not without dishonor may we withdraw an invitation once extended. But post a guard over the best royal plate. Perchance they'll prove more guestly than the locals, all of whom are either queer or dull, and ofttimes both."

Athough Barnevelt had expected the assembling of the expedition to consume a week, all the major matters had been taken care of by the end of the long Krishnan day. There were a dozen ships and boats for sale: an all-sail fisherman, seaworthy but slow; a naval galley-barge that would have needed a larger crew than the Earthmen cared to ship; a couple of wormy wrecks good for little but firewood . . .

"You pick her, pal," said Tangaloa, blowing smoke rings. "You are the naval expert."

Barnevelt finally chose an anomalous little craft with a single lateener mast, fourteen one-man oars, and a stench of neglect. However, under her dirt he recognized good lines and satisfied himself that her wood was sound.

He shot a keen look at the dealer. "Was this craft built for smuggling?"

" 'Tis true, Lord Snyol. How knew ye? The queen's men took it from a crew of illegals and sold it at auction. I bought it in hope of turning a small but honest profit. But for three revolutions of Karrim has it lain upon my shelf, for legal traders and fishers find it not sufficiently capacious for their purposes, while for military use is it too slow. Therefore I offer it cheaply—a virtual gift."

"What's it called?"

"The *Shambor*, a name of good omen."

The price the man asked did not strike Barnevelt as exactly giving the ship away, however. When he had beaten the dealer down as far as he thought he could, Barnevelt bought the ship and made arrangements for careening, scraping, painting, and renewing all questionable tackle. Then he and Tangaloa repaired to the Free Labor Mart and posted applications with the crier for seamen of exceptional courage and loyalty, because, as he made plain, the expedition entailed risks of no ordinary jeopardy.

After that they went to a second-hand clothing shop, where they procured the blue uniform of a courier of the Mejrou Qurardena. And as the uniform—the only one in stock—fitted Barnevelt fairly well while Tangaloa could not get into it, Barnevelt was elected to wear it for the invasion of the Sunqar.

When their dinners had settled and they had gone back to their room to put on their best clothes, they set out for the palace which, like most of Ghulindé, was lighted by jets of natural gas. They were ushered into a room containing Queen Alvandi, Princess Zei, Zakkomir bad-Gurshmani, and a paunchy, bleary-eyed, middle-aged Krishnan sadly setting out a game board.

"My consort Káj, such as he is," said Queen Alvandi, introducing the Earthmen under their Nyami pseudonyms.

"It's a great honor," said Barnevelt.

"Spare me these empty encomiums," said King Káj. "Once had I, like you, some small name in gests of war or sport, but all's done now."

"Rrrrrk," said a familiar voice, and there was Philo in his cage. The macaw let Barnevelt scratch among the roots of his feathers without trying to bite.

The king continued: "Play you chanijekka?"

Barnevelt, a little taken aback by Zei's rising to offer him her seat, peered at the game board. The latter looked somehow familiar: a hexagonal board with a triangular crisscross of lines covering the interior area.

"Father!" said Zei, who had just lighted her cigar on a gas jet. "How oft must I tell you 'tis pronounced 'chanizekash'?"

"The proper form of the name," said Queen Alvandi, "is 'chanichekr'."

"Be not absurd, Mother!" said Zei. " 'Tis 'chanizekash,' is't not, Zakkomir?"

"Whatever you say's right by definition, O star-jewel of the Zogha," said that young man.

"Weathervane!" said the queen. "Any noddy knows . . ."

King Káj snorted. "If I have but a ten-night to anticipate, then by Qunjar I'll call it what I please!"

"If you say it, 'tis probably wrong," said Queen Alvandi, "and I take ill your calling on a sanguinary god whom the righteous edicts of my predecessors have banished from the land! I have always understood 'chanichekr.' How say you, O men of Ny-amadzë?"

Barnevelt gulped. Feeling alittle like a man who has been asked to step into a cage to separate a pair of fighting lions, he replied: "Well—uh—in my land it's known as 'Chinese checkers'."

"Just as I pronounced it," said the queen, "save for your barbarous outland accents. Chanichekr shall it be to any who'd play with me. Choose you now, and red moves first."

She held out a fistful of markers, one of each of the six colors. King Káj drew red. He looked at it lugubriously, saying:

"Were I as lucky in the kashyó drawing as in this, I should not now face a wretched and untimely cease . . ."

"Stop your croaking, you wormy old aqebat!" yelled the queen. "Of all my consorts you're the most useless, in bed or out! Anyone would think you'd not had all the luxe the land provides in the year just gone. Now to your play. You're slowing the game."

Barnevelt inferred that Káj was one of those one-year consorts decreed by the curious customs of this land, and that the end of his term and of his life were fast approaching in the form of the kashyó festival. Under the circumstances he could hardly blame Káj for taking a dim view of things.

"Zakkomir," said Princess Zei, "you'll get nowhere with a move of that description. Why build you not a proper ladder?"

"Play your own game and keep your big nose out of mine, sweetling," retorted Zakkomir.

"The insolence of the princox!" cried Zei. "Master Snyol, would you term my nose large?"

"Matter of fact, I should call it 'aristocratic' rather than plain 'big'," said Barnevelt, who had been stealing furtive looks at the princess's boldly handsome features. He stroked his own sizeable proboscis.

"Why," she asked, "is a beak-nose a badge of birth in far Ny-amadzë? With us 'tis the contrary, the flatter the nobler—wherefore have I ever in my companions' laughter read mockery for my base-born looks. Perchance should I remove to this cold clime of yours, where my ugliness by the alchemy of social custom might to beauty be transmuted."

"Ugliness!" said Barnevelt, and was thinking up a neat compliment when Zakkomir broke in:

"Less female self-appraisal, madam, and more attention to your game. As the great Kurdé remarked, beauty of thought and deed outlasts that of skin and bone, be the latter never so seductive."

"And not pleased am I to hear customs made light of," growled Queen Alvandi. "Such mental mirror-posturing is meet for vain and silly males, but not for one of the stronger sex."

As Zei, looking a bit cowed, returned to her game, Zakkomir turned to Barnevelt. "General Snyol . . . O General!"

Barnevelt had fallen into a trance watching Zei and woke up with a start. "Huh? Beg pardon?"

"Tell me, sir, how go your preparations for the gvám hunt?"

"Mostly done. There's actually little left but to pay our bills, choose our crew, and oversee the overhaul of the ship."

"I'm tempted to cast my lot with you," said Zakkomir. "Long have I lusted for such adventure . . ."

"That you shall not!" cried the queen. " 'Tis much too perilous for one of your sex, and as your guardian I forbid it. Nor would it look well for one so near the royal house to engage in this disreputable traffic. Káj, you scurvy scrowl, my move to block! Would we could advance the festival's date to one earlier than that dictated by conjunction astrological."

Barnevelt was just as glad of the queen's interference. Zakkomir might be all right under his lipstick, but it wouldn't do to have strangers cutting in on the deal, especially as the expedition was not what it seemed.

"In truth," said Zei, "the dangers of the Banjao Sea are not to be undertaken in a spirit of frivolity. Could we persuade you two to give up this rash enterprise, sirs, high place could be found for you in our armed service, which being sore disordered at the moment needs captains of your renown to officer it."

"What's this?" said Tangaloa.

The queen answered: "My foolish lady warriors protest the men won't wed 'em for divers reasons, all addle-pated. There's factional quarrels 'mongst the several units and insubordinate jealousy amongst the officers—oh, 'tis a long and heavy-footed tale. The upshot is, I must bend my principles to the winds of human weakness and hire a male general to knock some silly crowns together. And as such employ to our own men is forbidden, I must seek my leader from foreign lands, however such choice may grate upon our pride. Do you perceive my meaning?"

King Káj, who seldom got a word in edgewise, spoke up: "How soon will you depart, my masters?"

"Not soon enough to avail you!" snapped Alvandi. "I see how blows the breeze, my friends. He'll think to seduce you into leaving early, having smuggled himself aboard in the guise of a sack of *tabid* tubers, and so provoke the righteous wrath of the Mother Goddess by evading the just price of his year's suzerainty. Know, sirs, you had better watch your respective steps, for this day have I signed the death warrants of three miserable males who sought unauthorized to slip from the land, no doubt to join the damned freebooters of the Sunqar. As for this aging idiot of mine . . ."

Káj stood up, shouting: "Enough, strumpet! If my remaining time be short, at least spare me your sluttish yap! Get the astrologer to finish the game for me."

He stalked from the room.

"Bawbling dotard!" the queen yelled after him, then beckoned a flunkey and bid him fetch the court astrologer. She said to Zei: "Find you young consorts, Daughter. These old ones like yon allicholy neither give pleasure in life nor prove toothsome when dead."

Barnevelt said: "You mean you *eat* him?"

"Certes. 'Tis a traditional part of the kashyó festival. If you'll attend, I'll see you're served a prime juicy gobbet."

Barnevelt shuddered. Tangaloa, taking the news quite calmly, murmured something about the customs of the Aztecs.

Zei's rich lips had been pressed together ever since the departure of Káj. Now she burst out: "Never will I have friends of mine to these family gatherings again! These travelers must deem us utter barbarians . . ."

"Who are you to reprehend your elders?" roared the queen.

"Sirs, but a ten-night past was she who speaks so nice one of a rout of young revellers who, instigated by this buffoon her adoptious brother," (she indicated Zakkomir) "did strip themselves egg-bare and mount the central fountain in the palace park, as they were a group of statues Panjakú means to set there. I had a lord and lady from Balhib, of oldest family, to walk in the park. So, say they, be this the great sculptor's new group, which we thought not yet completed? And whilst I stood a-goggle, wondering if 'twere a joke my minions had played upon me, the statues leap to life and cast themselves about us, loathly wet, with many unseemly jape and jest . . ."

"Quiet!" yelled Zakkomir, asserting himself suddenly. "If you women cease not from this eternal haver, I shall be driven forth like poor Káj. There was no harm in our acture. Your Balhibo lord did laugh with the rest when he got over his initial fright. Now let's talk of more delightsome things. General Snyol, how escaped you from the torture vaults of the Kangandites when they for heresy had doomed you?"

Barnevelt looked blankly at his questioner. The real Snyol of Pleshch must have been a Nyami general who had fallen afoul of the official religion of that country. After some thought he said:

"I'm sorry, but I can't tell without endangering those who helped me."

At that instant the court astrologer came in. Barnevelt sighed with relief at the interruption of another embarrassing line of conversation. The astrologer, an old codger introduced as Qvansel, said:

"You must let me show you the horoscope I have worked out for you, General Snyol. Long have I followed your career, and all has come about as predetermined by the luminaries of heaven, even to your arrival today at Qirib's capital and court."

"Very interesting," said Barnevelt. If only, he thought, he could tell the boy how wrong he was!

The astrologer went on: "In addition, sir, I should a favor deem it if your teeth you'd let me scrutinize."

"My teeth?"

"Aye. If I may so say, I am the kingdom's leading dentist."

"Thanks, but I haven't got a toothache."

The astrologer's antennae rose. "I know nought of toothaches or the cure thereof! I would tell your character and destiny from your teeth: a science second in exactitude only to the royal ology of the stars itself."

Barnevelt promised himself that if he ever did have a toothache, he wouldn't go to a dentist who examined his patients' teeth to tell their fortunes.

"Master Snyol!" barked the queen. "Your turn, as in truth you'd know were your eyes upon the game and not upon my daughter. Has she not the usual number of heads?"

They were invited back two nights later, and again the night after that. On these occasions Barnevelt was pleased to find that they did not have to put up with the morose king and the ferocious queen. It was just Zei, Zakkomir, and their young friends. Cautious questions bearing on the janrú traffic and Shtain's disappearance elicited nothing new.

Barnevelt wondered why he and George should be taken into such sudden favor at the palace. He was under the impression that royalty was choosy about its intimates, and he did not flatter himself that with his modest command of the language he had swept them off their feet by force of personality alone. Although George was socially more at ease than he, nevertheless they gave Barnevelt more attention than they did his companion.

Barnevelt finally concluded that it was a combination of factors. The social leaders of this remote city were bored with each other's company and welcomed a couple of exotic and glamorous strangers, arriving with impressive credentials, whom they could show off to their friends. They, especially the hero-worshipping Zakkomir, were impressed by the achievements of the supposed Snyol of Pleshch. And, finally, Zei and Alvandi were serious about hiring him.

He found the gilded youth of Ghulindé pleasant on the whole; idle and useless by his sterner standards, but friendly and charming withal. From the chatter he gathered that there were wild ones of this class as well, but such were not welcomed at the palace. Zakkomir, in his anomalous position as ward of the throne, seemed to pick the social list and to serve as a link between the outside world and Zei, who gave the impression of leading a somewhat shut-in life.

Barnevelt noticed that the princess became much livelier when her mother was not around—almost boisterous in fact. Perhaps, he thought sympathetically, she had a problem like his own.

Then something else began to worry him: He caught himself more and more stealing glances at Zei, thinking about her when he was away from the palace, and looking forward to seeing her again on his next visit. Moreover, they seemed to mesh spiritually. During the frequent arguments, he more and more found her and himself on the same side against the rest. (Tangaloa disdained to argue, regarding the whole spectacle with detached amusement and making sociological notes on the conversations when he got home at night.)

After several visits, Barnevelt even felt close enough to Zei to fight with her openly, and to hell with protocol. One night he beat her by a narrow margin at Chinese checkers, having nosed her out by a blocking move. She said some Gozashtandou words that he did not suspect her of knowing—unless she had learned them from Philo.

"Now, now," he said, "no use getting riled up, my dear. If you'd watched what I was doing instead of gossiping about the spotted egg Lady Whoozis has laid, you'd . . ."

Wham! Zei snatched up the game board and brought it down smartly on Barnevelt's head. As it was of good solid wood, not Earthly cardboard—and as he had no hair to cushion the blow—he saw stars.

"So much for your criticisms, Master Know-it-all Snyol!"

Barnevelt reached around and gave her a resounding spank.

"*Ao!*" she cried. "That hurt! Such presumptuous jocosity, sirrah . . ."

"So did your game board, mistress, and I'm in the habit of doing to others as they do to me, and preferably first. Now shall we pick up the little balls and start again?"

Seeing that the others were more amused than indignant, Zei cooled off and took the slap in good part. But, when Barnevelt had bidden her a ceremonious good-night at the door and turned to go, he got a swat on the seat of his shorts that almost knocked him sprawling. He turned to see Zei holding a broom and Zakkomir rolling on the rug with mirth.

"The last laugh is oft the lustiest, as says Nehavend," she said sweetly. "Good-night, sirs, and forget not the way back hither."

Dirk Barnevelt had been in love before, even though his mother had always managed to spoil it. He was not altogether foolish about such matters, though, and saw that nothing would be more tragically ridiculous than to fall in love with a female of another species. And one, moreover, who disposed of successive mates in the fashion of an Earthly spider or praying mantis.

Barnevelt worked hard on his crew, molding them into an effective unit. Knowing that his own shyness sometimes made him seem aloof and cold to those who did not know him well, he made a point of being chummy with the sailors, who seemed delighted that one of his rank should admit them to such unwonted familiarity.

After a day of training the crew in the harbor, the Earthmen's next visit to the palace found only Zei and Zakkomir visible, though the queen looked in once to bid a curt good-evening. The king appeared not at all.

"He's drunk, poor abject," said Zakkomir. "So should I be in his buskins. Of late he spends all his time in his chambers swilling and pottering with his collection of cigar cases. A rare assortment has he, too—marvels of jewelling and fine inlay work, and trick ensamples like one that plays a tune when you open it."

"Could I see them?" said Tangaloa.

"Certes, Master Tagdë. 'Twould pleasure the old fellow greatly. Showing off this accumulation is nearly his only joy in life, and few chances he gets. The queen scoffs at his enthusiasm and visitors, to flatter her, cloak themselves in similar agreement with her attitude. You'll excuse us, sir and madam, unless you also wish to come?"

"Let's not and say we did," said Barnevelt. The other two males strolled out.

"How soon do you sail?" asked Zei.

Barnevelt, feeling oddly breathless, replied: "We could be off day after tomorrow."

"You must not leave ere the kashyó festival be over! We have reserved for you a pair of choicest seats, next in honor after our royal kin."

Barnevelt answered: "It may seem uncouth of me, but watching your poor old stepfather butchered is a sight I could bear to miss."

She hesitated, then said: "Is it true we're criticized in other lands because of it, as says Zakkomir?"

"Matter of fact, some folks are horrified."

"So he says, but I doubted because he's a secret sympathizer with the Reform Party."

"The people who don't want to kill the king any more?"

"The same. Breathe nothing to my lady mother, lest in her rage poor Zakkomir suffer. They sent word to her through intermediaries that for the nonce they'd settle on elimination of the ceremonial devourment of the late consort. But she'd have none of it, and so beneath its fair-seeming surface our land does boil with treasonous plots and coils."

"What'll you do when you're queen?"

"That I know not. Though sensible am I of the causes urged against our custom, yet will my mother always retain much influence on the affairs of Qirib, so long as she does live. And, as she says, aside from considerations of true religion, there's nothing like slaying the topmost man yearly to keep the sex in its proper place."

"Depends on what you call proper place," said Barnevelt, thinking that Qirib needed a—what would be the opposite of "feminist"? "masculist"?—a Masculist Party.

"Nay," said Zei, "argue not like Zakkomir. Our realm's prosperity is proof positive of the rightful superiority of the female."

"But I can cite you prosperous realms where the men ruled the women, and others where they were equal."

"A disturbing fellow, are you not? As I said when you so rudely smote me upon the posterior, no Qiribu you!"

"Well, my disturbing presence will soon be gone. Actually, you can give me some useful advice. What's the connection between the Banjao pirates, the janrú traffic, and Qirib?"

She stared at her cigar. "Methinks we'd best change subjects, lest we get into perilous grounds where one's safety can only be assured by another's sacrifice . . ."

On the way home, Barnevelt said: "Let's shove off day after tomorrow, George."

"Are you mad? I wouldn't miss this ceremony for anything. Think of all the dinkum film we shall get!"

"Ayuh, but I'm squeamish about watching them kill and cook poor Káj in front of my eyes. To say nothing of having to eat a piece of him later."

"How do you know what he will taste like? Among my ancestors it was a regular custom for the winner of a sporting contest to eat the loser."

"But I'm no South Sea Islander! In my culture-pattern it's considered rude to eat people you know socially."

"Come, come," said Tangaloa. "Káj is not really human. Millions of Krishnans die all the time, and what difference does one more make?"

"Yes, but . . ."

"And we can't walk out on the queen. She expects us."

"Oh, foof! Once we're at sea . . ."

"You forget we're leaving a bond here, and Panagopoulos won't stand for our forfeiting it unnecessarily. Also our sailors will insist on being brought back home when we finish."

Unaccustomed as he had become to having George make a definite decision, Barnevelt gave in. He told himself he did so because of the weight of Tangaloa's arguments—*not* because he would thus be enabled to go on seeing Zei. Nevertheless he felt elated at the prospect of so doing.

The night of the festival, Zakkomir checked the costumes of Barnevelt and Tangaloa and found them adequate. "Though," he said, "they be not those customary, yet will the other practisants excuse you as foreigners who know no better."

"Thank Zeus they won't make us wear one of those toga effects," muttered Barnevelt. "I can just see myself trying to manage one in a gale."

Not Solomon in all his glory was arrayed like Zakkomir, in a sort of cloth-of-gold sarong, with jewelled armlets, gilt sandal-boots reaching halfway up his bare calves, a golden wreath on his green hair, and his face as bedizened with paint as that of a Russian ballerina.

He led them into the reception hall where royal aunts and uncles thronged. At last the trumpets blew and the king and queen marched through, the rest falling into place behind them. Káj wobbled as he walked and looked glummer than ever, despite the efforts of the royal makeup artist to paint a lusty look upon his visage.

Zakkomir showed Barnevelt and Tangaloa where to fall in, then went forward to take Zei's arm behind the royal couple.

As the amphitheater, where the kashyó festival took place, lay just outside the palace grounds, the procession went afoot. Two of the three moons showed alternately as the clouds uncovered them, and a warm brisk wind flapped robes and cloaks and made the gaslights flutter. Outside the wall of the palace grounds, many of the common people of Ghulindé stood massed, and a wedge of whifflers pushed a path through them.

The amphitheater was fast filling. On one side stood the royal box. The flat space in the middle of the structure was occupied by a stove and a new, red-painted chopping block. The people ranged about these accessories included old Sehri, the high priestess of the Mother Goddess; several assistants, some with musical instruments; the palace chef and a couple of assistant cooks; and a man wearing over his head a black bag with eyeholes and leaning on the handle of a chopper with a blade like a butcher's cleaver but twice as big. The cooks were sharpening other culinary implements. Amazon guards stood around the topmost tier of the theater, the wavering gaslights sparkling on their brazen armor.

Barnevelt found himself sitting in the second row a little to the right of the royal box, which was full of royal cousins besides the queen and the princess. The benches included a narrow table-like structure in front of each. Káj himself was down in the central plaza, sitting hunched on the chopping block with hands on knees.

Barnevelt said to Tangaloa: "I don't see how Káj can be stretched enough to give everybody a piece, unless they make hamburger of him and dilute it with more conventional meat. What else happens?"

"It's quite elaborate. They have ballet dancers acting out the return of the sun from the south, and the growing crops and all that sort of rot. You will like it."

Barnevelt doubted that; but, as the amphitheater was now full and the crowd quieting down, he did not care to argue the point. The high priestess raised her arms and called out:

"We shall first sing the hymn to the Mother Goddess: 'Hail to Thee, Divine Progenitrix of Gods and Men.' Are you ready?"

She swept her arms in the motions of an orchestra conductor. The musical instruments tweetled and plunked, and the audience broke into song. They sang lustily for the first few lines, then petered out. Barnevelt noticed that many were peering about as though trying to read their neighbors' lips, and guessed that, as in the case of "The Star Spangled Banner" and the "World Federation Anthem," a lot of people knew the words of the opening lines only. Tangaloa was unobtrusively filming the scene with his ring camera.

As the volume of singing diminished, Barnevelt heard another sound that swelled to take its place: the surflike noise of a distant human uproar. At the end of the first stanza, the priestess paused with her arms up. In the resulting silence the noise came nearer, resolving itself into individual roars and shrieks and the clang of metal. Heads turned; in the topmost tier, some stood up to

stare outward. Amazons bustled about and conferred.

Barnevelt exchanged a blank look with Tangaloa. The sound grew louder.

Then a bloody man dashed into the theater through a tunnel entrance, shouting: *"Moryá Sunqaruma!"*

Barnevelt understood, then, that the noise was caused by an attack of the pirates of the Sunqar.

The next minute he was pitched off his feet by a panic-push of the crowd. He fought his way upright again. In front of him Tangaloa gripped a corner of the royal box to keep from being swept away.

A renewed racket around one of the entrances, and a party of pirates pushed in against the opposition of the Amazons. Barnevelt saw some woman warriors go down before the weapons of the intruders, and others brushed aside. More pirates erupted through other entrances. Barnevelt felt for his sword, then remembered that he had been made to leave it at home. The Qiribo men were all unarmed; and, while some of the women wore swords, neither they nor the men seemed inclined to make use of them.

A pirate with a torch in one hand and a sheet of paper in the other shouted in the Qiribo dialect: "Stand! If you flee not, no harm shall come to you. We wish but two men from among you." He repeated this announcement until the hubbub quieted.

Other shouts came from outside. Barnevelt guessed that the pirates had thrown a cordon around the theater to catch runaways. He also had a horrid premonition of who the two sought by the raiders were.

Queen Alvandi and Princess Zei stood in their box, pale but resolute.

The bulk of the audience were still massed around the exits. In the center of the theater the cook, the executioner, and most of the priestesses had disappeared into the general mob; King Káj and the high priestess remained.

The pirate leader with the torch shouted: "We wish . . ."

And at that instant the gaslights went out.

The sudden darkening brought a few seconds of silence; then

a rising murmur that swelled to a roar.

"Snyol! You there, Snyol of Pleshch!" shouted a voice.

Barnevelt looked around. A few meters away from him stood King Káj, revealed by the fugitive light from one of the moons. The king bore a triumphant smile on his face and the executioner's chopper in his hands.

"Aye, you!" repeated the king. "Take the queen to the palace, and let your companion Tagdë take the princess!"

"How about you?" Barnevelt shouted back.

"I remain here. To me, all loyal Qiribuma! To me! Let's deracinate this gang of rogues!"

"I'm with you!" came Zakkomir's high voice, and the young man jumped down from the front of the box with a lady's sword in his hand. A few of the braver citizens joined them, and the remnant of the Amazon guard. With the king whirling the chopper at their head they bored into the scattered pirates. The clatter of weapons drowned speech.

Barnevelt, looking around, saw Tangaloa swarming up into the royal box, seizing Zei, and starting to hustle her off out through the private royal exit. Although Barnevelt would have preferred that job himself, he saw nothing to do but carry out the king's order. He climbed up after Tangaloa and caught the queen's arm.

"Come along, Your Altitude," he said

"But you— he . . ."

"Save the talk till later."

"I'll not come until . . ."

Barnevelt drew the queen's sword, a toylike little sticker, but at least it had a point. "You'll come or I'll spank you with this!"

They trotted down the tunnel through which the royal aunts and cousins had already fled. Outside, the seizure and search that the pirates had so carefully organized was fast breaking down with the extinction of the lights. People were running away in all directions, and here and there men fought with swords and pikes in the gloom. A Qiribo gentleman mistook Barnevelt for a pirate and came at him. Barnevelt parried the first lunge and a yell from the queen enlightened the man in the midst of a second.

Another character with a torch confronted them, saying: "Halt! Ah, 'tis he whom . . ."

It was the specialist, Gavao er-Gargan. Barnevelt's point got him through the belly.

He doubled over and fell, dropping the torch.

Then Barnevelt was engaged with another. The pirate lunged. Barnevelt parried and felt his point go home on the riposte. But the pirate, instead of falling, came back for more. You could never be sure of hitting a vital organ on a Krishnan unless you knew their distinctive physiology.

"Heroun, you devil!" shrieked the queen, apparently at the pirate.

"We'll argue later, you mangy trull!" panted the pirate, coming at Dirk with a *coupe*.

They were still at it when another Qiribu got the pirate over the head from behind with a small statue. **Splash!**

Somewhere a trumpet blew a complicated pattern of notes. The crowd had now pretty well thinned out; and the Sunqaruma, too, seemed to have gone elsewhere. Barnevelt saw a couple in the distance, running back down the colossal stairway that led from Ghulindé down to Damovang and the sea. He stepped over a body lying on the path, then over another that still moved. An occasional groan from the darkness around the shrubbery told of others left wounded.

At the front entrance to the palace, a cluster of Amazons formed a double semicircular rank around the portal, those in front kneeling and those behind standing, their spears jutting out like a porcupine's quills. At a word from the queen they opened to let her through.

"Saw you my daughter?" she asked the guard in charge.

"No, my lady."

Barnevelt said: "I'll go back and look for her, Queen."

"Go, and take a few of these with you. We need not all of them, now the rovers have withdrawn."

Barnevelt led a half-dozen of the girl soldiers back the way he had come. One of them carried a small lamp. He stumbled over a body or two and met only one person, who fled before he could be identified. The accoutrements of the girls clanked behind Barnevelt. He was sure he had gotten lost and was casting about for directions when a small twinkle, as of a fallen star, caught his eye.

He hurried over and found the bodies of the two pirates he had sworded. Beside them lay Gavao's torch, nearly out but putting forth one feeble tongue of flame.

The moonlight also showed Barnevelt a white square on the path. He picked up a piece of paper about a span long and wide and turned it over. The other side was dark.

"Lend me that lamp, please," he said, and by the weak light of its flame examined the paper.

It was a print of the picture the old photographer had made of him and Tangaloa in Jazmurian.

He tucked the picture inside his jacket, thinking: A good thing the queen hadn't known the Moryá Sunqaruma were after George and himself, or she'd have surely turned them over.

"George!" he called into the darkness. "Tagdë of Vyutr! George Tangaloa!"

"Be that my lord Snyol?" called a voice, and footsteps and clankings approached. However, it was not George Tangaloa but Zakkomir bad-Gurshmani, limping, with a small party including a couple of Amazons.

"Where's the king?" asked Barnevelt.

"Slain in the garboil. Thus, whilst he evaded not the doom marked out for him in the stars, at least he came to a happier end than that which gallowed him. The queen'll be wroth, howsomever."

"Why?"

"Because, item: it spoils her ceremony. And, item: 'twill strengthen the sentiment of the vulgar for male equality. 'Twas another male, the palace janitor, whose quick wit led him to shut off the gas. Moreover Káj knew what he was about. After he'd struck down twain of the robbers, he said to me: "If we win here, we'll next deal with the old she-eshuna,' by which I think he meant the queen and Priestess Sehri. And then a pirate blade did jugulate him as he pivoted. But enough of that—where are your friend and the princess?"

"I'm wondering," said Barnevelt, and called again.

The party spread out to search. After much poking among the bushes an Amazon called: "Here lies one without hair upon his pate!"

Barnevelt hurried over and found that sure enough it was Tangaloa asprawl on his face, his shaven scalp puffed into a bloody lump over one ear. To his infinite relief Barnevelt found that George's pulse was still beating. When an Amazon dashed a helmetful of fountain water into Tangaloa's face, he opened his eyes and groaned. His right arm was also bloody; he had been run through the muscle.

"What happened?" asked Barnevelt. "Where's Zei?" Zakkomir echoed him.

"I don't know. I told you I was a dub at sword play. I hit one bloke over the head, but the sheila's sword broke on his helmet and I don't remember any more."

"Serves you justly," muttered Zakkomir when this had been translated, "to use a light thrusting blade in such thwart fashion. But where's our princess?"

"Let me think," said Tangaloa, putting his left hand to his head. "Just before that happened, one of 'em grabbed her, and another shouted something about taking 'em both—everybody was yelling at once. That's all I know."

" 'Tis enough," said Zakkomir. "For from this can we infer they've seized her. Mushái, run to the top of the theater and see if all their ships have left their mooring. If not, there might be yet time. . . ."

But Mushái called down in a couple of minutes that the fleet of the Moryá Sunqaruma was now all well out to sea.

The queen was wild. "Cowards!" she screamed. "I should let slay the whole mangy pack of you—and you detestable strangers, too!" she added, indicating Barnevelt and Tangaloa, the latter of whom was having his arm bandaged. "For what's a monarchy without a monarch, save a worthless rabble, and what's a monarch whose subjects will not spend their blood to save her? Caitiff knaves, all my subjects! Burn the lot! Why should they live when my chick's gone?"

"Now, now," said Qvansel the astrologer. "Your Altitude, what had happened was writ upon the firmament and not to be avoided. The opposition of Sheb to Roqir did presage . . ."

"Shut your mouth! Enough time for star-gazing foolery when my girl's recovered. You, madam!" Queen Alvandi shot a thick forefinger at her spinsterly minister. "How account you for this arrant botchery?"

"Madam, may I speak without fear?"

"Say on," said the queen, though her angry-lioness expression did not invite candor.

"Then hear me, Awesomeness. What happened was predestined, though not for the reason given by our star-staring friend. For five reigns now has the right to bear arms in this land been limited to our own sex. Hence have your subjects male become unused to the shock of combat, while your armed females, though valiant enough, lack the size and stoutness to endure the onslaught of these rampant depredators."

The queen glowered. " 'Tis well you extracted from me a promise of immunity, or, by the six breasts of Varzai, I would tear the flesh from your aged bones myself for your treasonous talk! But let's consider what is to be done. And no counsel of overturning the basis of our state, either! I'll see Ghulindé razed to the ground and the heads of its people piled in pyramids ere I'll put out the beacon light our state does shed upon this sorry world by the exaltation of the better sex to its proper seat. How about an expedition to rescue her?"

"Could be," said the minister, "save that the Sunqaruma no doubt entertain some plan of holding Zei for hostageship or ransom, and would slay her should you press attack upon them."

The high priestess, Sehri, muttered something about expense, and the chief of the Amazon guards protested: "Though we yield to no mere males in intrepidity, Your Altitude, yet the Sunqar is a fearsome place to overcome, as it can neither be walked over nor sailed through. Methinks that the occasion cries more for guile than brute puissance."

"Guile?" said the queen, looking from face to face. "As, let us say, to slip a small group into this steamy stronghold on some fair-seeming pretext, and then away to snatch my daughter?" Her small glittering eyes came to rest on Barnevelt. "You, sir, come hither claiming you'll seek the gvám stone in the Banjao Sea to inflame the lust of lechers. You buy a suitable ship, amass gvám-hunting gear, and hire men—and also, my spies report, procure one used expressman's uniform. Now wherefore this last? Could it be that you twain also entertain some plot the Sunqar in disguise to enter?"

No flies on Alvandi, thought Barnevelt, giving the queen a noncommittal smile. "One never knows when such a thing will come in handy, Your Altitude."

"Humph! I take your evasion for assent. So, since you wish it, you shall do it. You are hereby commissioned to rescue the princess from the clutch of these misdemeanants."

"Hey!" cried Barnevelt. "I never volunteered for anything like that!"

"Who said you did? 'Tis my command and your obedience. You leave on the morrow."

"But I couldn't even think of going without Ge— my friend Tagdë, and he won't be ready till his arm heals!"

"Such delay might well be fatal. I'll lend you Zakkomir in his stead."

"I shall be glad to go," said Zakkomir. "'Twould be an honor to serve under the great Snyol."

Barnevelt scowled at the young Krishnan, then addressed the queen again: "Look here, madam, I'm not a citizen of Qirib. What's to stop me from going about my own business as soon as I'm out of your country?"

"The facts that, first, Snyol of Pleshch is known as one who keeps his plighted word, and second, that your companion remains with me as hostage, your acquiescence to assure. *Guards!*

Seize these twain, and fetch the executioner with his instruments of torment."

A couple of Amazons seized Dirk's arms. He struggled, but they were strong, and before he overcame his Earthly inhibitions against kicking a lady in the abdomen, more fastened onto him until he could not move at all. Others seized Tangaloa, who did not even try to resist.

Presently the man with the bag over his head appeared with a brazier full of hot coals, in which the business ends of an assortment of pincers and other instruments of interesting design were heating.

"Now," said Queen Alvandi, "do you submit, or must I stage a painful demonstration of my will?"

"Oh, I'll go," grumbled Barnevelt. "But if you want me to accomplish anything, tell me about the Sunqar. There's some connection between it and the janrú trade and Qirib, isn't there? You knew one of the men I was fighting with."

"He's right, exalted guardian," said Zakkomir. "This foray will prove perilous enough without sending this mighty man against his foes half-blind by ignorance."

"Very well," said the queen. "Release them, guards, but watch them close. Sit, my friends.

"Know that the janrú is but an extract made from that same sea vine of which the Sunqar is composed. And since the founding of the matriarchal monarchy, because that nature had unequitably made my sex the smaller, we have redressed the balance by the use of perfume mingled with this volatile essence called janrú. 'Tis not broadcast among the general, but any wench whose man develops fractiousness can draw a ration of it from the temple of the Mother Goddess, her churlish spouse to tame.

"The foundress of the dynasty, great Dejanai, did organize a party to invade the Sunqar, then a watery and weedy desert, to erect a floating factory the stuff to make. All went as planned, save that our women caring not for heat and damp and stench, the work came more and more to be performed by convicts exiled to this lonesome spot to expiate their crimes. In time the men outnumbered women two to one, whereat some base sub-

109

versive rebel stirred the silly males to rise by tempting them with tales of male superiority among the savage nations. So rise they did and seized the factory, the women there degrading to the state of common queans. (The worst of 't was, that many of 'em seemed to like it.) Our navy they repelled, and from us did extort a tribute in return for a meager trickle of janrú. We tried by gathering terpahla that grows on rocks along our coasts, to free ourselves from their rapacity—but only in the Sunqar does the vine occur in quantities sufficient.

"Since then the Sunqar has continued to defy us. Not only does it squeeze us juiceless for this wondrous substance, but serves as sanctuary for our malcontented males. Hence has its population grown and divaricated into other lines of enterprise: for ensample, gvám-hunting and plain piracy. In the days of my immediate predecessor did a chief named 'Avasp make a deal with Dur, whereby Dur did pay him tribute on his agreement to withhold his hand from Duro ships, but on all others in the Banjao Sea most balefully to prey. Thus does Dur reach out for a monopoly, not only in its own Va'andao Sea, but in the other waters of this hemisphere as well.

"All sorts of curious characters have assembled in this fearsome fastness. Not only discontented Qiribuma, but also tailed men from Zá and the Koloft Swamp, and even Earthmen and other creatures from the deeps of space. When 'Avasp died, the new chief chosen in his room was one of these—a scaly, odious horror from a planet called Osiris: a towering monstrosity named Shea-fasè who, 'tis said, maintains a rule of iron by a dreadful power of fascination. And this Sheafasè had far and wide outspread the tentacles of his enterprise, until he does amass the wealth of Dahhaq by the drug to Earthmen selling . . ."

Despite the queen's harrying, they did not sail the next day, nor yet the day after that.

For one thing, half the crew disappeared when they learned the real object of the expedition, so that new men had to be signed on and broken in. One of these, a bright young fellow named Zanzir, followed Barnevelt around asking questions. Barnevelt, flattered, gave the youth a good deal of his time until Tangaloa warned him against favoritism. Thereafter Barnevelt tried to treat the others with equal cordiality.

He also hired a new boatswain, Chask: a thickset, gnarly, snag-toothed man with his green hair faded to pale jade. Chask took hold of the crew and soon welded them into an effective rowing and sailing unit. All went well until one day while Barnevelt was in the cabin and the men were practicing evolutions on deck, he heard the sound of a scuffle. He went out to find Chask nursing a knuckle on the catwalk and Zanzir a bloody nose in the scuppers.

"Come here," he said to Chask. When the latter was in the cabin he gave him a dressing down: ". . . and my crew are to be treated like human beings, see? There shall be *no* brutality on my ship."

"But Captain, this young fellow disputes my commands, saying he knows better than I how to do what I've spent my life . . ."

"Zanzir's an intelligent boy. He's to be encouraged rather than suppressed. You're not afraid he'll take your job away, are you?"

"But sir, with all respect, ye cannot run a ship like a social club, with all entitled to a voice in deciding each maneuver. And if those in command let common sailors think they're as good as them, and entitled every order to discuss, then when comes the pinch . . ."

Despite inner qualms, Barnevelt felt he must show a firm front. "You have your order, Chask. We're running this ship my way."

Chask went out muttering. Thereafter the sailors seemed happier but also less efficient.

When the *Shambor* finally put forth from the harbor of Damovang with Barnevelt and Zakkomir aboard—and Tangaloa, surrounded by Amazons, waving his good arm from the pier—Barnevelt had accumulated several items of special equipment which, he hoped, would somewhat ease his task. There were smoke bombs made by a local manufacturer of pyrotechnics from yasuvar-spores, and a light sword with a hinge in the middle of the blade so that it could be folded and slipped down inside one of the expressman's boots. As a weapon it was inferior to a regular rapier, the hinge constituting a weak spot and the hilt lacking a proper guard. Barnevelt, however, doubted that the pirates would admit him to their inner circle fully armed.

He also bore a chest of gold and gewgaws, as a present from Queen Alvandi to Sheafasè, and a letter asking for terms for Zei's release. A Krishnan quadrant, simple but rugged and fairly accurate, would give him his latitudes.

Zakkomir, similarly clad and looking quite different without his face paint, waved a similar sticker, saying: "My lord Snyol, will you teach me to wield a sword in practiced style? For under our laws have I never had a chance for such instruction. 'Twas simple happenstance I wasn't spitted during the raid. Ever have

I nursed a perverse wish to be a woman—that is, not like the women of your land, or the men of mine, but a woman of mine, and to swear and swagger with rough muliebrity. Would I'd been hatched in your land, where custom to the male such part assigns!"

At least, thought Barnevelt, the kid's willing to learn.

The first leg of the trip was easy, for they ran free before the prevailing westerly along the coast of the Qiribo peninsula, where dark stunted trees overhung rocky promontories on which the spray broke. Zakkomir had a couple of days of seasickness, then snapped out of it. They stopped at Hojur to top off supplies.

Barnevelt studied his navigational guide and familiarized himself with the workings of the *Shambor*. Not far in the future all three moons would be in conjunction at full, which meant a real high tide—something that occurred only once in several Krishnan years.

In hull and rudder, the ship compared well with the yachts he'd sailed on Earth. The sail, though, was something else: a lateen sail of the high-peaked asymmetrical type used in these waters, in contrast to the symmetrical lateen sail of Majbur and the lug and square sails of the more boisterous northern seas. He learned that a lateen sail, however pretty, had but weak powers of working to windward. In fact, it combined many of the disadvantages of a square sail and a fore-and-aft sail with few of the advantages of either.

Chask explained: "Captain, there be six ways of tacking with a lateen sail, all impractical. Now, had we one of them Majburo rigs, with the two short sides equal, we could pay out the tack and haul in the vang, so that the low corner rises and the high one falls, meanwhile wearing ship. But with this rig must ye either lower sail altogether and re-rig on t'other side of the mast, or put half the men on the tack and haul aft to up-end the yard and twist it round the mast. Still, in the region of variables and calms whither we're bound, that high peak'll prove its worth in catching light airs."

At last they reached the end of the peninsula, where the Zogha

sloped down to the sea like the spinal scutes of some stegosaurine monster. They turned to starboard and headed south with the wind abeam. Barnevelt gave his men only an occasional turn at the oars, enough to keep them hardened but not enough to tire them. He'd need their strength later. The water was too rough for effective rowing anyway.

Then the emerald waters turned to slate, the wind fell, and they spent a day rowing in a fog through which a warm drizzle fell unceasingly. They spread a canvas tank to catch the rain for drinking water.

Barnevelt was standing in the eyes of the ship, peering into the mist, when the *Shambor* lurched suddenly as if she had struck bottom. Yells rose from the men aft.

On the port side of the ship, in the water, an elongated body was moving away. Covered with flint-gray leather, it might have been part of the barrel of a finback whale or a sea serpent. As it slipped through the water, the particular coil or loop that was arched up next to the ship sank down out of sight.

A scream jerked Barnevelt's attention to the stern. There in mid-air, its means of support hidden by the fog, appeared a crocodilian head with jaws big enough to down a man at a gulp. The head tilted to one side and swooped down onto the deck, a colossal neck coming into view behind it. Clomp! went the jaws, and a screaming sailor was borne back into the mist.

Barnevelt, caught by surprise, did not spring into action until the victim was on his way into the sea. Then he caught up a spare oar and ran to the stern, but too late. The shrieks of the victim were cut off as the dreadful head disappeared beneath the water.

"Row!" yelled Chask, and the oarsmen dug in their blades.

Barnevelt unhappily gave orders to mount a deck watch with pikes in case of another such attack. He went back to the bow for a while, then started back for the deckhouse.

He was just opening the door when a shuffle of feet and a clearing of throats behind him made him look around. There were Zanzir and three other sailors.

Zanzir spoke up: "Captain Snyol, the boys and I have taken thought and concluded that 'twere best for all if ye now do turn back homeward."

"*What?*" cried Barnevelt, not sure he had heard right.

"Aye, so we've decided. Is it not so, bullies?" The other three made the affirmative head motion. "Some of us feel poorly in this drizzle. Others have families at home. To press on through this ominous fog into a realm of uncharted rocks and bloodthirsty men . . ."

"And unknown deadly monsters, forget not," reminded one of the others.

"And unknown deadly monsters, like that which but now did snatch our comrade, were cruelty compounded. So we know that, being a good friend of ours . . ."

"Who admits we're as good as he," reminded the same prompter.

"Who admits we're as good as he, that ye'll heed our rede and

115

return us to our happy homes. Is't not true, bullies?" And all three indicated "yes."

"I'll be damned," said Barnevelt. "No, I will not turn back. You were warned at the start about our dangers, and now you shall see them through."

"But Cap old fellow," said Zanzir, laying a hand on Barnevelt's arm. "Between friends should there not be mutual trust and consideration? We've voted on it, and you're overborne by four to one . . ."

"Get back to your work!" said Barnevelt sharply, shaking off Zanzir's hand. "I'm boss, and by Qondyor's rump I'll—I'll . . ."

"Ye mean ye won't?" said Zanzir with an air of pained astonishment. "Not even to please your friends?"

"Get out! Hey, *Chask!* Put these men to work and discipline the next one who talks of quitting."

The men went aft, glowering back at Barnevelt who, upset and angry, flung into the deckhouse to work out a dead-reckoning plot. So that was what happened when you made pals of your men! All very fine while the going was good, but the minute the going got tough they were like a rope of sand. He'd heard it before, of course, but hadn't believed it, supposing that theory to be mere self-justification by aristocrats and tyrants. Now they'd be sore—and not altogether without cause—for he'd led them to think they could have their way and then rudely disillusioned them.

"I like this not," said Zakkomir, peering palely out the cabin windows into the mist. "Varzai knows on which side of Palindos Strait we'll make landfall, if indeed we run not upon the rocks. Would there were some means of closely fixing one's position east and west."

Barnevelt looked up from the plot he was comparing with his chart, and almost said something about marine chronometers and radio signals before he remembered where he was. Instead he said: "We're not due to reach the south shore of the Sadabao Sea for some hours yet. I'll slow down to take soundings before we get into dangerous waters."

"Let's hope you do, sir. We'd cut poor figures, setting forth with such brave impetus to save our damsel from disaster dire, only to find our immediate end in the maw of some monster maritime."

"Are you in love with Zei?" Barnevelt asked with elaborate casualness, though his heart pounded as he said it.

Zakkomir forced a smile. "Nay, not I! From long acquaintance I regard her as a sister and will lavish on the chick all brotherly affection. But love as between man and woman? To be the consort of a queen were difficult enough. To be that of one who's required by our customs to send her mate to death at end of year were quite impossible. The little Lady Mula'i, whom you've met at the palace, is my intended, if I can induce her to propose."

Barnevelt experienced a certain relief at this reply, though he knew it was silly since *he* did not intend to marry Zei. As he pondered his charts, he became aware of a clicking sound, which he finally identified as the chattering of Zakkomir's teeth.

"Are you cold?" he asked.

"Nay, only f-frightened. I sought to hide my mannish weakness from you."

Barnevelt slapped him on the back. "Cheer up—we're all frightened at times."

"Why, have even you, the great and fearless General Snyol, known fear?"

"Sure! Don't you suppose I was scared when I fought those six fellows from Olñega single-handed? Pull yourself together!"

Zakkomir pulled himself together, almost with an audible click, and Barnevelt continued his computations. When his dead-reckoning showed they were getting close either to Palindos Strait or to the shores adjacent to it, Barnevelt gave orders to take soundings. The first attempt touched bottom at fourteen meters. Thereafter they went slowly until the water shoaled to five meters and they thought they could hear the sound of a small surf ahead. There they anchored until a brisk north wind sprang up and blew the fog away in tatters.

"Said I not you were infallible?" cried Zakkomir, his courage regained.

Palindos Strait appeared in plain sight to the south and east of them. The strait was divided by the island of Fossanderan, the eastern or farther channel being the one used for navigation. The western channel was much smaller, and a note on Barnevelt's chart stated that its minimum depth was about two meters—too shallow for the *Shambor* unless tidal conditions were just right.

Zakkomir added: "What perplexes me is how you, a man from Nyamadzë where no large bodies of water exist, should add such adroit seamanship to your many other accomplishments."

Barnevelt ignored this comment as they ran through the eastern channel, off the wind, at a good clip.

Pointing to Fossanderan, Zakkomir said: " 'Tis said that on that isle it was the hero Qarar mated with a she-yeki, and from their union came a race of beast-men with human limbs and animal heads. 'Tis yet reported that there these monsters still hold riotous revels at certain astrological conjunctions, with din of drums and clash of cymbal making the long night hideous."

Barnevelt remembered the yeki he had seen in the zoo in Majbur: a carnivore about the size of an Earthly tiger but looking more like an oversized six-legged mink. "Why doesn't somebody land and find out?" he asked.

"Know you, sir, the thought never occurred to me? When this present task be over, who knows what we'll next essay? For under your inspiring leadership I feel brave enough to mate with a she-yeki myself."

"Well, if you think I'm going to hold a she-yeki while you experiment, you can think again."

The air grew warmer and more humid as they entered the belt between that of the prevailing westerlies and that of the northeast trades. Calms made them rely on oars alone for days at a time, and Barnevelt checked his supplies of food and water and worried.

Krishnan flying fish, which really flew with flaps of jointed wings, and did not merely glide like those of Earth, soared past the ship. Once Barnevelt sighted his nominal prey, a gvám, plowing whalishly after a school of lesser sea creatures and darting its barb-pointed tentacles to them to spear them and convey them to its maw.

Barnevelt said: "After one of those, the Sunqaruma don't seem at all terrible."

Floating patches of terpahla appeared more frequently, and then at last the jagged line of a fleet of derelicts on the horizon. As they came nearer, the vine grew thicker until they had to zigzag through it. Somewhere in the haze ahead lay the stronghold of the Sunqar pirates. Probably Zei was there, and possibly also Igor Shtain.

Presumably the Moryá Sunqaruma got in and out of their lair by an open channel. Although none of his informants had known where this channel was, it seemed to Barnevelt that he could probably find it by simply coasting along the edge of this floating continent.

Hence, when they reached their first derelict (a primitive seagoing raft with a tattered sail flapping feebly in the faint breeze) they turned the *Shambor* to starboard and inched along to westward. To port the vine grew almost solid, brown slimy stuff supported by clusters of little purple gas-bladders that looked like grapes.

Looking over the side, Barnevelt saw a flash of motion. It was a spotted eel-like creature, about as long as he was, swimming beside the *Shambor*.

"A *fondaq*," said Chask. "Their venomous bite is swift death, and they swarm hereabouts."

Barnevelt followed the creature's graceful motions with fascination.

After half a day of this, Chask called into the cabin: "Ship ahead, sir."

Barnevelt came out. It seemed to be a galley, long and manylegged. The *Shambor*'s crew muttered and pointed in the manner of frightened men. Barnevelt and Zakkomir went back into the cabin to put on their expressman's costumes, for the Krishnan had procured one too. Zakkomir did not want to wear his vest of fine chain mail under his jacket, arguing speed and lightness, especially if they fell in the water. But Barnevelt insisted, adding: "Don't forget our new names. What's mine?"

"Gozzan, sir. And my lord: To you do I confess that terror's grip again lies heavy on my windpipe. Do I falter or flinch, strike me down or ever you let our plan miscarry on account of my despicable timidity."

"You're doing pretty well, son," said Barnevelt, and went out again.

As they neared the galley, Barnevelt saw that this ship lay just outside the mouth of the channel he sought into the interior of the Sunqar. A pair of cables ran from the stern down into a large mass of terpahla, which at first seemed to be part of the Sunqar. As they came closer yet and heard the ratchety sound of a catapult being wound up, it transpired that the mass to which the galley was attached was separate from the rest. Barnevelt wondered if this mass of terpahla might not be kept there as a sort of floating plug for the channel, to be pulled into the mouth of this waterway as a defensive measure in case of attack.

The galley was a deck higher than the little *Shambor* and over twice as long—thirty or forty meters, Barnevelt judged. When a face looked over the rail of the galley and challenged the *Shambor,* he leaned carelessly against the mast and called back:

"A courier of the Mejrou Qurardena, with a consignment and a message from Queen Alvandi of Qirib for Sheafasè, chief of the Sunqaruma."

"Heave to alongside," said the face. Presently a rope ladder tumbled down to the *Shambor*'s deck and the owner of the face, a man in a helmet and a pair of dirty white shorts, with an insigne of rank slung round his neck on a chain, followed. Several other Sunqaruma leaned over the galley's rail, covering the *Shambor*'s deck with cocked crossbows.

"Good afternoon, " said Barnevelt pleasantly. "If you'll step into the cabin, sir, I'll show you our cargo. And perhaps a drop of some of Qirib's worst falat wine will lessen the tedium of your task."

The inspector looked suspiciously at Barnevelt but carried out his inspection, accepted the drink with a grunt of thanks, and sent the *Shambor* on its way with one of his men to act as pilot.

Up the channel they crept, the oarsmen looking nervously

over their shoulders between strokes towards the mass of ships and other floating structures that loomed a couple of hoda ahead. From among these structures several thin plumes of smoke arose, to hang in the stagnant air, veiling the low red sun.

To one side of the channel, a tubby little scow was engaged in a curious task. A chain ran from the scow to the shell of a sea creature, something like an enormous turtle, flipping itself slowly along the edge of the terphala and eating the vine with great chomps of its beak. The men in the scow were guiding the creature with boathooks. Barnevelt aimed his Hayashi camera at the creature, wishing he could stop to get better acquainted with it.

"That," said Zakkomir with a glance over his shoulder to make sure the Moryá Sunqaru at the tiller in the stern was not within hearing, "is how these villains keep the vine from overrunning their channel and trapping 'em. What shall we do if our scheme miscarry? Suppose, for example, the *Shambor* be forced to flee ere our mission be accomplished, leaving us in the strong-thieves' hands?"

Barnevelt thought. "If you can, try to rendezvous near that derelict sailing raft we came to early this morning. You know the one, Chask?"

"Aye, sir. But how'd one trapped in the Sunqar win to this place of meeting? Ye cannot fly without wings."

"Don't know. Perhaps if we could steal a light boat we could pole it through the weed . . ."

And then they came to where the channel opened out into the most astonishing floating city any of them had ever seen: the stronghold of Sheafasè.

The *Shambor* passed another scow, a big one, piled high with harvested terphala. The smell of the drying vine reminded Barnevelt of a cow barn back in Chautauqua County. A man sat on the end of the scow, smoking, and idly watched the *Shambor* go by.

Then came the war galleys of the Moryá Sunqaruma, moored in neat rows according to class. Adjacent to them, and spreading out in all directions through the mass of weeds and derelicts, were the hulks the Sunqaruma had converted into houseboats. Among these were rafts and craft made of timber salvaged from older hulls. This timber, by reason of variation in its age and origin, came in divers hues and gave such vessels a striped look.

Beyond the nearer craft, and barely visible between them, lay a complex of rafts and boats whose nature was indicated by the smoke and stench and sounds that issued from it. It was the factory where terpahla was rendered into the janrú drug.

A web of gangboards and ladders interconnected the whole great mass of ships living and ships dead. On the decks of the houseboats, women moved and children played, the toddlers with ropes around their waists in case they fell overboard. The smell of cooking hung in the still air.

Barnevelt whispered to Zakkomir: "Remember, the go-ahead signal is: *'Time is passing.'* "

Now there were Sunqaro ships on all sides. Barnevelt, looking sharply at them, concluded that the surest way to tell which was still capable of movement was to observe whether the vine had been allowed to grow right up to the sides of the ship or whether a space of clear water, wide enough to let oars ply without fouling, had been maintained around it. He estimated that the Sunqaruma had twenty-odd warships, not counting dinghies, supply ships, and other auxiliaries.

The Sunqaru in the stern guided the *Shambor* towards a group of the three largest galleys to be seen, moored side by side: ships comparable to Majbur's *Junsar* in size. By directing the *Shambor* to starboard, the pilot went around this group to where a small floating pier rested on the water beside the nearest quadrireme.

"Tie up here," said the steersman.

As the crew of the *Shambor* did so, the man who had piloted them jumped to the pier and ran up the gangway leading to the galley's deck to converse with the sentry there. Presently he came down again and told Barnevelt: "You and such of your men as are needed to carry yonder chest shall mount this plank to the ship's deck and there await our pleasure."

Barnevelt jerked his thumb. Four of his sailors took hold of the ends of the carrying poles along each side of the chest and straightened up with a grunt. Barnevelt, followed by the men, stepped onto the pier, Zakkomir bringing up the rear. At the gangway there was some fumbling and muttered argument among the sailors, because the structure was not wide enough for them in their present formation, and they had to crowd between the ends of the poles to make it.

On the deck of the ship they put their burden down and sat upon it. The rowers' four-man benches were empty, and the oars were stacked beneath the catwalk, but there was some sort of activity in the deckhouse forward. Presently a man wearing the insigne of a higher officer came to them and said: "Give me your letter to the High Admiral."

Barnevelt replied: "I'd be glad to, except that my orders are to deliver these things in person to Sheafasè. Otherwise Queen Alvandi won't consider any reply germane, because she wants to know with whom she's dealing."

"Do you presume to give me orders?" asked the officer in an ominous tone.

"Not at all, sir. I merely repeat what she told me. If you don't want to deal on those terms—well, that's for you and her to settle. I'm neutral."

"Hm. I'll see what says High Admiral Sheafasè."

"Tell him also the queen demands that I see the Princess Zei, to satisfy myself of her condition."

"You demand but little, don't you? 'Twill not astonish me if he has you thrown to the fondaqa."

"That's the chance we take in my business," said Barnevelt with ostentatious unconcern, though his heart pounded and his knees wobbled.

The officer went away, over the plank to the next galley. Barnevelt and his five companions waited. The sun, a red ball in the haze, touched the horizon and began to slide below it. Barnevelt, who had been surreptitiously shooting film, regretted its passing from a cinematic point of view (the Hayashi being a poor per-

former at night) even though darkness would much improve their chances of escape.

After the sun had disappeared and Karrim, the nearest and brightest of the three moons, had risen palely in the eastern sky, the officer came back and said: "Follow me."

The sailors shouldered their burden and followed Dirk and Zakkomir across the deck and the gangplank to the next galley. Here the officer led them forward to the big deckhouse between foremast and bow. A sentry opened the cabin door to let them in.

As he passed the sentry, Barnevelt started. The man was Igor Shtain.

Although he had been half-consciously bracing himself for a meeting with Shtain, Barnevelt almost staggered at the sight of his boss. He hesitated, staring stupidly and waiting for some sign of recognition, while the others crowded up behind him.

Had Shtain genuinely joined the pirates, and if so would he denounce Dirk? Was this his method of getting into the Sunqar for professional purposes? Or had Barnevelt made a mistake?

No; there was the same wrinkled skin—its ruddiness apparent even in the twilight—the same staring blue eyes, the same close-clipped mustache the color of slightly rusted steel-wool. Shtain did not even try to pass himself off as a Krishnan by wearing false antennae on his forehead, though he had on Krishnan clothes.

Shtain, saying nothing, returned Barnevelt's gaze with a blank stare of his own.

"*Ao*, Master Gozzan!" said Zakkomir behind him. Dirk awoke and stepped over the raised sill of the cabin door.

Inside, lamps had been lit against the failure of the daylight. In the middle of the cabin was a plotting table, around which stood three figures. One was a tall Krishnan in a garment like a poncho: a big square of fabric with a hole in the middle for his head and a labyrinthine pattern around the edge. Another was another Krishnan, not so tall and in shorts.

The third was a reptilian Osirian, much like the Sishen whom Barnevelt had met in Jazmurian. This one, apparently, had abandoned what to Osirians were the decencies of civilized life, for he wore no body paint upon his scales. Barnevelt knew him at once for Sheafasè.

Barnevelt struggled to swallow, in order to lubricate his dry mouth and throat. He was frightened less of the hell that was due to break loose shortly than with the fear that, in a situation that was becoming so complicated, he might absent-mindedly overlook some obvious factor and hence bring them all to disaster.

The sailors set down the chest upon the floor. He of the poncho said in a strange dialect: "Let the sailors go out and wait upon the deck."

The officer who had led them into the cabin shut and bolted the door, then got out writing materials from a drawer in the plotting table. Barnevelt guessed this man to be some sort of aide or adjutant, while the other three Sunqaruma really ran the outfit.

"Your message." It was the dry rustling voice of the Osirian, barely intelligible.

Barnevelt plucked the queen's letter out of his jacket and handed it to Sheafasè, who in turn handed it to the adjutant, saying: "Read it."

The adjutant cleared his throat and read:

> From Alvandi, by the grace of the Goddess Varzai Queen of Qirib, etcetera, etcetera, to Sheafasè, Chief etcetera. Astonished and chagrined are We that in a time of peace between yourselves and Us, your people should commit the wicked depredation of entering Our city of Ghulindé, robbing and slaying Our citizens, and seizing the sacred person of our daughter, the Royal Princess Zei.
>
> Therefore We demand, on pain of Our dire displeasure, that you forthwith release the princess and either return her to Our territory by your own expedients or permit the trusty bearers of this message so to do. Further, We demand sufficient explanation of this base predacious act and satisfaction for the wrongs inflicted on Our blameless subjects.
>
> Should there however lie between us matters wherein you deem yourself offended, Our door stands ever open for the hearing of legitimate complaints. To prove that not even this felonious deed has yet exhausted the reservoir of Our good-will toward yourself, We do by these trusty couriers send a liberal gift. Their orders are: to you in person to give this message and its accompanying largesse; from you in person cogent answer to receive; and not willingly to depart from you until the princess in the body they have seen, and received assurance as to her condition.

Silence ensued for several seconds. Barnevelt felt that the queen had made herself look rather silly, starting out full of fiery indignation and demands and ending weakly with a tender of tribute and an implied promise to pay more. Yet what could the poor lady do? She was trying to beat a full house with a pair of deuces.

He stepped forward, unlocked the chest, and lifted the top. The Sunqaruma crowded around it, peered in, picked out a few pieces and held them up to the windows or the lamps to examine them more closely and ran their fingers through the coins. Barnevelt hoped they would not remark the disparity between the size of the treasure and the size of the chest. For, while the treasure was considerable both in value and weight, gold is dense, and in a chest the size of a small Earthly trunk it barely covered the bottom.

Finally Sheafasè stepped back, saying: "Attention, gentlemen. Agree we not that our letter, already prepared, covers all points raised by this message?"

The Krishnan in the poncho made the affirmative head motion. The Krishnan in shorts, however, demurred.

"Sirs, 'tis my thought we have not given my proposal due consideration. The princess is the key to the wealth of the Zogha, and we shall rue the day we let this key slip through fingers trembling from over-haste . . ." He spoke the Qiribo dialect.

"Enough, 'Urgan," said the Osirian. " 'Tis also true that many a key has been broken in the lock by turning too forcefully when it did not fit. We can discuss your proposal further while awaiting the old drossel's reply."

While this dialogue had been going on, the adjutant had been taking another letter out of a drawer in a small side table. Now he handed this to Sheafasè, together with writing materials. The pirate chief signed this letter, and the adjutant sealed it up and handed it to Barnevelt.

Sheafase said: "Receive our answer. In case it should be lost under the flail of fate before you can deliver it, tell Alvandi this: That we'll keep her daughter safe from harm on two conditions. One: that the contract relevant to the sale of janrú be amended by a rise in price, for the late increase in costs to compensate. And two: that she render unto us the persons of two vagabonds who now frequent her court, calling themselves Snyol of Pleshch and Tagdë of Vyutr. As for releasing the princess, that's a matter wanting more consideration. The letter furnishes details."

Barnevelt heard Zakkomir at his side start as he digested this demand. Barnevelt thought: How about the famous Osirian pseudohypnosis? Sheafasè might have worked it on Shtain and now want to get hold of George Tangaloa and himself to apply it to them, thus neatly ending their investigation of the Sunqar and, furthermore, making thrifty use of them by turning them into Sunqaro pirates. Or, more likely, Shtain had been subjected to the treatment before he left Earth, to make him docile.

"I think that's all. . . ." said Sheafasè.

Barnevelt spoke up. "We haven't seen the princess, sir."

"So you haven't. Who, think you, is in a positon to make demands?"

"Wait," said the short Krishnan addressed as 'Urgan. " 'Tis not unreasonable, and won't hurt us. If we refuse, the harridan will think we've fed her daughter to the fondaqa, and negotiations will drag on forever while she tries to learn the truth."

He of the poncho said: "Let's decide quickly, for my dinner cools."

After a brief confab among the bosses of the Moryá Sunqaruma, the adjutant opened the door and spoke to the man on guard. Barnevelt heard the latter's footsteps going away.

"May we smoke while waiting?" asked Barnevelt.

Receiving permission, he passed his cigars around. Everybody took one except the Osirian. To help conceal his emotions, Barnevelt lit his stogie on the nearest lamp, drawing long puffs from it. Outside the twilight faded.

Footsteps approached again. The door opened, and in came Shtain, holding Zei firmly by the arm. Barnevelt thought his heart would burst through his chest, mailshirt and all. She still had on the flimsy tunic she had been wearing the night of the kashyo festival, though the coronet and other ornaments had disappeared, no doubt into Sheafasè's treasury.

Barnevelt heard Zei's breath catch as she recognized the "couriers," but like a good trouper she said nothing. Barnevelt and Zakkomir each touched a knee to the floor in the perfunctory manner in which one would expect a busy expressman to pay homage to captive royalty. The adjutant briefly explained the circumstances to her.

While the time for action was fast approaching, thought Barnevelt, the presence of Shtain would complicate matters. Barnevelt couldn't very well turn to Zakkomir, standing tense beside him, and say aloud: "When the time comes, don't kill the Earthman. Just knock him cold because he's really a friend of mine."

He moved, as though from sheer restlessness, to place himself between Shtain and Zakkomir.

Shtain, looking up at his face as he passed, said: "Have I not met you elsewhere, courier?"

As Dirk's heart rose into his mouth, Shtain turned away, muttering: "Some chance resemblance, I suppose . . ."

Barnevelt almost laughed aloud at the sound of his chief's speaking Gozashtandou with a thick Russian accent. Phonetics was not the intrepid Igor's strong point.

"Tell my lady mother," said Zei, "that I'm sound of wind, limb, and maidenhood and have not been ill-treated, albeit the cookery of this swamp-city makes a poor showing in comparison with ours in Ghulindé."

"We hear and obey, O Princess," said Barnevelt. He scratched his person in the groin region and turned to Sheafasè: "Our mission seems to be accomplished, lord, and therefore if you'll let us take aboard some drinking water we'll push off. Time is passing . . ."

Barnevelt had continued to scratch, and now to compound his ungentlemanly behavior he reached inside the lower edge of his shorts, at the same time taking a big drag on his cigar. His hand came out of his pants-leg grasping one of the smoke-bombs, which had been strapped to his thigh. With a quick motion he applied the fuze to his cigar until it fizzed.

Then, with the bomb still in his fist, he swung a terrific uppercut at Shtain's jaw.

The blow connected with a meaty sound, and the explorer slammed back against the wall and slid into a sitting position. Then Barnevelt tossed the bomb to the floor and reached down inside his boot for the little folding sword. Zakkomir had already whipped out his.

Barnevelt straightened his blade with a click of the latch just as the bomb went off with a swoosh, filling the room with smoke, and the remaining Sunqaruma burst into cries of warning and alarm and reached for their own weapons.

Nearest to Barnevelt, now that Shtain had been disposed of, stood the adjutant, drawing his sword. This weapon was only just out of its sheath when Barnevelt's lunge went home, the blade sliding between the ribs and going in until stopped by the hinge. Barnevelt jerked it out just in time to meet the attack of Igor Shtain, who had gotten back on his feet, coughing from the smoke and shaking his head, and now pressed forward. Although not much of a fencer, Shtain swung his cutlass with a force that threatened to break Barnevelt's little toy at every parry. Moreover he had the advantage that Barnevelt was trying not to kill him, while he labored under no such inhibition.

The short Krishnan, the one called 'Urgan, had been quick to reach for his hilt, but Zei seized his right wrist and hung on before he could get his blade free. He had finally thrown her off, but then Zakkomir's point had taken him in the throat. Then Zakkomir was engaged with the man in the poncho, both coughing.

Barnevelt cast a longing glance at the sword of the man he had killed, wishing he could snatch it up in place of the one he was using, but he had no chance to do so. Shtain was driving him into a corner. In desperation he threw himself into a *corps-a-corps* and struck with his free fist at Shtain's jaw, hoping to knock his man out. Shtain's jaw, however, seemed to be made of some granite-like substance. In fighting with Shtain, Barnevelt realized that the slight advantage he had over Krishnans, in consequence of having been brought up on a planet with a gravity about one-tenth greater, was cancelled out.

Sheafasè, who alone of the males in the room was not armed, came around behind Zakkomir and seized his arms. The man with the poncho lunged. Zakkomir, though pinioned, managed to deflect the first thrust. On the *remise* the man in the poncho got home, but Zakkomir's mailshirt stopped the point, the blade bending upward into an arch. Sheafasè tightened his grip. The man in the poncho drew back his arm and aimed for Zakkomir's undefended throat . . .

However, Zei had picked up a light chair that stood in a corner and now brought it down on Poncho's head. The man drooped like a wilted lily. A second blow brought him to hands and knees, and a third flattened him. Zakkomir continued to struggle to get loose from Sheafasè.

Barnevelt, still straining in his *corps-a-corps,* pushed Shtain off balance with his shoulder. As Shtain staggered, Barnevelt got a grip around his body with his left arm and freed his blade. The silver helmet went **glonk** as Shtain struck it with his cutlass. Then Barnevelt brought his right fist, which still held his sword, into action. A series of punches to the ribs, the jaw, the neck, and a final blow to the head with the brass pommel brought down Shtain for good.

Barnevelt whirled and leaped to Zakkomir's assistance. From the other side Zei had already whanged the Osirian in the ribs with the chair. As Barnevelt stepped around the plotting-table, Sheafasè tried to swing Zakkomir's body as a shield. But Barnevelt reached around his companion and thrust his point into the scaly hide. Not far: a centimeter or two. As Sheafasè backed up with a shrill hiss, Barnevelt followed, saying: "Behave yourself, worm, or I'll kill you too."

"You cannot," said Sheafasè. "You are under my influence. You are getting sleepy. You shall drop your sword. I am your master. You shall obey my commands . . ."

Despite the impressiveness with which these statements were delivered, Barnevelt found he had no wish to obey the Osirian's commands. Zakkomir, too, now had his point in Sheafasè's skin, and between them they backed him against the wall. The whole fracas had taken less than a minute.

"It's these helmets," said Barnevelt, remembering what Tangloa had told him about Osirian pseudohypnosis. "We needn't be afraid of this lizard. Zei, open the door a crack and call my sailors."

As the sailors approached, the man in the poncho groaned and moved.

"Kill him, Zei," said Barnevelt, a little surprised at his own ruthlessness. "Not that one—this one."

"How?"

"Pick up his sword, put the point against his neck, and push."

"But . . ."

"Do as I say! D'you want us all killed? That's a good girl." Zei threw the bloody sword away with a shudder. "Now," continued Barnevelt, "tie and gag the one who brought you here, the Earthman. I'll explain why later."

The four seamen stepped over the raised sill of the cabin door and halted as their eyes became accustomed to the dim light of the smoke-filled room and they took in the tableau. They chirped with surprise.

Barnevelt said: "Boys, shut the door and dump all this trash out of the chest. No, don't stop to pick up pieces! And don't let this monster look you in the eye, if you want to live."

As the chest was tilted over, the treasure slid out on the floor with a jingling crash.

Barnevelt continued: "Help the princess to tie that fellow up. Did you hear anything?"

One sailor said: "Aye, sir, we heard a sound as of voices raised, but nought that seemed to call for interference."

Zei said: "Be your purpose to carry me out in that chest?"

"Yes," said Barnevelt. "But—let me think." He hadn't planned on taking both Zei and Shtain, but he could hardly leave either without trying. He told the sailors: "Put the Earthman in the chest. Push him down as far as he'll go. Now, Zei, see if you can fit in on top of him . . ."

"Such vulgar intimacy with a stranger, and so unprepossessing a wight too!" she said, but climbed in nevertheless.

The lid would not go down with both, however.

Zakkomir said: "If you want the Earthman, leave him in the chest, and let the princess walk with us as though she had been ransomed. And let's escort the monster with our blades at ready, making a sweep of all three."

"Good," said Barnevelt. "Admiral, you're coming with us. You shall walk to our ship with my friend and I on either side, and at the first false move we let you have it."

"Where will you let me go?"

"Who said anything about letting you go? You shall have a voyage on my private yacht. Ready?"

The sailors picked up the chest containing Shtain. Barnevelt and Zakkomir each took Sheafasè by one arm, holding their smallswords hidden behind their forearms, the points pricking the Osirian's skin. Behind them came Zei and the sailors.

The party walked aft to the gangplank that led to the next galley. They proceeded across this plank, then across the deck of the adjacent galley to the gangplank that led down to the floating pier at which the *Shambor* was tied up.

As they neared the latter companionway, however, heads appeared over the edge of the smaller galley, followed by the bodies of men coming up from the pier. At first Barnevelt thought they must be a party from his own ship. However the light was still strong enough to show that they were not his men at all. A glance over the side of the quadrireme disclosed the mast of another small ship tied up to the pier next to the *Shambor*.

Barnevelt whispered: "Careful!" and pressed the point of his sword a little further into Sheafase's hide. He drew the Osirian to one side to let the other party pass.

The first member of the other party, going by at a distance of about two meters on the deck of the galley, started to make some sort of saluting gesture towards Sheafasè—and then stopped and yelled "You!" in a rasping voice, looking straight at Barnevelt.

It was, Barnevelt saw, his old acquaintance Vizqash bad-Murani, the ex-salesman, against whose occiput he had shattered the mug in Jazmurian.

With a presence of mind that Barnevelt in calmer circumstances might have admired, Vizqash whipped out his sword and rushed. Barnevelt instinctively parried, but in doing so he loosened his grip on Sheafasè, who instantly tore himself free. Zakkomir thrust at the reptile as he did so, inflicting a flesh-wound in the Osirian's side.

The other men of Vizqash's party ran in to help. The first to arrive struck at one of the sailors from the *Shambor*. His blade bit into the man's neck, half severing it, and the sailor fell dead. The other three dropped the chest, which landed on its side with a crash. The lid flew open and Shtain rolled out on deck.

Barnevelt parried a thrust from Vizqash, then got his point into his antagonist's thigh on the riposte.

"Run!" yelled Zakkomir.

As the wounded Vizqash fell, Barnevelt snatched a quick look around. Zakkomir was starting to drag Zei off. Sheafasè was dancing out of reach and whistling orders to the Sunqaruma, who were rushing upon the invaders. The three surviving sailors were running away; one dove over the rail. Hostile blades flickered in the twilight.

Barnevelt ran after Zakkomir and Zei, who bounded on to the gangplank leading to the big galley on which they had conferred with the pirate leaders. The three raced across the plank, then across the deck, and then across the plank to the third big galley. Feet pounded behind them.

"Hold a minute!" yelled Barnevelt as they gained the deck of the third galley. "Help me . . ."

He cut the ropes that belayed the end of the gangplank to the deck of the third ship. Then he and Zakkomir got their fingers under the end of the plank. A couple of Sunqaruma had already started across it from the other end, adding to the weight. With a mighty heave the two fugitives raised their end of the plank and shoved it free of the side of the ship. Down it went with a whoosh and a splash, and down went those who had started across it, with yells of dismay, into the weedy waters below.

A crossbow bolt whizzed past. Barnevelt and his companions ran to the other side of the ship they were on. Here a ladder led down the side of the ship to a scow, and from both ends of the scow a series of rafts led off into tangles of houseboats and miscellaneous craft.

"Which way?" asked Barnevelt as they gained the deck of the scow and paused, panting.

Zakkomir pointed. "That's north, the direction of that raft. You and Zei go to the next raft and crouch down out of sight, and when they come along I'll lead them in the opposite direction. Then can you and she try for our rendezvous."

"How about you?" asked Barnevelt uncomfortably. Not that he was keen to send Zakkomir off with Zei while he himself played the part of red herring, but it seemed hardly decent to let the young man sacrifice himself.

"Me? Fear not for me. I can lose them in the darkness, and under your inspiring leadership have I attained the courage of a very Qarar. Besides, my first duty's to the dynasty. Go quickly, for I hear them coming."

He pushed them, half unwilling, to the end of the scow. Unable to think of a better scheme, Barnevelt dropped down to the raft with Zei and hid under the overhang of the scow's bow.

Then sounds of pursuit increased, indicating that the Sunqaruma had brought up another plank to replace the one thrown down. Zakkomir's footfalls receded, and cries of: "There he goes!" "After him, knaves!" told the rest of the story.

When the noise died down, Barnevelt risked a peek over the end of the scow. People seemed to be moving in the distance, but the light was too far gone to tell much. He grasped Zei's hand and started off in the direction opposite to that which Zakkomir had taken.

After they had crossed from raft to raft and from scow to scow, they found that their path led up to the deck of one of the houseboats.

Zei said: "Should we not throw down more of these gangplanks?"

"No. It'd only stop 'em a minute, and would show where we've gone."

"There seem to be but few abroad this night."

"Dinner time," said Barnevelt.

They wound their way from houseboat to houseboat. An adolescent Krishnan brushed by them, giving them hardly a glance, and vanished through the nearest door, whence came the sound of scolding.

They continued on, over decks and across gangplanks and up and down ladders, until they came to a big roofed-over hulk without signs of life aboard. It had once been a merchantman from the Va'andao Sea, but now looked more like the conventional pictures of Noah's Ark.

They made the circuit of the deck, finding no more ways leading from this ship to any other. It lay in fact at the extreme north end of the Sunqaro settlement, and beyond it the only craft were scattered derelicts not connected with the "city." Barnevelt looked northward and in the fading light thought he could just see the tattered sail of the rendezvous raft on the horizon. Almost in line with it, the nose of a big derelict that was slowly sinking by the stern thrust up through the vine, a darker pyramid against the dark northern sky.

"This seems to be the bottom of the bag," he said. "What sort of ship is this, anyhow?"

The barnlike superstructure that had been built up on deck had no windows, but three doors: a small one on each side and a large one at one end. All three were closed with padlocks.

Barnevelt settled down to work on the door on the northeast side, where he would be out of sight of the settlement. The lock was a stout one, and he had nothing to pick it with even if he had known how to pick locks. The iron straps to which the lock was attached were nailed to the door and the door frame and so could not be unscrewed with his knife blade. With a stout enough instrument he could have pried them loose, but any attempt to do so with knife or sword would, he was sure, merely break a good blade.

As he ran his fingers over the door, however, he became aware of a roughness in the strap that ran from the door frame to the lock. By looking closely and gouging with his thumbnails he made out that the strap was badly rusted—so much so that he could pry flakes of rust off with his bare hands.

The simplest way, then, might be the most effective. He heaved on the strap until it bent outward enough to let him slide the fingers of both hands between it and the door. Then, with a firm grip upon it, he put one foot against the door and heaved. His muscles stood out with the strain.

With a faint crunch the weakened strap gave way. Barnevelt staggered back and would have fallen over the side had not Zei, with a squeak of alarm, caught his arm.

A minute later they were inside. It was pitch-dark save for the triple moonbeams that came through the open door, which was not enough light to tell them what they had gotten into. Barnevelt tripped over something solid and swore under his breath. He should have thought to bring a candle or the equivalent; but one couldn't think of everything . . .

That gave him an idea. He felt along the wall, sometimes bumping into things, and before long came to a bracket holding a small oil-lamp. After much fumbling with his pocket lighter he got the lamp lit, then quickly closed the door lest the light betray them.

This hulk was used for stores, piled in orderly fashion on the deck: barrels of pitch, nails, and other things; lumber, ropes of various sizes flemished down in neat cylindrical piles, spars, canvas, and oars. A big hatch lay open in the middle of the deck, and by stooping Barnevelt could see that the deck below was also lined with barrels, piles of firewood, bags, and so on.

"Interesting," he said, "but I don't see how it'll help us."

"At least," said Zei, "we have a place to hide."

"I'm not so sure. If Zakkomir gets away, they'll comb the whole settlement. Even if he doesn't, they'll know there were two more of us. Matter of fact, some people saw us on our way here. I told Chask to meet us on the edge of the Sunqar. . . ."

"Who's Chask?"

"My boatswain. I hope he got away when the ructions started. But even if he does show up at the rendezvous tomorrow, you couldn't expect him to stick around long once the sun was up."

"You know not if he escaped?"

"No. If there were a small boat we could steal, now. . . ."

"I saw none as we came, and 'tis said that to thrust such a craft through the vine were a thing impossible."

Barnevelt grunted. "Maybe so, but you'd be surprised what impossible things people do when they have to. I'll look."

He slipped out the door and made another circuit of the deck, peering off into the moonlight for a sign of a dinghy. None did he see; nothing but houseboats, the weed growing up to their sides. While he was about it, he took a good look at the ship's superstructure to make sure no light showed through from inside. Light *did* show faintly along the bottom crack of the southwest door.

Back inside, he uncoiled some rope and laid it along the sill of the southwest door, meanwhile telling Zei of his failure.

She said: "Could you not build a raft from these many stuffs and staples?"

"In six ten-nights, with a set of tools, maybe. Say, what were the pirates talking about when that one from Qirib—forget his name—spoke of using you as the key to the wealth of the Zogha?"

"That must have been ere I came in."

"So it was. This fellow seemed to have an alternative proposition he wanted to argue, but Sheafasè shut him up, I suppose so as not to spill their plans in front of me."

"That would be the Qiribo arch-pirate, who is (or rather was) one 'Urgan, not long since a respected commercial of Ghulindé. Taking ill the way his goodwife spent his money, as under our statutes she had a right to do, he fled to the Sunqar. The true inwardness of his plan I know not, save that from hints they dropped before me I think 'twas to have Sheafasè place me under his malefic mental suasion, declaring me true ruler of Qirib, seizing the kingdom, and dandling me before the people as a puppet their true rapacious plans to hide. Had not you and Zakkomir intervened, they might indeed have executed such chicane, for many Sunsaruma are from Qirib and so could give their enterprise the feeble surface tint of lawfulness. But how came you and Zakkomir hither?"

Barnevelt brought her up to date on events in Ghulindé, omitting to mention that to persuade him to come the queen had had to threaten his partner with hot pincers. He felt that that detail might take the fine romantic edge off her admiration.

He concluded: ". . . and so we got in by pretending to be Mejrou Quarardena couriers. My name is now Sn— Gozzan." Damn, he knew he'd get his aliases mixed up.

"And who's the Earthman whom you sought to fetch forth in the chest? Methought he was but a common pirate, unworthy of such pains."

"Long story. Tell you some day, if we live through this."

"Live or die, 'twill be a famous feat," she said. "Our tame bard shall make an epic of it, in heroic heptameters. A versatile wight you must be, Lord Snyol. From the mountains of Nyamadzë you come to the seas, and from the polar snows to this steaming tropic. From skids you take to ships . . ."

"*Ohé!* You've given me an idea."

Barnevelt jumped up and began examining the piles of lumber. After a while he settled on a width and thickness of board as suitable and dragged out several lengths of that size.

"Should be about two meters long," he mused. "They'd better be right the first time, too."

He looked around for a work-bench with tools, but such work was evidently done elsewhere in the settlement. Finally he fell to whittling with his knife.

"What do you?" said Zei. "Make skids wherewith to travel over the terpahla-vine? In sooth, a levin-flash of genius. If, that is, we fall not through a gap in the vine to provide a banquet for the monsters of the sea."

"Let's see your foot. Damn these flimsy sandal effects. . . ."

The hours slipped by as Barnevelt worked. When he again opened the northeast door, the light of the three clustered moons no longer shone in through the portal, for they had ridden across the meridian to the western half of the starlit sky.

Barnevelt planned his next steps with care. First he made the circuit of the deck once more, looking and listening for sights and sounds of pursuit. Finding none, he peered to northward across the moonlit waste of weed. It would be the easiest thing in Krishna to get lost while splashing around on the vines at night without map or compass. He could no longer see the pale speck on the horizon that he had thought to be the sail of the rendezvous raft, but the nose of the up-ended derelict still stood out plainly.

Then he knocked at the door, saying: "Put out the lamp and come."

Zei obeyed him. Together they lugged out the four skis, the two oars he had chosen for balancing poles, and an armful of rope. He belayed one end of a length of heavy rope to a cleat on the deck and let the rest of it hang down into the water.

Then he discarded his vest of chain mail, which would make swimming impossible, and with the lighter rope set about making ski lashings. He had already cut notches in the sides of the skis for the rope, since it would have to pass under the skis. His own skis gave no great trouble. Though he had never made a ski lashing before, he was sophisticated in the ways of ropes from his boating experience on Earth, and his expressman's boots afforded his feet the necessary protection.

Zei's feet, however, were something else. Although he had cut a couple of pieces of sailcloth which he wrapped around her feet to protect them from the rope, he still feared she would be chafed. However, there was no help for it. . . .

"The Sunqaruma are coming!" she said in a loud whisper.

He listened. Over the subdued ground noise of nocturnal Sunqaro activity came a more definite sound of many feet, a clink of steel, and a murmur of voices.

He frantically finished Zei's bindings and hurried to the hulk's side, his boards going clickety-clack on the deck.

"I shall have to go first," he said, and lowered himself over the edge, holding the heavy rope.

He let himself down to the weed and heard the skis strike water. Then he felt the coolth of the sea around his ankles. For an instant he thought the weed would not bear his weight; that if he let go the rope he would go right on in up to his chin.

The noise of the approaching men grew rapidly louder. Barnevelt could now make out different voices, though not the words.

"Make haste!" came the voice of Zei from above.

Barnevelt, choking down an impulse to bark at her: what did

she think he was doing? lowered himself further. The tension in the rope decreased, and he found himself standing on the weed with the water not yet halfway up his calves. He took a gingerly step, and then another, still holding the rope, and found that the vine afforded more substantial support away from the ship's side. He also learned that if one kept moving, one kept comparatively dry, whereas to stand in one place meant to sink gradually to one's knees in water as one's weight pushed the terpahla under.

"Hand me down my oar!" he said softly. When Zei had done so, he tried it and found it not a bad ski pole.

He judged from the sound that the approaching searchers were now coming across the gangplank on the other side of the hulk. That fact left them only seconds' leeway.

"All right," he murmured, "hand me down yours and the rest of the light rope. . . . Now climb down."

"Will you not stand under to catch me?"

"Can't. It would put too much weight in one place."

She began to lower herself down as best she could, her skis rapping against the hulk's side. On the far side of the hulk feet sounded on the deck, and Barnevelt caught snatches of speech:

". . . the gods know we've searched everywhere else . . ." ". . . if they be not here, they must have flown . . ." ". . . go around the deck in the other direction, you, lest they . . ."

Zei reached water level, took a staggering step on the vine, fouled the whittled nose of her right ski in the terpahla, and almost took a header.

"Watch out!" hissed Barnevelt frantically. "The terpahla's more solid over here. Here's your oar. Now come quickly."

They started hiking off to northward, their skis swishing over the weedy water. Barnevelt snatched a look back at the hulk. Although the hither side of it was now in shadow, there was a hint of movement around the deck and the sound of a door being opened. Someone called: "They broke in here! Fetch lights!"

Perhaps, thought Barnevelt, the Moryá would be too occupied with searching the hulk to notice that their quarry was escaping in plain sight; not expecting to see people walking on the water, they would not even glance out across the weed.

No such luck. A voice said: "What does this rope here? *Ohé*, there they go!" "Where?" "Yonder, across the terpahla!" " 'Tis a thing impossible!" "Yet there they . . ." "Witchcraft!" "Bows! Bows! Who bears a bow!" "No one, sir, for you did command . . ." "Never mind what I commanded, fool, but run to fetch . . ." "Can you not throw . . ."

"Keep on," said Barnevelt, lengthening his stride. Behind him the voices merged into a buzzing babel.

"Watch out for that hole," he told Zei.

The distance increased with agonizing slowness. Behind them came the snap as of a twanged rubber band, followed by a short, sharp whistle passing close.

"They shoot at us," said Zei, in a voice near tears.

"That's all right. They can't hit us at long range in this light." Barnevelt did not feel as confident as he sounded. He felt even less so when the next **whsht** came by so close that he could swear he felt the wind of it. What would they do if one were hit?

Whsht! Whsht! That mail-shirt would have felt good despite its weight.

Little by little the distance lengthened, and the invisible missiles ceased to whizz about their ears.

"We're safe now," he said. "Stand still and catch the end of this rope. Tie it around your waist. That's so if one of us falls into a hole, the other can pull him out. Thank the great god Bákh you're not one of these tiny girls! Off we go again, and remember to keep moving."

They plodded towards the bow of the up-ended derelict.

Zei remarked: "An uncommon sight it is to see all the moons full and in conjunction simultaneously. Old Qvansel avers that this event portends some great upheaval in the realm's mundane affairs, though my mother will not have it so, holding that Varzai governs all and that the old man's talk of astrological whys and wherefores be nought but impious superstition."

" '. . . and rhymes, and dismal lyrics, prophesying change beyond all reason.' Why does she keep him on the payroll if she doesn't believe his line?"

"Oh, he's a legacy from my grandmother's reign, and my mother, however harsh she may appear to those who do not know her intimately, cannot bring herself to cast adrift a longtime faithful servant. Besides which, be his star lore true or false, he's still a man of mighty erudit . . . *glub!*"

A sudden tug on the safety rope staggered Barnevelt. Zei had fallen into a hole. Talking women! Barnevelt thought savagely as her head appeared above the water with a strand of terpahla draped over one eye.

"Pull yourself out, Mistress Zei!" he snapped, moving his skis to keep a constant tension on the line. "On hands and knees, like that."

She seemed to be hopelessly tangled in her skis, but finally got squared away.

"Now, bring your feet around under you one at a time," he said. "That's it. Now grab your oar and stand up. Next time, keep your mind on where you put your feet!"

"Master Snyol!" came an offended voice. "Though you have rescued me from peril dire, no license does that grant you to address me as if I were some kitchen drab!"

"I'll address you worse than that if you don't obey orders! Come on."

She sank into silence. Barnevelt felt a little contrite over his outburst, but not to the point of apologizing. After all, he told himself, with these Qiribo dames you had to get the bulge on them at the start or, accustomed as they were to commanding, they'd walk all over you.

At that, it was probably the first time in Zei's life that any mere male had addressed her so roughly. It must have been quite a shock, he thought with a trace of malicious relish. He wondered why he felt that way, and presently realized that neither had he ever so spoken to a woman before. His pleasure must come from a subconscious satisfaction at asserting his masculinity against the female sex. He cautioned himself not to take his burgeoning aggressiveness out on poor Zei, who was not responsible for his upbringing.

He cast a look at her as she splashed beside him. With her gauzy tunic soaked and the light of the three moons upon her, she might almost as well have had no clothes on. Metaphors of goddesses rising from the sea crossed his mind . . .

Off to eastward, perhaps a hundred meters away, the surface suddenly heaved. Something dark and shiny—a head or flipper?—showed in the moonlight and then vanished with a loud splash.

"I think," he said, "we'd better both be careful about falling into holes . . . Wonder how Zakkomir's making out? I like the young fellow and can't understand why he seems so anxious to get himself killed."

"You came, did you not?"

Barnevelt paused before answering. "Ye—es, but then . . . Is there an—uh—understanding between you and him?" (He had already asked Zakkomir a similar question, but confirmation would be desirable.)

"Not at all," she replied. "As a loyal subject and familiar of the royal family he's naturally happy to risk his life for the crown."

Well, thought Barnevelt, such feelings no doubt existed among people brought up in a monarchy, even though he, as a native of a planet where the democratic republic had become the standard governmental form, found it hard to imagine.

They continued their plod and presently came to the bow of the up-ended derelict. Holding the rail, they pulled themselves up the steep deck to a hatch to rest.

Barnevelt looked north but was still not sure he could see the sail of the rendezvous raft. However, he had a good idea of its direction, and thought he could find it by frequent back-sighting. The settlement of the Moryá Sunqaruma was now a dark irregular outline on the southerly horizon. Barnevelt picked out the storeship, which he could still discern, as a mark to sight on.

"How are your feet?" he asked.

"Though this be no ballroom floor, yet they will abide."

"Okay, let's go."

They took off across the vine again. The clustered moons now hung low, and Barnevelt thought he saw a faint light in the East, reaching up from the horizon in a great wedge. After a while it faded; this must be the poets' "phantom of false morning." He continued to back-sight on the half-sunk hulk and the store ship.

The moons sank lower, and the pallor of the eastern sky this time looked like the real thing. The smaller stars of the unfamiliar constellations went out, and the sail of the rendezvous raft came into plain sight.

As they neared their goal, Barnevelt lengthened his stride in his eagerness to get aboard and take off his footgear. He drew ahead of Zei who, finding herself towed behind him, called: "Not *quite* so fast, pray!"

Barnevelt turned his head to answer, and at that instant his skis pitched forward. The water came up and closed over his head with a gurgle.

Before he came to the surface, something struck him a sharp blow in the back, and then he was tangled with human limbs. He knew what had happend: Being behind him, instead of to one side of him, Zei had not been able to resist the pull of the rope as he went into the hole but had been towed right in after him.

He finally got his head clear, broke a length of terpahla that had wrapped itself around his neck, and began to climb out. It was harder than he expected, for the skis got fouled in the vine and made normal movements impossible. When he finally got his feet under him and recovered his oar, he sidled away from the hole and helped Zei out by pulling on the rope.

When she had coughed up half the Banjao Sea and recovered her breath, she said: "I trust, my lord, you'll not deem it impertinent if I advocate that you, too, watch where you place your feet?"

He grinned shamefacedly. "Turn about's fair play, as we say in Nyamadzë. We're nearly there, thank the gods."

As the light waxed, he saw why he had fallen in. They were nearing the edge of the solid part of the Sunqar, and there were many gaps in the vine. Ahead, beyond the raft, the vine was not solid at all, but drifting in yellow-brown patches of all sizes.

At last they clattered on to the raft and sank down on its

moldering timbers with a simultaneous sigh of exhaustion. Barnevelt untied his ski lashings and turned his attention to those of his companion. She winced at his touch, and when he got the rope and the canvas wrappings off he saw that her feet had been chafed raw in several places.

"Great Qondyor!" he said. "These must have hurt! Why didn't you tell me?"

"To what end? You could not have borne me across this insubstantial floor of floating weed, and my plaint would only have distracted you from your proper task."

"You've got guts," he said, pulling off his boots and socks and wringing out the latter.

"I thank you." Then she laughed. "Look at your legs!"

In the increasing light he saw his legs were streaked with blue where the dye of the expressman's uniform had run.

A pre-dawn breeze sprang up, making Barnevelt shiver.

"Brrr!" said Zei. "And I had but just got dry from the previous ducking! Here, doff that wet apparel and suffer me to wring it out. Otherwise 'twill not dry for hours in this dank."

Suiting the action to the word she slid out of her own flimsy garb and wrung it over the side. Dirk's Chautauqua County past rose up and covered him with a blush as rosy as the dawn, while Zei, with no more self-consciousness than a one-year-old, hung her clothes on the raft's remaining mast stay and said: "What holds my lord from action? Are you maimed in your members?"

Barnevelt mutely obeyed.

As he took off his jacket, Sheafase's letter fell out. He crumpled it and threw it away. It would serve no useful purpose now and might cause trouble if it incited Queen Alvandi's curiosity as to why the Moryá Sunqaruma were so interested in her friends from Nyamadzë.

He said: "One good dose of sunburn on those sore feet would cripple you for fair. Maybe I could cut down this old sail to cover us—but no, I'd better leave it up for the time being so Chask can find us."

"And if your ship comes not?"

"I've been wondering. Maybe I could sneak back to the settlement at night to steal food and stores for re-rigging this raft or building a new one. Doesn't sound practical, though."

"Oh, so versatile a hero as yourself will overcome all obstacles. Meanwhile, how about sustenance? For I do hunger with a monstrous appetite."

"Now where would I find anything to eat out here?"

"But one of your proven resource and aptitude can surely devise some ingenious expedient . . ."

"Thanks for the compliments, darling, but even I have limitations. And don't look at me with that famished expression. It reminds me of that beastly custom of your nation."

"Nay, twit me no longer on that subject! The custom was not of my instigation. And fear not that towards you I entertain plans anthropophagous, for like a shomal bred for racing you'd prove all bone and gristle."

He yawned. "We'd better catch some sleep while waiting. You cork off first while I watch."

"But need you not the first repose? Yours has been the heavier . . ."

"Go to sleep!" roared Barnevelt, feeling very dominant.

"Aye, noble master." She gave him a worshipful look.

He sat down with his back against the mast, his eyes sweeping the horizon. Now and then he pinched or slapped himself to wake himself up. Memories of all the cartoons he had seen, showing a pair of castaways on a raft, paraded through his mind. As the sea water dried upon his hide, it left little itchy flakes of salt. When he scratched his scalp, he became aware that his coarse bronze fuzz was sprouting. He'd better find means of shaving it, or his non-Krishnan origin would soon become obvious.

"O Snyol!" said Zei in piteous tones, "I am too cold to sleep."

"Come on over and let me warm you," he said. Instantly he regretted it. With a swift octopoid motion, Zei slithered sidewise into the crook of his right arm. She was shivering.

"That's better," she said, smiling up at him.

Oh, is it? thought Barnevelt, in whose soul two natures—the cautious, calculating man of affairs and the healthy young animal—were locked in mortal combat. Blood pounded in his temples.

For an instant, the man of affairs ruled. "Excuse me," muttered Barnevelt, disengaging himself and abruptly turning his back on Zei to feel his clothes where they drooped from the stay. They were still damp, as might be expected so close to the surface of the sea. Nevertheless, he donned these dank garments, saying over his shoulder: "They'll never dry on the line at this rate. But if we put them on, our body heat'll dry them in time. Better put your tunic on, too."

"Ugh!" she said, fingering her torn chemise. "But if you say so, my lord." She slipped the gauzy garment over her head. "Now warm me again, sirrah, for my teeth begin to clatter like the castanets of a dancer of Balhib."

Once more they settled down at the base of the mast. The moons neared the horizon; the sun should soon be up. Zei gave a contented sigh and smiled up at Barnevelt. Before he knew what he was doing, he bent down and kissed her.

She neither pulled away nor responded. Instead, her face bore an expression of surprise and perplexity. She asked: "Is this, then, that Earthly custom called 'kissing,' whereof I have heard rumors?"

"Why, yes. Hasn't it spread to Qirib yet?"

" 'Tis practiced amongst the wilder spirits of the land, I'm told—albeit none of our courtly circle has yet monstrated it to me. Is it true that, amongst the Terrans, 'tis a kind of salute, signifying love and esteem?"

"So they tell me."

"Excellent. It is right and proper, forsooth, that all loyal subjects should love the members of the royal house. So, dear Snyol, have the goodness once more to prove your loyalty to the throne!"

The thought flickered through Barnevelt's mind that "love" had many meanings. He complied. Zei, he found, improved quickly with practice.

Again his blood pounded. Healthy-animal Barnevelt, thrown for the nonce, now rose up and grappled Man-of-affairs Barnevelt. The latter protested: In the name of all gods, Dirk, use some sense! If you go on like this and she doesn't resist—which she sure hasn't so far—it could cost you your head! Wait till you've gotten your affairs and those of your company straightened out. . . .

Healthy-animal Barnevelt advanced no arguments; he had no need to. By sheer brute strength, he forced Man-of-affairs Barnevelt to the mat. Barnevelt discovered that the partial covering of Zei's hidden glories, far from abating his desires, only stimulated them.

He shifted his position, for his right arm was going to sleep from the pressure of Zei's body. Then a fleck of brightness in the distance brought him up with a start.

"What is it, dearest friend?" said Zei.

Barnevelt reluctantly disengaged himself and pointed towards the little whitish triangle, standing up against the lightening sky on the western horizon. "If I'm not mistaken, that's the sail of the *Shambor*."

He gave her a long, lingering glance. However, Man-of-affairs Barnevelt was now firmly back at the helm. Grimly, Barnevelt began doing calisthenics. The rotten planking of the ancient raft creaked under his push-ups and knee-bends.

"What do you?" asked Zei. "Is that a matutine gesture of obeisance to the grim gods of far Nyamadzë?"

"You might put it that way. Nothing like a little exercise to—ah—get the blood circulating. Better try it."

At length he stopped, panting. "It struck me that this may not be our ship after all. So we'd better lie down behind the mast, so as not to show against the sky, just in case."

"What if it be our foes?"

"Then we'll slip into the water and take a chance on the fondaqa."

The sail grew swiftly larger as the dawn breeze drove it closer. When it drew near enough for the ship's hull to be discerned from where they lay, Barnevelt saw that it was indeed the *Shambor*. He waited, however, until he recognized Chask at the tiller before leaping up to whoop and wave.

Minutes later, the little ship nosed into the weed until her stem bumped the raft. Barnevelt boosted Zei over the rail and climbed aboard himself.

He grumpily told himself that he had had a lucky escape from forming an intimate connection with the princess, with the gods knew what dire results. But, at the same time, the less practical side of his nature—Romantic-dreamer Barnevelt—whispered: Ah, but you do love her, and not as subject and royalty, either! And some day, perhaps, you and she will be united somehow, somewhere. Some day. Some day . . .

As Barnevelt and Zei came over the rail, Chask called another man to the tiller, came forward, and cried: " 'Tis the Lady Zei herself! The sea gods have surely prospered out enterprise!"

He knelt to the princess while grasping Barnevelt's thumb, looking like some gnarled old sea god himself.

Barnevelt gave the rest of the crew a wave and a grin. "Greetings, men!"

The sailors, resting on their oars or standing by the lines, looked back in silence. One or two smiled feebly, but the rest seemed to glower. With a chill of self-doubt, Barnevelt reflected that he had never been able to get back on good terms with them since he turned down their demand for giving up the expedition.

Chask said: "Is it your pleasure that we make for Palindos Strait with all possible dispatch, Captain?"

"Absolutely!"

"Aye-aye, sir. Back oars!" When they were out of the weed: "Forward on the starboard bank . . . Now all together . . . Haul the sheet. Up the tiller . . . Now row for your worthless lives, ere the Sunqaro galleys find you. Avé, set course northeast, sailing full and by." He turned back to Barnevelt. "What befell you, sir, and where's the young fantastico who accompanied you?"

"Step into the cabin with us," said Barnevelt.

While Barnevelt salved and bandaged Zei's feet with supplies from the first-aid cabinet, Chask rustled them a snack and told his tale.

"We lay at the pier, ye see, until the other shallop ties up beside us, and a battalia of pirates disembarks to mount the gangplank to the big galley. Next we know, one of our seamen leaps from the galley's deck into the briny and clambers over our gunwale, crying that all is lost and we must needs flee. Whilst we hesitate, unwilling to push off whilst hope remains, down come the men of the Sunqar with weapons bared, crying to take us.

"At that we went, pausing but to cut the rigging of the other shallop, pursuit to incommode. Then forth we row, leaving tumult in our wake, to give the chasers slip under cloak of night. In sooth we hid behind a hulk that lay upon the terpahla's edge and heard the galleys go by close, searching for us. With dawn we issued from our hidey-hole and, seeing no Sunqaro ships, sought this rendezvous in recollection of our skipper's parting orders."

"Good," said Barnevelt. "But why did you keep your sail up after the sky had become light? That's asking for the Sunqaruma to come out and pick you up."

"The lads would have it, sir, misliking to do all the work of moving the ship themselves. 'Twas all I could do to bully and persuade them to turn aside from their flight to pick you up." Chask gave Barnevelt an accusing stare, which said as plainly as words: *You're the one who ruined the discipline on this ship, so don't blame me.* "And now, Captain, will ye not tell me what befell you?"

Barnevelt told as much of his story as he thought wise. "While we were arguing terms in the cabin, I threw a smoke bomb. In the confusion, Zakkomir and I killed a couple of the pirates. We cornered the Osirian chief and made him escort us out, with our swords in his ribs and the princess walking with us. But, as luck would have it, we ran into a man whom I had met before, far from the Sunqar, and who is now one of the pirates. Recognizing me and knowing me for no expressman, he gave the alarm. So we had to run for it. Zakkomir led the pursuers one way to give Zei and me time to escape in another direction, and we got away by walking across the vine with boards tied to our feet."

"The young popinjay has more mettle than I should have thought. What betid him at the end?"

"I don't know. Now tell me, why are the men so glum? You'd think they'd be glad to see us."

"As to that, two reasons: One, if ye'll pardon my outspeaking, they like this voyage not, for that it has already cost the lives of four—five, if ye count young Zakkomir. Ye know, sir, there's many a man who's brave as a yeki in his home port, in planning voyages of hazard, but who develops second thoughts when peril stares him in the face—like Kugh the Bold in the chantey. And though I count our greatest danger past, yet do they fear the Sunqar's heavy hand upon their shoulders ere they win to safety.

"And two: We have that young Zanzir, who mortally hates you because ye shamed him before his comrades after he'd boasted of his intimacy with you. Moreover, he's lived in Kätai-Jhogorai, where they have no kings or nobles, and there imbibed pernicious thoughts of the equality of all men. So he'll have it that the life of my lady Zei—no disrespect to you intended, mistress—that her life weighs no more in the scales of the gods of the afterworld than that of a common seaman, and that to trade it for four or five of theirs were no exchange but murder and oppression. And thus the crew he's disaffected . . ."

"What!" exclaimed Zei, her mouth full of food.

"Think no ill of me, my lady . . ."

She swallowed and said: "No fault do I impute to you, good Chask, I'm but astonished by the thoughts expressed. 'Tis either the inspiration of a genius or the droolings of a madman."

"Natheless, so they hold to be the law in Kätai-Jhogorai . . ."

"Why haven't you done something about this guy?" said Barnevelt, interrupting what promised to develop into a seminar on government. "Anybody knows you can't have democracy on a ship at sea."

Privately, Barnevelt admitted that he was not being honest. He had started out on the assumption that you *could* have it, and he still thought there was something to be said for Zanzir's point of view. But no good would come of admitting that now. Nothing would revive the dead; and besides the men, fairly warned, were here of their own free will.

Chask said: "I take the liberty, sir, of bringing to your mind your own express orders at the start of this expedition: No 'brutality,' ye said. So now the time for a swift thrust in the dark, that might this sore have cauterized, is past, specially as Zanzir's careful to keep within arm's reach of his more fanatic partisans . . ."

"Sirs!" cried a sailor, sticking his head in the cabin door. "A galley's on our trail!"

They hurried out. The morning sun showed a sail on the horizon, between them and the diminishing Sunqar. Barnevelt scurried up the mast. From the height of the parral, he could see the hull below the sail, end-on, and the bank of oars rising and falling on each side. From his point of vantage he also made out a second and more distant sail.

He climbed down and looked around the deck. Young Zanzir, at the moment bow oarsman on the port bank, returned his stare as if defying him to start something.

Barnevelt called the boatswain and Zei into the cabin, unlocked the arms locker, and got out swords for Chask and himself and a long dagger for Zei.

"Now you see what I meant about the sail. It occurs to me that our young idealist might jump us when the Sunqaro ships got close and turn us over to them in exchange for his own freedom."

"That could be," said Chask, "though honest mariners mortally fear the Sunqaruma, holding them not men but automata animated by the fiendish magic of the monster who rules the swamp."

"Well, if anybody makes a false move, kill him and throw him over the side," said Barnevelt. "After this, use *your* judgment in matters of discipline."

Chask gave Barnevelt a ghost of a smile, though he refrained from crowing openly.

"Now," said Barnevelt, "I'll make a plot, if you'll help." He turned to Zei. "You'd better put on some more seagoing clothes. That gauze thing is falling apart."

He unlocked the slop chest and got out the Krishnan equivalent of dungarees. Then he spread his charts on the table and went to work. A swell from the North tossed the *Shambor* about enough to make position-reckoning a bothersome chore. When Barnevelt had finished, Chask said, "If we go not soon upon the other reach, Captain, the Sunqaruma'll be in position to cut us off from the Strait."

"Let's make our tack, then," said Barnevelt. Not wishing to sunburn his nude scalp, he put on his battered silver helmet and went out again on deck.

The north wind, having freshened, blew spray from the bow slantwise across the deck. Water squirted in through the oar holes from time to time. With the seas so high, the oarsmen could no longer keep a regular rhythm but had to pause between strokes, oars in the air, until the coxswain called "Stroke!" at a favorable instant.

Barnevelt took another turn up the mast, holding the rungs tightly so as not to be jerked off by a sudden pitch. The wind sang in the rigging, the ropes creaked, and the sail was stretched tautly on its yard. Astern, the pursuing galley, though nearer, labored under similar difficulties. From time to time, Barnevelt could see a burst of spray as she dug her bow into a wave. Being a bigger ship, she dug in farther than the *Shambor*, which rode like a cork. The galley, he now saw, was a two-sticker with a big mainsail forward and a smaller mizzen aft.

When Barnevelt got down again, Chask called, "Ready about!" The boatswain had to ship several oars to get enough men to handle the sail in this wind. "Tiller hard down to leeward! Pay out the vang! Start the sheet! Cast off the weather stays!"

Watching this complicated maneuver, Barnevelt feared that a sudden gust might tear the sail, now streaming out ahead of the ship, flapping and booming like a huge triangular flag; or that the mast, now unstayed, might be carried away. In either case they'd be done for. They were drifting before the wind at no small speed, notwithstanding that the remaining oarsmen were backing water.

The deck rumbled under the feet of the crew, scurrying about and wrestling with the sail. At last they got the yard into vertical position and, by means of a complicated tackle, shifted it around to the other side of the mast, with yelling and grunting and heaving on the lines.

"Tiller up! Trim the sheet! Full and by!"

The yard came down to its normal slanting position, but on the other side of the mast. The mast stays were re-rigged, and the sail boomed and cracked as the wind filled it on the new reach. The men went back to their oars. How much simpler, thought Barnevelt, with a plain fore-and-aft rig, when all you had to do was to bring your helm up sharply and remember to duck as the boom swung across the deck. You could sail closer to the wind, too. He doubted they were making closer than six and a half points. Even an Earthly square-rigger (if any still existed)—could do as well as that and could also wear much quicker.

Zei, standing at his side on the poop, said, "O Snyol, wherefore this movement? Will not the Sunqaro ship cut across our path?"

"Not if he uses his sails. He'll have to tack at the same angle we do, and in this chop his oars alone won't be much good. . . ." He frowned at the sky, the sea, and his own rigging. "If we get a real blow, he'll have to run for home, but we shan't be much better off. You can't wear ship with this rig in a gale, and we'd have to run before the wind to stay afloat, which would land us right back in the Sunqar."

"What if the wind drops totally away?"

"Then he's got us too. He has over a hundred men on the oars, compared to our fourteen."

He wondered: If they kept ahead of the galley until night, could they slip away in the darkness? Not with three full moons all shining at once. With rain or fog it would be different, but the present weather did not look much like either. And, from the *Shambor*'s mast, the sail of the second following galley could still be seen.

"Your pardon," said Zei, "but I feel unwell and must needs retire . . . *wup!*"

"Use the lee rail!" cried Barnevelt, pointing.

When Zei had gone below to lie down, Chask came up and said, "Captain, there's one more item I'd ask you to consider. Not having taken aboard drinking water at the Sunqar, we run low. Men sweat away their water fast on a long oar-chase like this, ye wite."

"Ration it," said Barnevelt, watching the galley, whose bearing was changing fast as the *Shambor* cut across her course.

Now men were shinnying up the yards of both the galley's masts and furling the sails with gaskets, like little brown ants crawling up a straw. Although not without experience at the monkey work of sail-handling, Barnevelt was glad he was not up there with them, gripping the swaying yard between his knees like a bronco rider and clawing at the canvas.

Little by little the galley's sails shrank until they were bunched against the yards. Then the yards sank to the deck. The galley crossed the *Shambor*'s wake and continued north. Barnevelt figured that the galley would try to gain the weather gage of her quarry before hoisting sail again, as the difficulties of wearing a lateener would increase progressively with the size of the sail and would be even more onerous for the galley than for the little *Shambor*.

Devoted as he was to sailing, Dirk Barnevelt would have given a lot at that moment for a nice compact little Allis-Chambers or Maybach gas turbine in the stern to send them scooting for the Strait of Palindos regardless of wind and weather.

The long Krishnan day wore on. Barnevelt went into the cabin, slept, and shaved his head with sea water, lest the bronze hair and beard betray his origin. The men grumbled about the lack of water, shutting up when Barnevelt walked past with a hand on his hilt and a hard look on his face.

Then one of the planet's flying creatures, apparently blown out of its course, came aboard and clung to the rigging. It looked something like a small hairless monkey with bat's wings. Barnevelt killed time by luring it down from its perch and by evening had it eating out of his hand.

Evening came. The greenish sky remained clear. To the west, red Roqir set behind the galley, now closer and plowing along, its reset sails silhouetted blackly. The stars came out, shining with a hard brilliance unusual in this hazy latitude. Barnevelt picked Sol out of the unfamiliar heavens; from Star-map Region Eight, in which lay the Cetic planets, Sol was almost in line with Arcturus. The clump of moons came up: Karrim the big, Golnaz the middle-sized, and Sheb the little—like the three bears, thought Barnevelt, with himself in the rôle of Goldilocks.

The wind dropped a little. Looking off to the north, Barnevelt visualized a great high-pressure area lying over the Sadabao Sea, sending a sheet of cool dense air flowing southward towards the Sunqar.

"How long should a blow like this last?" he asked Chask.

The boatswain waved a hand in the Krishnan equivalent of a shrug. "Mayhap a day, mayhap four or five. 'Twill die of a sudden, leaving a week's calm on this stinking sea. I shall rejoice when we're back in the belt of steady westerlies."

The men were tiring, despite the fact that the *Shambor* still carried enough for two complete shifts at the oars. However, the galley drew no closer; her oarsmen must also be tiring.

"Besides," explained Chask, " 'tis unlikely they'd essay to run us down in the dark. A small craft like this can turn and dodge too well. And shooting catapults and crossbows at night, even with the moons, were wanton waste of missiles. Won't ye snatch some slumber, Captain?"

Barnevelt had been wondering whether he shouldn't put in a turn at the oars himself, though he knew Chask would disapprove. Moreover, he was not sure, now, whether such an act would raise or lower him in the eyes of the crew. His previous attempt to treat them as gentlemen seemed to have miscarried.

Besides, he did not think his muscles would add much to the *Shambor*'s oar power. While he was the tallest person aboard, and strong enough by most standards—having the advantage of being brought up on Earth with its slightly greater gravity—he lacked the great bulging shoulders and horny hands of these

professionals. In the end he followed Chask's advice, alternating with the boatswain on watch throughout the night.

All night the galley hung off their quarter, a blackness partly outlined by the phosphorescence of her waterline and oar-splashes. Neither ship showed any light.

At the end of his second watch, as the long night drew toward its close, Barnevelt awakened Chask and said, "I've been thinking that with another rig we could outsail those fellows."

"What's this, Captain? Some scheme from the polar regions ye'd broach amongst us? To change a rig in mid-chase like this, be your plan never so good, were to my thinking plain and fancy lunacy, if my frankness ye'll pardon. By the time your new rig were up . . ."

"I know, but look." Barnevelt pointed to where the galley's sails showed pink in the rising sun. "They're gaining on us, and by my reckoning we shan't reach the Strait before noon. At this rate they're sure to catch us before that."

"Be ye sure of that, sir?"

"Yes. Matter of fact, we're heading too far west and therefore shall have to wear ship again, which'll take us across their bows practically within spitting distance."

"Our situation's hard indeed, sir. What's to do?"

"I'll show you. If we plan our change-over carefully and then hop to it all at once, we may just get our new rig up before they catch us. And we shall have a better chance if we do it now before the wind rises and those guys get closer."

"Desperate conditions dictate desperate remedies, as says Nehavend. What shall be done?"

"Pick a couple of men you can trust and bring 'em into the cabin."

Half an hour later, Barnevelt's plan got under way. He was not himself so sure of it as he tried to sound, but anything was better than watching the galley crawl up with the inevitability of King Canute's tide.

His plan was nothing less than to convert the present lateen rig into a Marconi or Bermuda rig.

First, one of the men went along the foot of the sail, cutting holes in it at intervals, while another cut a coil of light line into short lengths that would go loosely round the yard, which in the new dispensation would become the mast. When everything was ready, Chask put up the tiller and swung the *Shambor*'s bow into the eye of the wind. The sail luffed and the rowers, knowing they had no more help from it, dug in their blades.

The galley, seeing the maneuver, put up her helm also and let her sails flap. Barnevelt realized with a sinking feeling that she could now cut across the hypotenuse of a right triangle to intercept them, since neither was now depending on wind.

"Lower away!" yelled Chask, and down came the great yard, stretching the whole length of the *Shambor*.

The sailors glowered at Barnevelt, and he caught one tapping his forehead. But the boatswain gave them no time to grumble. A rattle of orders sent some to cast off the stays and knock out the wedges that held the mast. Chask put men holding guys at bow, stern, and sides. Others hauled the mast out of its step and set the butt of it on deck beside the partners. The flying thing that Barnevelt had half-tamed flew round and round, squeaking excitedly.

Meanwhile, the sailor who had cut holes in the foot of the sail did likewise along the leech, while another cut the straps that held the sail to the yard. Then all hands except the rowers turned to, to step the yard in place of the mast. By hauling on the halyard, they hoisted the bare pole up to the head of the old mast, now serving as a gin-pole, and manhandled the butt end into the partners vacated by the mast. The tall spar swayed perilously; the men at the guys screamed; but the stick finally went home with a thump that shook the ship and was wedged into place. Then, by shifting the guys to the yard and slackening off the old halyard, they lowered the former mast to the deck.

The galley, with sails furled, crept closer. Barnevelt heard a faint hail come up the wind.

When the new and taller mast was in place, they triced the short edge of the sail to the ex-mast, reeving a light line through the holes in the sail and helically around the spar. Then they triced the intermediate edge of the sail to the ex-yard, now the mast, by reeving short lengths of rope through the holes in that edge and around this spar and tying them with reef knots to form rings. As these rings were installed, the men hoisted the sail.

"Make haste, rascallions!" shouted Chask. "Yare, yare!"

A louder hail came from the galley. The finishing touch was to lash the yoke that had formerly topped the ex-mast to the ex-yard, loosely enough so the ex-mast, now the boom, could swing, but tightly enough to hold it fast.

On the galley a catapult whanged. A black dot grew into a leaden ball which arced across the water and plunked in a couple of oars' lengths from the *Shambor*.

Barnevelt told Zei, "Go into the cabin, Princess."

"I'm no coward. My place is . . ."

"Into the cabin, dammit!" When he saw her starting to obey, he turned to Chask. "Think that lashing'll do?"

"It must suffice, Captain."

A sharp whistle, as of a whip, made Barnevelt wince. He saw a man on the bow of the galley start to wind up a heavy crossbow. A second bolt whizzed close.

However, the endless work on the new rig seemed finally done. The sail was fully hoisted. Chask shouted, "Belay the halyard!"

The sail hung limp, flapping gently. Another minute would tell whether Barnevelt's scheme was sound. He didn't like the look of that limber new mast, but it was too late for regrets now. He hopped up the steps to the poop and took the tiller from the seaman.

The catapult thumped again. The missile sailed past Barnevelt, skimmed the deck, and carried away a piece of the port rail with a splintering crash. The rowers flinched as it passed them, breaking stroke. The bow of the galley loomed close, clustered with men.

Barnevelt pushed the long tiller arm to starboard. The *Shambor* responded, her nose swinging to port. The wind ironed the ruffles from the sail, then filled it. The *Shambor* heeled sharply as the sail took hold, bringing water in the lee oar-ports and breaking the rowers' stroke again; then recovered as Barnevelt corrected his turn.

The whizz of crossbow bolts was punctuated by sharp drumlike sounds as the bolts tore through the taut sail. Barnevelt could see the two little holes from where he stood. *Let's hope they don't*

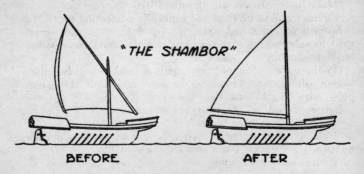

"THE SHAMBOR"

BEFORE   AFTER

start tears! he thought. *That sail's a precarious enough proposition
with all those ungrommeted holes in it.*

Chask, having gotten the crew straightened out, came to stand
beside him. He said, "Methinks we gain, sir."

Barnevelt took his eyes off the sail long enough for a quick
glance back at the galley. Yes, she did look a shade smaller . . . or
was that wishful thinking?

The sound of the catapult came again. Barnevelt caught a
glimpse of the ball flying past him. Then it headed straight for
the mast. All they needed now was to be dismasted by a lucky
shot!

Closer flew the missile to the mast . . . and missed it by an
eyelash, to graze the roof of the cabin with a loud bang and
bounce off into the sea. It was followed by another whizz of
crossbow bolts, one of which struck the wood nearby, plunging
down at a steep angle.

"They're lofting 'em at us, being too far for direct aiming,"
said Chask. "In another twinkling shall we be out of range entirely."

The next catapult missile splashed astern of the *Shambor*. Little
by little they drew ahead. Barnevelt, still tense as a spring,
glanced back. The galley, finding oars insufficient, was shaking
out its sails again.

However, as the minutes passed it became obvious that the
Shambor—with Barnevelt's eye on the sail and hand on the tiller
to get every possible degree of close-hauled sailing out of the
new rig—could now sail at least a point nearer the wind than her
pursuer. Hence the ships were on diverging tracks. The galley,
making good time, drew abreast of the *Shambor,* but too far down-
wind to be dangerous.

Barnevelt waited until the galley stood out in profile, then put
his helm up sharply. Without hesitation, the *Shambor* luffed and
heeled into the other tack. The galley shrank fast, because the
two ships were now sailing away from one another. Barnevelt
saw frantic activity on the galley's decks; but, by the time the
lateen sails had been laboriously shifted to the opposite reach,
she was too far behind for details to be made out.

As the sun climbed towards the meridian, the galley receded until her oars were hidden by the bulge of the sea. However, if anybody expected the pursuers to withdraw in baffled rage, they were disappointed. Unable to keep up with Barnevelt's short quick tacks, the galley plodded on under oars alone.

The *Shambor* seemed to be doing so well, though, that Barnevelt passed the word to reduce the oar crew to eight men to give the others more rest. He thought the men's attitude towards him improved a bit also.

Then it occurred to him that he was hungry. He had eaten hardly anything in the last tense forty-eight hours, and his animal self was beginning to protest. He turned the tiller over to Chask and started for the forward cabin, hoping for a bite in Zei's company.

"O Captain!" said a voice, and there were three sailors, including the argumentative Zanzir.

"Yes?"

"When shall we have water, sir?" said Zanzir. "We die of thirst."

"You'll get your next ration at noon."

"We ask it now, Captain. Without it we can't row. Ye wouldn't hold out on us, would ye?"

"I said," said Barnevelt, raising his voice, "you shall have your next water at noon. And next time you want to speak to me, get Chask's permission first."

"But Captain . . ."

"That's enough!" roared Barnevelt, his fury aggravated by the knowledge that the crew's undiscipline was partly his own fault. He went forward to the deckhouse, hearing behind him a mutter in which he caught the words, ". . . high and mighty emperor, is he? . . ."

"What ails my captain?" said Zei. "You look as sour as Qarar when he'd been deceived by the King of 'Ishk."

"I'll be all right," said Barnevelt, slumping down on a bench. "How about a spot of sustenance, girl?" He felt too weary to worry about the fact that this was not the usual way of addressing a princess. "That is, if you know how to rustle food."

"And why should I not?" she said, rummaging on the shelves.

"*Aaow,*" he yawned. "Being a crown princess and all that non-sense . . ."

"Canst keep a royal secret?"

"Uh-huh."

"My lady mother, mindful of the revolutions that have most piteously overthrown the ancient order in Zamba and elsewhere, has compelled me to learn the arts of common housewifery, so that come what may, I shall never be utterly at a loss for such elements as feeding and clothing myself. Would you like some of these dried fruits? Meseems the worms have not yet made them their domicile."

"Fine. Let's have that loaf of badr and the knife."

"Heavenly hierarchy!" she exclaimed when she saw what he proposed to tuck away. "But then, I ween, heroic deeds go with heroic appetite. All my life I've read legends of Qarar and his ilk, though knowing none besides our fragile local popinjays, I had, until I met you, come to think such men of hardihood existed nowhere but in song and story."

Barnevelt shot a suspicious look at Zei. Although he liked her the best of any Krishnan he knew, he thought he had made up his mind against any serious entanglement with the lady.

He said, "You don't look forward, then, to being queen with a freshly painted Qiribu each year for a husband?"

"Not I. Though even misliking it, I lack the force or subtlety to swerve events from their appointed course. 'Tis one thing to talk big, like the heroine in Harian's *The Conspirators,* of casting aside the comforts and prerogatives of rank for love, and quite another so to do in very fact. Yet sometimes do I envy common wenches in barbarous lands, wed to great brutes like yourself who rule 'em as my mother does her consorts. For while female domination is the law and custom of Qirib, I fear by nature I'm no dominator."

Barnevelt thought vaguely of suggesting a revolution in Qirib, with Zei in the role of Shaw's *Bolshevik Empress.* But he was too tired to pursue the matter.

"*Ao,*" he said, "only my fair share of the water!"

"But you're captain . . ."

"Only my fair share."

"Such scrupulosity! One would think you, too, had dwelt among the republicans of Kätai-Jhogorai."

"Not exactly, though I sympathize with their ideas." He patted a yawn and sprawled out on the bench while she cleared the table.

The next he knew, Chask was shaking him.

"Sir," said the boatswain, "the wind drops and the galleys press upon our wake!"

Barnevelt sat up, blinking. Now that he noticed, the motion of the ship did seem less and the noise of wind and wave lower.

He went out. Although they were still bucking a swell from the north, the swells were smooth from lack of wind to ruffle them. There was just enough breeze to keep the sail filled. Chask had already put a full crew back on the oars.

Behind them, the galley loomed about as distant as when Barnevelt had gone into the cabin. No doubt the *Shambor* had drawn farther ahead after he went in and then lost some of her advantage with the dying of the wind. Moreover the second galley, which they had seen the previous day, was now in sight again, its masts alone visible save when a wave lifted the *Shambor* to an unusual height.

Without wind, the galleys would soon catch them. Ahead, no sign of the northern shores of the Banjao Sea appeared. Yet the sun was high; it must be around noon.

"Tell 'em to put their backs into it," said Barnevelt.

Chask replied, "They do what they can, sir—but lack of water robs their sinews of their accustomed strength."

The reckoning indicated that, though Palindos Strait was not yet in sight, it must lie not far below the horizon. Careful estimates showed that they could just nip through the strait ahead of the following ship.

Chask said, "Then we shall be in the Sadabao Sea, but what

will that avail us? For yon cutthroats will follow us even to the harbor of Damovang."

"True," said Barnevelt, frowning over his chart. "How about running ashore and taking to the woods?"

"Then they'll put ashore, too, to hunt us down, and with hundreds to carry on the search there's little doubt in my mind of its outcome. What else would ye?"

"How about doubling around one of the headlands of the Strait and hiding in a cove while we're out of sight?"

"Let's see, sir." Chask pointed a stubby finger at the chart. "The easterly shore of the Sadabao Sea, along here, is rocky and hard to draw nigh to without staving your bottom. The westerly has some rock, much open beach, and few places to hide. Fossanderan may have such coves upon its northern flank, but never will ye persuade ordinary seamen to go ashore on that accursed isle."

"Oh, foof! Are they afraid of the mythical beast-men?"

"No myth, Captain. At least I've heard the sound they say is the drums of these demons. And myth or no, the men would not obey."

Barnevelt went out again, to be greeted by a chorus of hoarse cries: "Water!" "Water, Captain!" "Water, we pray!" "We demand water!"

The galley was crawling up once more. The wind had now ceased entirely save for an occasional light puff. The sail flapped limply, reminding Barnevelt of Chask's prediction of a week's calm.

He gave orders to ration out the men's noon sip of water, which he hoped would quiet them. Instead, they only grumbled the more for its paucity.

The galley was now all visible again, her oars rising and falling with mechanical precision now that the sea was comparatively smooth. The second galley, too, was closer.

A sailor in the bow called, "Land ho!"

There it was: a cluster of wooded peaks—the hills of Fossanderan. Barnevelt's little winged friend saw it, too, and flew off to northward.

Barnevelt went back into the cabin to correct his reckoning and lay his course for the eastern channel. Zei watched him wordlessly with large dark eyes.

He ran over his estimates again. This time it looked as though the galley would overhaul them in the throat of the eastern channel of the Strait. Then why keep trying? The usual hope for a miracle. The galley just might spring a seam or have a mutiny at the last minute . . .

Too bad the western channel wasn't deep enough to float the *Shambor*, so that he could lure the galley on to the bottom.

Well, wasn't it? With three moons in conjunction at full, Krishna would have record tides. And, while the tides in these seas were usually nothing much, because of the limited size of the seas and the complicated tidal patterns engendered by Roqir and the three moons, on this one occasion the tidal waves should all be in phase, producing a tide of Earthly dimensions.

Barnevelt got out the handbook he had bought in Novorecife. The sight reminded him of Vizqash bad-Murani, the Krishnan clerk who had sold him the book. Vizqash had then tried to betray him into the hands of a gang of kidnappers or slayers on a picnic; had later, in the guise of a masked gentleman, started a riot in the tavern at Jazmurian; and finally had turned up as a pirate of the Sunqar, to ruin Barnevelt's neat getaway with Zei and Shtain.

Barnevelt had no doubt, now, that all these events were connected. The Moryá Sunqaruma, he was sure, had had their eye on him ever since the *Amazonas* had landed him at Novorecife. He grinned at the thought that the very book that Vizqash had sold him might be the means of frustrating the fellow's knavish tricks.

The book, along with the rest of Barnevelt's gear, had been soaked when the Earthman had fallen through a hole in the terpahla during his flight. He found that he had to pry the pages—actually one long strip of paper folded zigzag—apart with care to avoid tearing them. Once opened up, however, the book was found to include not only tables for computing the revolutions of the moons, but also a table showing how much time the tidal waves caused by each luminary led or followed the movement of that moon in various places.

Majbur, Jazmurian, Sotaspé, Dur . . . Here it was, Palindos Strait. Barnevelt whooped when he saw that here Karrim's tide lagged behind that moon by less than a Krishnan hour, and the tides of Golnaz and Sheb by even smaller amounts.

"Chask!" he yelled.

Although Chask looked dubious, he had to admit that there was nothing to do but try the western channel, especially as they should hit it a little past noon. Then, and a little past midnight, were the times of the highest tides.

The *Shambor* swung to port and crept towards the channel, while the galleys crept towards the *Shambor*. The wooded hills of the peninsula that came down to the Strait from the west now rose into view. As they plodded over the glassy sea, the land rose higher until it looked as though the island were part of the mainland. Then, as they came still closer, the western passage opened out.

Still the galleys lessened their distance. Barnevelt looked back with a shiver. Would they have to duck another barrage of bolts and missiles?

One of the sailors called out, " 'Tis no use, Captain. We're spent!" Others joined the chorus of defeatism: "They'll take us long ere we reach sanctuary . . ." "Let's give up on terms . . ."

"Shut up, all of you!" said Barnevelt. "I got you out before . . ."

At that moment a sailor—not Zanzir, but an older and bigger fellow—began to harangue the crew. "This haughty captain cares nought for you, but only for his royal doxy. Let's throw them to the fish . . ."

Barnevelt at the start of this speech drew his sword and walked towards the man. The latter, hearing his approach, spun round and reached for his knife. Others among the crew did likewise.

Barnevelt made his last two steps running and, before the mutineer could either stab or throw, struck the side of his head with the flat of his rapier. The man staggered sideways, across the deck, through the gap in the rail left by the galley's catapult missile, and over the side. Splash!

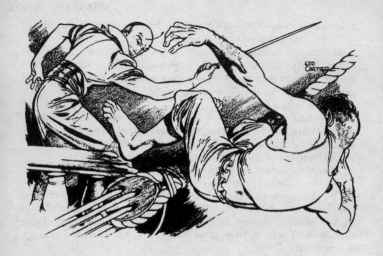

Barnevelt had not intended to kill the man, only to stun him. But he was perforce becoming callous; they couldn't stop to pick the fellow up, and now they would know he meant business. He only regretted it hadn't been Zanzir, who was no doubt at the bottom of the trouble.

"Anybody else?" he asked the crew.

Nobody answered. He walked up and down the catwalk, peering at the rowers. One whom he judged to be shirking he whacked on the bare back with the flat of his sword.

"Lay into it, you!" *Me and Captain Bligh,* he thought.

They passed a rock. Barnevelt said, "Chask, take the tiller. Put a couple of men in the bow to take soundings. I'll go aloft—oh-oh!"

"What, sir?"

"Our new rig has no ratlines. Get me a hammer, some spikes, and a length of rope."

Presently Barnevelt, his implements dangling from him, began to shinny up the mast. It was a foul job, since all he had to climb by were the rope rings holding the luff of the sail to the mast, and these provided poor purchase. When he was about two-thirds of the way up, he drove a couple of spikes into the mast and looped his rope from them to made a crude boatswain's chair. Though neither safe nor comfortable, he could now at least judge depths from the varying shades of green of the water ahead. From behind came the thump and splash of the galley's oars.

"A point to port," he called down. "Little to starboard. Steady as you go. . . ."

Any minute the ship might touch ground, probably snapping him off his perch. He kept peering for patches of dark water. A slight tidal current through the Strait to northward helped the *Shambor* along.

When he found a good channel, he snatched a look aft. The galley was still coming up, also picking its way, and a couple of hoda behind it came its sister ship. The cries of men taking soundings in the galley drifted up to the *Shambor* like an echo of the calls of her own leadsmen in the bow, except that the figures were different.

Barnevelt concentrated on a bad patch, where pale-green shoals seemed to block his way completely.

A sudden outburst of yells came up to his ears, "She's aground! The pirate ship has struck!"

Ha! he thought, his scheme *had* worked. Still he dared not take his eyes off the water ahead. He'd feel foolish indeed if he lured the pirate aground only to strand himself a minute later.

A jerk of the mast told him the *Shambor* had touched, too. "Pull hard!" he shouted. "A hair to starboard!"

The oars dug in and the *Shambor* came free. Ahead lay all the dark-green water anyone could ask.

Barnevelt drew a long breath and looked back again. The galley was backing water furiously, the sea foaming about her oar blades. Behind her the second galley, in response to flag signals, had turned to starboard and now showed her profile heading east.

Barnevelt guessed that the second ship had received orders

to go around by the eastern channel and try to catch the *Shambor* in the Sadabao Sea. Therefore it would not do to sail blithely on for Qirib as if their worries were over. Once the second galley sighted them in the open sea, they'd be in the same fix as before, without any shallow strait or north wind to rescue them.

What the *Shambor* needed was a hiding place where the water supply could be replenished. The men were not exaggerating their exhaustion. Barnevelt's own throat felt like something dug out of an Egyptian tomb. If his own sailors for superstitious reasons were afraid to land on Fossanderan, the pirates would probably feel the same way.

He told Chask, "Hard to starboard, and find me a cove on the north side of Fossanderan that might be the mouth of a stream."

"But Captain . . ."

"That's where we're going!"

Chask, shaking his head, swung the ship east. As they emerged into the Sadabao Sea, the promontories of Fossanderan hid the stranded galley. The breeze freshened a little. Sailing with the wind on the beam, they made good time along the rocky, wooded shores.

After most of a Krishnan hour, Barnevelt said, "That looks like a good place; a little valley that ought to have a stream."

"Say not I failed to warn you, sir," said Chask, and turned the *Shambor* shoreward.

At once the men, who had been very quiet since the mutineer had fallen overboard, set up an outcry: "The haunted isle!" "Our mad captain's taking us to the home of the demons!" "All's lost!" "He must be a demon himself!" "Anywhere but that!" "We'd liefer forgo water!"

Again Barnevelt faced them down, though the oarsmen relaxed their efforts until they were merely dipping their oars in the water. That, however, made little difference, because the breeze wafted them shoreward.

"The first man who backs water without orders," said Barnevelt, "gets this. *Zei!* Come out. We're going ashore. Get out the buckets."

The *Shambor* nosed gently into the embayment until tree branches swept the deck and swished against the rigging. Chask ordered the sail and the anchor dropped and then hurried forward. Barnevelt dropped off the bow into knee-deep water and caught Zei as she climbed down.

He shouted. "Fresh water!" and pointed to where a little trickly stream spread itself out thinly over a small sandy delta.

The men scurried to the bow to leap off also, drink, and fill buckets for the ship's water tank, which they passed to others on deck. Although he was as thirsty as they, a quirk of vanity made Barnevelt hold off from drinking until everyone else had done so. He turned a grin to Zei.

"We'll tell old Qvansel his three moons did save our skins—not by occult astrological forces, but by the good old force of gravity."

Chask came ashore last. He walked up to Barnevelt swinging an axe, and said, "I like this not, Captain. We should all be armed in case the beast-men appear. Yet with the crew in its present temper 'twere folly to serve out arms to 'em. Besides, we're low on stove wood, and methought . . ."

Barnevelt said, "I haven't heard any spirits of the waste and weald moan— Hey, what goes on?"

In a concerted movement, all the sailors rushed back to the *Shambor* and scrambled aboard. Before Barnevelt and Chask could even reach the ship, they were hoisting the anchor and backing water vigorously. The ship started to move.

Barnevelt and Chask seized the anchor before it disappeared over the gunwale and pulled on it, as though two men could counteract the thrust of fourteen vigorously wielded oars. Suddenly the tension in the anchor rope ceased, and Barnevelt and Chask sat down with a splash. Somebody had cut the rope.

As Barnevelt sat foolishly in the shallow water, the *Shambor* receded rapidly, the sailors jeering: "Fare thee well, Captain!" "May the demons give you pleasant dreams!" And Zanzir, loudest of all: "We thank you for the fine ship, Captain. We'll make our fortunes in't!"

There was no use swimming after the *Shambor*, which backed out into open water, hoisted sail, and swung round to head off northeast, close-hauled. Soon she was out of sight, leaving Barnevelt, Zei, and Chask on the doubtful shores of the island of Fossanderan.

Barnevelt said, "I should have run that young squirt through the first time he gave us a piece of his lip."

He wondered, now, what would happen to the *Shambor* in her new rig, which he had intended to change back to the old before reaching Damovang to avoid trouble with the Viagens over the introduction of an invention to Krishna.

"Nor should we have both come ashore at once," said Chask. "That last blunder was of my doing."

"Instead of apportioning blame," said Zei, "were't not more profitable to plan our next course?"

Chask said, "The princess is a fount of wisdom. The sooner we're off this accursed isle the sooner shall we be home. By the gods' own luck we have this axe and that length of anchor rope. I propose, Captain, that we build a raft, utilizing trunks of trees and the rope to bind them. Then shall we paddle to the western mainland and thence proceed to the Shaf-Malayer road, which runs not far west of here."

"Two logs is all we have rope for," said Barnevelt. "We'll have to straddle 'em as if we were riding an aya."

Chask found a likely tree and felled it. He was still trimming the glossy branches away when a hideous clamor arose from the woods around.

A swarm of creatures rushed out of concealment and galloped towards the three. They were of about human size and shape, but with tails, heads faintly resembling those of Earthly baboons, and hair in lieu of clothes. They carried stone-age clubs and spears.

"*Run!*" screeched Chask.

The three ran to the mouth of the stream and turned westward along the shore. The shore here took the form of a crescent-shaped beach, ending in a rocky promontory. Barnevelt and Zei, being taller than Chask, drew ahead of the boatswain as they raced along this beach, the beast-men howling behind. Barnevelt heard them gaining.

A sudden break in the noise behind made Barnevelt snatch a look to the rear. What he saw filled him with horror. Chask had stubbed his toe on a stone and fallen. Before he could get up again, the beast-men had reached him and were working him over. Barnevelt checked his stride and reached for his sword before realizing that Chask must be already dead under the shower of blows and thrusts, and for him to go back would be to throw his life away to no purpose.

He ran on. At the promontory, he and Zei leaped from rock to rock until they found before them another short stretch of beach.

"*Ao*, Zei!" he said. "In here!"

At the beginning of this curve of beach, the waves had undermined the bank beneath a big old tree, whose roots now dangled barely from the overhang and whose trunk leaned sea-

ward at an ominous angle. One good storm would send the whole tree crashing into the sea, but meanwhile the space beneath it formed a small cave.

The fugitives burrowed in among the rootlets, bringing showers of dislodged dirt down on their heads and disturbing many-legged creeping things. One of the latter got inside Barnevelt's jacket and squirmed about while Barnevelt swatted frantically. In its death throes it bit a crumb of flesh out of his chest, making him suck his breath in sharply in lieu of yelling.

When they were as far back as they could push, they found that they could no longer see the beach for the curtain of roots that hung down from the roof of their refuge like the baleen from the palate of a whale.

Well, thought Barnevelt, *if I can't see out, they can't see in. How about footprints?* Between the wet sand and the bank of which the tree formed a part there was a strip, not much over a meter wide, of soft dry sand, and they could hope that this would not betray them. They crouched in their hole, rationing breaths in an effort to be quieter than utter silence.

The noise attending the butchery of Chask died down. Bare feet trotted by, **slap-slap,** over the wet sand. Beast-men called to one another in their own tongue. For all Barnevelt knew, they were organizing an attack on the cave. Any minute now, he expected to have to start thrusting at the bestial heads as the creatures came crawling into their refuge. He could put up quite a scrap . . .

Then all sound died away, save the swoosh of the surf and the sigh of the wind. Nevertheless, the fugitives continued to crouch for hours.

Barnevelt whispered, "Just like 'em to be waiting out there to greet us!"

When the dimming of the light at last showed that afternoon was well advanced, Barnevelt murmured, "You stay here. I'm going out to scout."

"Take care!"

"You're durn tootin' I'll be careful. If I don't come back by tomorrow morning, try to swim for the mainland."

He pushed his way out, centimeter by centimeter, like some timid mollusk emerging from its shell. However, he could neither see nor hear any trace of his enemies.

The tide, which when they had sought refuge was almost lapping the mouth of the cave, had now receded many meters. Barnevelt skulked back to the place where Chask had fallen. The sand was roiled and stained with brown Krishnan blood running down to the water in a broad band, but no bodies were in sight.

Barnevelt followed the teeming humanoid footprints back to the mouth of the little stream. A few meters up the stream, where lay the trunk the boatswain had felled, he came upon the axe that Chask had been using, lying in the stream bed with the water rippling over it. He picked it up.

Barnevelt pushed upstream looking for spoor of the beast-men. He found broken bushes and blood from their burden, but the mold of the forest floor did not take footprints with any clarity, and soon the trail died out. Too bad, he thought, that he was not a trained jungle wallah.

While he cast about in perplexity, a sound came to his ears: a rhythmic booming, too sharp and high for a drum of the conventional type, too resonant for mere banging on a log. At first it seemed to come from all directions. After a while of turning his head this way and that like a radar antenna, he thought he fixed its direction and struck off uphill to the south-east.

An hour later he knew he was nearing the source of the sound. He drew his sword, to have it handy and so as not to let it clank in its scabbard. Creeping stealthily over the curve of a rounded saddleback he looked down upon the scene of activity that he was stalking.

On a level space, cleared of trees, the beast-men were dancing around a fire while one of their number pounded on a drum made of a hollowed log. Or rather, Barnevelt saw what he had supposed to be beast-men, but which now turned out to be ordinary tailed Krishnans, *Krishnanthropus koloftus*, like those of the Koloft Swamp and the island of Zá. They had been wearing carved animal masks when they made their attack and had now removed these and hung them on stubs of branches around the clearing. And, whereas the tailed men of Zá were semi-civilized and those of Koloft had at least been subdued by the authorities of Mikardand, the present examples of the species were carrying on their aboriginal traditions with full savage vim.

Across the fire, Barnevelt was distressed though not much surprised to see parts of his late boatswain hung on lines to sizzle. While Barnevelt was uncertain of the identity of some of the organs—Krishnans being less human inside than out—there was no doubt about their fate.

Barnevelt swallowed the lump in his throat and started back.

Back at the hiding place, Barnevelt said, "I found him all right. They're eating him."

"How dreadful!" said Zei. "And he such a worthy wight! What a bestial and abhorrent custom!"

"Too bad, but actually it's no different from what you do in Qirib."

"Not at all! How can you utter such blasphemous sophistry? Whereas the one's a solemn ceremony, the holy powers above to gratify, the other's but the swinish satisfaction of the alimentary appetite."

"Well, that's how some people look at it. But let's not argue—let's get out of here. It's pretty far to swim, and we don't want to leave our clothes and weapons behind. . . ."

"So why not finish the raft our slaughtered friend and deputy began?"

"Because the sound of the axe would fetch 'em running." He sniffed the breeze. "The wind's backed to the northwest, and we're on the northwest shore of the island. The woods look dry, and my lighter should be working."

"You mean to set the weald ablaze, to distract the tailed ones from our enterprise?"

"Matter of fact I'll set the damndest forest fire you ever saw. Bear a hand, gal."

For the next hour they prowled the shore, piling sticks and

dead shrubs where they would do the most good, until they had a line a hoda long running along the shore, bending inland at the mouth of the stream to aford room to finish the raft.

When that task was done, Barnevelt started at the east end of his line of bonfires and lit the first with his lighter. When it blazed up, he and Zei each thrust into it a torch of faggots and ran down the line, igniting blaze after blaze.

By the time they finished, the whole slope extending inland was a roaring hell, the fire leaping from tree to tree.

Barnevelt, his face red from the heat, sweated over his raft. There was not much more to be done: to cut two logs from the felled trunk, shove these into the water, and tie them together with the piece of anchor rope. Then he felled a sapling and trimmed the soft wood of the trunk down to a couple of crude paddles—too narrow in the blade to be efficient, but not even the long Krishnan day provided time for a better job.

"Off we go!" he shouted over the roar of the fire, and drove the axe blade into one of the logs to secure it. Zei straddled the logs forward. With their footgear hung around their necks, they paddled out from shore, the heat of the blazing hillsides beating with blistering force upon their backs. All of Fossanderan seemed to be red with fire or black with smoke.

The thick stems of the paddles were awkward; Barnevelt wondered if bare hands wouldn't have done as well. Every swell swirled up to their waists as they angled out from shore. When they were far enough to start west for the mainland, the swells made their craft roll precariously; every second Barnevelt expected the raft to roll clear over and dunk them.

Meter by meter they struggled westward as the sun sank. The first stars were out when they came to the western channel of the Strait of Palindos. This was just as well, Barnevelt thought, because the stranded galley was all too visible from where they crossed the channel.

The galley sat with lanterns hung about her. The low tide had left her hull exposed down to the curve of the bilge, and the settling of her weight upon her keel had made her heel over at an undignified angle. Beyond her, a dark-red shape in the twilight where the fires of Fossanderan shone upon her, lay the galley's consort. Hawsers stretched in graceful catenary curves between the two ships; the banked oars of both rested quietly upon the water.

Evidently, thought Barnevelt, the second galley had made a cast into the Sadabao Sea, had either caught the *Shambor* or had given up looking for her, and had come back to try to pull her stranded sister off the bottom. But the dropping of the tide had stultified this project, so now they were waiting for midnight and high water to try again.

Peacefully, Barnevelt and his companion paddled across the channel. When all three moons arose, now more widely spaced than they had been the previous night, the travelers grounded gently on the sand spit projecting from the mainland towards the blazing island.

Barnevelt dismounted stiffly from the raft and helped Zei off. He pulled on his boots, hauled the raft up on shore, and struggled with the knots of the lashings.

"What do you, O hero mine?" said Zei.

"I'm getting these ropes off."

"Wherefore lust you after two old pieces of rope?"

"Because, my dear Zei, in our fix we need all the equipment we can lay our hands on. And few simple things serve more practical uses in the wilds than a length of rope."

By working the point of his dagger into the knots, Barnevelt finally prized them loose. He found that he had two lengths of rope, each about as thick as his thumb and two meters long. Other accouterments comprised his sword and dagger, the axe, a pocket knife, and a pocket cigar lighter. He did not count the Hayashi ring camera, which had no survival value in the wilderness that he could see.

He would have given a lot for a compass, or even for a crude Krishnan watch with a single hand, which could be used as a compass at need. He had begun his journey with such a watch in his pocket, but the ducking he had received during his flight across the terpahla had ruined it, so he had left it behind on the

Shambor.

Barnevelt tied one of the ropes around his own waist and the other around that of Zei. "As I understood Chask," he said, pointing westward, "if we head in that direction long enough, we'll reach the road from Shaf to Malayer."

"So we shall—albeit, lacking road or trail, I know not how we shall win through this fearsome forest."

"Well, we can follow the north shore of the peninsula for a few hoda before striking inland."

This proved easier said than done. The shore itself was rocky, with only a few small patches of beach, which the rising tide was now covering. The tumbled masses of rock that divided the beaches proved such a trial to clamber over that the pair soon gave up the effort and struck inland.

Here they found conditions hardly better. The trees grew so thickly along the edge of the high-water mark that it would have taken a bishtar to force its way through the tangle. Further inland, the foliage was sparser at ground level and the footing easier. Here, however, the canopy of leaves overhead shut out the light of the three moons with such effect that the travelers, stumbling along in near-total darkness, were always tripping over fallen logs or stepping into holes.

All around them, small nocturnal creatures chirped, squeaked, rustled, and whirred. From time to time Barnevelt felt small wings brush his face. In the distance, larger animals crashed away unseen through the thickets.

After an hour of this struggle, a gurgle caught Barnevelt's ear. Presently he panted, "Here's a stream. What—what say we camp here?"

"I—I wondered when you would call a halt. So weary am I that scarcely can I raise foot from ground."

"You're a brave girl."

They drank. Then, scratched, bruised, sore, and utterly exhausted, they sank down at the base of a big tree. As Zei's head came to rest upon his shoulder, Barnevelt started to say something. Then he realized that Zei had already fallen asleep.

§ § §

Towards morning Barnevelt awoke, cramped, stiff, and shivering. A fresh breeze rustled the leaves overhead. The three moons had sunk in the west so that their oblique rays penetrated the canopy less than ever. Zei stirred, murmuring, "I freeze!"

"I'll fix that," said Barnevelt. "Let's find a better place and I'll make a fire."

"Won't the Sunqaruma see it?"

"I don't think so. The peninsula curves around so they couldn't possibly see this part of the shore from where they are. Here we are!"

Following the brook downstream to the thickets along the shore, he came to a place where a forest giant, in falling, had brought down several smaller trees and created a small clearing. Here was just enough light for his night-sensitized eyes to see what he was doing. He gathered sticks, broke them into convenient lengths, piled them in a heap, and applied his lighter.

This lighter was not unlike a Terran lighter but larger and cruder, of pre-industrial workmanship. He spun the little thumb wheel and brought forth a shower of sparks. The wick caught for an instant, then flickered out.

Barnevelt tried again and again, but no flame could he make.

"Hell!" he said. "Either it's out of fuel, or it got too wet during our paddle this afternoon. Let's see if we can't start a fire with the sparks alone."

After several attempts, he gave up and put the lighter away. He sat with chin in hand, thinking. At length he rose and began feeling and knocking against the standing and fallen trees roundabout.

"What do you, my noble lord?" said Zei.

"I'm going to try something, but it may not work. Let me have the lace of one of your sandals."

Time ticked past as Barnevelt chopped and whittled and tinkered. At last he had a wooden bow drill and a rough board, split from one of the fallen trees, with a notch near one end.

"Now find me some tinder—real dry stuff."

Presently he began sawing on his bow drill, holding the upper end of the drill in place by a lump of wood with a socket crudely dug into it. He sawed and sawed. Nothing happened.

"What . . ." began Zei.

"The spell," rasped Barnevelt, "won't work if a woman speaks within ten hoda of it."

He kept on sawing. The sky began to lighten in the east.

At last, as the stars were going out one by one, the bow drill began to smoke. A ruddy glow appeared at its lower end. Delicately, Barnevelt pushed tinder at it, blew gently upon it, and sawed some more on his bow. With the faintest **pop,** a tiny flame sprang into being, dancing with elfin steps over the little heap of forest-floor litter.

Barnevelt fed the flame, gingerly drew away his apparatus, and soon had a proper fire going. He drew a long breath, saying, "Thank the gods I was once a Boy Scout!"

"You were a what?"

"Never mind. Damn, I've blistered my hands. I—what's that?"

From the dark depths of the wood came a prolonged animal grunt, as if someone had unskillfully sawed on the lowest string of a 'cello.

Zei shrank back against him. "A hunting yeki!"

"You mean one of those long brown things . . ." Barnevelt loosened his sword in its sheath, peering into the dark depths of the forest. "More fire," he growled, adding fuel.

The fire blazed up. But, although they remained tense and staring for some time, no further sound broke the stillness, save the lapping of waves and the rustle of leaves.

"Where are we?" he asked at last.

Zei pondered. "I strive to recall the geography I learnt as a chick. Meseems this land hight the peninsula of Rákh."

"What about the local fauna? Are we likely to be stepped on by a wild bishtar?"

"Nay, I think not. 'Tis in the lands more distant from the cultured western shores of the Triple Seas—let's say Zhamanak to the south or Aurus to the east—that the great herds of these vast creatures roam. Natheless, the forests of Rákh harbor denizens fell enough, such as that which we but now did hear." She shuddered. "Let's hope your prowess will save me from the fate that, most of all, I dread—namely, of being devoured by a yeki."

"There, there." Barnevelt hugged, patted, and kissed her. "It seems to have gone away. Anyhow, as Lord Dunsany once said, 'It does not become adventurers to care who eats their bones.'"

"Who pray is Lord Donsené? Some Nyami bard?"

"Why, he was—but yes, of course, he was the greatest poet of the Nyamadzë." Barnevelt peered around. "Isn't there anything edible in this damned wood? I could eat an aya and chase his driver."

"So also could I!"

"Well, don't look at me like that. It reminds me of the way your mother looked at poor old Káj when he was about to be chopped up and served to the assembled court. Here, take my sword in case some beastie comes along. I'm going down to see what the Sadabao Sea has to offer."

He pushed through the thickets along the shoreline, waded into shallow water, and began rummaging among the sands and rocks. Presently he came back with a double handful of spiral shells not unlike those of an earthly snail. The creatures inside the shells, however, walked on many short legs instead of gliding along on their bellies like Earthly snails.

"What's the local word for these?" he asked.

"Those we term *safqa*. They're eaten in Suruskand, I'm told, although we care not for them in Qirib."

"Hm. Now, what's the first rule about eating strange things when camping out? Eat a little piece first and see what happens."

"If they eat them in Suruskand, they must needs be edible."

"Let's not be hasty. It might be a different species, or maybe they're good only in months beginning with a **kh.**"

He broke one of the shells with the hilt of his dagger, cut off a small piece of the rubbery creature within, and toasted it on a sharpened stick. At last he popped the brown, bubbling morsel into his mouth.

"Not bad, if you don't mind chewing a piece of old inner tube," he said.

"What's this about tubes, good my lord?"

"Sorry. That's a Nyami joke unintelligible to foreigners."

"When shall I receive my meed? For I am monstrously anhungered by the smell of cookery."

"You'll have to be monstrously anhungered for a while, till we see how the thing affects me. If I start to roll on the ground, foam at the mouth, and turn blue with pink spots, you'll know the local variety of safqa doesn't agree with me."

"Then, to pass the time, I desire that you pleasure me with tales of your adventures. As, for ensample, when you smote the powers of Olñega."

Knowing nothing about the wars between Nyamadzë and Olñega, Barnevelt said, "Oh, that's a long and heavy-footed tale. Just a lot of people running around in the snow and whacking away at each other, being too stupid to realize that they were accomplishing nothing save to feed their leaders' vanity. I found my visit to Novorecife and my journey from there to Qirib a lot more interesting."

"Did you come to know the Terrans face to face?"

"Sure. I even got quite chummy with Castanhoso, the chief Terran policeman. That's how I picked up that damned bird I gave your mother."

"How came this creature ever to dwell at Novorecife, so far from its native planet?"

"It seems there's a Cosmotheist missionary named Mirza Fateh, who travels about the Cetic planets cultivating his cult—you're not a Cosmotheist, are you?"

"Good Varzai, nay! The worship of the Mother Goddess is demanding enough for one of my rank. What said you this Terran was clept?"

"Mirza Fateh. Know him?"

"The name plucks at the strings of memory—but nay, I know him not. Pray continue."

"Mirza is no doubt a faker, but he seems to have had his share of trouble. His wife and child were killed in a train robbery between Majbur and Jazmurian. Anyway, he recently arrived with this cantankerous bird in a cage. But the medical authorities at Novorecife wouldn't let him take it with him unless he left it

185

at the station long enough to be sure it carried no sickness. So, being in a hurry, Mirza gave it to one of the Terrans there, and Castanhoso gave it to me."

"Then you do not find all Earthmen to be cruel, lying, arrogant, treacherous, cowardly villains?"

Barnevelt raised his eyebrows and the antennae glued to them. "Not at all. Earthmen come much like Krishnans. There's good, bad, and indifferent, and most of them a mixture of all three. Is this the opinion in Qirib?"

"Amongst the many it is. Although few would dare raise hand against an authentic Earthman, for fear of the deadly powers these creatures from the depths of space are thought to wield, yet are they held in much dread and despite. To be known in Ghulindé as a 'Terran lover' is to have children throw stones at you in the street.

"Howsomever, such japery is not my wont, for, whereas I've known no Earthlings closer than to nod the time of day to, meseemed that the opinion you've set forth must be the right one. But I'm retarding the wheels of your narrative, sirrah—so let us gather up once more the reins of your discourse and gallop off upon our fleet aya of thought."

Barnevelt told of the journey of himself and Tangaloa—alias Tagdë of Vyutr, another Nyamë—down the Pichidé River to bustling Majbur, thence by bishtar-train to the raffish port of Jazmurian, and thence by stagecoach to Ghulindé. He told of the disturbance in the inn at Jazmurian, when his mysterious enemy Vizqash, the same who had tried to have him waylaid at Novorecife and picked a quarrel with Barnevelt's roommate Sishen, a reptilian native of the planet Osiris and, so far as Barnevelt could tell, a harmless tourist.

He also told of the attempt to ambush him on the road to Ghulindé. He spoke slowly so as not to let slip some detail that would expose him as, not Snyol of Pleshch, but Dirk Barnevelt. Naturally he said nothing about his life on Earth, or about his early career as a high-school English teacher before he joined Igor Shtain, Limited; nor did he mention that he had come on this expedition partly to escape a domineering mother.

"No bellyache," he said at last. "So I guess these critters are safe. Here's your stick."

Sustained for the nonce by a meal of insubstantial sea food, they struggled westward all day. Although Barnevelt kept his eyes open for edibles, the forest of Rákh did not seem to provide many. Although he experimentally ate a few berries, he did not have the courage to try some loathsome-looking but possibly edible fungoid growths. A luscious-looking orange fruit turned out, when opened, to be all seeds and no pulp within. However, its hard, dry rind made a pair of usable drinking vessels.

By evening, the coast of Rákh had begun to trend northward so markedly that Barnevelt said, "Tomorrow, I guess, we'll have to strike inland if we're ever going to reach the Shaf-Malayer road."

"How will you find your way, once we part from the pilotage of this coast? For no mariner's needle have we."

"Steer by the sun, I guess. We'll keep it behind us in the morning and in front of us in the afternoon."

"And how for the midday, when life-giving Roqir stands stark overhead?"

"We shall have to spend that time resting and foraging. I never realized what hard work it is to be a food-gathering savage."

"True, dear speech-friend. Though were we natives of the wildwood, we should doubtless know of many edibles that in our urban ignorance we overlook."

"Like that," said Barnevelt, pointing to a many-legged thing that scuttled out of sight under a flat stone.

He had been watching for a stream. Presently they came upon one, which emptied into the Sadabao Sea a few meters from the base of a little sandy peninsula.

"Let's camp out on that," he said. "Then, if something comes at us, we shall at least get a look at it before it's upon us."

They made another skimpy meal. At the start of the journey on Rákh, Barnevelt had sworn to himself to keep his hands off Zei. Once they started lovemaking on the soft forest floor, the results would be what they had been for Atalanta and Meilanion;

and, while Barnevelt did not expect them to be turned into lions by some affronted deity, the results might be just as fatal in the long run. He was somewhat relieved to find that, between fatigue and ravenous hunger, his self-imposed abstinence was easier than he had feared.

Barnevelt found a tree that had died in youth, felled it, cut several lengths of firewood, and soon had his bow drill snoring away in its notch. His fire-making technique improved with practice, but he hoped that the weather would remain dry until they reached the road. He was hardly enough of an aboriginal to make fire by rubbing *wet* sticks together.

"We'd better take turns sleeping and watching," he said. "We were damned fools not to have done so last night."

At the end of his first spell of sleep, hunger and cold awoke Barnevelt. He looked up to see that Zei had fallen asleep, curled up against a rock. Tactfully, he said nothing but fed the fire and took up his watch.

He pondered a problem in logistics. This was: if they spent enough time foraging to furnish adequate meals, they would have no time left for hiking. If on the other hand they contented themselves with the few berries and safqa that could be gathered in a couple of hours' food-hunting, they would weaken day by day. Thus they would progress towards the road more and more slowly, until exhaustion felled them to die in the forest—perhaps only a bowshot from their goal.

If they could kill some larger beast, they could haul enough meat with them to keep them going. But how? In their progress they had from time to time started some smaller plant eater of the forest. But these animals, even when formidably horned or tusked, had always bolted. Barnevelt doubted that he could get close enough to one to use his sword. Even if he made a spear by lashing his dagger to a pole, that would not be much improvement. As for archery, Barnevelt did not even know which side of a bow the arrow is supposed to be shot from.

The hours passed; the stars wheeled overhead in glittering swarms. The three moons, now more widely spaced than ever, sank into the forest of Rákh. As the first light of dawn paled the eastern sky, Zei awoke.

"Why, you arrant treacher, not to awaken me for my proper stint!" she said, yawning. "I must have fallen into slumberland during my watch—for which odious recreancy you shall visit upon me punishment condign. What wouldst have of me?"

"If you'll . . ." He started to blurt out what he really wanted but thought better of it. *"Ulp.* One small kiss and we'll call it square."

She kissed him while he clasped his own hands together with knuckle-whitening force to keep from grabbing her. Then a sound brought her round. She screamed.

"A yeki!"

Barnevelt bounded to his feet, almost upsetting Zei into the fire. At the base of the little peninsula on which they camped, a great beast crouched. Although the light was too dim to make out details, Barnevelt had seen a yeki in the zoölogical park in Majbur and knew what they looked like.

Imagine a carnivore of the height and stoutness of a Terran tiger, but half again as long, with six relatively short legs. The head and paws could be compared either to those of an Earthly bear or, on a much expanded scale, a mink. Glossy short brown fur covered the beast.

The yeki, with its six short legs bent so that its belly almost scraped the ground, slunk forward like a cat stalking a bird. Barnevelt snatched a brand from the fire and threw it. He missed the yeki; but the beast leaped sidewise, snapped nervously, and grunted as the glowing billet whirled past its head. Then it resumed its stalk. Barnevelt's mind raced frantically as he threw another brand.

"Can they climb trees?" he panted.

"Nay—the cubs, perchance, but not the grown yekya. What . . .?"

"Keep throwing, and put more wood on the fire." Barnevelt snatched up the top of the young tree he had felled the previous

189

evening. The main shaft was a little taller than he was, with branches.

" 'Tis about to charge, O Snyol," said Zei.

"Keep throwing." Barnevelt, holding the treetop in his left hand, began lopping the branches with his sword: one swift slant-wise slash for each branch.

In a few seconds, he had a straight stem ending in an antlerlike cluster of branches, each cut off a foot or two from the trunk with a semi-sharp point.

"Now," he said, "see the big tree with branches near the ground?"

"Aye."

"We're going up it."

"How, when the fearsome beast obstructs our road?"

"You'll see. Take the axe and keep behind me."

Holding a blazing brand in his left hand and the trimmed treetop in his right, he stalked towards the yeki. The beast, not expecting its prey to advance upon it, gave back a step and reared up the part of its body in front of the middle pair of legs, snarling and roaring.

Barnevelt, tense as a drawn bow, thrust the treetop into the animal's face and waved his torch at it. It bawled, foamed, and batted at the cluster of prongs with one of its front paws.

"Get out! Scram!" yelled Barnevelt, thrusting again.

The beast moved sidewise like a crab, trying to get around the points. Barnevelt kept facing it, holding his torch out. Roaring terribly, the yeki gathered its legs for a spring; but Barnevelt advanced upon it and thrust for its eyes. It backed with a rippling motion, its hoarse bawling cries making the forest ring.

Inch by inch he worked around the beast. Each time it prepared to leap, he took the offensive and drove it back. At last he had himself between the yeki and the tree, and Zei between the tree and himself. He left off screaming at the yeki to bark at the girl, "Get up the tree! Quick!"

She obeyed. Following her, he backed up to the tree and threw the flaming stick at the yeki's head. The brand struck the beast on the nose and caused it to leap and snap wildly, slashing the air with its forepaws.

Barnevelt began to climb with one hand, still facing the yeki and holding out his whittled treetop. When he had gained the first few branches, he dropped his wooden weapon and scrambled up with both hands.

With a frightful roar, the yeki leaped in among the branches and reared its full height against the trunk. Barnevelt jerked his feet out of the way as its jaws clanged inches from his toes.

"Whew!" he said when he had gained a safe perch beside Zei. "Don't think I've ever been so scared in my life."

"My hero!" cried Zei, smothering him with kisses. "How can one so manifestly valiant even speak of fear?"

"You'd be surprised what goes on inside heroes, darling, even when they're rescuing maidens fair from monsters fell. How long is our friend yonder going to wait for us?" He indicated the yeki, sitting at the base of the tree and looking up with a hopeful expression.

"Until we weaken from hunger and thirst, or fall asleep, and so tumble into his ravening maw."

"We'll fool him. Tie yourself fast to one of the smaller branches with that rope around your waist. I told you they'd come in handy."

They secured themselves with the ropes and settled down to outwait the carnivore. The yeki seemed to be in no hurry.

Zei said, "Whence came the inspiration to trim that bit of tree into a spinous lance, wherewith to hold off the wrathful brute?"

Barnevelt chuckled. "In my country, men train beasts like that to do tricks in public shows. When such a yeki-tamer is in a cage with his beasts, he keeps a light chair handy to fend them off if they forget who's boss and attack him. They can't get past the feet of the legs and haven't sense enough to take the chair away from him. Well, when this fellow started for us, all I could think of was that I needed such a chair. Not seeing any kitchen chairs lying around, I improvised the next best thing."

Zei sighed. "The tales they tell of the prowess of General Snyol do not exaggerate. Tell me, have you a harem of voluptuous Nyami wenches at home, as do most men of mark, they say, in your far land?"

"Nope, not even one wench. I move around too fast."

Barnevelt gave the princess a sharp look. The old image arose in his mind, of a year of paradisiacal passion, followed by the attentions of the man wearing a hood with eyeholes and wielding an axe with an oversized blade.

She raised her brows and antennae at him. "Yet, from what I've seen, you do not find the female of the species unattractive."

"Depends on the female. If we had 'em like you in Nyamadzë, I'd have had a harem like Solomon's, long ago."

"Like whose?"

"An ancient king—never mind." He glanced down at the yeki, which showed no sign of abandoning its post. "I wonder if I could make a spear of my dagger and a pole after all and maybe spear him from above . . . No, I'm afraid it would only cost me my dagger and make him all the angrier."

For hours they sat on their perches, staring dully at the yeki, which stared back. Barnevelt dozed, woke, and dozed again, dreaming of steaks. Then a new smell prickled his nostrils.

"There's that which may yet put the monster to rout," said Zei, pointing.

"Oh-oh!" said Barnevelt, following her gesture with his eyes.

One of the flung brands had started a small fire in the undergrowth. A thin plume of blue smoke arose, and little flames danced with a faint pop and crackle.

"It may put him to rout, but it may also grill us," said Barnevelt.

The yeki, too, became aware of the fire. The big brown head swiveled from the pair in the tree towards the blaze and back again. The animal moved about uneasily, once rearing its height against the tree as if to make sure that its victims were indeed beyond reach.

The fire grew. A bush caught and went up in a sudden **floomp** and a flare of flame. Burning leaves fluttered up and spiraled down again to the forest floor.

The yeki prowled around the tree, stopping betimes to look at the fire, its nostrils quivering at the dreaded scent. At last, with a grunt of disgust, the beast trotted off through the woods.

"Better wait a minute," said Barnevelt, untying the rope that secured him.

"But the fire . . ."

"I know, darling. But we don't want Oscar charging back to snatch us just as we reach the ground"

He peered through the curtain of leaves. All was silent save for the sigh of the surf and the growing sound of the fire. "Okay, turn out the fire brigade. You fetch water in those cups while I beat the fire."

"Wherefore would you extinguish this blithesome blaze? Methinks 'twere useful, to rout any other unfriendly beasts that lurk nearby."

"Because that's what you do with a forest fire—put it out."

"But on Fossanderan . . ."

"For the gods' sake stop talking and get going with that water! I'll explain later. If an east wind sprang up, we'd be fried."

He beat at the fire with a heavy stick and stamped on it. The amount of water that Zei was able to bring each time from the sea, a few meters away, seemed absurdly small. But little by little they gained the upper hand.

An hour later, grimed and blackened, Barnevelt declared the fire out. After a bath in the Sadabao Sea and another breakfast of shellfish, they struck out again for the west, leaving the coast and steering by the sun.

Three days later, in the early afternoon, Barnevelt and Zei came out of the forest of Rákh beside the Shaf-Malayer road. Both were gaunt, dirty, worn-looking, and shabby. Zei carried a spear, which Barnevelt had made by lashing the hilt of his dagger to a pole, in case they met another yeki. But, having assembled the weapon, they had no occasion to use it.

Barnevelt sighed. "I suppose we ought to start hiking north, but let's sit here a while and hope to catch a ride."

He tossed his axe on the ground and sat down heavily with his back to a tree. Zei dropped down beside him and laid her head on his shoulder. He said, "Let's see the rest of those berries."

She handed over her seaman's cap, which she had been using as a bag. Barnevelt started fishing out berries, feeding them alternately to her and to himself.

He looked hard at one and threw it away, saying, "That's the kind that gave us a bellyache. Can't you just imagine the meals we'll have when we get to town?"

"Aye, verily! A fine roast unha, with tabids on the side, and a tunest in its mouth. The platter swimming in betuné sauce."

"And a bunch of those yellow what-d'you-call-'ems for dessert, and a big mug of falat wine . . ."

"Not the falat of Mishdakh, which is thin stuff, but that of Hojur, especially that of the year of the yeki . . ."

"Don't talk to me about yekis! I've seen all I want of them. We'll also have a loaf of badr, to sop up what's left . . ."

She raised her head. "What a blade! Here you sit, with a most royal maiden all but lying in your arms, and all you think upon's your beastly stomach!"

"Just as well for you."

"How mean you?"

"There's no guardian of virtue like starvation. If I had my strength you wouldn't be a maiden long."

"Braggart! Your thoughts would still center upon aliment. Oh, I saw the repasts you consumed aboard the *Shambor* and knew your nation's gluttonous reputation were but a pallid plantom of the fact."

"It's a cold country," he said.

"But you're not cold now!"

"And at least we eat normal wholesome food, and not our husbands."

"The kashyó's no feast, dolt, but a solemn ceremony . . ."

"I've heard that before, and I still think it puts you on a level with the tailed men of Fossanderan."

"Insolent carper!" she cried, and slapped him—gently, to show it was in fun.

"And," he continued, "I don't see how your royal line perpetuates itself if every time the consort finds the queen looking at him he wonders if it's the love light in her eyes or whether she's picking out a nice chop. That sort of thing must be unmanning."

"Perchance our men are less readily unmanned than those of your chill abode. A Qiribu on the verge of death retains his gallantry, whereas if you put a Nyamë on berries and shellfish for three days . . ."

"Four!"

"Four days, he's blind insensible to aught but food."

"Foof! You were imagining just as big a meal as I was."

"I was not! The repast of your fancy overtopped mine as the Zogha overshadows Mount Sabushi."

"How d'you expect to prove that?"

"A princess royal has no need to put matters to proof. Her word alone is adequate."

"Is that so? Then you'd better learn some new customs."

"Such as that Earthly usage called 'kissing,' wherein you've schooled me? Methinks I need more practice at this sport . . ."

After a while, Barnevelt said, "I'm afraid I'm not so near starvation as I thought."

"So? Seek not to violate the ancient customs of Qirib, or you shall learn the rough-and-tumble methods taught by our lanistae in the maiden warriors' palaestra. . . . Are you perchance carrying a gvám stone in your pocket?"

Barnevelt shifted his position. "No, I'm relying entirely on my native charm. Anyway, I doubt that such a stone really gives a man power over women, as the janrú does in reverse. Sounds like wishful thinking."

"Yet you abet this superstition by hunting the sea monster for its stones."

"Who am I to upset age-old beliefs? I had enough trouble back in Nyamadzë, as a result of trying to enlighten people about some plain and obvious facts. But speaking of your women warriors, I hope this experience has convinced you that manning an army with women—if you can man something with a woman—isn't practical."

"And what's the cause of that?" she asked.

"Because the men are bigger. If this were that planet where the females are ten times the size of the males, it would be different."

" 'Twas most unfair of Varzai this disparity to establish."

"Sure, if you must blame the gods."

"If not the gods, then whom?"

"That depends on what you believe about such matters."

"Do you not take the gods seriously?"

"No. I think things just happen."

"No wonder the Kangandites sought for heresy to slay you!"

"No wonder at all. But still, it's a wonder Qirib hasn't been swallowed up by some powerful neighbor, with that set-up."

"Our queens have averted war by a diplomacy of marvelous subtlety, using our mineral wealth to play one foe against another."

"Fine, but eventually some tough guy says, 'Fight or give up!' and that's all the choice you have."

"Do you present *me* with these grim alternatives, O scoffing nihilist, fear not but that I'll fight."

"Oh, no. I'd use that marvelous subtlety you were talking about to gain my ends. As for instance . . ."

"Malapert!" she said when she could speak again. "Could you not remain at Ghulindé to play this gladsome game with me forever?"

"Unh? That depends."

"On what? Another, I command—"

"If your mother abdicates, your consort mightn't like it."

"He'd have nought to say. My word were law."

"Still, it might be considered pretty familiar," he said.

"Well then, could you not teach the wight? Or better yet, become my first consort yourself?"

"Good gods, no! You don't think I want to end up on your sacrificial stove, do you?"

She looked surprised and a little hurt. " 'Tis an honor many would envy you. Art afraid?"

"Damn right! I like you fine, but not that much."

"Oh? Plain blunt fellows, Nyamen."

"Anyway I'm not eligible."

"That could be arranged," she said.

"And I thought your consorts were picked by lot."

"That, too, were no obstacle insurmountable. All's not what it seems in the drawing of the sort."

"So I've heard. But I still don't intend to spend a year as a lady's pup-eshun and then be killed. Can you imagine your hero Qarar doing such a thing?"

"N-nay, but . . ."

"It reminds me too much of a bug in my country called a mantis, of which the female eats the male during coiture."

Her eyes filled with tears. "You said you liked me, and we're really of one kind, you and I, despite our seeming differences exterior."

"So I do." He took time off to demonstrate the new game. "Oh, hell, I'm madly in love with you. But . . ."

"I love you too."

"As a man or as a steak? Unh!" She had punched him sharply in the short ribs.

"As a man, fool," she said. "At least a putative one, for the proof definitive has yet to be submitted."

"Well, that's something. And don't make cracks about my self-restraint, or I'm likely . . ."

"Hold, perchance there's a way out. Know you the agitation of the Party of Reform, to convert the execution to mere symbolism? Well, having seen a greater portion of the world and having heard the irreverent talk of yourself and other skeptics, I'm not so sure as once I was that the Divine Mother in fact demands this sacrifice."

"You mean you want to adopt the Reformers' program when you come to power?"

"Why not? Then you'd have no dire doom to dread."

"No," said Barnevelt firmly. "Look, sweetheart. In the first place your mother'll keep on running things, as you said yourself, even after she's abdicated, and I don't think she'd stand for such monkeying with custom."

"But . . ."

He placed a hand firmly over her mouth. "In the second, when I love a girl I want her permanently and not on a one-year lease. The idea of watching a parade of successors doesn't—ouch! You little devil, are you sneaking a snack in advance to see how I taste?"

"Nay, you mass of string and bone! I did but nip you gently to remind you that I, too, must breathe to live and cannot with that great hand clamped upon my countenance. As for your theories of love and life, that's a view extraordinary for a wandering adventurer. Most such, I've heard, prefer a short hot love and a speedy departure."

"I'm different. In the third place I intend to damn well be the boss and not one of your Qiribo househusbands. Which lets out your whole matriarchal system."

"If the women be housewives in the barbarian nations, why in equity should not the men be househusbands with us?"

"No reason at all, darling. If they put up with it that's their business. But I will not. Nor will I stand for being doped with that janrú drug."

"I'd swear by the six breasts of Varzai never to use it on you."

"How could I be sure of that? No, my dear, I'm afraid . . ."

Barnevelt sighed unhappily, for he now saw what showing his genuine fondness for Zei was getting him into. The real reason for his adamant refusal was the fact that they were of two different species. Yet, with Tangaloa in the clink, Shtain unrescued, and the Cosmic contract unfulfilled, he did not yet dare admit his Earthly origin, knowing the parochial prejudices of many Krishnans. Still, her nearness filled him with desire.

"What then?" she asked with a dangerous gleam in her eyes. "To what extent must one of my proud lineage abase herself before you?"

"You'll have to let me think," he stalled.

"You slippery equivocator!" She jumped up, gave him a sharp kick in the thigh, and started off. "The bigger fool am I, so to cozen me have let you! Here, sir, part our ways for good. I'll to

Ghulindé alone."

She started walking briskly northward along the road.

Barnevelt watched her straight receding back with mixed feel-ings. On one hand he should be glad she'd broken off this dan-gerous and unprofitable game. On the other he was horrified to hear his softer self call, "Come back, sweetheart! Let's not fight. How will you manage without money?"

She kept on. In a few seconds she would be out of sight around the next bend.

At the last minute, he put his hands over his mouth and im-itated the grunt of a hunting yeki. He did not really expect it to work and was all the more surprised when Zei jumped into the air with a cry of alarm, dashed back to him and flung herself into his arms.

"There, there," he said. "You needn't be afraid with me around. Let's sit down again and take it easy."

"Concerning our future relationship, my love . . ." she began.

Barnevelt laid a finger on her lips, saying, "I said I should have to think about it, and I meant that."

"I insist. . . ."

"Darling, you've got to learn in dealing with men from outside Qirib that they won't stand for your insisting. I have decided we won't talk about that subject for a while."

"Oh," she said in a small voice.

"Besides, when we're practically starved to death is not time to make vital decisions."

"Food again!" she cried, her irrepressible good humor fully recovered. "Said I not all Nyamen were gluttons? And now back to our game . . ."

Starvation or no starvation, Barnevelt thought, it was just as well for the ancient customs of Qirib that a few minutes later a shaihan cart, headed north, creaked up the road. Instantly he and Zei were on their feet thumbing. The driver spat and halted his animal.

"Clamber aboard, sir and madam," he said. " 'Tis long since the Mejrou Qurardena has honored my poor slow vehicle with a commission, but your uniform is credential enough for me."

Barnevelt had almost forgotten that he still wore the express-man's suit. No doubt the owner of the cart would bill the company for his mileage, whereupon a clamor would arise; but that was the least of Dirk Barnevelt's worries right now.

The stagecoach to which they had changed in Alvid stopped at the border between Suruskand to the south and Qirib to the north. On the Qiribo side of the line was the usual Amazon guard, the usual inspection, and the usual warning that Barnevelt's sword would have to be wired up in accordance with Qiribo law.

"And now," said the customs inspector while a guard went to fetch the wire kit, "Your names?"

Barnevelt had not given the question of identification a thought. Therefore he simply answered, "I'm Snyol of Pleshch, and this young lady is Zei bab-Alvandi . . ."

"What?" cried the inspector, her voice leaping an octave. "So she is! Your Altitude!" The inspector knelt. "We were com-manded to watch for you."

Barnevelt started to say, "Oh, let's not make a fuss . . ." but the Amazon continued:

"Girls! *The princess is saved!* Light a fire in the smoke box to send a signal message to the capital! But Your Preëminencies cannot continue on a vulgar noisome common carrier! Our dis-patch coach is at your service, and I myself will escort you. De-scend, I pray. Your baggage? None? What ignominy you must have suffered! Girls, hitch up the carriage. Saddle up—let's see—five ayá. Vaznui, you shall command the post till my return. Rouse the second watch from their slothful beds and bid 'em don parade uniforms, with boot and lance for escort duty. . . ."

Half an hour later, Barnevelt found himself speeding toward Shaf in the back seat of the official barouche, with the top down,

Zei beside him, and the customs inspector, her knees touching theirs, facing them from the front seat. The vehicle had a plain black-lacquered body with the royal arms in gold on the doors. A mere male drove the two oversized ayá, while the five customs guards, resplendent in purple and gilded brass, galloped before and behind. To clear the road when they approached a settlement, the leader of these blew a shrill little silver trumpet.

Although this was both faster and less smelly than the public tallyho they had just quitted, Barnevelt was not altogether pleased by the change, for his intimacy with Zei was now cut off. Besides, the accouterments of the escort clattered so that one had to shout to be heard, and on the dry stretches one had to breathe the clouds of dust the hooves of those in front stirred up. Finally, Barnevelt, had no escape from the chatter of the inspector, a gushy female. She garruled on about the gloom that had descended upon the realm with Zei's disappearance and the unbounded joy that would now reign . . .

At Shaf, however, Barnevelt observed that most of the people went about their own immediate business as if that were much more interesting than the vicissitudes of royalty.

By frequent changes of teams they kept up their headlong pace, save when a rain slowed them during the afternoon. The second day after passing the frontier saw them winding along the road on the north shore of the Qiribo peninsula, the same road on which the emissaries of the Moryá Sunqaruma under Gavao had ambushed Barnevelt and Tangaloa on their first approach to Ghulindé. This time, however, there was no interference. To the left crawled the emerald waters of Bajjai Bay; to the right rose the shaggy peaks of the Zogha.

Roqir was descending behind them when they came in sight of the capital of Qirib. Barnevelt had not seen Ghulindé from this angle, whence the colossal image of the god Qunjar showed his profile, brooding over the spired city on his knees like an overstuffed Buddha with a birthday cake in his lap.

To the left and lower lay the harbor of Damovang. As it came clearly into view, Barnevelt saw the harbor was crammed with shipping. Moreover, most of the ships were war galleys, making

a much larger fleet than the modest navy he knew Qirib to possess.

"What's all that?" he asked the customs inspector.

"Know you not? Of course, I'm a witless wench, how could you? 'Tis the combined fleet of the powers of the Sadabao Sea, which our magnificent monarch seeks to plat into a firm alliance for the extirpation of the scoundrels who've so grievously affronted us. She does but wait to be sure of the fate of my lady princess ere setting her martial machine into motion. Yonder lie the battleships of Majbur, of Zamba, of Darya, and of other powers of the western Sadabao. Never since Dezful the Golden reigned in riotous ribaldry in Ulvanagh has the sea groaned beneath such armament."

"What kind of ship is that?" asked Barnevelt, pointing. "The galley with a roof."

The ship in question did indeed look like an enormous galley with a flat roof over it.

The inspector giggled and said, "It is a ship of Prince Ferrian of Sotaspé, who's ever dazzling the world with some new thing. One of his subjects has invented a glider of novel design, differing from other gliders in that 'tis propelled through the empyrean by engines pyrotechnic. This galley is adapted to bear a score of such devices on its roof, wherewith, 'tis said, he hopes to assail these pirates in their swampy home by flying over them and lapidating them with missiles."

Thinking back, Barnevelt remembered pictures of a type of Earthly ship called the aircraft carrier, which dominated naval warfare in the twentieth century between the decline of the big-gun steam-driven ironclad battleship and the rise of the atomic-powered guided-missile ship. An aircraft-carrying galley, however, was a combination to stagger the imagination.

"But hold," said the inspector, "we must make arrangements for your arrival."

She called to the leading customs guard and gave her instructions to gallop on to the palace while the coach dawdled to give the queen time to get organized.

Thus, when the barouche drew up in front of the palace, all the elements of a royal reception were present: Amazons with lances presented, trumpeters blowing flourishes, and the royalty of Qirib and its neighbors drawn up on the steps in glittering array.

As Barnevelt glanced at his scarecrow garb, his old shyness rose up and (he was sure) made his knees shake visibly. He'd hardly cut a fine figure before the gilded highnesses on the steps. But then, he thought with a faint grin, maybe that was just as well. In the weatherbeaten expressman's suit and the battered and blackened silver helmet, nobody could overlook him. He braced himself, helped Zei down from the vehicle, and swept her up the steps.

Ta-raa went the trumpets. Barnevelt almost glanced over his shoulder to see if there wasn't a movie camera on a boom dolly hovering behind him, so cinematogenic was the scene. Then he remembered the camera on his own finger, and pressed the stud as he advanced toward the queen. A few paces from Queen Alvandi in the front rank, George Tangaloa flashed him a wink, while moving his fist in a way that showed that he, too, was filming the performance.

Barnevelt knelt to the queen while the latter embraced her daughter, then rose at the sound of Alvandi's stentorian voice:

". . . inasmuch as our state, inaccord with its divinely ordained institutions, does not possess an order of knighthood, I cannot confer it on you as a token of the favor and esteem in which I hold you, General Snyol. I do however hereby confer upon you honorary citizenship in the Monarchy of Qirib, with full rights appertaining not only to the male but to the female as well—together with a draft upon our treasury for fifty thousand karda.

"Now let me present you to these lords and princes gathered here. Ferrian bad-Arjanaq, Prince Regent of Sotaspé. King Rostamb of Ulvanagh. President Kangavir of Suruskand. Sofkar bad-Herg, Dasht of Darya. Grand Master Juvain of the Order of the Knights of Qarar of Mikardand. King Penjird the Second of Zamba . . ."

Having tucked the draft into his jacket, Barnevelt tried to impress on his memory the long roll of names and faces. The first Krishnan whose thumb he grasped, the famous Prince Ferrian, proved a youngish-looking fellow of middle height, slim, swarthy, and intense-looking, wearing a cuirass of overlapping plates, of black-oxidized steel damascened with gold. Next came Rostamb of Ulvanagh, big, burly, and wearing a straggly caricature of a beard, who looked at Barnevelt with dour intentness. After that, however, the unfamiliar names and faces merged into one big confusion in his mind.

The queen was speaking again, "Where's Zakkomir, Master Snyol?"

"I don't know, Your Altitude, but I fear the worst. We got separated while they were chasing us in the Sunqar."

"A woeful loss, but we'll keep hope for the nonce. Let's within, to restore your tissues before the banquet."

Banquet? Barnevelt feared there'd be speeches, and after all his narrow escapes from death it would catch up with him in the form of acute boredom.

They filed into the palace and were passed mugs of spiced kvad. Barnevelt had his thumb wrung by admirers until he thought it would come off. He could not get near Zei who, still in her seagoing rig, was surrounded by the gilded youth of the land packed four deep.

The President of Suruskand, a stout little party in horn-rimmed spectacles and vermilion toga, astonished Barnevelt by producing a little native notebook and a pen-and-inkwell set from the folds of his garment, saying, "General Snyol, since my elevation has my eldest chick besought me to exploit my station to gather for him autographs of the great. So, sir, if you'd not mind posing your signature hereon. . . ."

Barnevelt laboriously indited a series of Gozashtandou curleycues upon the proffered sheet.

President Kangavir looked at the result. "Whilst I hesitate to plague you further, sir, could you be so generous as to add thereto your signature in your native tongue?"

Barnevelt gulped, for he did not know how to write Nyami. After staring blankly for a few long seconds, he scrawled "Snyol of Pleshch" in ordinary English longhand. Luckily, the little president seemed to see nothing amiss.

"Excuse me, Your Beneficence," said Barnevelt and tore himself away. Since Zei had disappeared, he went over to speak to Tangaloa, who was quietly swilling his drink and waiting.

The big brown man was as stout and jovial as ever. Wringing Barnevelt's hand, the xenologist said, "My God, cobber, but you resemble a swagman!"

"You would, too, if you'd been with us. When did she let you out of pokey?"

"As soon as she got word by that smoke-telegraph thing that you and the sheila were safe."

"How's your arm?"

"Nearly as good as new. But you're the lad with things to yarn about. Let's have the dinkum oil."

Barnevelt gave a synopsis of his adventures. ". . . so we can

205

take it as proved that this Osirian, Sheafasè, is the boss of the buccaneers. Further, he's put Igor under Osirian pseudohypnosis, so that our cream of the Muscovite team doesn't know who he is any more. It was only those silver helmets that saved Zakkomir and me from the same fate."

Tangaloa clucked. "That'll complicate our efforts to rescue him, but I daresay something will turn up. Go on."

When Barnevelt told of setting fire to Fossanderan, he was surprised to see Tangaloa's good-humored face take on a look of stern disapproval.

"What's the matter?" said Barnevelt.

"That was a hang of a thing to do! Think of all the good timber you destroyed! On Earth we have to watch every stick of it. And what happened to the tailed men?"

"How should I know? Maybe they got roasted. Maybe they swam over to the mainland on the other side. What about them?"

"Why, there's a whole culture group that has never been investigated! They sound like the same species as those of Koloft and Zá, but the culture may be quite different. These groups are all enclaves of the tailed species that were left when the tailless Krishnans overran the country thousands of years ago. Perhaps our hosts here derived their cannibalism from the tailed aborigines they displaced. Oh, there are all sorts of possibilities—or there were until you burned the evidence. How could you, Dirk?"

"Jeepers!" cried Barnevelt. "What the hell d'you expect me to do, let these bloody savages eat me so you can come along later with your little notebook to study 'em?"

"No, but . . ."

"Well, it was them or us. As for the trees, Krishna's only got a small fraction of Earth's population, with three or four times the land area, so we needn't worry about its natural resources yet. Tailed men, foof!"

"You don't understand preliterates," said Tangaloa in his lecture-platform manner. "Usually this savagery, as people call it, is merely a protective reaction to the treatment they've had from so-called civilized folk. It was that way four hundred years ago with my own people in the Pacific. A shipload of Europeans would land to rob and murder and kidnap, and the next boat-load wondered why they were speared and eaten as soon as they came ashore. Probably those Fossanderaners had been raided by slavers . . ."

"So what? What could I have done?"

"You could have told 'em . . ."

"I don't speak their language and, even if I had, those bleeps would have whonked me first and asked questions afterwards. Matter of fact, that's what they did to poor old Chask."

"But when I think of the scientific data going to waste . . ."

"If there are any left when we finish our job, you can go down to Fossanderan and interview them in the most enlightened an-thropological style while they stew you in the tribal cauldron."

"A popular superstition. If a tribe is advanced enough to make cauldrons, they're beyond cannibalism. What happened next?"

Barnevelt told the tale of their adventures in the forest of Rákh. "The only thing that saved us," he said, "was stumbling on a cache of eggs. Four big ones. I don't know which of the local critters laid 'em. Anyway, mama was away from the nest, so we scooped up the eggs and legged it."

"How'd you cook them?"

"Set them on the ground beside the fire and turned them every few seconds. Turned out all right—they must have been freshly laid. Otherwise the yekya would be gnawing our bones in the somber forest of Rákh."

"Oh, nonsense, cobber, don't make such a big thing of it! A healthy young couple like you and the princess could have gone for weeks without food before you collapsed. We did on Thor, when they thought we'd stolen their sacred pie and we had to shoot our way out. We didn't even have shellfish and berries, let alone eggs to eat." Tangaloa looked down at his paunch. "I was actually slender when we'd finished that stroll. And, by the bye, how much film did you get?"

"Not enough. We were in the Sunqar only overnight, and after we got away I hardly gave the Hayashi a thought until now. The forest was mostly too dark anyway. I have some exposed rolls in my pocket, if the water hasn't gotten into the capsules. But what'll

207

we do about Igor? He'll have to be taken by force."

"That will take care of itself," grinned Tangaloa.

"How d'you mean?" said Barnevelt uneasily.

"The queen is pushing you for commander-in-chief of this expedition against the pirates."

"*Me*? Why me?"

"Because you're a famous general, if you've forgotten. As you're from a distant country, she figures these temperamental skites might agree on you when they wouldn't let one of their own group lord it over the rest. Penjird is jealous of Ferrian, Ferrian is jealous of Rostamb, and Rostamb is jealous of everybody."

"But I'm no admiral. I couldn't even keep control of the crew of a little fourteen-oared smuggler."

"They'll never know that if you don't tell 'em. Here they have been beating their brains out to think of a way through the sea vine, and you've solved it."

"You mean my skis? Maybe . . ."

Barnevelt hesitated. On one hand, the expedition would furnish a good excuse to get clear of Qirib before he fell so deeply in love with Zei that his will power could no longer extricate him. Besides, something had to be done about Igor Shtain and the Cosmic Features contract. On the other hand, his old shyness filled him with dread at having to stand up in front of hordes of strangers and shoulder vast responsibilities to which he was unequal.

"Of course it is all nonsense," said Tangaloa. "If Castanhoso had given me the name he gave you, I should have been chosen admiralissimo instead of you. As it is, having no military ambitions, I will happily shoot film while you wrestle with logistics."

The flash of jewels in the gaslight caught Barnevelt's eye. Here came Zei, freshly scrubbed and waved, in gauzy tunic and glittering tiara, dodging through a scrimmage of painted youths towards himself and George. Barnevelt whistled his admiration and quoted:

"Let never maiden think, however fair,
    She is not fairer in new clothes than old!"

"What's that, my lord?" she asked, and he translated. "A Nyami poet named Tennyson," he added.

She turned to Tangaloa. "Does he narrate our adventures, Master Tagdë? The telling could never in a millennium do justice to the doing, for compared to our struggles were the Nine Labors of Qarar as nought. Has he told you of the time, after we attained the mainland, when we were treed by a yeki? Or again how, after his lighter broke down, he made a fire by rubbing sticks together?"

"No—did you?" asked Tangaloa.

"Yes. The Boy Scout handbooks are right. It can be done if you have dry wood and the patience of Job. But I don't advise . . ."

"What's a boskat ambuk?" asked Zei.

"A Boy Scout Handbook?" said Tangaloa. "The national encyclopedia of Nyamadzë. Did you make a bow-and-arrow, Snyol?"

"No. I suppose I could have in a month, with nothing else to do, and a couple more months to learn to shoot it. But we'd have starved to death. There's nothing to eat on that damned peninsula except berries and nuts and the creeping things we found under stones along the shore." Barnevelt shuddered reminiscently. "And at that we had to take only a tiny taste of each kind of thing at first to find out which were poisonous." He glanced at the clepsydra on the wall. "I'd better get washed and dressed:

"The Bird of Time has but a little way
    To flutter—and the Bird is on the Wing."

As guest of honor, Barnevelt had the seat on the queen's right, with Zei on her left looking like one of the gauzier Greek goddesses. The rest of the company ranged in a crescent, jewels gleaming in the gaslight.

There were speeches, as Barnevelt had feared: one dignitary after another getting up and—often in a dialect Barnevelt could hardly understand—saying nothing with all the eloquence and elegance at his command. As Admiral Somebody from Gozashtand launched into his speech, the queen spoke to Barnevelt in a whisper that must have carried to the kitchen.

"I'll break this up early, so that the council meeting shall be started. Dost know that the staff of command's to be thrust into your grip tonight?"

Barnevelt gave a polite but inarticulate murmur, and said, "Is there anything you want me to do to clinch it?"

"Just keep your big sack of a mouth tightly shut and allow me to manage the matter," the queen replied graciously.

After the banqueters had been dismissed, the council meeting assembled in a smaller chamber of the palace. There were about a dozen present: all head men and high military officers of the neighboring states.

First the Gozashtando admiral, in a long speech, gracefully explained why his imperial master, King Eqrar, could not join the alliance because he was in the midst of negotiating a treaty with Dur, and—ahem—everybody knew what that meant.

"It means your royal niggard will endure piracy and pilferage rather than sacrifice some piddling commercial advantage," said the queen, "Whereas if he could see beyond that beak of his he'd know he stands to lose tenfold as much from unchecked lawlessness. Unless in plain poltroonery he fears Dur'll assault him for clipping their furacious friends' claws."

"Madam," said the admiral, "I cannot permit such contumelious gibes towards my master to pass unrebuked . . ."

"Sit down and shut up, or take the road back to your craven king!" yelled Alvandi. "This is a meeting of warriors, not of palsied recreants! Whilst we face the foe with what we have undaunted, he sits on his fat podex in Hershid with more force at his command than all of us together, but trembling in terror lest a bold move cost him half a kard. He makes me sick."

The admiral gathered up his papers, bowed stiffly, and walked out without a word. When he had gone, Prince Ferrian flashed the queen a sardonic grin.

"That's drubbing the old runagate!" he said. "No wonder the women rule in Qirib. Of course, had we frontiers in common with Dur, as has Eqrar of Gozashtand, well might we sing a less temerarious tune. Howsomever, let's to business."

"Right are you," said Alvandi. "Here upon my right sits he of whom I told you—the hero who has penetrated to the Sunqar's heart and lived to tell the tale. General Snyol, tell these lords in brief how you rescued my daughter."

Barnevelt gave a condensed account up to the incident of the improvised skis, then asked, "Do you know what skis are?"

All looked blank save Ferrian, who said, "I do. We had a Nyamë in our island last year who showed us how to shape boards for walking on soft stuff. Having none of that strange frozen rain called 'snow' in sunny Sotaspé, we coated a hill with fine wet clay and slid adown it. I blacked an eye and bent an ankle so that for a week I walked on crutches, though the sport was worth it. Is that how you escaped? By striding over the terpahla on these contrivances?"

"Yes. You see I took some boards and whittled . . ."

"I see it all! We'll equip our entire battle with skids and send 'em forward over the vine, while the silly Sunqaruma look on in amaze, having thought themselves impregnable in their marine morass. I'll take the training and command of these troops, and tomorrow set all the carpenters in Ghulindé to carving skids."

"Nay!" cried King Penjird. "While we all know you for a man of impetus and soaring spirit, Ferrian, yet never shall you command my soldiers!"

"Nor mine," said Rostamb of Ulvanagh. "Who's this young rashling who'd upset the tried and proven principles of war? I was commanding soldiery ere he'd broke the shell of 's egg . . ."

"Quiet, sirs," said Queen Alvandi. "For this selfsame reason have I inveigled hither this ugly wight from far fantastic lands of cold and ice. His worth's already demonstrate, by his known repute in deeds of dought and by his recent solitary foray . . ."

L. SPRAGUE DE CAMP

"I care not," said Penjird of Zamba. "Be he a very Qarar returned to the mortal plane, yet shall he not command my men. They're mine, recruited, trained, and paid by me through all vicissitudes, and none but me they'd trust. I am who I am!"

"I crave pardon, lords," said the Chief Syndic of Majbur, whose plain brown suit contrasted with the gaudery around him.

He went on quietly, "Most of those here hold their authority by hereditary right or lifelong tenure. To accommodate yourselves to the interests and desires of other men is not your habitude. Yet, without a single head, an expedition such as ours is doomed to prove abortive, as those versed in the lore of war can readily confirm. Therefore, if we'd sink our shaft in the pupil of the shaihan's eye, must we all our independence compromise, as we who politick in states of rule elective learn to do habitually. And for that purpose, who could better leader be than this one—a man of force and craft from distant lands, having no local ties to sully his disinterest?"

"Right, old money-bags!" said Ferrian. "While I'd liefer lose a tooth than lessen my authority, yet do I yield to your logic's overriding force. Will you stand with me in this, Penjird my lad?"

"I know not. 'Tis without . . ."

"Not I!" roared Rostamb of Ulvanagh. "How know we Snyol of Pleshch has truly earned the reputation that is his? Tales shrink not in telling, and we know him but by rumor that has wafted halfway round the globe. How know that he'll prove impartial as contends our friend from Majbur? For some substantial time has he frequented Qirib's court, and how know we what secret offers or relations bind him to the douri's interest?" Rostamb looked hard at Zei. "For that matter, how know we he's the authentic Snyol of Pleshch? I should have thought the General Snyol an older man."

Qeen Alvandi whispered behind her hand to Barnevelt, "Tell the old *fastuk* you left your papers in Nyamadzë, and challenge him for unfaming you!"

"What? But I . . ."

"Do as I command! Challenge him!"

Barnevelt, unhappily realizing that who rides the tiger cannot dismount, rose and said, "My means of identification were left behind in my native country when I fled. However, if anybody wishes to press a charge of lying against me, I shall be glad to settle the question privately, as one gentleman to another."

With that he whacked the council table with his sword, making the ash trays dance. Rostamb growled and reached for his hilt.

"Guards!" shrilled the queen, and Amazons leaped into the room. "Disarm these twain! Know you two bibacious recusants not the law? 'Tis only in deference to your rank that we let you come armed within our purlieus at all, and any further swinish male brawling shall result in heads' bedizening the city wall, though they be royal ones. Be seated. My lord Ferrian, meseems your head's the levelest of those here. Continue your argument . . ."

For hours they went round and round. First it was only the queen, Prince Ferrian, and the Chief Syndic for Barnevelt. Then they won over the President of Suruskand, then Penjird of Zamba, and little by little the others until only Rostamb of Ulvanagh held out.

King Rostamb snarled, "You're all bewitched by that perfume the harridans of Qirib use to subjugate their miserable men. When I came hither I thought 'twould be a fair and open enterprise 'mongst comrades and equals, 'stead of which I find a most nefarious palpable swindle whereby Alvandi hopes to gain control not merely of the Sunqar as she does openly admit, but also of all of you, to impose upon your hapless lands her own perverse iniquitous dreams of female rule. To Hishkak with it! Before that, I'll see the bloody flag of the Sunqaruma flying over golden Ulvanagh. You'll see I'm right, sirs, and meantime I bid you good night."

Out he went, his bristly chin in the air. The impressiveness of his exit was impaired by the fact that, not watching where he was going, he tripped on a fold in a rug and fell flat on his face.

As a result of the delays that plague every large-scale operation, more than a ten-night passed before the skis were built, the men taught to use them, the organizational wrinkles smoothed out, and the expedition against the Moryá Sunqaruma squared away. Barnevelt, having deposited his reward from the queen with the banking firm of Ta'lun & Fosq, worried because the hurricane season in the Banjao Sea was drawing close. He found, however, that there was little he could do either to help or to hinder; the commanders under him went about their several tasks regardless.

He was, he thought, a figurehead, though a necessary one to keep the others from trying to boss one another and quarreling. Even at the job of resolving disagreements he found he could do better by delegating the task to George Tangaloa, whom he made his aide. For George with his linguistic fluency and unfailing good humor proved an ideal soft-soaper of wounded feelings and reconciler of divergent views.

One day Tangaloa said, "Dirk, I think we can stoush the Sunqaruma all right. But how the flopping hell are we to keep our troopers from doing in Igor Shtain along with the rest?"

Barnevelt thought. "I think I know. We'll take a leaf out of the pirates' own book. Have you still got that photograph of Igor I left with you when I went after Zei?"

"Yes."

Then Barnevelt went to the queen and said: "Your Altitude, there's an old photographer in Jazmurian . . ."

"I know the one, for but lately did the Artists' Guild of Jazmurian hale him into court on charges that he'd hired a band of bravoes to assail them in the streets, their competition to abate. But when the case came up it transpired that the bravoes were but a pair of travelers named Snyol of Pleshch and Tagdë of Vyutr—names possessing a familiar sound—who did nothing but resist this Guild's extortionate demands. So my judge dismissed the case with a warning to those overweening daubers. What about him?"

"He's a spy for the Sunqaruma, and I wish you'd have him arrested . . ."

"Arrested, forsooth! I'll have the blackguard boiled alive till the flesh sloughs from his bones! Be this his gratitude for our even-handed justice? I'll have his head sawn off with a jeweller's saw, a hair's breadth at a stroke! I'll . . ."

"Please, Queen! I have another use for him."

"Well?"

"There's an Earthman in the Sunqar I particularly want taken alive. . . ."

"Why?"

"Oh, he did me a bad turn once and I want to work him over little by little, for years. So I don't wish one of our soldiers to give him a quick death. Now, I want the old photographer allowed to keep his head and go scot-free in return for a piece of work—to reproduce a picture of this Earthman. He can have all the help and materials he needs, so long as he turns me out three thousand prints before we sail. Then I'll distribute them among the assault troops, with the word there's a five-thousand-kard reward for this Earthman alive, but none dead."

"You have strange ideas, Master Snyol, but it shall be as you desire."

On the appointed day, Barnevelt led those who were seeing him off to the deck of Majbur's *Junsar*, which he had selected as a flagship. (The queen had been surprised and disappointed, expecting him to choose her own *Douri Dejanai*. He persisted in his choice, however, to avoid any appearance of partiality. Besides, the *Junsar* was bigger.) Everybody came aboard to drink and chatter like any sailing party.

Barnevelt wanted a private good-bye with Zei, with whom he had hardly had a private word since their return to Ghulindé. However, for a long time both he and she were enmeshed in polite conversations with others. At last he took the shaihan by the horns, excused himself, and said, "Will you step in here a minute, Princess?"

He led her into his private cabin, stooping to avoid hitting his head on the cross-beams.

"Good-bye, darling," he said, and swept her into his arms.

When he released her she said, "You *must* come back, my dearest love. Life will otherwise be savorless. Surely we can come to some agreement to meet your stipulations. Why should I not make you paramour permanent, when I'm queen, to reign over my affections perennially whilst my wittol spouses come and go?"

" 'Fraid not. Don't tell anybody, but I'm really a very moral fellow."

"If that concordat suits you not, such is the burning passion in my liver that I'd cast away my royal rank to tramp the world with you, or plunge into the dread deeps of space whence come the exotic Terrans. For my secret hope has ever been to be mastered by a man of might and mettle such as you."

"Oh, come, I'm not that good . . ."

"There's none like unto you! Qarar, if indeed he lived and be no figment of a poet's fancy, were no stauncher hero. But say the word . . ."

"Now, now, stop crying. We'll settle that when I see you again." He neglected to add that, if his plans worked out, that time would never come.

Her praise made him uncomfortable, for he could not help a guilty feeling that much trouble, including the death of Chask, might have been avoided had he handled the *Shambor*'s crew more skillfully. Although he did love her (damn it all!) he still thought the course he planned the best for all. He hoped, once Shtain were secured and the film shot, to fade quietly out of the Krishnan landscape and return to Earth.

. He kissed her with a fervor that would have done credit to the great actor Roberto Kahn, dried her eyes, and led her back on deck. The party broke up, those who—like Prince Ferrian—were going along, to scatter to their own ships; those who—like King Penjird of Zamba—weren't, to go ashore. With flags flapping, bands blaring, fireworks fizzing, thousands waving from the docks of Damovang, oars thumping, and one of Ferrian's rocket gliders circling overhead, the combined armada filed out upon the smaragdine sea.

•

Again the hills of Fossanderan came into view, this time covered with black stumps like an unshaven chin seen under the microscope. Only away to the left, towards the eastern end of the island, did the greens and browns and mauves and purples of growing Krishnan vegetation persist.

Barnevelt, leaning against the forward rail of the Junsar, said, "George, pass the word we're putting in to the cove on the north shore of Fossanderan to top off our water. I don't want to be caught short again."

"If they make a stink about the demons?"

"Oh, foof! Remind 'em I'm the guy who cleaned up on the demons single-handed. Of course the water parties will need guards."

The fleet drew up along the north shore of the island and gathered water while hundreds of rowers went ashore to catch a few hours' sleep on solid ground after putting up with crampsome dozes on their benches since leaving Damovang. Of the tailed men there was no sign, and the story of Barnevelt's exploit

seemed to have killed much of the popular dread of the place.

When the leaders gathered aboard the *Junsar* for a conference, the Dasht of Darya asked, "Suppose these villains ask terms?"

"Heave their emissaries into the sea!" said Queen Alvandi.

"Not in accord with the practice of civilized nations . . ." began the Majburo admiral.

"Who cares? Who calls these sanguinary filchers civilized?"

"A moment, madam," said Prince Ferrian. "A proper moral tone is no small advantage to an enterprise like ours, sobeit it costs but little. Offer 'em, say I, terms they'll refuse. Like —say—their bare lives alone."

And so it was decided.

When the water had been replenished and the sleeping oarsmen roused, the fleet put forth again. Behind the leading *Junsar* plowed the grotesque shape of Ferrian's oared aircraft carrier, the *Kumanisht*. The catapult in the latter's bow whanged, hurling a rocket-glider into the air on a practice flight, to circle over the fleet and drift in over the tail of the flight deck, where the handling crew caught it.

As they rounded the eastern end of Fossanderan into the larger channel of Palindos Strait, Barnevelt touched Tangaloa's arm and pointed. A small group of tailed men were spear-fishing in the shallows. The instant they saw the *Junsar* they scampered back to shore, to disappear among the trees.

Tangaloa said, "I say, couldn't we stop long enough for me to interview them? I'll take a guard. . . ."

"No! If we win the war, maybe we can stop on the way back. . . . Yes?"

An officer had come up to report that Captain So-and-so had sprung a seam and asked permission to turn back.

"Zeus!" said Barnevelt. "That's the fourth or fifth that's aborted. We started out with plenty of margin, but Rostamb ratted on us, and at this rate we'll be tackling a larger force than our own."

"We inspected them at Damovang," said Tangaloa.

"Sure. I suspect some of 'em have been sabotaged by people who want to stay out of the fight. I'll go look at this sprung seam."

Barnevelt made his inspection, told the captain to caulk his leak with sailcloth, and returned to the *Junsar*. As they emerged from the Strait into the Banjao Sea, he detached a couple of empty cargo ships to sail straight for Malayer, fill up with food and water, and then rejoin the main fleet at the Sunqar. Then he resumed his former position, elbows on the forward rail, staring somberly over the sea.

"What makes you so gloomy?" said Tangaloa. "You weren't this way when you set out before, though you were running a worse risk."

"Oh, am I? It's not the fighting."

"What then?"

"Hollow, hollow, all delight."

"I know, you're in love!"

"Uh-huh," Barnevet admitted.

"Well, what's that to be sad about? I have always found it fun."

"I've said good-bye forever to her."

"Why?"

"She had the idea I'd make a good consort. And . . ." Barnevelt struck his neck with the edge of his hand.

"I had forgot that angle. It could have been arranged."

"It *was* arranged! That was what I objected to."

"No, no. I mean if you played your cards right you could overthrow the matriarchy and end the custom. It is not a really stable set-up, the one they have in Qirib."

"You mean because the males are bigger than the females, as among us?"

"Not exactly, though that helps. Ahem. I meant this female-dominated society didn't grow naturally, but was suddenly imposed upon a different culture pattern as a result of a couple of historical accidents. The people's basic cultural attitudes are still those of the surrounding Krishnan states, where the pattern is approximate sexual equality."

"I see. It is the little rift within the lute, that by and by will make the music mute."

"Precisely. Now in Nyamadzë, on the other hand, I understand that . . ."

"Haven't the people's—uh—basic cultural patterns changed since Queen Dejanai set up the matriarchate?"

"No. That will take centuries yet. You see, most people get their basic cultural attitudes before they reach school age and never change them thereafter. That is why on Earth there are still traces of racial hostility and discrimination in spots, after all the good-will propaganda and legal measures of the last few centuries. And apparently culture patterns are transmitted on Krishna in the same way. So if you want to break up this pattern of basilophagous gynecocracy before it hardens . . ."

"Of *what?*" said Barnevelt.

"Sorry, bod, I forgot this isn't a meeting of the Anthropological Association. This pattern of king-eating petticoat rule, I should have said, can be overthrown by a resolute man, and you will have all the advantages—an inside position, a hero's prestige. . . ."

Barnevelt shook his head. "I'm a quiet sort of guy and don't care for the fierce light which beats upon the throne and blackens every blot."

"Oh, nonsense, Dirk. You love leadership. I have been watching you."

"Well, I don't intend to put my head in that particular noose so long as the queen uses that Unbridled Lust perfume to keep the men subdued. Anyway there are my obligations to the firm."

"True—I'd forgot Igor Shtain, Limited. Couldn't you persuade the sheila to chuck her job? Then you wouldn't have to be consort."

"Matter of fact she's already offered to. She'd have gone back to Earth with me."

"For God's sake, why didn't you take her up on it?" said Tangaloa. "She's a bonzer little squid. I shouldn't mind a bit of a smoodge with her myself."

"She's Krishnan, dammit!"

"So what? Relations are possible despite—or is there some rule in *Deuteronomy* against it?"

"It's not that. We're not interfertile."

"So much the better. One need not worry about . . ."

"But that's not what I want!"

"You mean you want a lot of little Dirks running around? As if one were not enough?"

"Ayuh," said Barnevelt.

"A sentimental yearning for vicarious immortality, eh?"

"Not at all. I prefer a stable family life, and poor old sex alone won't give you that."

"Ha ha," said Tangaloa. "What was that thing you were quoting to Castanhoso about loathing the bright dishonor of her love? You're still full of irrational inhibitions, my boy. We Polynesians have found . . ."

"I know. Your system of progressive polygamy may be all right for you, but I'm not built that way. So no egg-laying princesses need apply."

"A bigoted, race-conscious attitude."

"I don't care, it's *my* attitude. Good thing this expedition came along to separate us, or I should never have had the will power to leave her."

"Oh, well, it's your life." Tangaloa wiped his forehead. "This is hotter than the Northern Territory of Australia in January."

"South wind," said Barnevelt. "It'll make it tough for us all the way to Sunqar."

"We ought to do like those blokes from Darya. As soon as we were out of Damovang Harbor they reverted to their native costume, a coat of grease, and now they just leave the grease off."

At last the Sunqar appeared again upon the hazy horizon. Barnevelt, beginning to feel as if he knew these waters well, gave the course for the northwest coast of the floating island, where lay the entrance to the pirate settlement.

A glider returned to the *Kumanisht* with word, passed on to the *Junsar* by flag signals, that a ship was coming out to meet them. The ship itself followed hard upon the word of its coming.

221

As she approached, she furled her sails and headed straight for the *Junsar,* both slowing until they rested motionless with bows almost touching. The green truce pennon flew from the pirate's mainmast.

"Who be ye and what do ye here?" came a rasping voice in the Qiribo dialect from the bow of the Sunqaro ship.

Barnevelt told the herald with the megaphone beside him: "Tell him we're the allied navies of the Sadabao Sea, come to clean out the Sunqar."

"Clean us out!" came the yell from the other ship. "We'll teach you . . ." the spokesman for the Moryá Sunqaruma mastered himself with an almost audible effort. "Have ye terms to present ere the hand play begins?"

"If you surrender we'll guarantee your lives, but nothing more—not your liberty or property."

"Very kind, ha ha! I go to carry your generous offer to our chiefs."

The Sunqaro galley backed oars until she was several lengths away before turning; her captain evidently did not care to expose his vulnerable side to a hostile ram at close quarters, truce or no truce. Then the pirate's oars thumped and splashed furiously as the ship raced for the entrance to the weed.

The *Junsar* started to follow at a leisurely pace to give the Sunqaruma a fair chance to consider the ultimatum. Then Barnevelt became aware of another rapid thumping on his left as Queen Alvandi's *Douri Dejanai* foamed past in pursuit of the pirate.

"Hey there!" Barnevelt called across the water. "Stay back in line!"

Back came the queen's hoarse bawl, "That's Gizil the Saddler who served as herald! I'll sink his ship and . . ."

"Who's Gizil the Saddler?"

"A saucy runagate from Qirib and a notorious fomenter of discontent among our males! We'd have hanged the losel but that when he heard there was a warrant out for him he fled. He shan't escape us this time!"

"Get back in line," said Barnevelt.

"But Gizil will escape!"

"Let him."

"That I'll not! Who think ye you are, to command the Queen of Qirib?"

"I'm your commander-in-chief, that's who. Now stop where you are, or by Qondyor's toenails I'll sink you myself!"

"You'd never dare! Faster, boys!"

"Oh, no?" Barnevelt turned to Tangaloa and said, "Pass the word: Full speed ahead—load the forward catapult—secure to ram."

Although the *Douri Dejanai* had drawn ahead of the *Junsar* during this exchange of unpleasantries, the larger ship soon overhauled the smaller.

Barnevelt said, "Fire one shot over her poop. Try not to hit anything."

Whang! went the catapult. The great arrow, as long as a man, screeched across the narrow space between the two ships. Barnevelt had intended to miss the queen by a comfortable margin. However, whether because the target was too tempting or because the motion of the ship affected the crew's aim, the point of the missile struck Alvandi's cloak, ripped the garment from her shoulders, and bore it fluttering far out into the sea, where missile and cloak disappeared with a single splash. The queen spun and sprawled on the deck. One of her Amazons rushed to help her up.

She stopped her ship's oars, then shook a fist at the *Junsar*. Barnevelt saw grins everywhere, for Queen Alvandi's high-handedness was notorious even in a fleet whose leaders included such uninhibited individualists as Prince Ferrian of Sotaspé. Thereafter there was no more disobedience to Barnevelt's orders.

Me and Napoleon! he thought. If they only knew who he really was . . .

As they neared the Sunqar, the patches of terpahla became commoner until they occasionally fouled an oar. Through a long brass Krishnan telescope, Barnevelt saw that the ship that had met them was the one that stood guard at the entrance. This ship had resumed her former position and was pulling the detached floating mass of terpahla into the mouth of the entrance. Meanwhile a longboat was rowing up the channel.

The Sunqaruma were standing on the defensive. Barnevelt passed the word: "Carry out Plan Two."

With much signaling and trumpeting, the fleet changed formation. Two groups of ships that had been modified from regular galleys to troop carriers by cutting down their oarage drew off on the flanks, while Barnevelt in the *Junsar* led the Majburo squadron straight for the plug that blocked the channel into the Sunqar.

The pirate galley still stood guard inside the channel, a tackle of ropes connecting her with the plug. Beyond her, other ships moved about the channel.

Barnevelt wondered if the Sunqaruma would try a further parley, but then the *Junsar's* captain pointed out to him the maroon war pennant flapping lazily from the mainmast head of the guard ship.

"There's your answer, my lord," said he.

An instant later a catapult thumped, and lead balls and feathered javelins began to arc across the intervening water. As these got closer they were accompanied by arrows and crossbow bolts. Under the *Junsar's* captain's directions, some men of the crew rigged a bulwark of shields around the bow so that Barnevelt and the others could watch more safely.

"Shall we shoot?" said the captain.

"Not so long as they're kind enough to do our ranging for us," said Barnevelt.

He swung his telescope, trying to see if the squadrons were following the plan, though with the haze that the warm wind had brought he could do almost as well with his naked eyes.

A missile plunked into the water between the *Junsar* and her starboard neighbor. "Shoot," said Barnevelt, and the catapults on the bows of the Majburo squadron went off.

Barnevelt knew that frustrated feeling that comes upon commanders-in-chief when they have given the last order they can expect to have obeyed with reasonable fidelity at the beginning of a battle. They want to make last-minute improvements in plans; but then it is too late, and the outcome must be left largely to common fighting men.

Things began to hit the bulwark of shields with resounding bangs. Aft, a crash and an outburst of yells told that the defenders' fire had gotten home.

Barnevelt, peering over his breastwork, found that only the plug of weed and a few meters of open water separated him from the galley that guarded the portal. This galley shot fast, things going overhead with a continuous swish and hum. Four Majburo galleys had come up to the plug and were shooting back, though being end-on they could only use their forward catapults, and there was not much room for archers to deploy on their forecastles.

Men scrambled down the bows of the attackers onto the rams with hooks and rakes, dug these into the terpahla, and pulled up streamers of the golden-brown slimy stuff with its purple floats. These they passed up to others above them in an effort to get a firm grip on the plug. In front of Barnevelt a man gaffing the sea vine was transfixed by a shaft and fell into the water. Another took his place.

A prolonged *swish* overhead made Barnevelt look up. It was one of Ferrian's gliders making a sweep over the enemy, its rockets leaving a trail of the yellow smoke of yasuvar powder. As it passed over the guardship, something like rain fell from it. Barnevelt knew that this was a handful of steel darts, of which Prince Ferrian had prepared great numbers for his aviators.

Another glider went on to the main settlement, where it dropped something. There was a burst of smoke and the sound of exploding fireworks, though Barnevelt could not see whether these pyrotechnics had done any real damage.

Bang! A leaden shot from a hostile catapult smashed through the bulwark, two shields away from Barnevelt, and went rolling along the forecastle like a bowling ball. A couple of men struggled to replace the broken shield. Below, other men were lying in the water among the vines. Barnevelt saw one of them jerk in a peculiar fashion and caught a flash of spotted hide. Drawn by the blood, the fondaqa or venomous eels were gathering.

A Majburo galley had belayed a number of strands of sea vine to its decks and began to back oars; but, as the tension increased, the vines broke one by one until none was left. Another glider hissed overhead. As it passed over the guardship, a spray of missiles reached up ineffectively for it.

"My lord Snyol!" cried the *Junsar*'s captain. "Here comes Prince Ferrian."

Barnevelt ran aft just as Ferrian, slim and swarthy, popped over the stern, the sun gleaming on his damascened armor. Below, the crew of the longboat that had rowed him over from the *Kumanisht* rested on their oars under the *Junsar*'s stern.

Ferrian took a few seconds to get his breath back, then said: "A strange fleet nears from the North, my lord. One of my fliers saw it from his height."

"What sort of fleet?"

"We know not yet, but I've dispatched another glider to see."

"Who's it likely to be? King Rostamb, ashamed of himself, come to help us?"

"All things are possible, but more likely 'tis the fleet of Dur, come to save their piratical friends."

Dur! Barnevelt had not thought of that possibility. Up forward, the racket of the fire fight with the Sunqaruma continued.

He said, "I'll go back to the *Kumanisht* with you to see about this. Carry on here," he told Tangaloa. "Send out a signal for the troopships not to disembark their ski troops until further notice."

It would hardly do, he thought as he climbed down the rope ladder into the longboat, to be attacked from the seaward side in the midst of that delicate operation.

Aboard the carrier he fidgeted on the flight deck, ducking out of the way during glider operations. Finally the glider that had been sent north to scout came back, drifting in with butterfly grace until seized by the deck crew.

The aviator climbed out, saying, "Another quarter-hour and I should have been in the sea for want of fuel. My lords, the approaching fleet's indeed that of Dur, as could be ascertained from their sails, cut square in fashion of the stormy Va'andao."

"How many?" asked Ferrian.

"I counted fourteen of their great ships, plus perhaps an equal number of small craft."

Barnevelt calculated. "If we can keep the Sunqaruma bottled up, that should leave us a margin to deal with Dur."

"You know not the great ships of Dur," retorted Ferrian. "Their biggest galleys are manned by nearly a thousand men, and one of those could destroy a squadron of ours as a man treads bugs under heel. With due respect, therefore, my lord, let's see a demonstration of this preternatural resourcefulness whereof Alvandi told us, lest the setting sun illumine the unjoyous spectacle of you, me, and all our brave people furnishing food for the fondaqa. What, sir, do you command?"

Food for the fondaqa? Barnevelt pondered, his long chin in his hand. Maybe two could play at that game.

"Tell me," he said. "For nearly an hour your gliders have been dropping things on the Sunqaruma without effect . . ."

Ferrian replied hotly, "My gliders are the greatest military invention since Qarar smote the dames of Varzeni-Ganderan with his magic staff! They'll make us as fearsomely puissant in the arts of Qondyor as the damned Earthmen! But as you say," (he calmed down) "they're not fully perfected. What would you do?"

"How much load do they carry?"

"For a short flight, the equivalent of one man besides the pilot. What's in your mind?"

"We have a lot of water jars in the supply ships. If we dumped half or two-thirds of the water out, they'd weigh about as much as a man—at least the smaller . . ."

"But wherefore a bombardment of water jars? Though you yerk the nob of one or two foes . . ."

"But if the jars were full of fondaqa?"

"*Hao*, now speak you sooth!" cried Ferrian. "We'll cut up the cadavers of the fallen for bait and use those hooks wherewith your sturdy Majburuma seek to claw apart the sea vine . . . Captain Zair, more ship's boats! Our admiral has an order for the fleet! Yare, yare!"

"But, my lords!" cried Captain Zair with an expression of horror. "The men mortally fear these creatures, and with good reason!"

Barnevelt took a hitch in his mental pants. "Oh, foof! I'm not afraid of them. Get me a thick leather jacket and a pair of gauntlets and I'll demonstrate."

As usual, once he had grasped the basic idea, Prince Ferrian took the bit in his teeth and ran away with it. He rushed about, haranguing everybody to break out fishing tackle, to bend the heads of spears for gaffs, and to get the order to the rest of the fleet.

All this took time. First Barnevelt had to demonstrate how to handle a fondaq without getting bitten, thanking the gods for his experience with Earthly sharks and eels. By the time the crews of the ships along the edges of the weed were hooking, gaffing, and spearing the wriggling, snapping monsters and popping them into water jars, another glider returned to report that the Duro fleet would soon be in sight.

Barnevelt glanced at the high, hot sun. "With this south wind," he told Ferrian, "we should have another hour to get organized. I'm going to divide the fleet and put you in charge of the part sent against the Duruma."

Seeing Ferrian's antennae rise quizzically he added, "Our main weapon against them will be the gliders, which you understand better than anyone. I'm going back to the *Junsar* because I think when the pirates see most of the fleet going off, they'll try a sortie." He turned to the skipper of the *Kumanisht*. "Captain Zair, signal all admirals to come here."

A longboat loaded with jars pulled up under the stern of the *Kumanisht,* the coxswain chanting, "Fish for sale! Nice fresh fish for sale! One bite and ye're a dead carcass!"

The sailors fell to work transferring the jars to the carrier. One of the smaller ships pulled alongside with another load of amphorae. The rows of jars along the flight deck began to grow.

The commanders came aboard, one by one. Barnevelt explained his plans, cutting short arguments. "That's all—carry on."

As he lowered himself into the longboat, hails came from the mastheads of the allied fleet: "Sail ho!" *"Sail ho!"* ***"SAIL HO!"***

The Duro fleet had been sighted.

On the *Junsar,* the missile fight went on. All the ships were looking battered where catapult bullets had carried away parts of their rails or stove in their deckhouses. One Majburo ship had her mizzenmast knocked over, another her forward catapult smashed, while the decks of the enemy seemed to be heaped with wreckage.

From the *Junsar*'s poop, Barnevelt and Tangaloa watched the main fleet get under way, the big *Kumanisht* in the middle, the others spread out across the sea in a crescent formation with horns forward. On the horizon, little pale rectangles appeared: the sails of Dur.

After two hours, the men of the Majburo squadron had torn away about half the weed of the plug, which brought them closer to the Sunqaro guard ship and made the fight hotter.

The Majburo admiral said, "My lord Snyol, methinks they make a sally, as you predicted."

Beyond the guard ship, down the channel came the galleys of the Sunqar in double column. Barnevelt could not count them because the hulls of the leading pair obscured the rest, but he knew he was outnumbered. The allied armada was caught between Dur and the pirates as in a nutcracker.

Tangaloa paused in his motion-picture making to say, "Those blokes will try to make contact with us, then line up, ship to ship, so they can pour an endless supply of boarders into us."

"I know. Wish I could persuade you to wear some armor."

"And if I fell into the water?"

Barnevelt somberly watched the Sunqaruma approach. If he could only think up some bright idea . . . If the pirates did break through his blockade, would they fall on the allied fleet from the rear or flee to parts unknown? It wouldn't matter to him; he'd be dead.

The noise forward died down. The guard ship's people had stopped shooting in an effort to turn her around so that she should not block the way for her sisters. Her oars moved feebly, leading Barnevelt to guess that most of them had less than their normal complement of rowers.

Barnevelt told the Majburo admiral, "Have 'em stop shooting to clear wreckage, build up the bulwarks, and gather more ammunition. How's it holding out?"

"Well enough, sir, with all the bolts and arrows that prickle my ship like the spines of the irascible 'evashq."

"Lash our six ships together the way I told you and push forward against the plug. And remind the men about that man we want taken alive." Barnevelt felt his sword edge.

The Majburo ships made fast, all the rowers except those on the outside banks of the outside pair shipping their oars because there was no longer room to ply them. The remaining rowers began to drive this super-catamaran forward, pushing the plug of weed and the crippled guard-ship ahead of it up the channel.

But soon the two leading pirate ships thrust their rams into the weed from their side and began to push back. Having more oars in use, they halted the movement of the plug and started it back towards the open sea.

Barnevelt asked, "What are you doing, George?"

"Just an idea of mine," said Tangaloa. He held a broken length of catapult arrow about a meter long, to the end of which he was tying a light rope several meters long.

"Here they come," said Barnevelt.

The two leading Sunqaro galleys had pushed the plug and the six Majburo ships back far enough down the channel so that it opened out enough to let one of the smaller following pirates slip past and work around the plug, albeit fouling its oars in the vine at every stroke. Little by little it crawled through the narrow lane in the terpahla until its bow touched that of the outermost starboard ship of the Majburo squadron.

Barnevelt and Tangaloa had hurried to the outermost ship, crowded with men released from oar duty. As they arrived, spiked planks were flung across from ship to ship. Trumpets blared and boarding-parties rushed from each end of the planks. They met with a crash in the middle. Men clinched and tumbled off the planks, to thump against the rams below or splash into the weedy water. Others pressed up behind them while, on the forecastles of both ships, archers and crossbowmen sent missiles into the thick of the opposing fighters. The archers of the Majburo ship's neighbor added their weight to the fire.

Tangaloa elbowed his way through the throng at the bow. At the rail he unlimbered his improvised whip and sent it snaking across the gap. **Crack!** The end coiled around the neck of a Sunqaru, and a jerk pulled the man over his own rail. **Splash!** He gathered up the rope and let fly again. **Crack! Splash!**

Barnevelt had worked himself into an adrenal state where he

was eager to fight, but the crowd at the bow blocked his way. Between the superior firepower of the Majburuma and Tangaloa's whip, the Sunqaruma on the planks began to give way, until the Majburuma poured into the waist of the pirate galley, sweeping Barnevelt along in the current. He stumbled over bodies, unable to see for the crowd or hear for the din.

The pressure and the noise increased as another force of pirates swarmed over this ship's stern from another Sunqaro ship. As Tangaloa had predicted, the pirates were passing from ship to ship to bring their full force into use. Barnevelt found himself pushed back towards the bow of the Sunqaro ship, until the rail pressed against the small of his back. Now, while a sudden push might send him over the side, he could at least see. The after half of the ship was full of Sunqaruma fighting their way forward.

Unable to reach the crowded gangplanks, Barnevelt put his sword away, climbed over the rail of the Sunqaro ship and down onto the ram, stepped over a corpse, leaped to the ram of the Majburo ship, and climbed up. The forecastle was still crowded, the Majburo admiral, armored like a lobster, bellowing orders in the midst of it all.

Tangaloa leaned against the rail, smoking. The latter said, "You shouldn't have done that, Dirk. The commander-in-chief ought to stay back where he can command-in-chief, and not get mixed up in vulgar fighting."

"Matter of fact, I haven't been near the actual fighting."

"You will be soon. Here they come!"

A wedge of Sunqaruma had bored through their opponents and gained the planks. The Majburuma on the planks were struck down or hurled off or pushed back onto their own ship, and then the pirates were after them, fighting with insensate ferocity. At their head stormed a stocky Earthman with a red face seamed with many small wrinkles.

"Igor!" yelled Barnevelt, recognizing his chief behind the nasal of the helmet.

Igor Shtain saw Barnevelt and rushed upon him, whirling a curved blade. Barnevelt parried slash after slash, and now and then a thrust, but the blows came so fast he could do no more than defend himself.

Step by step Shtain drove him back towards the stern of the Majburo ship. Barnevelt's helmet clanged from a blow that got home. Once or twice Shtain laid himself open to a riposte, but Barnevelt's hesitancy cost him his chance. If he could only hit the guy with the flat over the head, as he had done with the artist in Jazmurian . . . But he'd break his sword on Shtain's helmet.

Barnevelt was vaguely aware that fighting had spread through-out the mass of Majburo ships. He threw occasional glances over his shoulders lest somebody stab him from behind. He caught a glimpse of Tangaloa staving a pirate skull with his mace; of a pirate thrusting a Majburu over the side with the point of his pike.

Shtain continued, with demoniac force, to press him back. Barnevelt wondered where the hell a man of Shtain's age got such physical endurance. Though much younger and a better fencer, Barnevelt was beginning to pant. His aching fingers seemed hardly able to hold the sweaty hilt, and still Shtain came on.

The poop of this ship was raised only half a deck. Barnevelt felt the steps to the quarterdeck behind him and went up them, step by step, parrying Shtain's swings at his legs. It was unfair to have to fight a man who wanted to kill you while you were trying to avoid killing him.

Back across the quarterdeck they went. Barnevelt thought that if he didn't disable Shtain pretty soon, Shtain would kill him. He began thrusting at Shtain's arm and knee. Once he felt his point hit something, but Shtain kept coming as furiously as ever.

The rail touched Barnevelt's back. Now he had no choice be-tween the wicked blade in front and the Banjao Sea behind. In back of Shtain appeared the bulk of Tangaloa, but for some reason George simply stood there on the quarterdeck.

Shtain paused, glaring, shifted his grip on the saber, and threw himself upon Barnevelt. Still Tangaloa stood idly. This time it would be one or the other. . . .

There was an outburst of trumpet calls. At the same time

something flicked out, cracked, and coiled itself around Shtain's left ankle. The rope tautened with a jerk, yanking Shtain's foot from under him and sending him asprawl on the deck. Before he could rise, the huge brown form of Tangaloa landed on him, squeezing the wind out of him like an accordion.

Barnevelt leaped forward, stamped on the fist that held the saber, and wrenched the weapon out of Shtain's hand. He pulled off the helmet and smote Shtain smartly with the flat of his blade. Shtain collapsed.

All over the Majburo ships, the Sunqaruma were running back towards the gangplanks leading to their own vessels. A little fighting still flickered, but for the most part the Majburuma, having lost a quarter of their number, were glad to let their foes go unmolested. The ships were littered with swords, pikes, axes, helmets, bucklers, and other gear, and with the bodies of friends and foes.

As Tangaloa tied Shtain's hands behind his back, Barnevelt asked, "How'd you get so handy with a whip, George?"

"Something I picked up in Australia. Beastly business, fighting. A scientist like me has no business getting mixed up in it."

"Why the hell did you stand there like a dummy when you first arrived? The guy nearly got me!"

"I was shooting film."

"What?"

"Yes, I got a marvelous sequence of you and Igor battling. It will make our Sunqar picture."

"Jeepers cripus!" cried Barnevelt. "I like that! I'm fighting for my life and losing, and all you think of is to shoot film! I suppose . . ."

"Now, now," said Tangaloa soothingly. "I knew such an expert fencer as yourself was in no real danger. And it came out all right, didn't it?"

Barnevelt hardly knew whether to rage, to laugh, or to be flattered. He finally decided that since George was incorrigible he might as well drop the subject. He asked, "Why are the Sunqaruma running away? I thought they'd won!"

"Look behind you!"

Barnevelt looked around, and there came the entire allied fleet, gongs beating time for the oars. In the center wallowed the carrier *Kumanisht*, towing a huge square-rigged galley with great eight or ten-man oars staggered in two banks.

The pirates, having all regained their own ships, pried the gangplanks loose and pushed off from the Majburu galleys with poles, pikes, and oars. Presently the whole lot were splashing back up the channel towards the main body of pirate ships.

For the first time in hours Barnevelt noticed the sun, now low in the west. The fight had lasted most of the afternoon.

The sun had set. Shtain was safely stowed in the *Junsar*'s brig. Barnevelt's wounds—a couple of superficial cuts—had been bandaged. Barnevelt presided over a meeting of his admirals in the big cabin on the *Junsar*.

"How about it, Lord Snyol?" cried Prince Ferrian. "The men will have it you led the boarders into the Sunqaro ship, smiting off three piratical heads with one blow and generally winning the fight single-handed. Is't true?"

"They exaggerate, though Tagdë and I did personally capture that Earthman we were looking for."

"Won't you let me boil him in oil?" said Queen Alvandi. "The pirates of our own world be bad enough, but . . ."

"I have other plans, Your Altitude. Prince Ferrian, tell me what happened at your end."

" 'Twas no great affray—rather a comedy worthy of Harian's genius. You know that Dur uses slave rowers on those monstrous ships, for not even their ill-gotten wealth suffices to hire so many thousands of free oarsmen. And the usage is, when going into action, to run a chain through a shackle on the leg of each thrall, binding him securely to his bench by means of a bronze eye set in the wood.

"Now, these Duro ships were bearing down upon us like a charge of wild bishtars; but, seeing nought but our masts on the horizon, like a picket fence, they thought themselves well provided with time to make ready, when down upon them swooped the first of my intrepid lads in his glider, to drop his jar upon the flagship. It struck square among the rowers' benches, ere the slave masters had half finished shackling their rowers, and wrought most wondrous confusion, the fondaqa squirming and snapping, the slaves screaming and those bitten writhing in their death agonies, the slave drivers rushing about with their whips, and all in turmoil.

"Then came two more such love epistles, and the slaves went genuinely mad and mutinied. Those still free unshackled the rest, whilst others assailed the drivers and marines with bare hands, hurling some to a briny doom and others rending in bloody bits. The Duro admiral saved his gore by doffing his cuirass and leaping into the sea, where a dinghy picked him up.

"Meanwhile other fliers had dropped their jars. While some of these fell in the water, others struck home, with admirable results. For, even if the slaves in the other ships were bound, still the presence of these loathsome sea creatures destroyed all order and made maneuver flat impossible. In short, the novel nature of this onset so demoralized the foe that some of their ships began to flee before we came upon them.

"Others, seeing the carnage still raging on the flagship and not knowing that the admiral had been saved—for he'd left his personal flags behind—hesitated, and when the *Saqqand* of Suruskand rammed another of the great ships, the latter doing nought to avoid the dolorous stroke, and breaking up in consequence, away the rest of 'em went. We boarded the flagship, where still the anarch battle raged, quelled both disputing parties, and towed her back with us. Our total loss was one of my fliers, who missed his alighting and drowned, poor wight."

Next morning, as Roqir redly burst the bounds of the hazy horizon, the trumpets of the allied fleet sounded the assault. Up the channel rowed the Majburo squadron, the battered *Junsar* in the lead.

Meanwhile, along the edge of the solid terpahla on both sides

of the entrance to the pirate stronghold, in a far-reaching crescent, troops with skis on their feet lowered themselves from their ships on to the weed. They teetered and splashed on the wet and wobbly footing. Some fell and had to be helped up again. At length they began to move forward, hundreds of them in three lines: the first line carrying huge wicker shields to protect themselves and those behind them from missile fire; the second line with pikes; the third with bows.

From the pirate stronghold came no sound. During the night the Sunqaruma had drawn most of their ships together in a kind of citadel, the biggest galleys in the middle, around them a ring of smaller ships, and around these again an outwork of rafts and scows. This formation would prevent the attackers from sinking the pirate ships by ramming, at least until the low craft around the edge had been gotten out of the way.

Closer came the *Junsar;* still an ominous silence. The men splashing over the terpahla came closer from their side, lapping around the settlement so as to approach it from opposite sides.

L. SPRAGUE DE CAMP

As she came within catapult range, the *Junsar* slowed to let the bireme *Saqqand* pass her: the same ship that had so doughtily rammed a Duro galley thrice her size the previous day.

From the outlying houseboats around the edges of the settlement came the **thrum** of crossbows, and bolts streaked towards the lines of advancing ski troops. Barnevelt realized that not all the pirates had withdrawn to the central citadel, but they would fight delaying actions around the edges of their city. The archers among the ski troops shot back over the heads of their own men.

A catapult went off in the citadel. A giant arrow soared down the channel to dive into the water beside the *Saqqand*. And then the creak and thump of catapults and the snap of bowstrings began their din again.

The *Saqqand* nosed up to the nearest of the rafts around the citadel. The *Junsar* made her bow fast to the starboard quarter of the smaller ship, while Queen Alvandi's *Douri Dejanai* made fast to her port quarter. Other ships nosed up behind these two, like a parade of elephants, and their people threw planks from rail to rail so that fighters could pour up towards the citadel as they were needed.

Barnevelt, in the *Junsar*'s bow, heard the yell and clatter of combat around the far fringes of the settlement as the ski troops reached the outlying ships and strove to secure a lodgment on them. He could see little of this, however. Behind him his warriors lined up to go down the rope to the *Saqqand*'s deck, while on the *Saqqand* herself they began to climb over the bow to the raft.

Then from the citadel burst the greatest storm of missile-fire Barnevelt had seen: catapult missiles, bolts, arrows, and sling bullets. The whistle of missiles merged into a continuous ululation. The deadly rain swept over the raft and over the *Saqqand*'s deck, dropping men everywhere. The survivors pushed forward and closed up, to be mown down in their turn. The lucky ones dashed across the raft to climb the rail of the small galley on the other side. Sunqaruma rose to meet them.

Barnevelt found himself yelling, "Go on! Go on!"

Now another element appeared: From the citadel a large

rocket with a spear shaft or catapult arrow for a stick soared down the channel, leaving a trail of thick smoke. It went wild, as did the next, but then one struck the *Junsar*'s deck forward of the poop and burst with a roar, showering the ship with burning fragments. The men lined up on the catwalk, awaiting their turn to attack, scattered, and the *Junsar*'s crew had to turn to to put out a dozen small fires. Another such rocket hit the bow of the *Douri Dejanai*. The smoke and flame broke up the supporting fire from the ships.

Finally the attack broke. The men streamed back, dozens of them hobbling with arrows sticking in them, while other dozens lay scattered about the *Saqqand* and the raft, dead or too badly hurt to flee.

Under the bombardment from the citadel, it took hours to organize another attack. Barnevelt saw that the men of the leading group were furnished with big wicker shields like those of the ski troops. These latter had secured a footing here and there around the settlement. More than that Barnevelt could not find out, as communication between them and the ships from which they had come could only be effected by a runner plodding over the terpahla on skis.

The second attack got under way shortly after noon. The men with the big shields got into the small galley on the other side of the raft and almost drove the pirates out of it before a counterattack sent them running.

The long Krishnan day wore on. Barnevelt got out all the rowboats in the fleet and ordered a combined attack, the longboats to row around the citadel and disembark their men at various points.

This time the attackers did secure a foothold on the small galley nearest to the channel, which they still held when the sun went down and the longboats, those still afloat, rowed back down the channel. But then another counterattack in the fading light drove the allied troops out of the ship they had occupied, and everything was as it had been at the start.

At the evening conference, the Dasht of Darya reported that

the ski troops had occupied most of the outlying ships. Queen Alvandi said, "O Ferrian, why don't your brave fliers land their kites in the middle of the citadel, thus taking our foes in the only rear they present to us?"

" 'Twould serve no good purpose. Coming down singly, and mayhap smashing their craft and having to crawl by degrees from the wreckage, they'd be butchered like unhas at a country fair."

"Or do they fear the handplay, preferring to do their fighting at a safe distance? A mort of my brave girls lie dead out yonder because your delicate heroes'll fight only when they can drop things on the heads. . . ."

"Enough, hag!" shouted Ferrian. "Who put the Duro fleet to rout? I'll match my fliers against your pseudo-warriors . . ."

"No warrior you, but a contriving calculator . . ."

By banging on the table and shouting, Barnevelt restored order. Nevertheless, the admirals were quarrelsome over their failures and snarled at each other and at Barnevelt for hours without getting anywhere. Barnevelt realized that his ski-troop idea, while bright, had not been quite good enough to carry that strong defense with one push, at least not with the number of men he had available.

He stood up with the air of one who has listened long enough. "Tomorrow we attack again, using everything at once. Prince Ferrian, load up your gliders with darts and fireworks, and get more jars of fondaqa to drop. My lord Dasht, make your ski troops move forward from their present positions if you have to poke 'em in the rump. Post ski archers around the inner edges of the terpahla to throw more covering fire into the citadel. Queen Alvandi . . ."

After the admirals had returned to their ships, Barnevelt strolled out upon the deck of the *Sunqar*. He looked at the wan stars and thought of Zei. The few days since he had seen her last had done nothing to abate the fires within him; on the contrary. Fantastic thoughts ran through his mind, of swooping down on Ghulindé with some personal followers, snatching up

Zei, and bearing her off to Earth. Silly, of course . . .

Sounds in the darkness indicated that men were fetching back dead and wounded from the *Saqqand* and the adjacent raft, the live ones to be tended and the dead to be stripped of usable equipment before being consigned to the fondaqa. Sounds of carpentry came from the pirate citadel of ships.

"Have a cigar?" said Tangaloa's musical voice.

"Thanks. If I could get away with it I'd call this off."

"Why? You are doing fine—a bosker hero and all that rot."

"We've got Igor, and our film, and that money the queen gave us . . ."

"You mean you've got it! It belongs to you, not the firm."

"A nice idea," said Barnevelt. "Whether Panagopoulos would agree is something else."

"Don't tell him. Speaking of money, do you suppose we could claim that reward we offered for the capture of Igor, since we did the capturing? It would have been charged to the company if somebody else had caught the bloke."

"I'm *sure* Panagopoulos wouldn't allow that! But, as I was saying, it's not our fight any more. All we're doing is to help these poor benighted Krishnans to kill each other, and maybe stop a stray arrow ourselves. Why don't we load Igor into a boat and silently steal away?"

Tangaloa said, "I should like to get some proper pictures inside the settlement. Those you took are half-pie articles."

"What about those you've been taking?"

"Inadequate. Cosmic wouldn't accept them. Besides, anything like that would rouse the suspicions of the admirals, and with gliders to scout for them they'd easily catch us. Some of them are violently anti-Terran, and I hate to think what would happen if we were dragged back and—ah—unmasked."

"I could say I'm feeling poorly and turn the command over to Ferrian, since he thinks he can do anything better than anybody else."

"You forget—Igor is still under Osirian pseudohypnosis. I don't know whether it wears off . . ."

"It does," said Barnevelt, "but I understand it leaves you full

241

of neuroses unless you get another Osirian to break the spell."

"Precisely! Therefore we must get Sheafasè alive and force him to restore the Old Man's mind."

"I don't know. There are other Osirians, and I've drunk delight of battle with my peers enough to last me for some time."

"Look here, battler, while I don't like to throw my weight, I fear we must go on with this. Even if you are admiralissimo of the fleet, don't forget I'm your boss in Igor Shtain Limited."

Barnevelt was astonished to see the easy-going Tangaloa, for the first time, pull rank. George must take his xenological investigations—if nothing else—seriously.

"Oh, *tamates!* I've taken most of the responsibility and you know it. If it comes to a fight I know worse fates than not working for Igor."

"Then let's not fight, by all means," said Tangaloa pacifically. "If you can arrange one sunny day in the citadel for me, I'm easy as far as the war is concerned."

"Okay. I'll watch for a chance to effect such an agreement."

"Good-o. And now if you will excuse me, I have a date."

"You *what?*"

"A date. With one of Queen Alvandi's lady troopers, for some xenological work. I find them really quite feminine, in our sense of the term, under the warlike getup. Which—ahem—merely proves what I said the other day about the stability of basic cultural attitudes. Cheerio!"

Next morning a heavy overcast, a high fog that barely cleared the mastheads, confined Ferrian's fliers to their ship and reduced the effectiveness of long-range missile fire. By the leaden light it was seen that the besieged had erected bulwarks of timber, slotted for archery, around the outer rails of the ships forming the citadel. They had also rigged boarding nets and had fixed numbers of pikes with their points projecting outward, to aggravate the hazards facing the attackers.

After the usual delays, the trumpets sounded. Again the men advanced. Bows twanged, catapults thumped, swords clanged, and wounded men screamed.

By evening the allied forces had cleared the Sunqaruma out of all the outlying positions and had secured a precarious lodgment in the citadel itself. But again the cost had been heavy, and the Sunqaruma could by no means be deemed beaten.

The admirals, a couple of them nursing injuries, gathered for the post-mortem in a worse mood than ever, snapping at each other like crabs in a bucket. "Why supported you not my men when I signalled for help?" "My lord Ferrian, what good are your damned idlers lounging on the *Kumanisht* while better men and women die among the spears?" "Madam, should I use a scalpel to split kindling? One of my fliers is worth six common soldiers . . ." "Where's the genius of the great General Snyol?" "We should cease these vain assaults and starve the dastards out!" "A cowardly counsel!" "Who's a coward? I'll have your liver . . ."

Barnevelt was trying without much success to establish order when the sentry announced, "A boat from the Sunqaruma, my lords, seeking a parley."

"Send them in," said Barnevelt, glad of the interruption. If the enemy were softening up to the point of asking terms, the battle should soon be over.

Steps sounded outside. The sentry announced: "Gizil bad-Bashti, High Admiral of the Moryá Sunqaruma!"

"Gizil the Saddler!" shrieked Queen Alvandi. "Recreant treacher! Just wail till I . . ."

"Vizqash!" said Barnevelt, for the small, scarfaced fellow in the doorway was the Krishnan he had known off and on as Vizqash bad-Murani.

The man, wearing his lordly hidalgo manner, took off his helmet and made a mock bow. "Gizil bad-Bashti, otherwise Gizil the Saddler, otherwise Vizqash the Haberdasher, at your service," he rasped. "I greet my old acquaintance Snyol of Pleshch, otherwise Gozzan the Express-Courier, otherwise . . ."

He trailed off and sent a knowing grin at Barnevelt, who introduced him round and said, "Since when have you been chief of the Sunqaruma, Gizil?"

"Since the fourth hour today, when our former chief, Sheafasè the Osirian, expired of an arrow wound received yesterday."

"Sheafasè dead!" asid Barnevelt, and exchanged a look of consternation with Tangaloa. If the Osirian chief no longer lived to cure Shtain of his affliction, there would have to be a radical alteration in their plans.

"Yes," continued Gizil-Vizqash. "Promotion has been swift, for grievous has been the loss among our chiefs. Gavao did perish in our raid on Ghulindé. Qorf and 'Urgan the mighty Snyol did slay when he snatched the princess from our grasp. And even the Earthman, Igor Eshtain, who'd risen swiftly after his late enrollment in our company, was missing after the first day's battle. So—here am I, High Admiral.

"And speaking of the raid of Snyol upon our stronghold: In going through one of our provision ships in preparation for this siege, we found a youth asleep upon a sack of tunesta, clad as an expressman. Questioning revealed that he was the companion of your General Snyol, the suppositious Gozzan, on their foray. Becoming separated from his comrades, he'd hidden in this ship since then, subsisting on our stores. He says he's Zakkomir bad-Gurshmani, a ward of Qirib's throne. Be that the truth, Queen Alvandi?"

"It could be. What have you done with the boy?"

"Nought as yet. His safety answers for my own, in case you should by reasoning sophistical convince yourselves that faith need not be kept with such as we."

Barnevelt said dryly, "Interesting, but that's not why you came here. Are you surrendering?"

"Surrender?" Gizil's antennae rose. "A horrid word. I speak, rather, of honorable terms whereby this bloody conflict may be terminated."

"A pox upon this chaffering!" cried the Suruskando admiral. "Let's terminate him with a length of rope and press the attack with pitiless ferocity. They must be low on men or muniment, to offer terms."

"Wait," said Queen Alvandi. "You do forget, sir, they hold my sweet ward Zakkomir."

"What, you turning soft?" cried Ferrian. "You speaking for prudence and moderation, old battle-axe?"

Barnevelt broke in, "Say your say, Master Gizil."

"Let's consider our positions," resumed the pirate admiral unruffled. "By the grace of Da'vi you did rout our rescuers, the fleet of Dur. But it follows not they'll scamper all the distance to their stormy home. Rather is it likely that their admiral will think him of the loss of rank or head awaiting him at home and turn again for one more blow.

"Now, one need not be able to see through a plank of qong wood to know that you've had grievous losses in the last three days of combat, perhaps a quarter of your total force dead or disabled. Therefore I now expect, even if you set out at once on your return, you'd find many ships with oars but partly manned. Another day of this contention will find you in a parlous plight indeed.

"Then as to our situation. 'Tis true we are surrounded and, supposing Dur does not return, we must depend upon our own resources, while you can replenish and reinforce. It is also true that we've expended men and weapons. 'Tis even true that we've been driven from our outposts by that brainsome scheme of sending men across the weed with boards upon their feet. Who thought of that must be a very Qarar reincarnate.

"Still, by making use of cover, we have kept our losses small. As for weapons and missiles, we'd taken the precaution, in setting up our floating citadel, to include within it all supplies of such contrivances, and also ample food and water.

"Let us assume, to make your case most favorable, that you can in the long run overcome us. What then? Remember that your troops confront despairing men with nought to lose, and who will therefore fight to death—whilst yours, however brave, are not inflamed by such a desperate animus. This, combined with the advantage of a strong defensive stand, means that you will lose a pair or trio for every one of us you slay. You'll be lucky if such slaughter, in addition to bleeding your realms of their most stalwart battlers, do not to blank dissent and open mutiny incite them ere the siege be over.

"Then, what seek ye here? Queen Alvandi, we surmise, covets the Sunqar itself, and also her ward Zakkomir unperforate. You others seek our treasury and fleet, and also wish to rid yourselves of the menace of our jolly rovers on the seas. Speak I not sooth? So if you can center the shaihan's eye without further bloodletting, were't not sheer perversity and madness to refuse?"

"What are your terms?" asked Barnevelt.

"That all surviving Moryá Sunqaruma, unharmed, be set ashore upon the mainland, each man to be allowed to take family and personal possessions, including cash and weapons."

Gizil looked narrowly at Barnevelt and chose his words with care. "Snyol of Pleshch is widely known as a man of most meticulous honor, a quality sadly lacking in these degenerate days. For that reason alone do we propose to place ourselves upon your mercy, for if the veritable Snyol avers he will protect us, we know he will."

Again that knowing look. Barnevelt realized Gizil was saying: *Carry out your end of the bargain, as the real Snyol would, and I won't spill the beans about having known you at Novorecife as an Earthman.* Smart gloop, Gizil-alias-Vizqash.

"Will you step out, sir?" said Barnevelt. "We'll discuss your offer."

When Gizil had withdrawn the admirals sounded off: " 'Twere a shame to let slip the prize when 'tis almost in our grasp . . ." "Nay, the fellow has reason . . ." "That stipulation about personal moneys will never do. What's to hinder them, when Gizil goes back, from dividing the entire treasury amongst 'em?" "The same with their weapons . . ." "We should at least demand the leaders' heads . . ."

After an hour's argument Barnevelt called for a vote, which proved a tie. The queen was now for peace, since the Sunqaruma held Zakkomir.

"I say peace," said Barnevelt. "As for details . . ."

When Gizil was readmitted, Barnevelt told him they would take the terms with two exceptions: the Moryá Sunqaruma might not take their money and weapons, and those originally from

Qirib should be set ashore as far as possible from that land—say on the southeast shore of the Banjao. This last was at Alvandi's behest, as she did not want them to drift back to Qirib to make trouble.

Gizil grinned. "Her Altitude seems to think that, having once escaped her yoke, we *wish* to return thereunder. Howsomever, I'll take your word to my council. Shall we prolong this truce until the matter be decided?"

So it was agreed, and out he went.

Next day the opposing forces lay in uneasy silence, both of them repairing damages and strengthening their positions. Shortly after noon Gizil came out again, and a flutter of flag hoists called the admirals to the *Junsar*.

Gizil said, "My lords, your counterterms are hard—too hard to be endured by warlike men with weapons in their fists. Therefore do I present to you an amended offer, thus: That our men take with them money to the sum of one gold kard apiece, that they shall not starve while seeking honest work, and weapons to the extent of one knife or dagger each, that they shall not be utterly defenseless. And that only able-bodied ex-Qiribuma like myself be sent to those distant shores whereof Alvandi speaks, wounded ones being set ashore nearer home in civilized regions."

"We accept," said Barnevelt quickly before the admirals had time to speak. Some of them looked blackly at him, the queen especially assuming the appearance of a snapping turtle. But with peace so nearly in his grasp, he did not intend to let it slip. If they didn't like it, well—George and he would soon be going, and it mattered little to him if future Krishnan history books denounced him.

"Do you give your solemn promise, O Snyol of Pleshch?" said Gizil.

"I do."

"Will you come with me aboard my ship and repeat your promise to my chiefs?"

"Sure."

"Ohé!" said Prince Ferrian. "Art not thrusting your head into the yeki's mouth? Trust you the rascal so far?"

"I think so. He knows what they'd have to expect if they tried any monkey business at this stage. If I don't come back, you're boss."

Barnevelt went with Gizil to the citadel and climbed through the pikes and outer defenses to the big galleys forming the keep of this floating fortress. He saw signs of much damage, and dead and wounded pirates; withal, there were lots of live ones left. Gizil had not stretched the truth too far.

Introduced around the circle of officers, he repeated his promises. "Of course your men must submit to search," he said.

They drew up a written agreement covering the terms of capitulation, signed it, and took it back to the *Sunqar* for the admirals to sign too. This was all a tedious and time-consuming business.

Zakkomir, perky as ever but with the pussycat roundness gone from his face, was released. Barnevelt got him aside, saying, "Want to do me a favor?"

"My life is yours to command, Lord Snyol."

"Then forget that the pirates were interested in getting hold of Tagdë and me. Get it?"

The business of searching the Moryá Sunqaruma to make sure they were not carrying more money and weapons than they were allowed, and loading them into various allied ships, took the rest of the day. Because the pirates from Qirib—who comprised nearly half the total—were to be sent to a special destination, Barnevelt borrowed a troopship, the *Yars,* from the Suruskando admiral.

Queen Alvandi insisted upon manning it with her own people: men to row and Amazons to guard the passengers. She said, "I shan't be satisfied until I hear from my own girls that these villains have been landed at a place whence it'd take 'em years to regain Qirib."

§ § §

By the red evening light of Roqir, the unwounded ex-pirates filed aboard the *Yars* near the mouth of the channel. There were three hundred ninety-seven men, one hundred twenty-three women, and eighty-six children, which crowded the ship even without the Qiribo rowers who were going along to bring her back.

Barnevelt ate alone, Tangaloa being off shooting movie film. After his meal, Barnevelt had himself rowed from the *Junsar* down-channel to Alvandi's *Douri Dejanai*. He had not previously seen the queen's private cabin, now streaked with black from a fire set by the Sunqaro rockets. He was surprised to be greeted by a raucous cry of *"Baghan! Ghuvoí zu!"*

There was Philo the macaw chained to a perch at the side of the room. He looked at Barnevelt first with one eye and then the other, finally seemed to recognize him, and let his feathers be scratched.

In came Queen Alvandi, saying, "You and I are the only ones who can handle yon monster. You have a subtle power over such creatures, and me he fears. Guzzle yourself a mug of prime falat, in the carafe yonder. I suppose you'll preside over the meeting to divide the spoils of this eve?"

"Yes, and I dread it. Everybody'll be grabbing at once. I'm comforted, however, by the knowledge that this'll be about my last act as commander-in-chief."

"Oh, no need for dissonance. Tell 'em your decision and make it stand. I ask but my fair share—all the Sunqar, plus my proportionate part of ships and treasure."

"That's what I'm afraid of."

She made a never-mind gesture. "So that you demand not a fourth for your private portion there'll be no discord."

"Matter of fact I wasn't going to ask any for myself."

"What? Art mad? Or be this some subtle scheme to rive one of us of our throne? Seek you to subvert the popinjay of Sotaspé?"

"I never thought of such a thing! I like Ferrian!"

"What have likes to do with high politics? No doubt Ferrian likes you too, which fact wouldn't hinder him from slitting your weazand for the good of Sotaspé. But then it matters not, for I have other plans for you."

"What?" said Barnevelt apprehensively. Alvandi had a way of carrying through her plans in spite of hell or high water.

"Relinquish your share of loot, if you will, with a hoity-toity affectation of simple honesty, like Abhar the farm lad in the fable. But see to it that what would have been your share goes to me. Then 'twon't matter for it will all be in the family. Though you did vex me sore this afternoon when you gave in to the thieves on their demand to let wounded Qiribuma land upon the nearer mainland."

"I came here to ask about that," said Barnevelt. "The wounded ones are no problem, since they'll be mixed in with the rest. But I've been calculating, and the *Yars* with the unwounded ones will never get to where you want to send them with enough food and water for all those people. Therefore we must either divide them among two ships, or . . ."

"Nonsense!" cried Alvandi in her Queen-of-Hearts manner. "Think ye for an instant I mean to set these ravening predators ashore, my realm to infiltrate and subvert? Am I daft?"

"What d'you mean?"

"The captain of the *Yars* has my orders, as soon's he's out of sight, to pitch these miscreants into the sea, and their drabs and brats with 'em. For a carbuncle nought serves but the knife."

"Hey! I can't allow that!"

"And why not, Master Snyol?"

"I gave them my word."

"And who in Hishkak are *you*? A foreign vagabond, elevated by my contrivance to command of this expedition—and now our labor's over, chief no more, but one of my subjects, to do with as I will. And my will in this case . . ."

Barnevelt, feeling as if a cold hand were clutching his windpipe, jumped up, spilling his wine. "What's that about it's being all in the family?"

"So you've guessed? 'Tis plain as the peaks of Darya that my daughter Zei's in love with you. Therefore I choose you as her first husband, to serve in accordance with our ancient and unalterable custom until your function be performed. The lot's a fake, of course. And let's hope you provide a better meal at the end of your service than would the unlamented Káj have done!"

Barnevelt stood, breathing hard. At last he said: "You forget, madam, I'm not a Qiribu, nor is this Qirib. You have no jurisdiction over me."

"And *you* forget, sirrah, that I conferred Qiribo citizenship upon you when you returned to Ghulindé with Zei. By not refusing then, you did incur the usual obligations of such status, as the most learned doctor of laws would agree. So let's have no more of this mutinous moonshine . . ."

"Excuse me, but we'll have a lot more of it. I won't marry your daughter and I won't let you massacre those surrendered Qiribuma."

"So? I'll show you, you treasonous oppugner!" Her voice rose to a scream as she hurried across the cabin to fumble in a drawer.

Barnevelt at once guessed that she was after a container of janrú perfume—perhaps a bottle or a water pistol—to spray him with. One whiff and he'd be subjected to her will as if he were under Osirian pseudohypnosis. She was nearer the door than he at the moment; what to do?

"*Grrrrk!*" said Philo, aroused by the shouting.

Barnevelt thought of the one defense he had against such an attack. He leaped to the parrot's perch, seized the astonished bird, pressed his long nose in amongst its breast feathers, and inhaled vigorously.

Philo squawked indignantly, struggled, and bit a piece out of the rim of Barnevelt's ear, as neatly as a conductor punching a ticket.

Barnevelt released the bird as Alvandi rushed upon him with an atomizer, squirting at his face. His eyes were red, his nose was dripping, and blood ran down his ear from the notch the bird's beak had made. He whipped out his sword, grinning.

251

"Sorry," he said, "but I cadt sbell a thig. Dow get back id your bedroob, ad dot a word out of you, or Zei'll be queed without your havig to abdicate."

When he reinforced the command with a sharp jab in her midriff, she went, muttering maledictions like a Gypsy grifter being marched off to the paddy wagon. In the royal bedchamber he collected sheets, which he tore into strips: ". . . my best sheets, inherited from my grandmother!" wailed Alvandi.

Soon her plaints were smothered by a tight gag. In another quarter-hour he bundled her, trussed and bound, into her own clothes-closet and locked the door.

He told the sentry at the cabin door: "Her Altitude feels udwell, ad seds word that od do accout is she to be disturbed. By boat, please?"

He returned to his own ship filled with an odd bubbly elation, despite the peril in which he stood, as if in quelling the queen he had also defeated his own mother once and for all.

252

On the *Junsar*'s deck he found Tangaloa, who began, "I've been looking for you . . ."

"Matter of fact I've been looking for you too. We've got to get out of here. Alvandi thinks she's going to massacre all those surrendered Sunqaruma from Qirib and make me her son-in-law, complete with chopping block."

"My God, what shall we do then? Where is the old bat?"

"Tied up in her closet. Let's load Igor into our boat and—let me see—the *Yars* is at the mouth of the channel, isn't it? We'll row down there. You distract Alvandi's girl warriors while I arrange with Vizqash—I mean Gizil—to take over the *Yars* and sail back to Novorecife."

"With the ex-pirates as crew?"

"Why not? They're homeless men who'll probably be glad of our leadership. They'll believe me when I tell 'em I've switched to their side rather than let 'em be killed, because that's the sort of damn-fool thing the real Snyol would do."

"Good-o!" said the xenologist. They hurried below.

"Get me a pair of handcuffs," Barnevelt told the sergeant-at-arms. With these they went into the brig, where Shtain sat apathetically upon his bunk.

"Put out your hands," said Barnevelt, and snapped the cuffs on Shtain's wrists. "Now come."

Shtain, who had sunk into a torpor, shambled back up on deck with them and over the side into the longboat.

"Pull down the channel to the *Yars*," Barnevelt told his rowers. "Quietly."

"How did you avoid a whiff of that *nuit d'amour* perfume while you were tussling with the queen?" asked Tangaloa. When Barnevelt told him he laughed. "I'll be damned! That is the first time I ever heard of a bloke being saved from a fate worse than death by feathers!"

To facilitate loading, a small floating pier had been towed down the channel and made fast to the side of the *Yars*. The rowboat pulled up to this, and its passengers got out.

The sentry on the pier flashed her lantern towards them and

challenged, then said, "I crave pardon, General Snyol. Oh, Taggo! Girls, 'tis Taggo come to sport with us!"

"So that's what they call you?" said Barnevelt. "Try to inveigle 'em into the deckhouse. Tell 'em you'll teach 'em strip poker or something." He raised his voice. "Admiral Gizil!"

"Here I be. What would you, General Snyol?"

"Come down here and I'll tell you. It's all right, girls— everything's under control. Go topside and play with Taggo while I hold a conference."

The Krishnan dropped lightly from the rail of the *Yars* to the pier. When the Amazons were out of earshot, Barnevelt told him what had happened.

Gizil struck his palm with his fist. "A prime fool I, not to have thought of such waggery! Now that we know, what's to be done? Here lie we with nought but eating knives to fight with, under guard, surrounded by unfriendly ships. What's to stop them from working their will upon us?"

"I'll stop them."

"You?"

"Yes. Will you and your men follow me?"

"You mean you'll take our side instead of theirs, solely on a matter of honor?"

"Certainly. After all I am who I am," said Barnevelt, using a favorite Krishnan cliché.

"Let me grasp your thumb, sir! For now I do perceive that, though you be no more Snyol of Pleshch than I, but a vagrant Earthman, yet have you the true spirit that rumor credits to the noble Nyamë. Fear not. Your secret's safe with me. 'Twas for such urgency as this I did withhold it in the council with your admirals. What's to be done?"

"When Tagdë gets those women into the cabin, we'll call a conference with your officers—have you still got an organization?"

"Of sorts."

"We'll tell them what's up, and at the proper time we'll bar the cabin door, cut the mooring lines, and shove off. If anybody asks questions I'll handle 'em."

From the cabin came sounds of ribald revelry. Barnevelt reflected that discipline had surely gone to hell in the fleet in the last few hours, but he supposed that was a natural let-down after the tension of the campaign.

The word was passed. Barnevelt added, "Assign the men to the benches and have 'em get their oars ready to thrust through the ports. The first man who drops an oar gets left. Who's got a sharp knife? Cut the ropes and push the pier away with a boathook. The first pair of oars out first . . . Cut the lines to the weed . . . Now row. Softly—just enough force to move the ship . . . Here, stuff rags into the ports to deaden the sound. No rags? Use your women's clothes. If they object, smack 'em . . . That's right. Now another pair . . . Take that kid below . . ."

As the *Yars* crept snail-like out into the fairway and down the channel, a hail came from close aboard.

"What is it?" asked Barnevelt, peering over the rail at the ship they were passing. A man's head showed in the light of a riding lantern. "I'm Snyol of Pleshch, and all's well."

"Oh, my lord Snyol . . . I thought . . . Be that not the *Yars,* with the pirate prisoners?"

"It's the *Yars,* but with her regular crew. The prisoners haven't been put aboard yet, and we're going out for a practice row."

"But I saw them filing aboard this afternoon . . ."

"You saw them boarding the *Minyán* of Sotaspé, where they'll be quartered for the time being. There she lies now!" He pointed up-channel towards the vague black mass of hulls.

"Well," said the man in a puzzled tone, "if ye say all's well, it must be so."

And the ship dropped astern to mingle with the rest of the fleet.

"*Whew!*" said Barnevelt. "Right rudder—steady as you go. All oars out. Number three port, you're fouling up the stroke! Now pull! Stroke! Stroke!"

They issued from the mouth of the channel, leaving behind the mass of the allied navy moored along the edges of the terpahla, the ships' lanterns showing like a swarm of fireflies frozen in position. As the breeze still blew from the south, Barnevelt ordered the sails set wing-and-wing to take full advantage of it and turned the *Yars* north. Under the blanketing overcast, the Sunqar receded into the darkness.

Barnevelt watched it go with mixed feelings. If their luck held, they'd stop at Majbur and then go straight up the Pichidé to Novorecife, where he'd pay off the Sunqaruma.

Sometimes he thought he was tired of blue-green hair and olive-tinted skins, bright skimpy clothes, clanking cutlery, and windy speeches delivered with swaggering gestures in rolling, rhythmic, guttural Gozashtandou. He glanced towards where Sol would be were it visible. New York with its labyrinthine tangle of transportation, its suave eating and drinking and living places, and its swift wisecracking conversation, would look good . . .

Or would it? He'd be returning to a New York almost twenty-five years older than the one he'd left. Although his friends and relatives, thanks to modern geriatrics, would mostly be still alive and not much aged, they'd have scattered and forgotten him. He'd be separated from them by a whole generation, and it would take him a year just to get oriented again. Shortly before he left, he'd bought a hat of the new steeple-crowned shape. Now such hats were probably as archaic as derbies—which might in their turn have been revived. He understood why people like Shtain and Tangaloa, who made a business of interstellar trips, formed a clique of their own.

And his mother would probably be there. While he had accomplished the tasks formally set him—to solve the Sunqar mystery, rescue Shtain, and fulfill the Cosmic Features contract—he had not yet solved his personal problems. Or rather he'd solved his mother problem by removing himself light-years away from her, but his impending return would cancel that solution.

He also suffered an odd feeling of loss, as if he were missing a chance. One of his old professors had once told him that a young man should obey the romantic impulse at least once:

> "Come, fill the Cup, and in the fire of Spring
> Your Winter garment of Repentance fling . . ."

As by telling his boss to go to hell, or by joining a radical political movement. And here he was, letting prudence and foresight get the better of him.

On the other hand, George's suggestion that he bring a creature of another species to Earth and live with her there daunted him utterly. Such a life would be just too damned complicated for him to cope with, especially if his mother . . .

At least, he swore, this time he'd use his head in his relations with his crew: Be kind and affable, but firm and consistent, allowing no undue familiarity.

Gizil came up to report. Barnevelt asked, "Weren't you the masked man I conked with the mug in Jazmurian?"

Gizil grinned shamefacedly. "I hoped your lordship had not recognized me, but such is indeed the fact. I was to make a disturbance—as ye saw me do by picking a quarrel with the Osirian—while Gavao did drug your drink, but the lard-head must have doctored his own by error. 'Twas like an imbecile Balhibu so to do."

"Were you really going to kill Sishen?"

"No-o, I suppose not, though it did my liver good to see the eldrich monster quake with fear."

"One would think you didn't like Osirians, though you worked for one."

"Perforce—for once having clamped his claws upon our helm, Sheafasè gained such power over us by his fascinative talents that there was no shaking him, though many of us privately opined his reckless course would bring us to disaster, as indeed it did. Had the dice of Da'vi not turned up a double blank, thus terminating his existence, he'd have compelled us to the last man to resist."

"What were you trying to do to Tagdë and me?"

"To abduct, or failing that to slay. I trust you'll hold it not against us, for we did but as Sheafasè commanded—commands we could not shirk for the mental grip he held upon us. By his acquaintanceship with Earth, he knew full well the plans of Igor

257

Eshtain the Sunqar to explore, and laid his gins accordingly."

Gizil went on to explain the inner workings of the janrú ring, an organization that included Earthmen, Osirians, and Krishnans—how they had kidnaped Shtain and put him under pseudohypnosis on Earth; how they had planted Gizil, under the name of Vizqash, at Novorecife to watch for people sniffing on Shtain's trail, and so on.

". . . one of the heads of the ring is an officer on that Viagens ship—a *chivenjinir*, I think they call—what's that?"

Pandemonium from the cabin announced that the Amazons now knew they had been deceived.

Two ten-nights later, the *Yars* put in to bustling Majbur, having been blown out of her course by the tail of the season's first hurricane and having twice fled from unidentified fleets on the horizon.

Barnevelt and Tangaloa went ashore, dragging Shtain between them and leaving Gizil in charge of the ship. Barnevelt had come to have a good deal of respect for the ex-pirate, despite the Krishnan's lordly airs, predatory past, and assorted attempts to murder him.

They proceeded to the office of Gorbovast, official agent in Majbur of King Eqrar of Gozashtand and unofficial agent for the Viagens Interplanetarias.

"By all the gods!" cried Gorbovast, startled out of his habitual suavity. "The Free City's fleet arrived two days agone with a wild and wondrous tale of how you twain did lead the allied fleet to triumph over the Sunqar and then, over some darksome dispute with old Alvandi, did truss her like an unha on the way to market, steal a ship of Suruskand manned by pirate prisoners, and vanish into air attenuate. And here you be! What led a wight of proven probity to turn his coat in such amazing fashion?"

Barnevelt told the commissioner about the queen's plan to kill the surrendered Sunqaruma.

"Ah well," said Gorbovast, " 'tis said you are to singular idealisms given. Who's this frowsy fellow in gyves? The Free City forbids unlawful restraint upon free men, even Earthmen. . . ."

"This," said Barnevelt, "is the Shtain we were hunting."

"Igor Eshtain, eh?"

"The same. The janrú ring captured him, and the Osirian members of the ring made him into a pirate by their mental powers, so now he doesn't know his old friends. Sheafasè's dead, but we met another Osirian, Sishen, in Jazmurian some ten-nights back. I think he was on his way to Majbur. D'you know if he's here?"

"No, but we can learn. Let's to the Chief Syndic's chambers, across the street."

The Chief Syndic, whom they had seen last in Ghulindé, greeted them with even more amazement than had Gorbovast. When the situation had been explained, he sent for his chief of police, who sent for one of his subordinates, who said yes, this Sishen was staying at the Chunar and could be brought in within the hour.

"Don't frighten him," said Barnevelt. "He's a timid soul. Tell him some old friends want to see him."

"Ahem," said the Chief Syndic. "While I mislike to dampen so auspicious an occasion, yet duty forces me to bring up certain matters." He fumbled in his desk. "I have here a letter from the President of Suruskand, requesting help in recovering his stolen ship."

Barnevelt dismissed the question of the *Yars* with an airy wave. "He shall get his ship back. Meanwhile I'll pay him rent for it. Have you a draft blank?"

After puzzling over the strange printed instrument, arranged quite differently from an Earthly check, Barnevelt wrote out a draft to the Republic of Suruskand, on Ta'lum and Fosq for five hundred karda. "Send him this and tell him I'll settle the balance later."

"I trust he'll take your—uh—rather cavalier treatment of the matter in good part," said the Chief Syndic. "I have here another letter that concerns you, sir. It arrived but this morn, in diplomatic cipher—from Zakkomir bad-Gurshmani, a ward of Queen Alvandi. After the usual preamble he says:

" 'Since our return to Ghulindé, I have been doomed to grisly

259

death, to wit: chosen by this false lottery as Princess Zei's first consort, to wed her on the day of her accession, on the tenth of Sifta.' (That, as you'll perceive from yonder calendar, is six days from now.) 'You know, Master Syndic, the fate awaiting one on whom that honor falls at end of year. Nor is Zei happier than I in this predicament, but we are helpless puppets in my guardian's royal grip, for she will keep all the leading strings in her own fists even after she has nominally resigned. There is one, however, who might us rescue: the mighty Earthman traveling under the pseudonym of Snyol of Pleshch.' That, I take it, means you, sir?"

"That's right," said Barnevelt.

The Chief Syndic made a deprecatory motion. "Fear not to acknowledge the fact in the privacy of our chambers, for Gorbovast and I are enlightened men who strive against the prejudiced disfavor in which Terrans are by many held. Some of our best friends are Earthmen, for we take the view: Because some of the louts act with unseemly arrogance, insolently boasting of the superiority of all things in their own fearsome world, should the whole enseamed race be damned unheard?

"Howsomever, let's to our embroidery return. I quote: 'I did not know this hero was an Earthman till Zei told me after my rescue from the Sunqar, though I did before suspect it. Here's the kernel. He is a Terran, and so is Zei—a fact I have long guarded as a courtly secret. She is no chick of Queen Alvandi, who is barren as the rocks of Harqain, but an Earthly waif procured from slavers and reared as the queen's own, being taught from early years to disguise herself as a native of this planet. For Qirib's law not only dooms the consort yearly. It likewise damns the queen who within five years of her accession fails to lay a fertile egg.

" 'The princess tells me she did learn this pseudo-Snyol's true nature during the rescue and assumed he likewise learned of hers. And therefore was she all the more perplexed by the inconsistent sentiments he manifested towards her. . . .' "

The Syndic looked up. "I presume you know to what he refers, sir? To continue: 'Since he is an Earthman, it seems likely that he would direct his course towards Novorecife and his fellows. We therefore beg you with all the ardor we command to watch for him. Should he reach Novorecife without your interception, essay to get a word to him in the stronghold of the Terrans. For thus you may save, not merely my own worthless life, but the happiness of my lady princess.

" 'I add that Queen Alvandi also knows of Snyol's true nature and was therefore all the more eager to obtain him as a consort for her daughter, for she would rather have foreign rule in this Qirib than jeopardize her matriarchal principles. Failing to hold him, she has chosen me as second best—a choice I should find flattering did not the vision of the chopper spring uppermost in my thoughts. Since Zei—for whom my feelings are of sib affection only—could not be fructified by one of my species, I ween Alvandi plans to smuggle in another waif to carry on the line.'

"There you have it," said the Syndic. "What you do now is up to you. I beg you, if you turn your back upon this world, not to reveal these matters, which contain most dire subversive possibilities."

Gorbovast said, "I suspect who Zei really is."

"Who?" said Barnevelt sharply.

"Know you that Earthly missionary for a cult of more than normal incoherence, Mirza Fateh? Whose wife was slain and daughter carried off by robbers in the Year of the Bishtar?"

The Syndic made the affirmative head motion. "Zei would be of the right age and type, though my information was the child was sold in Dur and there did die. Where's Mirza Fateh now?"

"He was in Mishé," said Gorbovast. "It transpires, General Snyol, that you may be in a position to bring about a most affecting family reunion."

"We'll see," said Barnevelt, whose mind had been whirring like a generator. "I sort of think young couples are better off without too many parents cluttering up the landscape."

Tangaloa said: "If you want to check, say to Zei: *Shuma farsi härf mizänid?*"

"What's that?"

"That's 'Do you speak Persian?' in Persian. I lived in Iran once. But you won't have a chance, because I don't see how you will see the sheila before we push off for Earth."

Barnevelt was still practicing the sentence when Sishen came in. The Osirian, resembling a man-sized bipedal dinosaur, took one look at Barnevelt and leaped upon him as he had upon Tangaloa that time in their room in Angur's Inn.

"Hey!" yelled Barnevelt, trying to wriggle out of the reptilian embrace.

"Oh, my dear rescuer!" hissed the Osirian. "How good to see you again! Not for a minute has my gratitude wavered in the time since we parted in Jazmurian! I love you!"

"Let's not be so demonstrative about it," said Barnevelt, detaching himself by force. "If you really want to do me a favor, here's an Earthman under Osirian pseudohypnosis who's forgotten his life on Earth and thinks he's a pirate of the Moryá Sunqaruma. Can you cure him?"

"I can try. May we have a room to ourselves?"

While the reptile led Shtain out, Barnevelt inquired after the *Shambor*. The little Marconi-rigged smuggler, however, seemed to have disappeared without a trace. Barnevelt suspected that the mutineers had probably capsized or otherwise wrecked her as a result of their unfamiliarity with the rig. At least that would save him from trouble with the Viagens.

Half an hour later Shtain came out of the room shaking his head and rubbing his bristly scalp. He wrung the hands of Barnevelt and Tangaloa.

"God!" he said, "it's good to be normal again! It is the damnedest feelink, to have part of your mind that knaws perfectly well what's goink on, but can't do a damn think about it. You boys were fine, wery fine. I could not have done batter myself. When do we shuff off?" Shtain's thick Russian accent was as dense as ever.

"I don't know about you two," said Barnevelt, "but I'm going back to Ghulindé with my Pirates of Penzance."

"What?" shouted Shtain. "Dun't be ridiculous! You're coming

back to Earth with us . . ."

"I am not!"

"Wait, wait, both of you," said Tangaloa. "Let me handle him, Igor. Look here, cobber, don't take this business about Zakkomir and Zei seriously. We've got our film. We've had our adventure; and now you can return to Earth to live on your laurels. . . ."

"No," said Barnevelt. "In the first place my mother lives on Earth, and in the second I'm going to rescue Zei."

"There'll be another sheila along in a minute!"

"Not the one I want."

"If you do rescue her, will you bring her to Earth on the next ship?"

"I think not. I've about decided to make my fortune here on Krishna."

Shtain had been hopping about with clenched fists in an agony of suppressed emotion. Now he burst out: "Are you crazy mad? What will Igor Shtain Limited do without you? Where would I ever get soch a ghawst-writer again? I'll double your salary! You can't walk out on us like that!"

"Sorry, but you should have thought how valuable I was sooner."

Shtain began to swear in Russian.

Tangaloa said, "Ahem, Dirk, you know these Earthly adventurers who run around backward planets exploiting the natives are inferior types who can't compete with their own kind back home. They take advantage of Earth's more sophisticated culture, which they themselves have done nothing to create. . . ."

"Oh, foof! I've heard that lecture too. Call me inferior if you like, but here I'm quite a guy, not a shy schizoid Oedipean afraid of his ma."

"It's still no life for a man of intellect. . . ."

"And just think. Although we busted Sheafasè's gang, the Sunqar's still in Krishnan hands, so we haven't settled the janrú problem. Since Alvandi's a fanatical—uh . . ."

"Gynarchist?"

"Thanks, gynarchist, she'll go on making and selling the drug. Her objection to Sheafasè was not that he sold it to the interstellar smugglers but that he charged her all the traffic would bear."

"What of it? We have our information. The rest is up to the World Federation and the Interplanetary Council."

"But think how it'll simplify matters if I'm running the Sunqar!"

"There's that." Tangaloa turned to Shtain, whose lips were still spitting Slav consonants like a machine gun. "We might as well let him go—the romantic bug's bitten him. In a couple of years he may get tired of it and drift back to Earth. Besides, he's in love."

"Why did you not say so? That's different." Shtain sighed like a furnace. "When I was yong I was in loff too—wit three or four girls at once. Good-bye, my boy! I hate your guts, but I loff you like my own son."

"Thanks," said Barnevelt.

"If you come around in a year, I will first break your nack and then give you back your old job. George, how the hell do we gat to Novorecife?"

Six days later, two ships pulled into Damovang Harbor. One was the *Yars*, the other a stock boat full of ayas, which Barnevelt had bought for his private army with part of Alvandi's reward. The flag that flew from the masts of these ships made the folk of Damovang scratch their heads, for it was the ancient flag of Qirib, used back before the days of Queen Dejanai and the matriarchate.

The ships came quietly up to the vacant wharf. A line snaked ashore and was caught and belayed by one of the loafers to be found on any pier. Then out of the first ship tumbled a swarm of armed and armored men. Before their points, the people about the docks scattered with screams like a flock of frightened aquebats.

"Hurry up with those ayá!" yelled Barnevelt, clad in steel from head to knee.

From the second ship, more men were leading the beasts to the wharf. As they arrived, Barnevelt's most heavily armed men climbed or were boosted into the saddles.

(After a long argument between Barnevelt and Gizil over the merits of an assault on foot from the sea versus one mounted from the land, they had decided to combine the two in an amphibious cavalry assault. Barnevelt's hardest task had been to compel his men to wear armor. Being mostly sailors bred, they distrusted the stuff because they knew how quickly it could drown them if they fell overboard during a sea fight.)

"Follow me!" called Barnevelt. Gizil behind him blew a trumpet. The force clattered up the nearest street in double column. Behind them came the rest of the army on foot.

"What means this?" screamed a voice, and there came a trio of Amazon guards to block the way.

"The men of Qirib come back to claim their own!" said Barnevelt. "Out of the way, girls, if you don't want to get hurt."

One Amazon poked a pike at Barnevelt, who chopped off the spearhead with a swift slash, then whacked the brass helmet with the flat of his blade. The girl rolled on the cobbles. As his aya plunged forward, he spanked the second girl. As the third turned to run, he reached out and caught the hair that flowed from under the helmet.

"Just a minute, beautiful," he said. "Where's this wedding between the new queen and her consort?"

"At the t-temple of the Mother Goddess in the upper city."

"Gizil, lead the way. And make it snappy with those handbills."

Certain of Barnevelt's men began pulling fistfuls of handbills out of saddlebags and tossing them fluttering into the air. They read:

MEN OF QIRIB, ARISE!
Cast Off Your Shackles!
The Day of Liberation has Come!
Today, after five generations of female tyranny, a dauntless band of exiles has returned to Qirib to lead the glorious revolution for

EQUAL RIGHTS FOR MEN!
**Arm yourselves and follow us! Today we shall hurl from its
base the ugly image of the false vampire goddess whose degrading worship and obscene rites have so long served as a
pretext for a vicious and unfair oppression . . .**

Barnevelt held down his impulse to gallop madly ahead, leaving his foot troops behind. As the column, brave with pennon-
bearing lances, wound up the slope to the spired city in Qunjar's
lap, he looked back and saw that behind his own foot came a
straggling column of male civilians waving chair legs and other
improvised weapons. Some people ran away as he approached,
while others crowded up to see. Men cheered while women shook
fists and spat threats.

In the plaza in front of the temple of Varzai, Barnevelt reined
in. Across the plaza, ranged in a semicircle in front of the entrance, a body of Amazons was getting into formation. An officer
rushed up and down, pushing the girls into place. All held their

spears outthrust, as on the night of the pirate raid on Ghulindé; those of the rear rank held their pikes over the heads of those in front, who knelt.

Barnevelt signaled Gizil to hold the men back while he trotted across the plaza.

"How's the wedding coming?" he asked the officer.

" 'Tis even now being solemnized. What's this incursion?"

Barnevelt looked back. The logical way to attack the Amazons would be by archery, holding his cavalry back in case they tried to charge on foot. But his pikemen and arbalesters were only now beginning to file into the square, and to organize such a barrage would take several minutes. He made up his mind.

"Disperse!" he shouted. "We're coming in!"

"Never! We defy you!"

Barnevelt whirled and galloped back. "Form a square!" He backed his aya into the center of the front rank and brought down his visor with a clang. "Ready? Walk!"

Plop-plop went the hooves on the flagstones. It would be nice to work such a coup without bloodshed; but this was Krishna, where they had not attained the squeamishness towards violent death that Earth took pride in.

"Trot!" These six-legged mounts had a hard, jarring trot, as the saddle was right over the middle pair of legs.

"Canter!" The pikes ahead looked awfully sharp. If the girls did not break before they arrived, and if the ayas did not shy back from the hedge of points, there'd be a messy moment. He hoped he wouldn't be thrown off and trampled.

"Charge!" Down came the lances. The gallop of an aya's six hooves had a drumlike roll. Barnevelt slacked up until he could see the points of lances on either side of him; no use being absolutely the first to hit the line.

Closer came the line and closer. He'd try not to kill the pretty girl facing him . . .

Crash! The pretty girl warrior disappeared. Barnevelt knocked one pike point aside with his left arm while another glanced from his armor. His aya stumbled and was pulled up again with a furious yank on the reins braided into the animal's mustache.

For an instant, the world was all Amazons and ex-pirates turning somersaults. The middle of the Amazon line disappeared as the ayas rolled over it; the other girls dropped their pikes and shields and ran.

A riderless aya ran past. A dismounted man was hitting an Amazon with a broken lance shaft. Another was getting back on his animal. There were a couple of dead ayas and several Amazons lying still.

Raising his visor, Barnevelt snapped orders to Gizil to call off the fighting, tend the injured, and mount a guard around the temple and the plaza. Then he led a squad into the temple.

The audience sat frozen as the animals and their riders in steel plate clattered down the central aisle to where Queen Alvandi, Zei, Zakkomir, and some priestesses of Varzai stood in a group.

"Saved!" cried Zakkomir.

Alvandi spoke: "Never shall you carry through this antic enterprise, detestable Earthman! My people will tear you to pieces!"

"Yes? Come and see what your people are doing, madam." He grinned down at her, then turned his aya and led the group back up the aisle, crowding past the column of his own men who had followed him in. At the portal he said, "See?"

His own men had formed a square around the portal, and beyond it the plaza was packed with male Qiribuma. Gizil was haranguing them, and from the way they yelled and waved their cudgels they seemed to like it.

"What mean you to do?" said Alvandi. "Frighten me with threats you cannot, for my superior social order is dearer to me than life itself."

Barnevelt said, "Madam, I admire your courage even if I can't approve your principles. First, you're a usurper yourself, because you've never laid a fertile egg and therefore should have been executed long ago." (The queen quailed.) "Instead, you bought a kidnaped Earth girl, a small child, and reared her as your own. Will you demonstrate, Zei? Like this."

He reached up to his forehead and wrenched off the false antennae. Zei did likewise.

"Now," he continued, "I won't kill you merely because you

should have been sent to the chopper by your own silly law. Since the present regime is proved illegitimate and unlawful, it's time the old order changed, yielding place to new. I'll help them draw up a constitution. . . ."

"With yourself as ruler?" sneered Alvandi.

"By no means. I won't have the job. I'll just give advice—for instance to exile you. Then I'll take Zei, some ships, and some volunteers, and take over the Sunqar."

"But that's mine by treaty with the admirals . . ."

"*Was*, you mean. It's state property, and my followers, who being both Qiribuma and Sunqaruma are qualified to decide its fate, have given it to me."

The queen turned to Zei. "At least, daughter, you'll not willingly yield to the wicked importunities of this crapulous vaporer?"

"And why not? No daughter of yours am I, but one of another race whom you've sought to use as a puppet to prop your own power, even to forcing me into an alliance miscegenetic. I prefer my own."

"Zakkomir?" said Alvandi.

"The same for me."

"You're all against me," said the queen, drooping. She turned to Barnevelt with a last flicker of defiance. "What have you done with my warrior girls you carried off? Deflowered them and fed them to the fish?"

"Not at all, Queen. They're all married to my ex-pirates."

After doing what had to be done to secure order in Ghulindé—such as hanging a couple of liberated males who tried to celebrate their freedom by robbing shops—Barnevelt visited with Zei in her apartment.

When she could talk she said, "My lord and love, if indeed you love me, why, knowing I was of Earthly origin, did you hold off until Zakkomir's letter reached you? Another instant and the link had been forged."

"How was I supposed to know you were human? You couldn't expect me to yank your antennae to see if they'd come off!"

"By the same means I knew you for such."

"What was that? Did my ear points come loose or something?"

"Nay, but when we dried our apparel on the raft in the Sunqar, and again when we washed the soot of the fire from our bodies, I saw that you possessed a navel!"

Barnevelt clapped a hand to his forehead. "Of course! Now that you mention it, I can see how a person hatched from an egg would have no use for one."

"Nay further, knowing that *you* knew *I* had one, I recked that you knew all and could conceive no reason for your strange evasive diffidence. Perhaps, methought, he's been reared in Nyamadzë, even as I was in Qirib, and thinks himself more Krishnan than Terran. Perhaps he's a cogwheel in some vast plot; or perhaps he does but find me ugly."

"Ugly! Oh, darling . . ."

"In any case, 'twas plain as the peaks of Darya that, whereas you and I each knew the other's true race, you wished natheless to maintain this pretense of deeming us Krishnans still. Albeit curiosity consumed me, I durst do no more than hint. Thus it was that I said we were of the same kind, and neither was quite what he seemed."

"I remember you did, but I didn't catch on. My mind was on—other things." His eyes devoured her until she colored.

"Well, when you let these hints fall as dead as an aqebat struck by the fowler's bolt, I acceded to what I took to be your wish. For I loved you so that—despite my noble resolution to guard my chastity, as a princess must needs do—had you pressed me to yield a maiden's ultimate gift, I should not have known how to gainsay you."

Barnevelt drew a long breath. "I understand now. Put it down to sheer stupidity on my part—though perhaps in the long run it was a fortunate mistake. But how'd you hide your navel when you went swimming or pretended to be a statue in the park?"

"I wore a patch of false skin, but for the kashyó I'd left off my little patch, seeing no need for it under that formal gown."

"I see. While we're confessing impostures, that wasn't a real yeki that growled on the road to Shaf, when you started to leave me. It was I doing imitations."

"Why, I knew that!" she said.

Presently, Barnevelt said, "Now we have to figure out how we can get married—we are going to get married, aren't we?"

"I wondered when you'd bethink you of that," she said in a marked manner. "Well, sirrah, since you at last had the wit to ask me, the answer's aye, and aye again. But what's the obstacle?"

"We're Terrans, and I've read somewhere that only Terrans can legally marry other Terrans. The only people of Krishna who could splice us—with any legal effect under Earthly law, that is—are Commandante Kennedy and Judge Keshavachandra at Novorecife. And we hardly want to go all that distance in the wrong direction, when we're bound for the Sunqar."

"How about Qvansel the astrologer, or one of the priestesses?"

"No good. Your marriage with Zakkomir wouldn't have been legal, either. Let me think . . . There are some jurisdictions on Earth where a man and a woman can become legally married by standing up in front of witnesses and saying so. It's called common-law marriage. The Quakers have a similar system, and they're highly respectable. So that would have as much legal effect as anything our Qiribo friends could do. Wait here."

A few minutes later, he fetched Gizil, Zakkomir, and the court astrologer back to Zei's apartment.

When they were lined up, he said, "Now stand up and give me your hand, darling—the left. Do you, Zei bab-Alvandi, take me, Dirk Cornelius Barnevelt, to be your husband?"

"Aye. Do you, Dirk, take me to be your wife?"

"I do. With this ring . . ." (he slipped the Hayashi camera off his finger and on to hers) ". . . I thee wed." And he swept her close.

Another ten-day, and the freshly painted *Douri Dejanai*, at its dock in Damovang Harbor, prepared to cast off its lines. In the stern, Barnevelt bid farewell to his Krishnan friends.

Gizil said, "We all deem you a man of superhuman self-restraint, elevating me to the presidency in lieu of taking it yourself."

"I'm not a Qiribu, remember," said Barnevelt. "They'd have gotten tired of being ruled by a damned Earthman and thrown me out. Besides, they chose you."

"Thanks to that constitution you prescribed for us."

"Well, you asked for the latest model of republican constitution, so I obliged. I hope it works. Drink up, pals—we're shoving off."

The visitors went ashore. The ship pulled out from its berth, followed by the remaining two ships of Barnevelt's little fleet.

When people could no longer be recognized for the distance and the sun was setting behind the Zogha, Barnevelt turned away, threw an arm around Zei, and went below. He paused at Philo's cage to scratch the roots of the macaw's feathers (the queen having left the bird behind when she fled from Qirib) and then at the cage of his latest acquisition, a pair of bijara, bought at the same pet shop in Ghulindé where he had found the lost Philo.

Zei said, "Think you this new law you've given the Qiribuma will last like the rocks of Harqain?"

Remembering Tangaloa's remarks about basic cultural attitudes, he said thoughtfully, "Considering that they don't have a tradition of democratic self-government, I shall be pleasantly surprised if this shiny new constitution stands up to the strains of human weakness and ambition for many years. But this purblind race of miserable men will have to manage as best it can."

"What sort of rule will you establish in the Sunqar? Come, sir, more attention to me and less to your insensate beasts, specially since the Earthly monster makes you sniffle. At your present rate of accumulation, I foresee the day when the Sunqar's greatest renown will be as a park zoölogical."

"Sorry." He drew out a chair and poured her a drink. "I think I'll set up what on Earth would be called a stock corporation, with you and me holding a majority of stock. We'll be capitalists. Say, Zei . . ."

"Yes, dearest Snyol—I mean Dirk?"

He smiled at her slip. Then it occurred to him that "Zei" was probably not her original name, either—though, if it suited them both, there was no point in digging up some forgotten Persian praenomen. With so many pseudonyms in his circle—his own, Tangaloa's, Gizil's—it was hard enough to keep track of names. To aggravate matters, the men of Qirib had all changed their surnames from matronymics to patronymics.

Out of curiosity, however, he said, *"Shuma farsi härf mizänid?"*

She gave a little start. "Why yes—*what* was that, beloved? 'Tis a tongue I seem to recall once knowing, but now all's hazy. Didst not ask me if I spoke some speech?"

"Tell you some day," he said, running his fingers luxuriantly through his new bristle-brush of hair. Since she had stopped dyeing hers, Zei's, too, had begun to come in with its normal glossy black.

"Why did Alvandi adopt an Earthly child instead of a Krishnan one?" he asked.

"She did adopt a Krishnan babe, but it died a ten-night before the ceremony of Viewing the Heir. So Alvandi in great haste and secrecy besought the trafficker in slaves to give a surrogate. He sent me, not telling her I was of Earth, and by the time she learned her error 'twas too late and he'd vanished with his price. Ofttimes have I wondered who my authentic parents were."

Here was a chance to play God by reuniting a family, for there was no doubt in his mind now that she was Mirza Fateh's daughter. However, it might be better to let sleeping eshuna lie. He'd want to look Papa Fateh over with care before inviting him to move in with them. From what he'd heard about the missionary, he doubted whether he'd be a vast improvement on his own mother or Queen Alvandi.

A hectic week of politicking had left him little time to think about the future. For one thing, to help finance his Sunqar project, he had made a deal with Shtain to shoot additional film and send it to Earth from time to time, to pay for which Shtain had set up a drawing account for him in the bank at Novorecife. Tangaloa particularly wanted film and data on the tailed Fossanderaners. For another, the Mejrou Qurardena was suing him in the courts of Qirib for impersonating one of their express-men. . . .

"Dirk," said Zei, "happy though I am that we're now a peaceful, settled, wedded pair, in a way I miss the excitement of our flight from the Sunqar. Never have I lived with such intensity. Think you such feelings will ever come again?"

"Stick around, darling," he said, lighting a cigar. "The excitement's just beginning."

A Krishnan year later, a drunken fat man in the Nova Iorque Bar at Novorecife was declaiming, "All nonsense, letting these barbarians do as they please. Oughta send the army and civilize 'em. Make 'em adopt modern plumbing, democracy, mass production, and all the rest. And some good up-to-date religion . . . Say, who's that?"

He indicated a tall, horse-faced Earthman in Krishnan costume, with a small notch in his left ear, drinking with Commandante Kennedy and Assistant Security Officer Castanhoso.

The notch-eared man was saying, ". . . I did not invite him! He read about us in that paper they publish in Mishé and put two and two together. The next thing I knew, he showed up on a ship from Malayer saying he was my long-lost father-in-law. And since Zei's crazy about him, there's no getting rid of him. Matter of fact I don't mind Mirza so much, and he was at least able to splice us properly, so there'd be no more question of whether we're properly married. But those funny people who come to visit him . . ."

"Why do you not put him to work?" asked Castanhoso.

"I will, as soon as . . ."

"That," said the fat man's companion, "is the famous Dirk Barnevelt, president of the Sunqar Corporation. He's just pulled a big deal with the Interplanetary Council. Like to meet him?"

"Sure. Like to meet anybody *human*."

"Oh, Senhor Barnevelt, may I present Senhor Elias? A new arrival."

"Glad to know you," said Barnevelt, squeezing the pudgy hand.

"You're one of these guys who lives among the natives?"

"You can put it that way," snapped Barnevelt, and started to turn away.

"No offense meant, son! I just wondered if you consider 'em better than your own kind."

"Not at all. Some find them easier to live with than Earthmen, some don't. I do, but I don't think them either better or worse. It all depends on the individual."

"Sure, sure. But aren't they awfully primitive? National sovereignty and wars and nobility and all that crap?"

"Matter of fact, I like them that way."

"You're one of these romantic guys?"

"No, but I guess I like pioneering."

"Pioneering." The fat man sank into sodden silence. Barnevelt, finding his new acquaintance a boor and a bore, made a withdrawing movement. But Elias asked, "What's that new deal? Wong was telling me about it."

"Oh. Know the Sunqar?"

"A big mess of seaweed, isn't it?"

"Ayuh. There were some people who made janrú out of the terpahla vine. . . ."

"Say, I know you—the guy who eloped with a native princess, only she turned out human after all. Excuse me, what was the deal?"

"Well, I'm now lord high whatsit of the Sunqar and was willing to stop janrú-making and turn over the names of the smuggling ring. But I wanted something in return, so I persuaded the I. C. to let me have engineering help to set up a soap works in the Sunqar. The vine gives us unlimited potash, and there's no soap on Krishna. So . . ."

Again Barnevelt started to withdraw, but the fat man clamped a grip on his arm. "Gonna be the planet's soap magnate, eh? When you finish with the Krishnans, they'll be all civilized like us and you'll have to find another planet. Say, when'd you—

uh—marry this dame?"

"About a year ago."

"Any kids?"

"Three. And would you mind letting go my arm?"

"Three. Let's see. Is this the planet with years twice as long as ours? No-o, the years are *shorter* than on Earth. Three, eh? Haw haw haw . . ."

Barnevelt's ruddy countenance turned purple and his knobby fist smashed into the fat face. Elias reeled back, upset a table, and crashed to the floor.

"For God's sake, Dirk!" cried Kennedy, moving to interfere.

"Nobody insults my wife," growled Barnevelt.

"But," said the fat man's companion, "I don't understand. You did say three, and, that is, you know . . ."

Barnevelt turned on him. "We had triplets. What's funny about that?"

Paksenarrion, a simple sheepfarmer's daughter, yearns for a life of adventure and glory, such as the heroes in songs and story. At age seventeen she runs away from home to join a mercenary company, and begins her epic life . . .

ELIZABETH MOON

THE DEED OF PAKSENARRION

"This is the first work of high heroic fantasy I've seen, that has taken the work of Tolkien, assimilated it totally and deeply and absolutely, and produced something altogether new and yet incontestably based on the master. . . . This is the real thing. Worldbuilding in the grand tradition, background thought out to the last detail, by someone who knows absolutely whereof she speaks. . . . Her military knowledge is impressive, her picture of life in a mercenary company most convincing."—**Judith Tarr**

About the author: Elizabeth Moon joined the U.S. Marine Corps in 1968 and completed both Officers Candidate School and Basic School, reaching the rank of 1st Lieutenant during active duty. Her background in military training and discipline imbue The Deed of Paksenarrion with a gritty realism that is all too rare in most current fantasy.

"I thoroughly enjoyed *Deed of Paksenarrion*. A most engrossing, highly readable work."
—**Anne McCaffrey**

"For once the promises are borne out. *Sheepfarmer's Daughter* is an advance in realism. . . . I can only say that I eagerly await whatever Elizabeth Moon chooses to write next."
—Taras Wolansky, *Lan's Lantern*

*   *   *   *   *

Volume One: Sheepfarmer's Daughter—Paks is trained as a mercenary, blooded, and introduced to the life of a soldier . . . and to the followers of Gird, the soldier's god.

Volume Two: Divided Allegiance—Paks leaves the Duke's company to follow the path of Gird alone—and on her lonely quests encounters the other sentient races of her world.

Volume Three: Oath of Gold—Paks the warrior must learn to live with Paks the human. She undertakes a holy quest for a lost eleven prince that brings the gods' wrath down on her and tests her very limits.

*   *   *   *   *

These books are available at your local bookstore, or you can fill out the coupon and return it to Baen Books, at the address below.

All three books of The Deed of Paksenarrion ____
SHEEPFARMER'S
  DAUGHTER   65416-0 • 506 pages • $3.95 ____
DIVIDED
  ALLEGIANCE   69786-2 • 528 pages • $3.95 ____
OATH OF GOLD 69798-6 • 528 pages • $3.95 ____

Please send the cover price to: Baen Books, Dept. B, 260 Fifth Avenue, New York, NY 10001.
Name_____
Address_____
City_____ State_____ Zip_____

MAGIC AND *COMPUTERS* DON'T MIX!

RICK COOK

Or . . . do they? That's what Walter "Wiz" Zumwalt is wondering. Just a short time ago, he was a master hacker in a Silicon Valley office, a very ordinary fellow in a very mundane world. But magic spells, it seems, are a lot like computer programs: they're both formulas, recipes for getting things done. Unfortunately, just like those computer programs, they can be full of bugs. Now, thanks to a *particularly* buggy spell, Wiz has been transported to a world of magic—and incredible peril. The wizard who summoned him is dead, Wiz has fallen for a red-headed witch who despises him, and no one—not the elves, not the dwarves, not even the dragons—can figure out why he's here, or what to do with him. Worse: the sorcerers of the deadly Black League, rulers of an entire continent, want Wiz dead—and he doesn't even know why! Wiz had better figure out the rules of this strange new world—and fast—or he's not going to live to see Silicon Valley again.

Here's a refreshing tale from an exciting new writer. It's also a rarity: a well drawn fantasy told with all the rigorous logic of hard science fiction.

February 1989 • 69803-6 • 320 pages • $3.50

Available at bookstores everywhere, or you can send the cover price to Baen Books, Dept. WZ, 260 Fifth Ave., New York, NY 10001.

AN OFFER HE COULDN'T REFUSE

They were functional fangs, not just decorative, set in a protruding jaw, with long lips and a wide mouth; yet the total effect was lupine rather than simian. Hair a dark matted mess. And yes, fully eight feet tall, a rangy, tense-muscled body.

She clawed her wild hair away from her face and stared at him with renewed fierceness. Her eyes were a strange light hazel, adding to the wolfish effect. "What are you *really* doing here?"

"I came for you. I'd heard of you. I'm . . . recruiting. Or I was. Things went wrong and now I'm escaping. But if you came with me, you could join the Dendarii Mercenaries. A top outfit—always looking for a few good men, or whatever. I have this master-sergeant who . . . who *needs* a recruit like you." Sgt. Dyeb was infamous for his sour attitude about women soldiers, insisting that they were too soft . . .

"Very funny," she said coldly. "But I'm not even human. Or hadn't you heard?"

"Human is as human does." He forced himself to reach out and touch her damp cheek. "Animals don't weep."

She jerked, as from an electric shock. "Animals don't lie. Humans do. All the time."

"Not *all* the time."

"Prove it." She tilted her head as she sat cross-legged. "Take off your clothes."

". . . what?"

"Take off your clothes and lie down with me as *humans* do. Men and women." Her hand reached out to touch his throat.

The pressing claws made little wells in his flesh. "Blrp?" choked Miles. His eyes felt wide as saucers. A little more pressure, and those wells would spring forth red fountains. *I am about to die. . . .*

I can't believe this. Trapped on Jackson's Whole with a sex-starved teenage werewolf. There was nothing about this in any of my Imperial Academy training manuals. . . .

**BORDERS OF INFINITY by LOIS McMASTER
BUJOLD
69841-9 • $3.95**